THE GOLDEN AGE

A NOVEL

GORE
VIDAL

DOUBLEDAY

NEW YORK LONDON TORONTO SYDNEY AUCKLAND

THE
GOLDEN
AGE

A NOVEL

PUBLISHED BY DOUBLEDAY
a division of Random House, Inc.
1540 Broadway, New York, New York 10036

DOUBLEDAY and the portrayal of an anchor with a dolphin
are trademarks of Doubleday, a division of
Random House, Inc.

Grateful acknowledgment is made for permission to reprint: "It Was a Glad
Adventure," "Hector's Song," "Doomed, Doomed, Doomed," "Circe," and
"Finale: It's the Going Home Together," by Jerome Moross and John
Latouche, © 1953 (Renewed), Chappell & Co. and Sony/ATV Tunes
Publishing LLC. All Rights Reserved. Used by Permission.

BOOK DESIGN BY DEBORAH KERNER

Library of Congress Cataloging-in-Publication Data
Vidal, Gore, 1925–
    The golden age : a novel / by Gore Vidal.
       p. cm.
    1. United States—History—1933–1945—Fiction.   2. United States—
History—1945–1953—Fiction.   3. Newspaper publishing—Fiction.
4. Washington (D.C.)—Fiction. 5. Women publishers—Fiction.
6. Mothers and sons—Fiction.   7. New York (N.Y.)—Fiction.   I. Title.
PS3543.I26 G65 2000
813'.54—dc21   00-043071

ISBN 0-385-50075-0

THE GOLDEN AGE

A NOVEL

THE FAMILY TREES

CHARLES SCHERMERHORN SCHUYLER

(1813-1877)

DENISE DELACROIX   M. (1)   WILLIAM SANFORD

(c. 1851-1877)   *(1838-1897)*

FREDERIKA BINGHAM   M.   BLAISE DELACROIX SANFORD

(c. 1885-)   *(1877-c. 1978)*

KITTY M. JAMES BURDEN DAY

(1882-1950)

JAMES, JR.

(died young)

CLAY OVERBURY   M. (1) ENID SANFORD   PETER SANFORD   M. (1) DIANA DAY (2)

(?-1958)   *(1918-1950)*   *(1922-)*   *(c.1917-1977)*

(also married
Elizabeth
Watress after
Enid's death)

ALICE FREDERIKA SANFORD   CAROLINE

(1938-)   *(c. 1954-)*

FOUR CHILDREN

M. 1840   CAROLINA DE TRAXLER

M. (2) EMMA DE TRAXLER SCHUYLER   M (1)   HENRI PRINCE D'AGRIGENTE

(1840-1878)   *(?-1870)*

PLON

(1862-1919)

ANDRÉ

(1868-?)

CAROLINE DE TRAXLER SANFORD   M.   JOHN APGAR SANFORD

(1878-1950)   *(1865-?)*

M. (1)   BILLY THORNE

(last heard of in 1980)

(divorced 1950)

TIMOTHY X. FARRELL M. (2) EMMA DE TRAXLER SANFORD M. GILES DECKER

(1903-?)   *(1893-?)*

(divorced 1923)

AARON BURR DECKER

(1922-)

AARON BURR DECKER

(1960?-)

O N E

Timothy X. Farrell suddenly visualized the opening shot to the film that he had planned to make of Daphne Du Maurier's lush novel *Rebecca*. He had just pulled into the driveway to Laurel House, set high above the slow-churning Potomac River, and there before him in the icy silver moonlight was the start of *his* movie had David O. Selznick not outbid him for the movie rights and then hired Alfred Hitchcock, of all people, to direct. Plainly, a true disaster was now in the making.

Attendants parked cars in front and to the side of the mock-Georgian façade of the house of what would have been his brother-in-law, Blaise Delacroix Sanford, had Timothy and Blaise's half sister, Caroline Sanford, ever had time to get married in those busy years when, together, they had created a film studio that, for a time, nearly changed movie history until . . . What was the name, he wondered, of Olivia De Havilland's sister? The one who was now the lead in *Rebecca*.

Timothy parked at the front door. He could almost hear what's-her-name's voice over the screen: "Last night I dreamed I had gone back to Manderley"—or whatever the line was. Purest junk, of course. Timothy preferred his own "true to life" *Hometown* series of movies, but the public was supposed to be more at home with beautiful houses and beautiful people and a dark mystery at the heart of it all; not to mention a great fire that reveals a terrible secret. Even so, he had wanted desperately to direct *Rebecca:* something un-Farrellesque in every way.

The butler was since his time. "Sir?"

Timothy gave his name. Then: "Is my film crew here?"

The butler was now all attention. "Oh, yes, Mr. Farrell! This is an honor, sir. To meet you. Your camera people are setting up in the library." The drawing room was full of Washington grandees, some elected; some born in place, like Alice Roosevelt Longworth, wearing for once the wrong blue; some newly arrived from abroad now that England and France were at war with Germany. Nevertheless, for an average American like the butler, the defining, the immortalizing presence of The Movies took precedence over everything else. "Shall I show you into the library, sir?"

"No, not yet. I must say hello. . . ."

Timothy had forgotten the rapid lizardlike Washington gaze when someone new enters an important drawing room. Conversations never drop a beat and all attention remains fixed on one's group and yet the newcomer is quickly registered and placed and then set to one side, until needed. The Hollywood stare was far more honest, more like that of the doe frozen in a predator's sight line. Fortunately, Timothy's face was not absolutely familiar to anyone except Frederika Sanford, Blaise's wife, who now moved swiftly through her room filled with guests, many in military uniform, some drably American, some exotically foreign, like the embassy attachés. War or peace? That was the only subject in this famous "city of conversation," or the new phrase that Frederika used when she embraced the brother-in-law that never was: "The whispering gallery has been roaring with the news that you were coming here to make a film."

Frederika was now a somewhat faded version of her original bright blond self. Timothy recalled how Caroline had always preferred her sister-in-law to her half brother Blaise. But then Frederika was a born peacemaker while Blaise liked to wage war, preferably on every front. At the far end of the room he was regrouping his forces beneath a Sargent portrait of his father. Blaise was now stout; mottled of face— had he taken to drink? He looked like one of Timothy's Boston Irish uncles. To the troops attending him, Blaise was laying down the law as befitted the publisher of the *Washington Tribune*, which was still *the* Washington newspaper despite the efforts of Cissy Patterson, whose *Times-Herald*, published in bumpy tandem with William Randolph Hearst, was only just—at last—making a profit.

Cissy was standing beside Blaise. She was almost as red-faced as he, and even across the room, Timothy could hear the growl of her laughter. Cissy was a reluctant supporter of the Roosevelt Administration while Blaise had been, more often than not, a critic of the New Deal. But on September 1, Germany had invaded Poland. Two days later, England and France had declared war on the aggressor; and the New Deal was history. There was now only one issue: should the United States cease to be neutral and help finance England in the war against Germany? Cissy was beginning to revert to her family's isolationist roots; her cousin Bertie McCormick's Chicago *Tribune* had already declared war on both the President and the British Empire, while her brother, Robert Patterson, creator of the New York *Daily News*, was, true to the family's Irish heritage, no friend to England. Timothy himself was less provincial than these great Irish publishers, possibly because, unlike the McCormick-Patterson clan, he had been brought up poor enough to have no passionate interest in anything but himself.

"Basically," he heard himself saying to Frederika, "it's got to be a pretty neutral documentary. L. B. Mayer says I have to be fair to all the people who want us in the war and to all the ones who don't. I'm not to offend a single ticket-buyer."

"What do *you* want?" Frederika's practiced vague stare suddenly focused on Timothy as he took a glass of ginger ale from a passing waiter.

"I'm neutral. Pretty much," he added.

"Like America!" Frederika laughed. "Come say hello to Blaise. He's delighted you're making this film. Just as long as you do it entirely his way."

"Which is?"

"He changes from day to day. We've got three thousand English people here in town, all working out of the embassy."

"To get us into the war?"

"Splendid party, Mrs. Sanford!" A huge, dark-haired, ruddy-faced Englishman complimented his hostess while giving Timothy the swift Washington lizard's gaze that asked two simultaneous questions: Who are you? Can I use you?

Frederika introduced Timothy to John Foster. "He's . . . *what* at the embassy?"

"Legal Counsel is the latest title Lord Lothian thought up. Of course, it was a busy day. I gather you're making a film about the great debate hereabouts. . . ."

"Word spreads," murmured Timothy, indeed surprised that the embassy knew.

"I'm a great fan of yours, Mr. Farrell. In fact, you and John Ford are my favorites. But then trust the Irish to make the best American westerns."

Foster moved on. Timothy laughed. "Irish! What can he mean? We don't get much chance to ride horses?"

"You don't like the English." Frederika nearly frowned, something conscientious ladies of a certain age no longer dared do. "Washington is a battlefield these days."

"Who's winning?"

"Ah . . ."

Exuberantly, Blaise shook Timothy's hand in both of his. "My favorite non-brother-in-law!"

Tactfully, the others withdrew, leaving the two men in front of the fire, whose warmth reminded Timothy of how chilly the Potomac Heights could be on what was now the historic Fourth of November, 1939, when Congress had narrowly revised the Neutrality Act, at the President's urging. Now it was possible for belligerents in the European war—so solemnly declared and as yet so sensibly *un*begun—to get arms on a "cash-and-carry" basis from what key aides of President Franklin Delano Roosevelt were now calling the Arsenal of Democracy.

"He's going to get us into this thing. I know it. He thinks he's another Wilson, as if the original wasn't bad enough." Timothy noted that although Blaise was drinking only champagne, he was, in his decorous way, drunk. Since Timothy was about to go to work, he drank only a "horse's neck"—ginger ale with lemon twist.

"I thought you—and the *Trib*—are for helping the Allies against Hitler."

Blaise's eyes scanned the room, as though looking for someone. "Well, yes. If it comes to that. But the real enemy isn't Hitler."

As a onetime secret convert from Catholicism to Marxism and then onward to nothing, Timothy mentally timed Blaise's familiar hymn, currently being chanted by every other American grandee: the real enemy of the United States, and of God himself, the two being identical and indivisible, was not Hitler and Nazism but Stalin and his irresistible creed calculated to enthrall the world's mindless masses, godless communism, which would take away everyone's money.

As Blaise chanted his litany, Timothy noticed a familiar figure looking out a French window at the silver river below; it was someone Timothy knew but someone who ought not to have been there, or, at least, someone he did not associate with Washington or Laurel House or politics but with . . . The man turned toward him and raised his hand in a near-military salute and Blaise wound up with a quick amen. "There's Balderston," he said. "He's in movies, too."

Timothy wondered what the screenwriter John Balderston was doing at Laurel House. Mike Romanoff's Beverly Hills restaurant was more his usual venue. Recently he had written such popular films as *The Lives of a Bengal Lancer* and *The Prisoner of Zenda*. He had also been eager to work with Timothy on a film about King Arthur but Jack Warner had told them, sadly, that Errol Flynn was far too gone in alcohol "for me to lend him out. I mean, it would be just like in one of your westerns, Tim, where they give all the cows all that salt so they get so thirsty that they drink all this water to make them heavy so you can get a higher price per ton having watered your stock. Well, Flynn's scotched his stock. I'd never loan him out to a friend."

Warner's humor was always on the heavy side. A relatively unscotched Flynn had then gone on to make a dozen successful films in quick succession and the King Arthur film was never made.

"You'll be seeing Caroline, I suppose."

"If I get to France on this trip." But Blaise was now in deep conversation with Senator Borah, the Lion of Idaho.

Actually, if the budget was sufficient, Timothy did want to interview Caroline at home in Saint-Cloud-le-Duc, the seventeenth-century chateau where she and Blaise had grown up. Fate had so arranged matters that each was born to a mother who had died shortly after giving birth, first Blaise and then, two years later, Caroline, whose famously beautiful mother was daughter to an illegitimate son of Aaron Burr. Timothy had always wanted to make a film about Burr, who had chosen to take his stand at such an illuminating right angle to American history, but, unfortunately, no studio would touch the story of a man mistakenly thought to be a traitor.

The amiable Balderston was more like an Englishman than an American, the result, Timothy assumed, of his years as a London-based foreign correspondent. "I know what you're doing here." Balderston's upper plate at least had a professional American look to it, fully adhesive and not too dazzlingly British white.

"And I *don't* know what you're doing here." Timothy obligingly completed the dialogue.

"Well, I'm not making a film about . . ." He indicated the room. "But I wish I were."

"Have you chosen sides?"

Balderston put a cigarette in an ivory holder, rather like the one the President affected. "Well, I'm prone to the British, I suppose. But since you're Irish . . ."

"I'm not prone to the British. I'm not anti either, since my family left the bogs of our ancestral island. On the other hand, I'm anti-Hitler."

"I half-heard Mr. Sanford lecturing you. I hadn't realized that communism is so much worse than Hitler."

"Rich Americans all sound like that this season."

"Do you think they *believe* it?" Balderston was oddly urgent.

"I wouldn't know." Timothy felt himself cut loose in deep waters. What *was* going on this night at Laurel House?

"You were married to Caroline Sanford, weren't you?"

"We kept, as they say, company. Not quite the same thing."

"Sorry." Balderston actually blushed. Then he looked about him. "Anyway, here's the real—not the phony—war. In this room. There's Senator Borah, taking money from the Nazis to pay for his isolationist line."

Timothy was never shocked by what film producers or even politicians did, but for a senator to take money from a dictator like Hitler was, perhaps, going too far. "I've known the Lion of Idaho for over twenty years." Timothy was mild. "He's a total isolationist. Why would he take money for doing and saying what he does and says anyway?"

"I defer," said Balderston, "to your long years, in and out . . ."

"Mostly out."

". . . of this Jacobean court."

"Jacobean?" Timothy found the adjective inappropriate for something as essentially mundane as the American political system. "Will there be poisonings? A sword through the tapestry? Statesman murdered in a bathtub?"

Balderston laughed. "Nothing so good, I'm afraid. But even so, I've counted three Axis agents here tonight."

"How many British?"

"Only John Foster, and he'll tell you everything that he is trying to do to get us into the war, with absolutely no success. Then, if all else fails, he does a nice imitation of Senator Borah. John is a model spy."

The young assistant director approached Timothy. "We're all set up in the library, Mr. Farrell."

Timothy gave the AD his list of those who had agreed to speak to camera—for and against American participation in the European war. Blaise's office at the *Tribune* had been happy to do the preliminary work. Thus far, no one had turned down Timothy's invitation, particularly when they were told that the format would resemble Henry Luce's *March of Time*, easily the most popular of all newsreel programs, a new one shown each month in every movie house in the land. But where *The March of Time* dealt with a subject for no more than fifteen or twenty minutes, Timothy and his sponsors—an eclectic mix that included pro- and anti-war investors as well as L. B. Mayer's studio, MGM—were willing for him to make a ninety-minute feature that could then be cut into smaller segments. The voice-over narrative would be done by the notorious young radio actor Orson Welles, who had terrified the nation the previous year with his "reportage" of a Martian invasion of New Jersey. "I picked what I thought would be a perfectly incredible target for conquest. You see how wrong I was. Everyone believed that Martians lust for dominion over Passaic, New Jersey." Then Welles agreed to narrate Timothy's film. "We must call our film 'War or Peace?'"

"Why not 'Peace or War?'" Timothy suggested.

Welles grinned. "Less on the nose, I agree. I'm against Hitler, you know."

"I'll tell him, when I interview him."

Welles's eyes were suddenly very round and protuberant, like a vast Pekinese confronting dinner. "You've got *Hitler?* To interview?"

"Why not?" Timothy lied. He had been in the movie business almost thirty years, longer than the youthful Welles had been alive. But presently, after a prodigious number of stage and radio triumphs, Welles would be making his first film in Hollywood, after first narrating Timothy's film. Meanwhile, Timothy's muttered questions and asides would be the only narration in the library with its dark wood paneling and portrait of Aaron Burr over the fireplace. Later, Welles's voice would be dubbed in.

The five-man film crew, as always when left on their own, had overlit the room. Timothy brought down the lighting, aiming for the sort of Götterdämmerung effect that he had first concocted for Caroline in her ill-fated *Mary Queen of Scots*. After first making a success of the nearly defunct Washington *Tribune*, she had followed her mentor William Randolph Hearst to Southern California, where each had made silent films, she as an unexpectedly popular actress, he as producer of the serial *The Perils of Pauline*. In due course, she had gone into partnership with the ambitious Timothy X. Farrell. Their *Hometown* series was still much admired. Then she had gone home to France and the freelance Farrell had turned to documentaries.

Timothy now relit Blaise's library so that Washington statesmen would resemble the gods on Olympus, which was how they saw themselves and pretty much looked to be until they started to talk and one sadly realized that Jupiter, king of the gods, was just another saloon barfly, eager to buzz the new camera in town.

Timothy pulled a red leather wing chair into place beside the fire, noting contentedly that whoever sat in the chair would look agreeably diabolic if the key light were to be raised.

Blaise tapped on the door; then entered his now transformed study. "Looks like that movie you were doing when Frederika and I came out and stayed at the Ambassador."

Timothy now realized that the first interview would have to be with his host. "All right, Blaise. Sit there, by the fire. . . ."

"But . . ." But Blaise had already seated himself in his throne: king of the gods. "Now, Tim," he began.

But Timothy was already rearranging Blaise in the chair. Did he dare light each grandee in exactly the same way? Would that make the wrong point? After all, Senator Borah was pro-German. The newspaper columnist Walter Lippmann was pro-British. John Foster was exuberantly British. Senator Vandenberg was . . .

The Senator was standing in the doorway, drawn to camera as proverbial moth to flame. "Blaise." He was portentous. "Is there . . . ?"

"No. No." Blaise turned to Tim. "Let Senator Vandenberg go first."

But the gentleman from Michigan was firm. "Let me watch. I haven't done a *March of Time* in months now. Not that this is the same thing, Mr. . . . ?"

Timothy shook the professionally outstretched hand. "Farrell. No, sir. This is a special 'Peace or War' documentary. Just a number of different points of view on whether we should help Britain or not."

Timothy was aware of a tall fair handsome woman just back of the Senator. "So if you don't mind the hot lights, why don't you and Mrs. Vandenberg sit . . ."

"Mrs. Sims." The Senator was smooth. "A dear friend of Mrs. Vandenberg's. Her husband's counselor at the Canadian Embassy. . . ."

As the couple made themselves comfortable on a sofa, Blaise gave Timothy a rapid wink. This then was the Senator from Michigan's celebrated mistress, Mitzi, duly named in the notes that had been prepared for Tim by a dedicated researcher. One could never know too much about the players in a film, particularly a real-life one, involving—how *un*real it suddenly seemed—the lives of millions of people. But, again, Timothy reminded himself to remain neutral. Between Hitler and the British, even a South Boston Irishman was inclined to the lesser of two evils. But then—the question he must never cease to pose—why should the United States be involved at all in yet another European war, twenty-two years after the depressing conclusion of their first Great War, in which over fifty thousand American soldiers had been killed while bringing the nation no reward other than the prohibition of alcohol for a dozen years, thus increasing crime as well as its punishment, and giving birth to a new and lawless land? No, he warned himself. Don't impose. Be like the eye of God. Don't judge. Don't miss a thing.

Then, lights adjusted, he cued Blaise to speak to camera, which he did with almost the same professional ease as his sister Caroline, aka Emma Traxler, the exotic Alsatian star of the silent film *Huns from Hell*. Timothy fed Blaise few questions other than generalities. Could Hitler conceivably defeat France, much less England? Should we help France and England arm or remain neutral?

As part of Timothy's preparation, he had read a year's worth of *Tribune* editorials. The new phrase "Arsenal of Democracy" was acceptable, said Blaise, "but England must pay its way on a cash-and-carry basis." No surprises.

Timothy looked through the camera's lens; the picture was everything he had hoped. Blaise looked, if not Jovian, Olympian; perhaps Bacchic. So far so good. People seldom listened to professional public figures unless, like Roosevelt, the speaker had learned to talk very slowly with all sorts of oddly stressed emphases in order to be heard precisely as well as seen. Out of frame, in the shadows, Vandenberg's bespectacled owl-like eyes were trained attentively on the scene as he sat up straight, allowing the loose parabola of his stomach to rest on thin gangling arms and legs held in disciplined place like the stiff starched collar that supported his bullfrog jowl.

Blaise spoke so smoothly that Timothy paid no attention to him. But then, as the film was changed, Blaise suddenly sat up straight in his chair, always a sign, Timothy had learned in the few "real-life" documentary movies he had done, that the speaker had started to think as well as resonate air.

Timothy took the clapper and clicked it an inch away from Blaise's nose. "Blaise Sanford, November fourth, 1939. Take two."

Blaise looked the camera in the eye. "All of my sympathies are with the Allies, as they were in 1914. I find particularly repellent Mr. Hitler's regime, and though, in the long run, Stalin is the greater menace, I take it for granted that as we are too far away for Hitler to ever dream of attacking our shores, there is no danger to us in any foreseeable future. So thanks to geography, the Washington *Tribune* remains neutral with a natural bias to our allies in the last war, the first—and let's hope last— World War."

In the shadows, Vandenberg stirred. Timothy could smell Mitzi's gardenia-based perfume.

"In the years since that war, we have been bombarded by books and films, by propaganda, if I may use the right word, to the effect that all war is a bad thing, since people do get killed. For close to twenty years we have been hearing how quiet it was on that western front. We've also been looking at morbid picture books of the dead and the dying in the trenches of France. A generation has been convinced that any war is some sort of historic error. Well, it's very hard to interpret history as you live through it, day by day, as I have done. All I know for sure is that the curtain has gone up again on the second act of that grisly war. Once again France and England confront Germany. What are *we* to do? I can only hope that a generation overwhelmed with anti-war—with pacifist sentiments as the young are today will accept the fact that, should fate so ordain, we may yet, all of us, be called upon to fulfill our national destiny. But that time, thank God, is not yet here. I also trust that Mr. Roosevelt has the sense to realize how eighty per-cent of all Americans are against our taking sides, much less taking part, in the slaughter to come." Blaise stopped.

"Cut," said Timothy. "First-rate, Blaise."

Vandenberg was on his feet applauding. "Never knew you were so sensible, Blaise. You sound just like me. Doesn't he, Mitzi?"

"Particularly back home in Grand Rapids." Mitzi was mildly

sardonic. Timothy wondered what so . . . elegant seemed the word . . .
a lady saw in this caricature of a Midwestern senator.

Blaise mopped sweat from his face. "Between the fire and your
lights, I'm burning up. I must say I surprised myself. I left Franklin a
loophole to get us into the war."

Vandenberg shook his head. "I don't think he'll use your loophole
once he's made up that devious mind of his about what will help him
most to get a third term. Well, we're going to stop him dead in the Senate, at least in my Foreign Affairs Committee . . ."

"Yours, Van?" Mitzi was sharp. "You're only the ranking minority
member."

Mitzi smiled at Timothy. Yes, he thought, she is attractive. So who
is she . . . ?

Vandenberg was now in the chair beside the fire. He was all clumsy
expertise. As Blaise slipped out of the room, murmuring something
about Senator Taft, Vandenberg was instructing the cameraman.
"Could you go higher with your lens? I've got a bit of a chin problem."
He shook his pink ballooning jowls.

Timothy looked through his viewfinder. "Don't worry, Senator,
we'll give you a bit more shadow on your left side. I can see you're an
old pro." Timothy flattered the statesman much as he would the latest
studio ingenue. The only essential difference between the professional
and the amateur was that the professional was genuinely modest and
tense while the amateur—ham, no other word—like Vandenberg was
totally at home and at ludicrous ease.

Vandenberg tended to drone. He also liked to thrust his chin forward, belligerently, often at odds with what he was saying. He was, it
quickly developed, a friend to the Allied cause in his *heart*, but in his
head he believed only in Fortress America, a nation so powerful that
Hitler would never dream of attacking its alabaster cities, its fields of
amber grain.

"We must make ourselves strong militarily. We must not be isolationists." The voice was grave and the spectacles shone in the fire-
light as he launched a phrase that, plainly, he thought would resound
throughout history for all time. "We must be . . . *insulationists!*" A
dramatic pause; then he bowed his head as Timothy said "Cut."

Briskly, Vandenberg turned to Mitzi. "I thought that was pretty good."

"Superb, Arthur." It was Timothy not Arthur who detected the irony in the word "superb." What, he wondered, was their true relationship? Was she a spy, too? After forty-eight hours of Washington, D.C., Timothy had been told of a dozen secret agents, mostly working for England though several, apparently, served Germany. Since there was nothing much to spy on, their task, presumably, was to influence the national leaders to support whichever side the agent happened to be working for.

"The British are spending a fortune here," said the isolationist Senator Robert A. Taft, thought by all to be next year's Republican candidate for president. A bald, shy-mannered, professorial type with an unexpectedly tenacious manner, he was, in every way, a true opposite to his huge cheerful father, the twenty-seventh President, William Howard Taft.

"I plan to call for a Senate investigation of the various British and French agents here in Washington and, of course, New York and Hollywood. I have reason to believe that the editorial policy of the New York *Herald Tribune* is entirely dictated by the British secret services, with one aim only—to get us into the war on Britain's side."

Timothy collected a dozen "heads," his name for those who spoke to camera. John Foster was exuberant and witty. "Of course I'm a propagandist for England. That's because I am English, you see. Then, of course, we do need your help. That's why we're so awfully keen to get it. You know, at the embassy, each of us has been issued a cloak and a dagger. Also, let me warn you, we never sleep. Because we do want your ships and your planes *but* we don't want your troops. Heaven forbid! Give us your arms—your legs too—and we'll do the job. Think of us as your Bengal Lancers, fighting evil out there in the desert—or in the Tiergarten of Berlin."

Timothy was struck that each of the others, excepting Taft, seemed to be holding back some vital piece of information. The interventionists were nervously aware that eighty percent of the country was unwaveringly isolationist. Those who opposed joining the war in Europe were careful not to seem in any way friendly to Hitler, and that included Borah, whom Timothy had last seen sixteen years earlier in this same library; he was then very much in his leonine prime and famous for his proud boast "I'd rather be right than president," as well as for his affair with the volatile Alice Roosevelt Longworth. She had borne him a daughter, a situation calmly accepted by her husband, the speaker of the House, Nick Longworth, who had raised the child as his own. Now Longworth was dead; the Lion was moth-eaten while Alice was by far the best of the talking heads.

Timothy filmed her last. "Of course, Cousin Franklin is going to get us into the war over there so he can run for a third term next year. Two terms were good enough for my father, not to mention George Washington, and two terms are more than good enough for him if not for the long-suffering American people. But . . ." Dramatically she narrowed her gray-blue eyes. "Let me tell you a secret. Franklin is very ambitious. There! I've given the game away. He wants to be president for life and if it takes a war to keep him in the White House forever, a war we shall have!"

Thank God for Alice. Timothy found himself grinning with pleasure; she was a born star. She was also the last on his list, and so he escorted her back into the party. "Do you really think he's working to get us into the war?"

Alice had switched off her charm. The huge Roosevelt teeth were now covered by thin lips that made her mouth seem sulkily protuberant. "Yes." The answer was curt. "They say my father loved war. I think it was adventure that he loved. But those were simple days, fighting savages, far, far away. The 1917 business should have taught us a lesson. But all Franklin learned from Wilson was that war gives you the powers of a dictator. War can also win you an election, particularly if you swear to the American people that you're in favor of peace as Wilson did in '16 and Franklin will next year."

"But the people . . ."

"Always do what they are told. They have no choice, I suppose. I can't think why Hitler and Stalin go to such trouble with their secret police to keep people in line when all you need is just one Walter Winchell or just one darling Helen Reid at the *Herald Tribune* to spread British propaganda."

"But the people don't really fall for it."

"By the time Franklin's been reelected, they will. Don't worry. Something will have happened."

"Like 'Remember the Maine'?"

"Not if I can help it."

Senator Taft was standing next to them. "Sorry, Alice, I was eavesdropping."

"Quite all right. You and I think alike. *And* we're always right."

Taft introduced them to a smiling, silver-haired man. "Ralph Williams. He thinks he's running me for president, even though I'm standing as still as I can."

Timothy noted a twinkle in Taft's eye, not visible thus far in his career to any camera's eye. Some people projected charm like Alice and the President; others rejected charm, like Taft.

"We've got the nomination pretty well wrapped up," said Mr. Williams. "Mrs. Longworth, I certainly hope you'll make a speech for us at the convention . . ."

"I'll speak. But only in Theodore Roosevelt's name. You're all we've got, Bob."

"There's Arthur Vandenberg." Taft looked very grave.

"Poor Arthur's the only man I know who struts sitting down." They laughed at the old joke. But Alice had yet another turn to the screw. "We're the party of America First. The party of staying out of European messes. But Arthur is leaving us. Can't you see? The Senator from Michigan is one of us only for now but by next summer the Senator from Mitzi-gin is going to be an all-out interventionist. He's hooked."

Taft looked somewhat ill at ease. Plainly sexual gossip offended his native gravitas. But Timothy was now beginning to understand the odd tension between Vandenberg and his mistress in the study. "I don't think a lady, no matter how charming . . ."

"And devoted," said Alice, "to England, could not *not* get him to switch sides."

It was the dignified Mr. Williams who underscored the argument. "It is well known, I'm afraid, that the fabulous Mitzi is a British agent, specifically assigned to convert the Senator."

"I ought not to be listening to this." Senator Taft joined the crowd that was now moving toward the dining-room buffet, where the season's novelty was on display, hickory-smoked turkey, courtesy of Smithfield.

"Let me take you in." Frederika took Timothy's arm. "When will we see this documentary of yours?"

"Before the conventions, I hope."

Frederika nodded. "Yes, afterwards might be too late . . . won't it?"

Timothy was suddenly aware that he had plunged into a world absolutely strange to him. None of this was remotely like the normal dull Washington of Warren Harding and Calvin Coolidge. Somehow, everything had been dramatically changed by the mysterious cripple in the White House, who fascinated everyone as he spun his webs all round an entire world that was now rapidly converging upon the city in an effort to get his spidery eminence's attention so that, yet again, the maps of old Europe—and who knew what else of the world?—might be redrawn. As if to dramatize the extent of the sovereign's range, Frederika introduced Timothy to a pale Chinese who spoke perfect English.

"That was T. V. Soong," said Frederika, after a ceremonious greeting and departure. "He's Chiang Kai-shek's brother-in-law. The Chinese want us to help them fight Japan." Frederika looked amused. "I wonder if Franklin isn't biting off a bit more than *we* can chew."

"Why chew at all?" Plainly, the whole world was now enfolding the United States in its affairs and not, as so many of Blaise's guests thought, the other way around. Suddenly, despite the boredom of the Vandenbergs and Tafts—no, not boredom, studied reserve, since no one was about to give away the game whatever it might prove to be— history was beginning to move, if, indeed, it could ever be said to stop. But what was happening now was on a scale unlike anything in the experience of Timothy X. Farrell, creator of *Hometown*, the first of a series of films about an average American family as it coped, year after year, with a nation in constant flux. Caroline and he had worked, subtly they hoped, to change the way the audience perceived their world. Now President Roosevelt also had some sort of equally imperial vision for a people that, in Timothy's view, had no such sense of themselves. But then could any country be said to have a character, much less a spontaneous collective plan? Hitler spoke endlessly of a common German destiny that must have sounded to even the dimmest German like one of Wagner's more unworkable plots.

"You, sir, gave us our best country." A red-faced man approached Tim.

"Are you a mind-reader?" Tim wondered how this stranger could have, so easily, guessed his thoughts.

"I'm Griffiths." They shook hands. "Harold Griffiths, the *Tribune*'s film critic. I've seen and studied all your films, including the silents."

Tim recalled something vaguely unpleasant associated with the name. "Luckily, the great days of Emma Traxler were before my time. I mean, how do you review a film star who is also your publisher? But when the two of you did your last *Hometown*, and she went home to France, I couldn't help thinking, had the two of you gone on producing, what an era we might have had." Griffiths took a glass of whiskey from a waiter's tray and Tim took one, too: work was done for the night. "I thought you were about to make something of this incoherent country."

Tim was beginning now to recall a long dull review of his work in a magazine not usually associated with movies—*The Atlantic Monthly*? He gulped whiskey; burned his throat; experienced a change in mood, for the better. "Yes," he said, aware that he had missed a flow of words. "Yes," he repeated, eyes on a pretty middle-aged lady as she escorted a stocky pale-faced man, plainly drunk, to a chair by the library door.

"That's one of J. P. Morgan's partners." Griffiths seemed to know a great deal about subjects unrelated to movies. "He has a weakness, as you can see. But he's been very active in getting us into the war on the British side."

The Capitalist, thought Tim; in his head, the word was printed on a title card as in the silent days of film.

"Were you really stopped by the success of the Andy Hardy movies, by Mickey Rooney of all people?"

Tim remembered to smile like Gary Cooper, a thin costive smile. "Let's say Mr. Mayer's series about *his* America was better box-office than mine. The public likes fantasy."

Tim's crew were now leaving. He made arrangements to meet them the next day at the Mayflower Hotel. "We'll be working mostly in the Capitol." He thanked each of them, remembering even the names of the pickup technicians. They left, but Harold Griffiths did not. He hovered near. Tim usually avoided movie buffs, but here in a city where politicians reigned, he did not altogether mind the attentions of someone who actually knew who Timothy Farrell was.

"Will you make another—I hope you don't mind me sounding like an eager reporter—of your what-the-people-are-really-like films, or *should* be like, as my friend Jim Agee wrote in *Time*."

Tim recalled a flowery but shrewd description of his work in *Time*. Since reviews were unsigned in that Jovian magazine, this was the first time that he had heard that there was indeed a writer and not a committee who had written so warmly of the Farrell populist genius.

The drunk businessman was now pulling himself together. The lady was carefully arranging his dark curly hair. Suddenly, he blinked his eyes, and gave her a smile of considerable charm; he was sober now. Fast work, thought Tim, enviously.

"There's no room right now for one of my pictures. This is the year of fantasy."

"Do you still think that what you put on the screen can change the way the audience sees itself?"

Tim, who had always hoped that this was true, laughed and lied: "Of course not. Except in a very general way. Anyway, Judge Hardy and Andy are the way Americans want to see themselves."

Harold Griffiths nodded to show his—disbelief? Tim could not read him, and did not try to. "Would your Hometowners be isolationists today? I mean, if you were making one of your films this minute, what would you show—reflect? About what's going on in the old hometown?"

"If I were just *reflecting*, I'd show how indifferent they always are to Europe and its problems. This morning only seven percent want us to go to war against Hitler."

Which of his interviewees had just told him that? They were beginning to blur in a comfortable bourbon haze. Blaise approached them.

"But then, you don't just reflect, do you? You try to alter the way people see themselves. That's why I wrote how your *Dust Bowl* was better than *Grapes of Wrath* ?"

"Alter? Why, I'm not so vain as all that, Mr. Griffiths."

But the passionate devotee of film had caught sight of his employer and moved away. Meanwhile, Blaise had paused to say a word or two to the now sober—or apparently sober—Capitalist; then Blaise joined Tim.

"He's on the board of Fight for Freedom." Blaise indicated the Capitalist. As a sometime heavy drinker, Tim recognized a fellow "functionary," as he thought of himself, an alcoholic who still did his work well. Although drunk through most of the shooting of *Dust Bowl,* he had managed to bring the picture in on time and under budget, and yet, to this day, he had little memory of ever having made it.

Blaise was on his own track now. "Everyone's choosing up sides. Much too soon from my point of view. The Fighters for Freedom want us to go to war tomorrow to help England and France and I'd rather wait, while you, being Irish, want England to sink beneath the waves."

Tim laughed. "I don't know what I think. But certainly not that."

"This film of yours—the one now—isn't taking sides?" Blaise betrayed an uncharacteristic anxiety.

"How can I? Each of you says what he thinks and . . ."

"The rest is up to your *Hometown.*"

"I don't think," said Tim, poignantly aware of how thoroughly he had failed to accomplish his self-appointed mission to recreate his country through lights and shadows on a million screens, "that the Hometowners are ever consulted when it comes to death and taxes."

"Isn't that what *we're* here for?"

"Maybe what you're here for."

Blaise changed the subject. "She's here, you know. In the town."

"Who's here?"

"Your wife."

"I never married, remember? You mean your half sister."

Blaise reddened. "Yes. Caroline arrived two days ago, from France. She asked about you. First thing, actually."

Tim felt nothing but vague pleasure at the thought of seeing again not so much a onetime mate as a longtime unvaryingly constant, if seldom present, friend. He had not seen Caroline since she had turned over to him her share of the Sanford-Farrell Studio—by then worth nothing—and gone back to France at a time when she was almost alone in predicting that there would be, yet again, a great war; she had also made the point that as she had spent the first German-French war on a movie set, pretending to be a gallant nurse in search of her son in no-man's-land, she meant, this time, to be home at Saint-Cloud-le-Duc, where, she said delightedly, "the real front is bound to be. I have progressed."

Blaise took a card from his waistcoat pocket. "Here's her special number. Don't lose it. Because if you do, I don't know how to get hold of another one."

"Why? Where is she staying?"

"At the White House. Where else? With the Roosevelts, of course."

2

Caroline looked at her latest face and found it good . . . enough. Since she had long since killed off her movie star self, the need to worry about her appearance was minimal. Although she had, through sheer will, absolutely forgotten her age—sixty? No. Fifty—she managed to maintain herself so that she could pass for younger, though younger than exactly what was no longer a useful concept or benchmark. The jawline was still as firm as it was in *Huns from Hell*. She was ageless, she decided, turning away from the dressing-room table and dusty mirror . . . everything in Eleanor Roosevelt's White House was dusty, including the Queen's room, so named for the present British queen, who had slept there the previous June. Eleanor Roosevelt had insisted that Caroline stay with the family. "As long as you like. You cheer up Franklin, and of course I love having you here just down the hall." Then Eleanor promptly disappeared down a West Virginia coal mine, leaving President Roosevelt to cheer up Caroline, who had come to Washington to transact business with Blaise, never an easy matter.

The Queen's room occupied the northeast corner of the second floor. In honor of its recent royal occupant, some prints of Queen Victoria were haphazardly hung on the walls. Caroline recognized Eleanor's absentminded touch. The clock on the mantel was ten minutes slow. Caroline wondered if this was deliberate. The British royal family kept their clocks ahead of time, ten minutes fast, to create anxiety about punctuality. Fortunately, to counteract the misleading White House clocks, a bell always rang to announce the President's arrival in a particular room. He had been, for some minutes now, in the oval study down the hall from the Queen's room. This meant that it was seven-fifteen p.m. The sacred cocktail hour when the President would putter about with bottles and shakers and greet whoever happened to be staying in the house as well as the odd guest who might be joining the family for dinner.

Caroline opened the Queen's-room door to find herself face to face with a Secret Service man in a wrinkled gray suit. He blushed. "Sorry, ma'am."

"You are on the job, sir." Caroline stepped around him. As always, she was struck by how small the White House was. The corridor on what Americans called the second floor and she thought of as the first floor ran from west to east. For some unfathomable reason, the east end was higher than the west end and had to be reached by steps. At either end there was a semicircular window that gave surprisingly little light— dusty panes? At the corner of the southwest end, Eleanor had a two room suite with a view of the Cabinet room and the President's office as well as, from her bedroom, the sloping South Lawn and, just beyond it, the somewhat pointless obelisk to George Washington, which Eleanor always found, she liked to say in all her wise innocence, deeply comforting.

The President's bedroom was just up the hall from Eleanor's suite; connected, however, not with hers but, through a small door, with the oval study across from the Queen's room. The long dark corridor was decorated with dull paintings of interest only to the inhabiting family, while bookcases of different sizes contained the latest unread product of the nation's publishers, tribute to the First Reader. The southeast corner contained the Lincoln bedroom, which Franklin said had actually been Lincoln's office and Cabinet room, now combined into one large and one small bedroom. "There is a ghost, of course," he had added.

"Lincoln's?"

"I've never seen it. More likely a disappointed office-seeker. They never let you alone, in life or in death."

"A very proper ghost," said Caroline, "for such a house." The President had quoted her twice since. But then he collected phrases and anecdotes to decorate his strategically defensive, as she thought of them, monologues. Or, as Eleanor put it, "It is often so important for Franklin to keep on talking in order *not* to allow certain people to tell him certain things."

Caroline liked the oval study best of all the admittedly dismal family rooms. Paintings of the Roosevelt family, of ships, of John Paul Jones hung on the walls. There was a fire in the fireplace and the room smelled of wood smoke and furniture wax that, somehow, kept the heavy Victorian pieces from gleaming. To the left of the fireplace there was a sofa and a curious metal stool on which the President's legs could be arranged.

Opposite the hall door, the President sat at a table desk, strewn with papers as well as two telephones that had never yet rung, at least when Caroline was in the room. Plainly this was the one place in the house where Franklin was allowed to escape his high office. She still thought of him as the handsome flirtatious young man whom she had known so long ago. But now that he was literally historic, she found no difficulty in addressing him correctly.

"Good evening, Mr. President." She even felt for an instant that she should curtsy in the awesome presence of Franklin Delano Roosevelt, a figure who towered even when seated in his wheelchair. It was the head and neck that did the trick, she decided, with a professional actor's eye. The neck was especially thick while the famous head seemed half again larger than the average, its thinning gray hair combed severely back from a high rounded forehead. Roosevelt removed his pince-nez, worn, Eleanor had sighed, as a reminder of his political mentor, President Woodrow Wilson. "We hope Franklin won't make the same mistakes poor Mr. Wilson did."

"Such as going to war?" Caroline, like everyone else in the world, wanted to know what the President intended to do about the European war in which, thus far, no gun had been fired. Caroline suspected that no one, including the President, had the slightest notion what was going to happen next. The next move would be, as usual, Hitler's.

"Caroline!" The resonant voice filled the room as Franklin rolled himself out from behind his desk. She was well used, by now, to the fact that the totally paralyzed legs were like two sticks beneath the extra-thick flannel of trousers calculated to disguise the heavy metal braces that he always wore whenever he knew he would have to be got to his feet in public. Tonight he was not wearing the braces. But then he had always been at home with Caroline since they had first met twenty years earlier when he had been the vigorous athletic assistant secretary of the Navy. She had found him charming if somewhat light-weight and altogether too conscious of the great name he—and Eleanor—together and separately bore. She was President Theodore Roosevelt's niece; Franklin was merely that president's fifth cousin. Eleanor and Caroline did enjoy one thing in common: Eleanor Roosevelt Roosevelt had married a cousin as had Caroline Sanford Sanford; only Eleanor's marriage to Franklin had been a state affair while Caroline's marriage of mild inconvenience to a dim cousin was the result of her unexpected pregnancy by a handsome married statesman, James Burden Day, now a senator, eager to replace Franklin in the White House next year unless, of course, the master politician were to run for a third term, something no president had ever done before. "Nor will I run," he had assured Caroline her first evening in the White House, "unless there's war. . . ." But, thus far, there was no shooting war, though she knew it was coming, and so she carefully answered his questions about the part of France where she lived and the mood of the people, which she described, accurately she thought, as "resigned."

In order to minimize the effect of his useless legs, the President never used a proper wheelchair. Instead he had taken a plain armless chair to which rollers had been added as well as discreet side wheels which he could turn by hand to get himself about. Since he appeared supremely unconscious of his disability, others ceased to notice it. But there was a great deal of careful stage-managing so that the public would not notice. If he was to be photographed seated, a valet would lift his right leg and decorously cross it over his left. Trouser cuffs were pulled down to touch the tops of his shoes, hiding the ends of the braces. When he "walked," he would start out of view of the public, his arm through that of an aide or one of his large sons. Then as he stepped into the limelight, head thrown back, the great smile glittering, he would swing first one leg forward, then back as he simultaneously swung the other forward so that he appeared to be walking in a some-what swaying nautical manner.

Eleanor had confided, "The worst times are at the end of a speech, particularly in the old days. Franklin must hold himself up with both hands on the lectern and still be able to use one of them to turn the pages of his speech, all the while trying to keep his balance on those braces, which are locked just before he starts his walk, which is a terri-ble effort. Then, when he finishes, we have to get him off the stage—that's usually fifteen feet to be negotiated. In the old days when we all wore such huge skirts, the ladies would surround him—at least the tall ones like me—and we'd screen him from the audience while two men would then carry him into the wings. That was then, of course. But, even now, with all the Secret Service, it's still not easy." Eleanor's matter-of-factness always charmed Caroline, who would have been tempted to dramatize the situation had she been an actor in so extraor-dinary a script. Nevertheless, there was sufficient drama in the fact that although there must be numerous photographs of the President caught off-guard in his rolling chair, none had ever appeared in an American newspaper. Why? she wondered. Instinctive self-preservation? In a world where dictators strode and strutted toward war, Americans instinctively did not want to publicize the fact that their own leader could not even walk.

"We have only the cocktail hour," said Franklin, "before Eleanor's young communists join us for dinner."

That morning Caroline had heard on the radio in Blaise's office reports from a congressional committee deeply concerned with something known as "un-American activities." Various youth organizations had been testifying about *their* suspect activities. Apparently, the September pact between Germany and Russia had been a political earthquake on Capitol Hill, where the President's New Deal, already sternly labeled communist by American conservatives, was now looking especially vulnerable. With what seemed, to Caroline, either exemplary courage or plain lack of judgment, late the previous evening Eleanor had come down from New York in order to attend the meeting of the House committee, thus demonstrating her sympathy with the young witnesses who wanted no part in old Europe's war.

Early that morning, in a green dress, she had left for the Capitol with Caroline, who wanted to hear her testify, but Eleanor had said, "You're better off at the *Tribune*, influencing Blaise. I'll drop you off."

As it turned out, Mrs. Roosevelt caused a sensation in the Caucus Room: First Ladies were almost never seen in the legislative halls of the republic. She had been received courteously by the congressmen, who had invited her to sit with them on their dais. Gracefully, she had said that she preferred just to sit in the back where she could keep her cold gray alert eyes upon the congressmen while projecting her patented brand of motherly solicitude for the young firebrands.

"Now she's asked six of them to dinner." Franklin sighed theatrically.

"Are they communists?"

"Some, I suppose. Or they think they are this week. I shall be benignly noncommittal."

"Your greatest role."

"Do you think so?" Franklin placed a cigarette in a holder. Caroline lit it for him. "We have some other actors here tonight. For dinner, there's Melvyn Douglas and his wife, Helen Gahagan. Loyal New Dealers, I'm happy to say. She's very political and never too shy to advise me. Now you tell me about Daladier." The President's love of gossip, Caroline had decided, came from the fact that as he could not move about, either literally or symbolically as president, he must pump others. Although he often acknowledged that the peripatetic Eleanor acted as his eyes and ears, he also acknowledged, privately to Caroline, that Eleanor was far too noble ever to meanly gossip, "and since you are too far away in France, all I've got, at the moment, is Liz Whitney. She drives over from that place of hers in Virginia and just barges in. Without an appointment. Then she asks me about all the news that was in the papers that morning, which she never reads. Patiently, I tell her. Then she rivets *me* with all the problems that Jock Whitney and David Selznick had in making *Gone With the Wind*, which is about to open at last."

During this, a black steward had placed a tray full of bottles and glasses on the President's desk, to which he now returned. "I think a martini will hit the spot." The Roosevelt special. Caroline loathed gin but gamely drank the President's astonishing concoction, whose secret ingredients were two brands of vermouth, each sweeter than the other, and a dash of absinthe to destroy the palate. As he shook the martini, he returned to Daladier, the premier of France.

"We say that he is more the Veal," said Caroline, "than what he likes to be called, the bull of Vaucluse."

"Yes. Bullitt says he's scared to death of Hitler. But who else is there?"

"Léon Blum." Caroline was particularly fond of the socialist intellectual, whose Popular Front government had been denounced in America as—what else?—communist, even by Blaise. Caroline had long since given up trying to explain the difference between communism and socialism to Americans.

The President tasted his martini. "Now that is just about right." He poured her a glass. They toasted peace.

"I wouldn't mind talking to Blum, face to face. Particularly now. But we're all so cut off from each other. So far apart, geographically. So many misunderstandings. You're back with Tim Farrell, I gather?"

"No. No. Just friends, as they say. You were going to ask him to dinner tonight."

"If I was, I did." Franklin laughed. "I'm not sure how much he'll like Eleanor's young friends."

"But that's exactly what he wants. He's making a documentary. About the war. About how Americans feel about the war."

The President moved his chair directly across from Caroline's. He rubbed his eyes; for an instant he looked to be without energy. "I don't envy him," he said at last. "A film *now?* When anything can happen." He shook his head. "Look at Finland. Whoever dreamed that Russia would invade them? Certainly not our State Department," he added, with an unpleasant smile. "But then whoever dreamed they could defeat a Russian army? For the moment, anyway." He raised the martini shaker and turned to Caroline. "Another sippy?"

At that moment two giants, Mr. and Mrs. Melvyn Douglas, appeared in the doorway.

"Come in, Helen, Mel. What shall I make you?" The President was once again his airy light-hearted social self, as he prepared yet another Roosevelt special, all the while talking to the handsome Helen Douglas while her husband introduced himself to Caroline. She had never found him attractive on the screen—nose too large, lips too thin—but his voice was seductive, and he was also the only American-born movie star who had no difficulty playing high comedy, when allowed. Had he been older, he would have been a perfect leading man for Emma Traxler, the Black Pearl of—where was it her publicity had said she was from? Alsace-Lorraine?

"I grew up watching your movies," he said; then frowned. "There I go, you weren't making movies when I was a kid back in Georgia and you were a child in—where was it?"

"Washington, D.C. I was the child publisher of the *Tribune* before 1917 and Hollywood and the birth of my dreaded other self, Emma Traxler."

"I've just met your brother, Blaise."

"Did you quarrel?"

Douglas blinked his eyes; then smiled a thin-lipped smile. "Yes. How did you know?"

"He doesn't like the Roosevelts. You do."

"And you do?"

Caroline gave him the Emma Traxler left-three-quarter-right-eyebrow-raised close-shot look, quite aware that, with age, she must now resemble the moon's far side if it had one. "I never said, Mr. Douglas, that Blaise liked me either."

He laughed. "One of those families." The room began to fill up. A pair of bureaucrats, each with a wife, had shyly entered the presence. Franklin was now jovial, as he peddled yet another Roosevelt special— rum, vermouth, and pineapple juice. He seemed to absorb energy from an audience.

"He *is* an actor," said Caroline to herself, unaware that she was sharing her not particularly original insight with Douglas, who said, "Of course he is. But one who gets to write his own play."

"His? Don't you think Hitler and Stalin are going to get co-credits for this one?"

"Certainly not if the Screen Writers Guild arbitrates!"

Caroline changed the subject; complimented him on a film that he had just made in which, according to the press, the moody Swede, Greta Garbo, had finally laughed on screen. "That was a lot more than I ever did," said Douglas, raising a practiced eyebrow.

"Is she so dull?" Caroline was fascinated by Garbo's androgynous charm.

" 'Selfish' is more the word." Why, Caroline wondered, was she herself no longer young and in competition with this new generation? But Tim had now joined them and her instant of self-pity passed. Douglas moved on to join his wife, whose lips had never ceased to move since she had stationed herself beside the President.

Tim was little changed. "I'd like to work with him." He indicated Douglas. "He shouldn't let himself get trapped in all those drawing-room comedies, particularly as a second lead."

"He does get Garbo at the end of *Ninotchka*."

"Yes," said Tim, "and she's getting the boot from Metro soon."

Caroline was slipping more and more into her previous existence. Soon they would be discussing the grosses of films and the latest studio preview, in Bakersfield. Meanwhile, she was interested to learn that Garbo's principal audience was European, not American, and once the war became hot the studios would no longer be able to distribute their "product" abroad and so the expensive Garbo would no longer be asked to make movies for MGM. "Anyway, she *says* she wants to retire. Where's the President?"

"He's over there." But the President was not over there at the desk. In fact, he was nowhere in the room. An usher approached Caroline and Tim. "He is in the West Hall with Mrs. Roosevelt. They'll be going down to dinner presently."

Caroline explained Eleanor's young people to Tim, who said, "I wish I could film them."

"Tonight's out of bounds." As they started to the door, Tim stepped in front of a strange metal piano. "What's that?"

"A mechanical pipe organ. A gift to the President. He told me that for his entire first term, he tried to learn to play it, but so far the thing has defeated him. I suspect he's tone-deaf."

"Can we talk?"

"After dinner. He goes to bed early."

The West Hall was simply the west end of the long corridor, closed off by two ill-matching Chinese screens. The sounds of the young were clearly audible as well as the high-fluting tones of Eleanor herself.

"I think we can start down now. Let's walk. The lift tends to get stuck."

"It's just like home. *My* home, that is. In South Boston."

"It is," said Caroline, "democracy."

The dinner was reasonably chaotic. Eleanor presided at one end of the family dining table, her six young Americans to her left, Melvyn Douglas and the bureaucrats to her right. Tim had been placed next to Caroline.

The President made his entrance after everyone was seated. As an aide pushed his chair into place at the head of the table, everyone rose. He waved for them to be seated. "Lovely to have you here," he said with a most genuine-looking smile in the direction of Eleanor's brood.

Next to the President, Mrs. Douglas continued her conversation into his right ear while he addressed, down table, the Youth of the Nation, radical division.

"I gather you young people distinguished yourselves this morning before Mr. Dies's Committee . . ."

"Only he wasn't there," said Eleanor.

"He knew he had met his match when he heard you were coming."

"Hardly. Actually, I was ever so mild."

"I'm sure the rest of you were not so mild." The President looked at the youthful witnesses—to what? wondered Caroline. Some were, no doubt, actual communists, or had thought they were, until communist Russia and Nazi Germany had made their alliance in August and the American left had behaved like an anthill struck by lightning. Before this astonishing event, the Youth Congress had, more or less, followed the communist line, supporting the New Deal at home while supporting France and England against Hitler abroad. Now, if Blaise was to be believed, directions from Moscow were instructing the faithful to join the isolationists. Mrs. Roosevelt, as one of the guiding spirits of the Youth Congress before the infamous pact, was in a delicate position. She had already been bitterly denounced by political conservatives as well as by pro-Nazi groups like the German-American Bund. Thus far, she had sailed serenely above the tempest, but the unexpected alliance of communists and Nazis could not be so easily sailed through.

"I must say they all behaved very well." Eleanor was maternal but, again, Caroline caught the cold alert eye even as she dripped honey; she was constantly calculating and assessing. "Why, one of them even suggested . . ." She turned to the scruffy boy beside her. "Tell them, John, what you proposed to the committee."

John was not as nervous as Caroline would have been at President Roosevelt's table for the first time. "Well, Mr. President, I proposed to the committee that a resolution be submitted to Congress for the abolition of the House Committee to Investigate Un-American Activities."

"What happened?" Franklin was leaning forward, elbows on the table, a characteristic gesture when he was particularly interested in what someone else was saying.

"Well, sir, the acting chairman, a gentleman from Alabama, was very polite and he said that that was my right as an American citizen, and he would let what I say go onto the record in spite of what he called my slanderous remarks."

"I love it!" Franklin turned to Melvyn Douglas. "If I could only put a sheet over my head and hide in the back row."

"I'm sure," said Douglas in his most suave voice, "you would have been greeted as an honored emissary from the Ku Klux Klan."

The conversation became general except for Mrs. Douglas, beautiful eyes flashing with intelligence and firmness of purpose, as she continued to speak into the President's constantly moving right ear.

The food was, as always, inedible. Caroline had had a long experience of the infamous Roosevelt table, which dated back to when Eleanor had discovered that her husband was committing adultery with her social secretary, a Maryland beauty called Lucy Mercer. Eleanor had then moved like a conquering army onto a battlefield where she imposed her conditions of peace. If Franklin chose, she would grant him a divorce so that he could marry Lucy, who would then become the stepmother of their five children, and Eleanor would go her solitary way. At this point, onto the field came Franklin's mother, the formidable Mrs. James Roosevelt, who told her son that if he went through with a divorce, she would disinherit him, which meant that he would have no money of any kind and lose forever the Hudson Valley estate at Hyde Park. Finally, no one needed to point out to him that a divorced man could not have a career in politics. "So," Caroline murmured to Tim, "he gave up Lucy, I think."

"You think?" As a rule, Tim disliked gossip of the who is with whom and why sort. But this was part of the history he was starting to record.

"I said *think*," said Caroline, carefully drowning a heavily fried chicken croquette in a viscous sea of white cream sauce that was slowly coagulating into library paste, "because—I think—he still sees her, they say."

"How do *they* know?"

"How do they always seem to know everything? Lucy married happily but apparently, every now and then, the two meet. She's supposed to have sat in the back of a car at his first inauguration and watched it all."

"How very romantic."

"I think it is. Anyway, he and Eleanor lead separate lives. She's always on the move. Even so, they are very much a team. I can't fathom what they think of each other. There is a basket beside his bed and whenever she's here, she fills it every night with notes, things to be done, people to see. Oh!"

Caroline had seen what she'd been longing for Tim to see: The Salad. It had materialized at the President's end of the table. From afar, it looked to be a milky mound, studded with golden and red splotches like some rare disease. "Part of Eleanor's revenge for Lucy has been Mrs. Nesbitt, a cook from Hyde Park, now the housekeeper who commands the kitchen where . . . Well, look!" Caroline gazed at the drowned but still intact chicken croquette. Tim had already eaten his.

"It wasn't so bad. Just like Holy Cross."

"I'm sure nothing like The Salad was ever seen at Holy Cross. It is Mrs. Nesbitt's most belligerent creation."

"It appears to have the stigmata, a very Holy Cross touch."

"Watch the President."

The black waiter had presented the huge mountain of a salad to the President's back.

"What's in it?" Tim had put on his glasses.

"Mostly mayonnaise from a jar, with slices of tinned pineapple, carved radishes—the ones with spongy interiors—and, sometimes, deep under the mayonnaise, there is cottage cheese decorated with maraschino cherries, to add gaiety to this Hudson Valley Staple."

The President, aware of the waiter on his left, turned expectantly. When he saw The Salad his smile ceased; sadly, he shook his head, lips moving to frame: "No, thank you."

"Now watch Eleanor," Caroline whispered. Their hostess was watching her husband with relish. She had already got halfway through her own salad and now she was watching him grimly: would her husband take his punishment? He would not. When the waiter was obliged to move on, Eleanor simply looked more than ever resolute.

Tim was awed. "She is taking a great revenge."

"It's positively Greek, isn't it? Euripides. The Furies."

"Actually, I think I'm going to like this." Tim helped himself generously to The Salad. Out of the corner of Caroline's eye, she saw that Eleanor was smiling with approval: Tim was making a hit.

At the end of dinner, the President vanished and Mrs. Roosevelt and her brood retired to the oval study, the Douglases in attendance.

"I'm here," said Caroline outside the door to the Queen's room. "Come on in. We're not expected to join the seminar. Eleanor has a nicely haphazard way with guests. You come and go as you please. Some have actually stayed a month or more. There are also a dozen rooms on the floor above." They sat before an unlit fire. Rose was the predominant color in the room. "The President's secretary lives up there above us, in a nice suite."

"Missy Le Hand." To Caroline's surprise, Tim knew her name. But then he lived in America full-time and read the press, while she was now once more a foreigner.

"She's the actual wife, at least when it comes to arranging his life, keeping the sons out of jail, running the office, telling him which angry letters not to send. She's very wise."

"Mrs. Roosevelt . . ."

". . . is not jealous. Relieved, I'd say. They get on very well, the two wives."

"Positively French," said Tim, reprising Caroline.

Caroline found it curious to be once again in such close proximity to someone with whom she had, for the most part contentedly, lived and then, for no reason other than geography, parted from. "You see, I had to go back to France," she heard herself say.

"I don't think I ever asked you why you had to." Tim was cool. "Why?"

"Did I never tell you?"

"If you did, I've forgotten."

As they had parted for no reason, they were now for no reason reunited, each trying to inhabit a previous self, and each quite willing to say exactly what was thought if not necessarily felt.

"I suppose I felt, or thought," Caroline edited herself, "that I'd come to the end with movies as I had with publishing the *Tribune*."

Tim removed the cellophane from a small thin parchment-brown cigar; he bit off the end. "Nobody gets to the end with movies. But they do get to the end of us pretty fast." He puffed blue smoke.

"I thought I was old then. I see now I wasn't, really."

"At least not so old as you are now."

"Thank you. I needed that. Life is less than fair to women."

"I don't need to hear that. At least not from you to me. Maybe from Emma Traxler to Melvyn Douglas. What *are* you doing here?"

"I have found a book."

Tim looked alert. "To be filmed?"

"No. To be published. A manuscript. It was in a box. At the chateau. The memoirs of my grandfather, Charles Schermerhorn Schuyler. The historian."

Tim nodded. "Wasn't he the illegitimate son of Aaron Burr?"

"The same. In 1876 he left Europe, where he lived, with his daughter Emma. She was a widow. He was a widower. They were flat broke. It was the year of the American Centennial. So he came home to write about his native land and she came looking for a husband." Caroline wondered how much she should tell.

"She got the husband, didn't she? Your father, with all that money and the French chateau and all those . . . was it railroads?"

"Yes. But to begin with he had a great many New England encaustic tiles. Whatever they are—or were."

As Caroline told Tim her story, she began, inadvertently, to start turning the narrative into a movie, aware that she was now decades too old to play her dark—the adjective always used to describe her beautiful, but dark in every sense—mother. Perhaps she could cast herself as Mrs. Astor, the sovereign of New York society. "My father wrote his impressions of the country that legendary year when the Republicans stole the presidential election from the Democrats."

"Political movies do even worse at the box office than baseball movies." Tim parroted movie wisdom; yet he himself was always eager to show on the screen how people actually lived, a political action if there ever was one, and some of the time he had even attracted large audiences.

"Mr. Capra has proven otherwise." Caroline knew how sincerely Tim disliked Capra's syrupy films about Washington.

"I hope your story isn't for him."

"No. It is too . . . dark." That adjective was now filling up her head. "Emma got William Sanford to marry her. That part was easy. But the hard part, the dark part, was when she killed her best friend, his wife, Denise, who died giving birth to my half brother Blaise."

Tim whistled blue smoke; then stubbed out his cigar. "How did she kill her?"

"Deliberately withheld information, withheld the medicine that would have saved her. By the end of his memoir, my grandfather knows the whole story. He had found out what she had done and, worse, had not done. And it killed him."

There was a long silence, broken finally by laughter from the oval study. "So Emma married Sanford, gave birth to you, and lived happily ever after."

"No. After I was born, *she* died of complications. There's a dark sort of symmetry in this story. Anyway, I shall publish it, though my daughter will be shocked."

"What about Blaise?"

"It's my mother, not his. Besides, the Burrs fascinate him. My grandfather once worked in Burr's law office. He's done a sort of biography of him, as hero, with Jefferson and Hamilton as villains."

"That's what Burr would think."

Caroline nodded. Actually, she had always found her ancestor far more humanly attractive than any of the other founding fathers even though there was little doubt in her mind that he had been, at times, quite mad. "Now you know why I came back."

"I'd hoped we could reopen the Sanford-Farrell Studio. After all these depressions and financial panics, rapes and murders and drug addictions that we have lived through, the movies are now a huge business. It takes real genius to fail—commercially that is."

There was a rap at the door. It was Mrs. Roosevelt. Caroline and Tim rose. "I'll wash out the ashtray," said Tim, dutifully going to the bathroom with the remains of his dead cigar.

Eleanor laughed. "Don't bother. This is an old politicians' retirement home. People do nothing but puff cigar smoke at you, while Franklin smokes far too many cigarettes."

Eleanor sat down. "I've just come to say good night. I hope my lame ducks—as Franklin calls them—weren't too dull for you."

"Fascinating, Mrs. Roosevelt. For me," said Tim, "especially now."

He told her about the documentary. Caroline was surprised at how knowledgeable Eleanor was about filmmaking, but then she had spent the last dozen years in front of newsreel cameras. Eleanor thought it would be a good idea for Tim to do a series of short interviews with some of the leading interventionists. "But only the very . . . uh, subtle ones, if you know what I mean."

"I shall need a list."

"That's one thing we do rather well around here. I'll see you get one."

"Could I interview you?"

"Oh, I'm far *too* subtle on that subject. Also, my young people really hate the idea of any sort of war with anyone and I must say they tend to influence me—up to a point—rather than the other way around. After all, they know that they will be the ones who will have to fight." She rose. "I'll get you your list, Mr. Farrell. Good night, Caroline." She was gone.

"Neither one ever says what he means and yet they both appear to be so candid, so . . ." Caroline tried for a new word: "Transparent."

"I find him pretty opaque. But then I've only seen him in action once, fighting off The Salad."

For an instant Caroline wondered if she and Tim could ever live together again. She was, of course, far too old for him, too old for any sort of sex, or so she had convinced herself. But that need not be the link or, indeed, anything at all, as she had observed in the case of the interesting, if sometimes baffling, friendship between Franklin and Eleanor. Each in a separate bedroom, and often city, yet sharing an entire nation between them while, privately, he had Missy Le Hand for an efficient selfless wife and Eleanor had, it was rumored, several lady friends, of whom a journalist named Lorena Hickok was the one that she most saw; traveled with; allowed to use a spare bed in her White

House suite as well as in her getaway cottage at Hyde Park. This sort of relationship came as no surprise to Caroline, who had attended the same girls' school as Eleanor, the creation of a distinguished lesbian named Mademoiselle Souvestre. The atmosphere of the school had been something of a hothouse where usually nipped-in-the-bud emotions blossomed and flourished, all intensely described in an unpublished novel by one of the teachers, who had given it to André Gide to read, who had then given it to Caroline, with a smile: "Your old school, I believe." But none of this had been, or would ever be, Caroline was certain, shared with the American people, although at least one journalist, Joe Alsop, cousin to Eleanor, liked to go on and on about her Sapphic attachments, which, he claimed, included a fan-dancer from the recent World's Fair.

"Why haven't you married?" Caroline was more to the point than she had intended. "Of course, it's no business of mine."

Tim smiled his crooked smile. "Lapsed Catholics don't make good husbands."

"Is that an answer?"

"An observation. Besides, I don't want children. Why haven't *you* married again?"

Was this her chance? "I seem to have done all that. With you. With others before." She then erased the subject from her mind. She would continue as she was.

"There is something going on here." Tim changed the uncomfortable subject.

"Here . . . where? The White House?"

"Yes. And Washington. It's about the war."

"Everything's about the war now."

"No." He walked over to the window; pulled aside the curtain. Mrs. Nesbitt's patented Hyde Park dust glittered an instant in the lamplight. Across the avenue Lafayette Park looked bleak and wintry. "Who used to live here? In this room?"

"In a hundred and thirty-nine years there have been thirty or so presidents—just about every one, I should think." Then a memory stirred. "You know I was engaged to Del Hay."

"Before my time."

"Yes." She was cool. "It was very long ago." But she could not bring herself to give the date when she became engaged to Del. That would have frightened Tim. She felt unpleasantly historic. "Anyway, Del's father was John Hay, who came to Washington with President Lincoln. He was one of two secretaries, and he told me that this was their room, and how when the President couldn't sleep, which was often—he had terrible nightmares, like Mr. Roosevelt, who keeps dreaming that there's a man coming in through the transom to kill him and he wakes up screaming. Anyway, Mr. Lincoln would come in here, wearing only a long nightshirt, looking like an ostrich with his long thin legs and the nightshirt bunched out in back. He would sit down and read something funny to them, to take his mind off the war. . . . So what do you think is going on?"

Tim turned his director's gaze on her, intent, impersonal. "The British are secretly getting us into their war. Yes, I know that I've been filming mostly isolationists so far, but they are convinced that the British secret services are busy buying up members of Congress, planting horror stories in the press, making films . . ." Tim started to light a cigar; thought better of it. "It's the business about the films that convinced me. Because that's something I know. Remember Balderston? He was at your brother's. He's in on it, too. He's always been an Anglophile, which is his business, not mine. But everything he makes— or wants to make—is a celebration of gallant little England, not to mention France and all those Scarlet Pimpernels."

"I don't see how poor Norma Shearer having her head chopped off by the French mob will make Americans pro-French."

"No. But it will make them anti-mob, anti-Bolshevik, anti-Russia."

Caroline reminded him of their old ambition to influence—even re-create—people.

"This is more specific than we ever were. It's more like what's-his-name. Wilson's man in Hollywood who saw to it all those anti-Hun movies were made. George Creel, his name was." He sighed. "I wish I knew what was in the President's head."

"I suspect he wishes that he knew too. He acts mostly on instinct, even impulse. Yet he takes his time. He doesn't dare be too far ahead of the public. Yesterday when someone asked Eleanor what the President thought about the Russian invasion of Finland, she said, 'The President doesn't think. He decides.' Of course, he wants to be a second Woodrow Wilson. But a successful Wilson."

"And go to war for England?"

"For himself. Which will include us, of course. Then he'll want a new League of Nations, which he will personally take charge of to make sure it doesn't fail."

Tim rose. "I get the feeling that I'm in some sort of witches' coven. Everyone is sharing secrets—big secrets—speaking in a code to which I don't have the key."

"No one's apt to give it to someone Irish, who doesn't want us to go to war."

"Being Irish has nothing to do with it. Being the maker of *Hometown* does. I want to keep Americans home. To make improvements about the house. Who is Ernest Cuneo?"

Caroline shrugged. "Every day I hear another one hundred unfamiliar names."

"He works, at times, as a lawyer for the President. He's also working for BSC . . ."

"British Security Coordination." Caroline laughed. "Now, I said that only out of vanity. To impress you when I shouldn't have let you know that I even know what it is." She rose. "Yes, I am a witch, too. A kindly one. I just hope you're not with the Germans in all this."

"Of course not. I think I must get to know Mr. Cuneo."

"He's a friend of the newspaper columnist Drew Pearson, who used to be Cissy Patterson's son-in-law."

"I knew you'd know."

Caroline wondered if by saying far too much, she had put Tim in harm's way. He was quite right about the gathering of the witches. All sorts of black magic was in the air, and though she was more observer than participant she had quickly realized how great the stakes were for everyone involved. The world was about to be turned upside down in a way never seen before. "One must serve oneself." She kissed Tim on the cheek and said good night.

Would things now become as bad as they had been when John Hay and the other one—Nicholas? Nicolay?—slept in this room, wearied with news of bloody defeats at the South, disturbed in their sleep by the cries of Abraham Lincoln, as he dreamed his terrible dreams just down the hall? Caroline took a sleeping pill to ward off the ghosts of ancient nightmares, not to mention premonitory whispers of those as yet undreamed.

3

"Third table on the left. I'm bald." The voice on the telephone had a strong New York City accent. Tim entered the Mayflower's Presidential Room, where breakfast was served to all sorts of visitors to the city as well as to important residents, doing business. At the third table to the left, a thickset half-bald man with narrow eyes was seated beside a familiar-looking thin man whose gray hair was thinning in contrast to his moustache, which bristled like that of a British colonel in a film.

"Mr. Cuneo?" Tim approached the table. Both men stood. Cuneo introduced Tim to the moustache, which belonged to the journalist Drew Pearson, who shook Tim's hand rather absently while giving him a very sharp look indeed; the contrast between handshake and scrutiny was oddly disconcerting.

"I'm on my way, Mr. Farrell," said Pearson. "Looking forward to that documentary. When are you releasing it?"

"June, MGM says."

"Wish it were sooner. All hell's going to break loose long before that." Pearson made his wary way across the room. Tim usually read Pearson's syndicated muck-raking political column "Washington Merry-Go-Round," co-authored with someone called Allen.

"Sit down, Mr. Farrell." Cuneo's smile was amused and amusing.

"I like Pearson."

"Do you? He'll take a lot of convincing that you really do. He's more used to being hated. Look at him dodging around that table because Senator McKellar is sitting there. Drew's afraid he'll get bit. And McKellar's rabid on the subject of Drew. A lot of people are."

"Right-wing people, anyway." Tim was not sure how best to play Ernest Cuneo. After three months of asking questions, he had come to think of Cuneo as somehow the center of everything; certainly he kept cropping up in the oddest places. Originally a legal adviser to Mayor La Guardia of New York, he had joined the White House as special legal counselor to the President. He was also involved, somehow, with British intelligence and the American interventionists. He was said to be close to J. Edgar Hoover of the FBI, also to the country's other powerful journalist, Walter Winchell.

"I'm Drew's legal adviser." Cuneo ordered chipped beef on toast; inspired by Mrs. Nesbitt's cuisine, Tim did the same. "'Adviser' is a safer word than 'lawyer.'" Cuneo chuckled. "Drew is sued for libel about once a week, and now that he's on radio he's sued for slander, too. The lawsuits never stop. Luckily, he loves a fight, good Quaker that he is. I give him advice on how to win the suits. I also tend to pick up odds and ends of information that are useful to people. I saved Drew from that General . . . I have a block about his name. The pompous ass—you know; the chief of staff who attacked the bonus veterans . . ."

"Douglas MacArthur."

"The same. Drew went after him. MacArthur filed suit. We discovered that he had this Eurasian mistress out in Manila. We told him we'd go public. End of suit. Was I on the list?"

The transition was so quick that Tim almost missed it. "List?"

"Mrs. Roosevelt's. People to talk to. 'Subtle' people." Cuneo waved to the large John Foster in the middle distance.

"No. You weren't." Had Caroline talked to Cuneo? If she had, how did she know him? Through all of this Tim remained, he hoped, poker-faced. "No. You weren't on the list. I guess you know Caroline Sanford."

Cuneo nodded. "I even went to Saint-Cloud-le-Duc last year. What a place!"

"I've never seen it." There were definitely two quite separate Carolines. He had known the American one intimately; had never met the French one.

"It was a perfect day. She'd invited Léon Blum, at my request, and he arrived with André Gide. It was certainly an educational day for me. I only wish Blum were still in charge over there in France. He's got Hitler's number. The others don't—or they do but they think they can handle him, which they can't. What can I do for you, sir?"

Tim produced his White House list of names. He read them off to Cuneo, who told him, briefly, even sharply, who was worth talking to and why. Tim made notes. The chipped beef came. The whole room now smelled of roast coffee and cigarette smoke. The steady murmur of masculine voices was like a distant thunder.

"I've pretty much finished with the isolationists."

"Lucky you got Borah back in November. He's dying as we speak." Tim noted that Cuneo was never tentative. He never said "I hear that" or "They say." He simply made flat statements. "Once he's dead you might try to find out if he took cash from the German government. We know he did. From several sources. But we have no proof so far. No safety box full of cash. I have some leads if you're interested."

"Since he's always been an isolationist, why would he take money to do what he'd have done anyway?"

"This is Washington, Tim. Are any of Mrs. R's Youth Congress kids on your list?"

"One. But I haven't seen him."

"I wouldn't. Not now. They're too mixed up with the communists, which means Russia. So they'll be pro-Hitler for the next few months until Hitler double-crosses Stalin and starts his invasion of Russia and then Mrs. R's kids will all have to switch again."

Tim was doing his best to absorb so many mind-boggling revelations. "Hitler, having just signed a pact with Russia, now plans to invade Russia?"

"In the zoo, study your beast. Haven't you read his book, *Mein Kampf*? It's all in there. He gives the whole game away. But hardly anyone has ever got through the book, while the few who have read it never take him seriously. He tells just how he plans to carve up Russia. Enslave all the Slavs. Annex the Romanian oil fields, which he really needs. Get rid of all the Jews . . ."

"How?"

"However he can. He's been selling a lot of German Jews to the West. But we're not taking in as many as we should. I fear the worst. But people think I'm an alarmist to be alarmed by what is so plain to see. Anyway, thanks to some nice undercover work, Hitler won't be invading Russia this summer as originally planned. He hadn't figured on England and France going to war over Poland, so he'll have to defeat them first. Then he'll go after the real prize, Eastern Europe." Again the amused smile. Tim wondered if Cuneo was making fun of him. Since September 1939 many scenarios had been prepared by various pundits but no one had yet sounded as positive, if not plausible, as this pudgy bald man who seemed to know everything as well as everyone.

"You don't think England and France can beat Hitler in a fighting war?"

"No. England's too small. England's also broke. France is weak. With Blum they might have. . . . Anyway, let's not indulge in what-might-have-been stuff. Without our help, money, ships, planes, information"—the last word he gave special emphasis to—"they'll go down." Cuneo was no longer smiling. He suddenly looked like the gangster Al Capone. "We need this film of yours to help with public opinion."

"So that the boys will enlist in the Army and follow Roosevelt into war?" Tim realized that he was being less than cool.

"I know your inclinations are isolationist. Why not? Most Americans are, and you're the recorder—if not the inventor—of a real America out there." Cuneo knew Caroline well enough to have obtained a good blueprint of her onetime lover. "But we'll be driven into this no matter what."

"In which case, Mr. Cuneo, why are you—and the British and all the others—swarming about Washington and Hollywood and the New York *Times* . . . ?"

"*Our* paper is the New York *Herald Tribune*." Cuneo chuckled. "You'd think that the *Times*, with a Jewish owner, would be helpful but Sulzberger is afraid of not seeming to be 'even-handed,' as he calls it, so we rely on Mrs. Reid and the *Tribune* to get our views to the people."

"To the wealthy Anglophiles of New York, anyway—as Senator Borah would have said."

Cuneo crossed himself, eyes to the ceiling. "Heaven forbid that we are so elitist. Anyway we have Walter Winchell and Drew for the great public. Walter's column is in a thousand papers. That's twelve hundred words or more a day, six days a week. Then there's his Sunday radio broadcast, which I also help with. Millions hear us."

"You do this for nothing?"

"I do it for the President. Not to mention the lawsuits my clients get themselves into which I have to get them out of. Drew's the worst. Walter sounds fierce when on the attack but basically he's an actor. Drew is a believer. Drew's righteous. Drew's a killer."

Tim was impressed, the object of Cuneo's exercise. But to what end? He asked; got an answer. "We need your help, that's all." Cuneo opened a briefcase on the banquette beside him. "Let's see what your horoscope says. You don't have to bother to give me your date and time of birth because I have it all here." He was looking through a notebook. "Here we are. Sagittarius, Moon in the House of . . ." He muttered to himself. Then: "You will be unusually receptive to new ideas. Your native Sagittarian skepticism will quickly see through someone who is trying to influence you. That must be me."

"Probably." Tim remained cool. "I'm not a believer in astrology, you know."

"Neither am I. But Hitler is, and so are most of the people who read Walter Winchell with moving lips. Also, a surprising number of politicians. Washington's the city of clairvoyants. Life's so uncertain for politicians." Cuneo shut his notebook. "We're syndicating nationally a distinguished Hungarian astrologist. Number one in his field. Hitler always reads him. Lately, our Magyar sees good things for us. Very good things."

"This stuff . . . works?" Tim was surprised.

"Why not? Sort of like the polls, only not so tough to control. We have quite a time getting the good Dr. Gallup, when he polls our innocent folks, to ask our questions the *right* way."

Tim was now at home. Hollywood studios had been using polls for years and they knew that the way a question was asked predetermined the answer. Movies and politics were uncertain activities not, if possible, to be left entirely to dangerous chance.

"We have some input with Elmo Roper's poll. But that's because his major client is *Time, Life, Fortune* magazines and Henry Luce is with us, at the moment. Roper says that sometimes he will do a poll to serve Harry's interests only to find that Harry's changed his mind and re-slants the poll. At Gallup we have a more discreet arrangement. We all think, Tim, that your picture could make quite an impression this spring."

"I certainly hope it will. . . ." Tim was uninformative. Cuneo chewed rather than smoked a fresh cigar.

"The *real* figures—from Gallup and the rest—are not so good. For the Allies, that is."

Curious to see how Cuneo meant to play him, he played Cuneo. "Well, we're an isolationist country, and since we got nothing out of the last war, why go that route again?" Tim used the familiar isolationist line.

Cuneo nodded. "So why help England pull her chestnuts out of the fire again? I often coin memorable phrases. Actually, we got quite a lot out of that war. We got Prohibition and Al Capone and Brother Wilson's war on the Bill of Rights, and then—the main feature—the Depression! Pretty good I'd say for a few months over in France during the off-season. You're giving the isolationists a break, I hope?"

"I have to. For a movie like this to work it can't be one-sided. Can't *look* to be one-sided."

"*I love fair play!*" Cuneo did a surprisingly accurate imitation of the President's voice at its most richly ecclesiastical.

Tim laughed in spite of himself. "Will he run this November?"

"Well, if all goes as planned, yes, he'll run for a third term and he'll win."

"All *what* has been planned?"

"First, we'll have to take a good look at Hitler's astrological chart for 1940. Our astrologist is busy working on it even as you and I do the Mayflower special breakfast tour of the world's horizon. After all, Hitler can still be killed. We've even got a man standing by to do the deed. No Hitler no war, or maybe no war. And no war means Franklin will go home to Hyde Park, to his stamp collection, along with Judge Sam Rosenman, who will then write his memoirs for him, with some help from Harry Hopkins if he lives that long."

"But suppose Hitler survives?"

"He'll probably conquer most of Europe. I can't think why he wants to. Imagine governing France! No one's been able to do that since Napoleon, and he only did it by conquering Europe, for all of five minutes. Anyway, if England's attacked, Franklin will do what no president's ever done. He'll run for a third term so as to save the world for freedom and democracy, not to mention for this and for that." Cuneo was, Tim thought, a bit too blithe in the face of so much catastrophic history.

"So he's already planning to run?"

"If there's war, yes. It's all in a speech I wrote that was delivered July twenty-fifth, 1938, at Traverse City, Michigan, by Governor Frank Murphy. 'Without Roosevelt in 1940,' he trumpeted my notes, 'we will be unprepared when Hitler invades—as he means to—the Western Hemisphere.' Oh, it was a great speech. Played well in the press. Of course, poor Frank Murphy lost the election, but you can't have everything, can you?"

Tim had already written down the date and place and the name. Currently, Frank Murphy was a Roosevelt appointee to the Supreme Court. Was Cuneo lying? Or, more to the point, when exactly did he lie and when did he tell the truth?

"You should talk to Jim Farley. By the way, I'm legal counselor to the Democratic Party. Farley's sort of my boss, and he's running hard for the nomination. Roosevelt's convinced him he won't run. Franklin does like to raise people's hopes. Keep everybody off-guard. Farley, of course, would be hopeless as president."

Tim knew, as everyone did, that the postmaster general and patronage dispenser would be a particularly hopeless candidate because he was an Irish Catholic from the hated city of New York and nothing had changed in the nation since Al Smith, another New York Catholic, had gone down to a dismal defeat in 1928, thus propelling FDR into the governorship of New York, and subsequent glory. Cuneo mentioned one or two Democratic rivals Tim might want to talk to. Then he signed the check for their breakfast.

"Not long ago, Walter Winchell came to town and he wanted to meet Drew Pearson. Two historic figures, you know. After all, their combined newspaper circulation reaches just about everyone on earth, or so the two boys like to think. Anyway, as their mutual legal adviser, I invited them here one morning, to my regular table. This table. Drew was nervous. Walter was full of jokes. Then I tactfully crept away. Well, the next day when I came in for breakfast, George here . . ." Cuneo gave the smilling waiter the signed bill, ". . . says, 'Mr. Cuneo, you never saw such a performance as those two put on over which one was *not* going to pay that check! Finally, around noon, they got out all these nickels and dimes and pennies, piled them up on the table, and split the bill.'" Cuneo shook his head. "They make millions, those two misers!" He reached into his pocket and pulled out a card on which had been written a name and a New York City telephone number. "This fellow should be very interesting for you to talk to. Lively. Bright. He's tied in with the Morgan Bank. He's also on the executive board of Fight for Freedom . . ."

"Another interventionist." Tim was flat.

"But with a difference. He's heartland American."

"With the House of Morgan?"

"Every house must have a heart, as the old ditty goes." Cuneo rose. "If you like, keep in touch. I might be helpful with this. And with that, too. Now I've got to soothe Drew over there in the corner, cowering behind the palm tree." They shook hands, then Cuneo crossed the room, greeting every other table, while a bemused Tim looked at the card in his hand. "Who the hell," he said aloud, "is Wendell L. Willkie?"

T W O

Caroline's old office in the *Tribune* building had been kept exactly as it was when she had finally sold out most of her remaining shares in the newspaper to Blaise, with the understanding that even as a minor stockholder she would be considered, when she chose, what indeed she was: the creator of the modern *Tribune*, and its co-publisher. Blaise seemed more pleased than not to have her back, if only as a pipeline to the White House.

On one wall there had been placed a map of Europe; each day, Harold Griffiths would move about different-colored pins to show the advance of the German armies across the Rhine and the retreat of the French and British armies toward the sea. Above the map there was a modernistic clock, first revealed at the World's Fair in New York the previous summer. It told the hour in every one of earth's zones as well as the dates. Thus far, it was May 10, 1940, in Washington, D.C.

As Caroline entered the office, it was six p.m. in Saint-Cloud-le-Duc and noon in the District of Columbia; she noted that the Germans were deep into France itself. Harold was busy putting blue British pins in a diagonal line, running south of Belgium toward the English channel. "Well, the Maginot Line was impregnable after all," he said, turning to face Caroline, who enjoyed his unrelenting good humor—even wit—as the world fell apart.

"So it was." Caroline sat in a leather armchair next to her elaborately carved Victorian desk, the property of the founder of the original *Tribune* back in the days of Andrew Jackson.

"Clever of Hitler to just go around it and then come down from the north." Griffiths sat beneath the map.

"Why didn't it occur to the French that he'd occupy Belgium and Holland first?" Caroline was genuinely puzzled. "No one ever thinks of the obvious, I suppose. Except a military genius."

"Genius!" Harold was contemptuous. "If *I* thought of it, anyone could. They simply don't think of anything, and now who cares about French politicians?"

But Caroline was apprehensive about her friend Léon Blum; he was a Jew, and if Hitler should . . . She put the thought out of her mind. France was still a world empire and a great military power. Hitler would be stopped, just as the Kaiser had been twenty years earlier. She saw it clearly: the fighting would drag on until the United States finally came into the war. Then trenches. Mud. Barbed wire. Poison gas. But could history repeat itself? For one thing, the speed with which the German tanks were moving through Europe was something new under the sun. She looked at the map. In April, in a few hours, Denmark had been overrun. Norway had taken a little longer. Now the Germans were approaching Paris as the defeated British troops raced for the English Channel and what would be, for the lucky ones, a most perilous voyage home.

Caroline was now going through her in-box. The world may be afire, but social Washington never stopped its formal round as people arranged themselves each day in different houses to scheme, to pass on information, to advance who knew what astonishing causes. There was a telegram from Tim. He was in New York, cutting his film. He had decided "War or Peace?" was too portentous a title. What should he call it?

"Where are the Italians in all this?" Harold asked the question that everyone was now asking. Mussolini had not gone, as expected, to the aid of his Berlin ally.

"Don't they always stay out until they know who is going to win? They are very sensible that way." Caroline tried to recall exactly what it was that Italy had done in the Great War to get onto the winning side.

"That's what the British say about us."

"John Foster is endlessly tactless."

"That's why they made him a diplomat. Did you hear what Lord Lothian told the press yesterday?"

Caroline quite liked the unmistakably attractive if eccentric ambassador. "He said what they all say. England needs ships, planes, bullets but not men, which of course England does, particularly now."

Harold shook his head. "No. He said that at the press conference, the official one. Later, he held a second press conference which he began with 'Well, boys, Britain's broke. It's your dollars we want.'"

Blaise had shown Caroline a secret report from the American Treasury to the effect that Britain had lost one-fourth of its wealth and so could not even pay the interest on old loans from the United States; presently, England would default. If that were to happen . . .

Blaise entered the room. "Chamberlain's out. The King has sent for Winston."

Harold left the room.

"Not Halifax?" Ever since the recent British military fiasco in Norway, Prime Minister Chamberlain's days had been numbered. Caroline thought that he should have gone after the Munich meeting where he had failed to "appease" Hitler, with his brisk businesslike sellout of Czechoslovakia. As Chamberlain left the Munich Conference, wielding his umbrella like a shepherd's crook for the cameras, Hitler was said to have said, "If that old fool ever comes back here, I'm going to kick him down the stairs and jump up and down on his stomach in front of the Pathé news camera." From the beginning of Hitler's career, Caroline had noted with professional eye what a remarkable screen actor he was; certainly, for a professional rabble-rouser he had a surprising range of effects, including such delicate rhetorical instruments as irony and even not-so-bad jokes. Unfortunately, the West had not taken him seriously until too late. Only Blum had seen the coming danger, but the French were not a people who took well to being told anything that they did not already know. Caroline had watched the Bastille Day parade of 1939 from a friend's Paris flat, and though it was made colorful by Moroccan and Senegalese troops, there were no latest-model tanks, only cavalrymen with curved sabers, guarding the open car in which the Premier, Daladier, glumly rode, unaware that in less than a year's time Hitler himself would be able to drive through the streets of Paris. Caroline wished that she had had a premonition of things to come. But she had not been able to imagine the unimaginable. Besides, as of May 10, 1940, Paris was not yet occupied. A miracle could still light up the skies.

"The government has left Paris." Blaise was reading her mind. "No, I don't know where your friend Blum is. We can't even find the Premier. Last we heard from our man in Paris he was sticking close to the fleeing government, which means we've lost him, too, for the moment." Blaise crossed to the map. Found a dot to the northwest of Paris, "Rennes? Is that where they are? The Associated Press is helpless. Hopeless."

Caroline then tried to ring Saint-Cloud-le-Duc. All overseas lines were busy. "Isn't there someone we could radio?" She sat at her desk.

Blaise prowled the room, unusually red of face, while the once blond hair was now the color of ashes. He was definitely stout, no longer the handsome youth that both sexes had once found desirable.

"But you got through to London."

Blaise nodded; sat down again. "We have—or had—a special line. There was a proper row in the House of Commons. Chamberlain tried to hang on. But it wasn't his own party that did him in, it was Labour. Labour wants Churchill to form a coalition government."

"How pleased he must be." Caroline had never cared for the half-American British politician who, when it seemed opportune, had no conscience about changing parties. It seemed in character that as he was currently a Conservative, he would be Labour's first choice for prime minister. She could imagine the confusion at Westminster: the old Tories had wanted the Earl of Halifax, the new—plus Labour—wanted

the colorful Winston, who had only recently been recalled from political limbo by Chamberlain to be First Lord of the Admiralty, a post that
when he had held it in the World War had provided him with a wide
margin—if not indeed a whole page—on which to commit all sorts of
gaudy military errors. Now he had been catapulted to an even higher
place. Caroline shuddered at the thought.

"Two journalists," she announced, grimly.

"Two journalists—what?"

"Churchill and Mussolini are both professional journalists. They
think in headlines. Startling phrases. Exaggerations."

Blaise frowned. "Has neither ever worked for a living?"

Caroline was amused. "I think that what we do is very hard work.
But, no. Neither has ever had a profession. Only drum-beating in the
press. And politics. Much the same thing."

"Winston's long-winded. But he has wit. I never dealt with Mussolini. Did you, before I came aboard?"

Caroline nodded. "We picked up several of his pieces when he was
editing that socialist paper in Milan. I'm afraid he has no jokes. But he
did send me a novel he had written. Something about a cardinal with
a mistress. Could I help him find an American publisher? He longed to
be another Rafael Sabatini. Now, of course, he's Julius Caesar."

"By such small threads . . ." Blaise went to the long table beneath
the window, where a tentative mockup of the next day's front page was
laid out. Churchill was the feature story. Three right-hand columns
beneath a large constantly changing head. At the moment only the
name floated in a sea of white.

"What about 'Winston is Back'?" was Blaise's contribution.

Caroline said, "Winston who? Back from what? Assume no one
knows anything. The English keep track of their public figures. We
don't. You know, he's been making money lately by writing film
scripts."

"I thought he just wrote books. Very long books. But then he's
always broke. Wonder if we can get him to . . ."

"Too busy. At last. But he's doing . . . or was doing . . . something
for the Korda brothers. Two Hungarians. In Hollywood. About Lord

Nelson. And Lady Hamilton. The English girl who's in *Gone With the Wind*."

"Instead of Liz Whitney. Harold Griffiths keeps me informed of movie trivia whether I like it or not. What about something simple? 'Churchill Prime Minister,' subhead 'Chamberlain gives way to coalition government.'" Blaise turned back into the room. "Have you seen the Roosevelts?"

"Not since I moved out. They are marvelously kind, in their absentminded way. People keep accumulating at the White House until the beds are all full, then Eleanor drops a hint or two and the beds empty out."

"What's the Wardman Park like?"

"Gloomy. I'm in the annex. The Vandenbergs are down the corridor. We meet over the kitchen fence, you might say. She is surprisingly shrewd. He's having an affair with a Canadian woman and Hazel Vandenberg knows everything and simply smiles."

"Grand Rapids is very like Paris in these matters." Blaise was amused. "How do you know she knows?"

"I've been with the three of them. In Hazel's kitchen. We *all* have our kitchens. I think Mitzi—the charmer's name—is not what she seems."

Blaise sat in a chair opposite Caroline. She noticed that he had developed a tremor in his left hand. "What is all this about?"

Caroline tried to look mysterious but realized that she had failed: her face was no longer the youthful pane of glass behind which she could produce so many moods—even thoughts or near-thoughts—for the mass audience that had once been hers until age had struck her down in much the same way that the executioner's ax had taken care of Mary Queen of Scots on the screen while a giant philharmonic orchestra thundered the somewhat too folksy "Loch Lomond."

"I'm not sure," she said, looking out the window at Ninth Street, crowded now with traffic and, despite stern city ordinances enjoining quiet, much horn-blowing. She must speak to the composer, she thought, her mind slipping, for an instant, backward in time to Hollywood days. She realized now—decades too late—that all she had needed for the scene was a single bagpipe upon whose dying mournful note the ax would fall, transferring Emma Traxler forever from the constellation of living film stars to those of legend, radiant old light from a long-dead star.

"Can I trust you?" Caroline liked impossible questions.

"It depends on what."

"Do you want us in the war or out?"

"Oh!" He made a snorting sound. "I'm on the fence."

"A mugwump."

"No. Of course I want the Allies to win. Of course, but . . ."

"It is the 'but.' Always. Isn't it?"

They sat in silence while the various clock faces on the wall recorded different times around the world. History was rapidly moving no matter how still they sat.

"The French government—wherever it may now be—sent me here *pour influencer* . . . English!"

"To influence. I assumed that. Between you and Tim you should be . . . well, influential. Do you plan to influence me?"

Caroline smiled at her half brother, whom she had come to like once the fierce war over their father's estate had ended not long after she had become, all on her own, a successful newspaper proprietor, fulfilling what had been *his* dream.

"I shall try, of course. . . ." She was demure. "But you are hardly an isolationist. It's Franklin I try to work on."

"The President!" Blaise laughed. "He knits socks for England. He sends them bundles."

"I don't think so. He is so secret."

"Is that why he talks so much?"

"What better way to keep a secret than to talk all the time? The problem is he can never get too far ahead of popular opinion, particularly in an election year."

"Will he run his political fixer, Farley?"

"Dear Blaise, it will be Roosevelt, again."

Blaise stood up smartly. "You *know* this?"

"I don't *know* anything, but I can . . . work things out. First, he's the only person, he thinks, who can get us through a war. But, more important, to him at least, if he goes home to his beloved Hudson River, he'll be dead in a month."

"What's wrong with him?"

"Nothing. Everything. While I was staying at the White House, I invited Dr. Ericson to come by, to look him over. Obviously without his knowing it. But they had a long loving handshake, while Ericson looked deep into his eyes and took his pulse and told him just how much the country needed him. Diagnosis: dangerously high blood pressure. Perhaps angina, too. Deadly fatigue as well as a possible melanoma—that black mole over his left eyebrow."

"I shouldn't think running for a third term was the best sort of cure."

"It is the only cure for someone who has nothing to live for except power. In this case supreme power when the war comes."

"Can we write this?"

"No." Caroline was blunt. "My opinion is not a fact."

"Dr. Ericson . . ."

"Won't talk. No. This is just for us to know. You and I. Background. Anyway, I'm intrigued by Mrs. Sims."

"He just died, by the way, Mr. Sims. Only sixty. Interesting man."

"He was in charge of the code room at the Canadian Embassy. I suspect his wife, the bewitching Mitzi, will now go back to Canada."

"Are you some sort of secret agent?" Blaise was amused.

"I? Who have never been able to keep a secret of any kind? No. But I'm doing what I can for my country—my *other* country, that is. Friends in the French government thought I might be helpful, which shows how desperate they are. They want me to use my influence on the Roosevelts, as if I had any."

"While keeping track of Arthur Vandenberg's harem."

"If the Republican convention were held now he'd be their candidate for president."

"So the ladies are supposed . . ."

"To convert him. But Franklin thinks he's not convertible. I'm not so sure."

"Arthur is a professional isolationist. The worst kind. They get elected by saying they are going to punch King George in the snoot, as the Mayor of Chicago so elegantly put it." The President was at his desk in the oval study, absently pouring a bottle of rum into a pitcher of some sort of magenta-colored fruit juice. He never remembered to measure. On the sofa by the empty fireplace, Harry Hopkins was going rapidly through a stack of newspapers. A crumpled dark suit did nothing to disguise the fact that he had become skeletal; only bright sharp eyes suggested that he was not only still alive but alert. Officially, he was the secretary of commerce and sat in the Cabinet. Actually he was, after Eleanor, the President's other self, somewhat the worse for having had most of his cancerous stomach removed the previous summer. A principal architect of the New Deal, as the President's largely unsuccessful plan to end the Depression was called, Hopkins was the man in the shadows, forever whispering into the President's ear, as they experimented with programs and secretly manipulated friends and enemies. Caroline found him charming if only because he did not find her so; since she was of no immediate use to him, he was simply polite to her. In time, she would charm him. Unlike so many of the virtuous social workers that had come into the Rooseveltian orbit, Hopkins loved the rich perhaps too well, as the President sometimes teased him. He liked to visit friends in great houses on Long Island. A widower with sons and a young daughter to look after, he was thought to be on the lookout for a rich wife, but between his never-ending work as well as flesh-consuming cancer, what time that he had left on earth was devoted to the President, who was now pouring out his extraordinary cocktail for Caroline's presumed delight.

"That should do the trick." Roosevelt turned to Hopkins expectantly.

"You know I haven't the stomach for it, Mr. President." Hopkins went on reading.

"We who have so often heard the chimes at midnight together." Roosevelt gave a theatrical sigh. "By the way, when are you planning to visit that little cheese shop on Forty-second Street?"

"Soon. I can see you are starving to death." Hopkins put down the newspapers. "Well, it looks like the Republicans will now nominate Thomas E. Dewey, the boy prosecutor from New York."

"He worries too much about the way he looks, or so I'm told." Roosevelt chuckled. "He is only three feet tall, of course. With a moustache, something no successful politician has worn since Grover Cleveland."

They spoke of other possible Republican candidates. Senators Vandenberg and Taft were duly named and dissected by the two professionals. Then other dinner guests began to fill the room, and Roosevelt, as bartender, was kept busy.

Caroline sat on the sofa beside Hopkins. He smelled of medicine. "Have you been psychoanalyzed?" he asked.

"No. Have you?"

"Yes. Over and over again."

"That means it doesn't work. Or does it?"

"It's the *way* that it doesn't work that matters." He began a soliloquy. Caroline poured her magenta cocktail into a potted azalea. Then one of the telephones on the President's desk rang. The room was suddenly still. This was something that seldom happened after seven-fifteen p.m.

"Yes? Oh, Steve."

Hopkins swung his legs to the floor. "Steve Early," he said at—if not to—Caroline.

Caroline had met the press secretary; found him courtly and uninformative, as press secretaries were meant to be. The President was listening intently. No one spoke. Finally, he said, "Tell them first thing tomorrow. You'll release our statement then." There was a pause. "*After* dinner? But that will be around four in the morning over there." The President listened; chuckled. "A night owl obviously. Anyway, express my kudos." He hung up. The guests chattered.

"Mr. Churchill?" Caroline feared more psychoanalysis.

"*Prime Minister* Churchill. The President's already spoken to him once today."

"What will he do? About France?"

Hopkins put his feet on the President's special metal stool.

"Something dramatic. After all, as he keeps reminding the President, he is a direct descendant of the first Duke of Marlborough."

"He'll invade France, too?"

"Only to liberate. Unfortunately, he's broke. England's broke, that is. And how do we get money to them?"

"A loan?"

"The Senate will never . . ." He trailed off, thinking hard.

"Surely you can always buy a piece of that empire of theirs." Caroline and Blaise had already been composing an editorial to that effect. Patriotically, she was willing to share their inspiration with the President's gray eminence.

"Canada maybe?" For the first time Hopkins looked at her with interest.

"Well, nothing so large. So empty, most of it. Perhaps Newfoundland. Or the Bahamas."

"Yes." Hopkins stared at her. "Weren't you in the movies?"

Caroline had, at last, got his attention. "Yes. But I'm now myself again. The publisher—founder of the *Tribune*."

"But Blaise . . ."

"Co-publisher. I've only come back to—"

"We'll need all the help we can get. Here's a delicate problem. There is no way that we—this administration anyway—will let England go down. We can always handle the isolationists here at home—"

"With a third term?"

Hopkins ignored this. "With some protective camouflage for Churchill, for England. The fact is they haven't been a great power since 1914. But we all kept pretending they were until Hitler came along. Up till then the whole thing has been a sort of bluff. That's why we keep going on about a special relationship between the English-speaking nations, only . . ."

"What is the delicate situation?" Caroline had guessed.

"Disguising the fact that we are the world empire now and they are simply a client state. A bunch of offshore islands. Certainly they are close to us in many ways, but they aren't necessary to us. To be blunt, we can survive—even thrive—without them, which is the wicked wisdom of the intelligent isolationists who are not just for America First, as they like to say in their speeches, but for *Amerika über Alles.*"

"I had not realized," said Caroline, at last introduced to an entirely new thought, "that they were so . . . profound."

"They aren't. The drum-beaters aren't. But there are a few, like crazy-as-a-fox Henry Ford, like your fellow publisher in Chicago, Colonel McCormick, like Tom Lamont, who means to find—or mold—a Republican candidate in his own image." Hopkins stopped. The gray-yellow skin of each cheek now sported a red smudge, like rouge clumsily applied. "That's further down the road, of course. Like next month."

"Harry!" The President was being wheeled out from behind his desk. "Bring Caroline in to dinner, and when you're in New York don't forget to visit that little cheese place."

The other guests followed the wheeled throne.

"What little cheese place?"

As Caroline helped Hopkins up, his arm felt like a bone wrapped in flannel.

Hopkins laughed. "Well, it isn't a cheese place, and it isn't little, and it isn't in Forty-second Street. But the President, like our Lord, talks in riddles and parables. It's actually Greengrass's delicatessen on the West Side of Manhattan, where I buy him smoked salmon and all the things that God created Eleanor to keep him from eating because he likes them. We would starve around here without Barney Greengrass, known to every real New Yorker as the Sturgeon King."

2

Tim and his camera crew arrived at St. Paul, Minnesota, two hours late. "Air traffic" had been the vague excuse. But the skies from New York had been empty and no planes seemed ever to have used the dusty airport, where weeds grew to unusual heights and a listless wrinkled stocking hung from a flagpole, registering no wind. They were met by a small van and Gardner Cowles, who, with his brother John, published *Look* magazine, something of a publishing wonder and already a serious rival to Henry Luce's *Life* magazine.

Tim sat in the front seat next to Cowles, who drove them through the flat dull green countryside, shimmering in damp heat.

"We expect a full house," said Cowles. "We also got you rooms in the same hotel where he'll be speaking."

"This is the start, isn't it?"

"Well, we hope it's the start of something. It's his first campaign speech."

"A bit late." The Republican convention was only six weeks away.

"Very late. But at least we got you out here before you finished your film. Our theory is that Dewey and Taft will deadlock at the convention and then he'll be the dark horse. But even a dark horse has got to be visible before he can be *the* dark horse. So we're starting him off out here. He comes from the Midwest, you know. Indiana."

"And Wall Street," Tim could not help but add. Ever since he had been given the card with the name Wendell L. Willkie scribbled on it, hardly a day had passed that he hadn't read a major magazine or newspaper story about the rustic Hoosier who had been for some years president of Commonwealth and Southern, a Wall Street public utility holding company which had done battle with the government's Tennessee Valley Authority—and lost. Plainly Willkie was now the candidate of those publishers like Henry Luce as eager for war as they were for an end to Rooseveltian socialism. But despite the best efforts of Luce and the Cowles brothers, even those who read their magazines and newspapers still had no vivid idea of who or what Willkie was.

During filming, Tim had been fascinated by the gap between what interested the inventors of the news and the public itself, which largely ignored all the political medicines and cure-alls on offer in glossy magazines. But then something startling would always have to happen—like flying across the Atlantic alone—before the public finally registered a new name. Even the master of the news, Roosevelt himself, came and went in the public's fickle consciousness.

For Tim, a Wall Street businessman from Indiana seemed like the last person on earth that the people would turn to if war came, and he was now certain that the United States was being carefully positioned to be not only the so-called Arsenal of Democracy but a provider of shock troops as well. Paris had just fallen. England was now under siege; and here he was in St. Paul, Minnesota, checking into the Lowry Hotel, the heart of the heartland, someone had said—as a joke?

"He'll be speaking here in the ballroom," said Cowles, "at eight."

The crew went about their work of setting up; made no easier by the presence of a proprietary radio team from CBS. "We've bought a half hour of radio time tonight." Cowles and Tim sat at the back of the seedy ballroom.

"Five hundred seats," said Cowles, looking at the forlorn rows of folding wood chairs. "Empty . . . for now."

Tim was amused. "Well, that's my business, too. Getting people to pay to sit in chairs so that they can look up at shadows on a screen for two hours."

"It isn't easy, is it?"

"No. It's not. Why Willkie?"

"Energy. Intelligence."

"There's always a lot of energy on tap, and even intelligence."

"He's self-made. He reads everything. He's . . . well, every now and then you meet someone who's sort of like an electric eel. You know?"

"I've never met one. Does he give you a shock?"

Cowles sighed. "Not the best analogy. But, yes, he does. In a way. Wakes you up."

"Isn't he really a Democrat?"

Cowles shrugged. "He was until a year or so ago. But that's not a problem. Not these days. Because of the war, everybody's shifting around. Some very strange politics are going on these days."

They were joined by a dapper gray man in a pinstripe suit who seemed of no particular age; the result, Tim had observed in certain actors, of having gone bald early in life, thus minimizing facial lines while the camera—that is, the eye—is distracted by a quantity of smooth scalp and so settles for an illusion of youth.

"Mike." The newcomer addressed Cowles by his nickname; cast a curious eye at Tim; sat down in the row just in front of them.

"Just can't stay away from St. Paul, can you?"

"The bracing sea breezes are a tonic, I must admit."

Cowles introduced his cousin Tom Lamont to Tim, who wondered why the name sounded familiar. Cowles explained Tim's film to Lamont, who asked intelligent questions: "Mustn't seem too one-sided, of course," he murmured as Tim's lighting man short-circuited his klieg light in a blaze of blue flame, prompting a series of oaths which the technicians from CBS Radio merrily cheered.

Tim hurried to join his crew. New lighting was again improvised. Inevitably, Tim found himself working against the clock. Nothing was ever easy on location. He also hoped that he was not wasting his time with this mysterious political invention of the Eastern press. Mysterious because in the matter of war or peace, they already had Roosevelt, a president preparing in his circuitous way for war. Why did the magnates want to divide the President's vote with what was bound to be a far less resonant echo of the real thing?

Cowles then invited Tim to join his brother John and Mr. Lamont to share the blue-plate special at a nearby diner while the hotel lobby began to fill up with the evening's audience, curious to see the latest political phenomenon if *Time, Life, Fortune, Look,* and the New York *Herald Tribune* were to be believed.

"It's easier to get one of us to stop the isolationists," said Cowles, "than for Mr. Roosevelt to get Republicans to switch over to the party of the New Deal."

"But one way or the other, if Wendell is nominated, we're covered," said John Cowles. "That's the point, really. Isolationists will all stay home come November."

"But if he's *not* nominated?" Tim had decided that the self-effacing Mr. Lamont was the leader—the warlock of this coven. Caroline's image had stayed with him.

"It could be very hard for England." Lamont separated a hamburger from its bun with a knife and fork, like a practiced surgeon making a first incision. "Dewey is an isolationist, if he's anything—an unanswerable question. Taft is a zealot. Vandenberg drifts along with the majority . . ."

"Which is isolationist."

Tim had discovered that the one thing that did not work with these highly suspicious and often surprisingly subtle nobles was polite agreement. They were more at ease with opposition. In defense of their case, they became ingenious in argument.

"So the polls tell us," said John, with a secret smile.

"Ours or theirs?" Mike's laugh was hardly secret.

It was Lamont who chose ingenuity. "The great imponderable at the convention—aside from our man if he takes off in the next four or five weeks—will be Mr. Hoover."

Apparently the Cowles brothers were not prepared for this piece of news. Each said the same thing: "You're not serious."

"I may not be serious but President Hoover is very serious about being nominated again and then beating the man who beat him eight years ago. Hoover can still rally a lot of Republicans who went over to Roosevelt and are now ready to come back, just to stay out of war."

It had never occurred to Tim to film Hoover and now it was too late. He only hoped Lamont was wrong. The return of Herbert Hoover to the presidency would be a macabre miracle on the order of the raising of Lazarus, and to have missed it in his film . . . His mouth had gone dry.

Two state troopers appeared in the doorway of the diner. All eyes turned on them as the diner's owner hurried forward to greet the tall blond young man they were escorting.

"His Excellency the Boy Governor of Minnesota." Mike Cowles rose, as did the rest of the table. Harold M. Stassen was now headed towards them while his two guards stationed themselves back of the table, eyes on the door to the diner, where who knew how many assassins lurked.

"Harold!" The Cowles brothers were amiable, Mr. Lamont polite, rather like the ambassador from some minor power, trying not to be noticed at a great powers conference. As Harold Stassen warmly shook Tim's hand, he confided: "You know that movie of yours, *Hometown*, was probably the single decisive factor in my going into politics."

Tim shyly acknowledged the thrill of having inadvertently made so large a contribution to history. Actually, as Stassen was now thirty-three, he could very well have been influenced by a movie that, Tim liked to say, had gone from box-office failure to classic without an intervening success. Such films often haunted the imagination of those who saw them at an impressionable age. Tim had felt the same when he saw D. W. Griffith's *Intolerance,* vowing that not only would he make films himself one day, but he would never allow himself to get involved in such a gorgeously haunting mess.

Stassen sat between the Cowles brothers and showed them the text of his introduction. "Only five minutes," he said. "Radio time is expensive. I realize that." Tim slipped away, aware, as was everyone who read *Time, Life, Fortune,* and *Look,* that he had been, for a moment, in the company of the next president but two or, perhaps, the more cynical politicians said, three. Stassen was a true political miracle, everyone agreed, and the same age, Tim noted with a flash of Holy Cross piety, as our Lord when He was crucified.

The ballroom was full; the heat was intense and the largely Scandinavian audience sweated rather more, Tim thought, than did leaner Mediterranean types.

The stage was poorly lit but, Tim decided, the lack of clear definition might make the point that here was something slapdash and unprofessional—like the candidate.

Tim stood just back of the proscenium arch, maintaining eye contact with his cameraman in the center aisle, on a rickety wooden stand above the audience.

Governor Stassen was introduced. Boyish but statesmanlike; he shone like a figure out of some obscure Norse legend as he took his cue from the CBS radio director down front and began his speech. Then, out of the shadows of backstage, appeared Wendell Willkie, clutching a speech. Tim had the sense that he had seen him before until he realized that, by now, there had been so many thousands of pictures of Willkie that he must have seemed entirely familiar to everyone who read glossy magazines. Dark curly hair was cut in farm-boy style, one lock carefully trained to fall over his right eyebrow, pale blue eyes set in a round face; ingratiating smile punctuated by a Lincolnesque mole; only an exaggerated amount of jowl attached to a square Prussian jaw suggested that its owner was no stranger to fiery waters; he was also very much what was politely known as a lady's man if all—or even some—of the rumors that Tim had heard were true. Willkie was exactly Tim's age, forty-eight. He was also ten years older than his closest rival, Thomas E. Dewey. The Grand Old Party was uncommonly rich in boys this season while all the Democratic leaders were visibly aging, their famous faces etiolated from too much exposure to too many flashbulbs.

"I hate this shit." Willkie's Indiana accent was as countrified as his haircut.

"Campaigning?"

Willkie held up his speech. "No. Having to *read* a speech. I've never been able to. Never. I warned Mike. But . . . oh, this is Russell Davenport, Mr. Farrell." Willkie was not yet a professional politician but he had all the right instincts: he had got Tim's name right. Davenport was tall and rather opulent-looking, as befitted the editor of a magazine called *Fortune*. "The speech," he said in a grave cultured voice, befitting the secretary of state in a Willkie Cabinet, "is very good."

Tim moved around the curtain. He had told his crew to take their cue from the CBS director, who was now holding up five fingers—each one a second—as Stassen plunged into his peroration, filling the airwaves with his vision of a golden America, of a joyous future with freedom and democracy for absolutely everyone in the Republican Party.

Beside Tim, Willkie took a deep breath; then, on exhalation, he whispered, "Oh, shit," again, and as the applause began and Stassen stood back from the lectern, the bearlike Wendell Willkie lumbered firmly into Stassen's place. He was not, Tim noted, in the least nervous. Even Roosevelt's hands sometimes shook but the smiling Willkie, as he now sailed into American history, seemed quite aware of an audience that plainly liked what they saw. But they did not like what they then heard. Willkie read as badly as he had predicted. The agreeable croak of his voice, so unlike the usual politician's mellow sales pitch, started early to go wrong as he missed words, split sentences in two, stumbled from line to line.

Tim wondered how anyone could have thought that this blunderer might begin to compete with the master in the White House whose vast depths of benign insincerity could never be entirely plumbed by any mere mortal.

Willkie's glasses had slipped to the tip of his nose by the time the CBS director made the throat-cutting gesture that signaled the end of the torture. "I thank you," snarled Willkie.

"We're off the air," said the CBS director, his back to the stage. The soundmen gathered up their equipment. The audience applauded perfunctorily while rising to escape the overheated hall not to mention the dire speaker. In the wings opposite, the Cowles brothers were talking intently to Stassen, who was shaking his thick pink boyish head.

But Willkie, instead of leaving the stage, removed his glasses, took off his jacket, and draped it over the lectern. Then he picked up his speech and hurled it out over the audience. As the offending pages floated in the air, he stretched his arms wide like a bear coming out of hibernation. "Well, that's that, ladies and gentlemen. As you could hear, that was all spinach. Now that we're off the air we can really talk." He stepped back from the lectern while the astonished audience sat down.

Tim waved to his cameraman to keep recording.

"So I can talk straight to you without all that damn fine language I have to use for radio."

"Thanks, Wendell," said Davenport, sourly.

"*Your* language?" Tim was amused.

"Yes. So, now what is he going to do? He has no text and the wire services are all out there."

They didn't have long to wait. Willkie began to prowl the stage from left to right and back again, keeping sharp eye contact with section after section of the audience.

"Now you know and I know that we've got to get rid of that bunch in Washington—and we've got to do it soon. This November, in fact." There was a sharp round of applause.

As Willkie paced up and down the stage, he attacked the New Deal; the President's Machiavelli, Harry Hopkins; the arrogance of bureaucrats. One by one he struck at everyone and everything that this audience most hated. But on the one great issue, war or peace, he was both blunt and sly.

"Every time Mr. Roosevelt damns Hitler and says we ought to help the democracies in every way we can short of war, we ought to say: Mr. Roosevelt, we *double*-damn Hitler and we are all for helping the Allies, but what about the sixty billion dollars you've spent and the ten million persons that are still unemployed?' "

The hall erupted. Shouts. Rebel yells. Cheering. Even Tim felt the force of the man's . . . character? Or was it art?

Willkie had now pulled the unreluctant Boy Governor from the wings. He thanked him for his introduction. Congratulated him on his potential greatness, so plain to all. He laid it on. Then, sweat streaming into his eyes, the deceptive lock of hair plastered to his right eyebrow, he declared in a voice that needed no amplifier: "I can think of no one better than you for the job you've just been given, which is to make the keynote address at our convention in Philadelphia next month. You speak for our country's youth, which means you speak for tomorrow as well as for today. But I warn you, if you attempt to put the party on record as saying that what is going on in Europe is none of our business, then we might as well fold up!"

A huge breaking sound wave from the applause caused both men to step backward. Then Willkie, with a wave to the crowd, marched offstage, hands upheld, like a winning boxer after a knockout. Safe in the wings, he croaked to Davenport, "Bottle of whiskey."

In Willkie's suite a contented postmortem was taking place. The hero was reducing his adrenaline level with alcohol while the Cowles brothers, Lamont, and Davenport discussed the coming schedule, which, Tim could see, was being expanded to take in the whole country "with," as Mike Cowles said, "no written speeches."

"Swell." Willkie's voice was coming back. He drank bourbon neat.

Davenport reminded the brains trust that there would have to be written speeches to give to the press, otherwise the candidate's progress would go unnoticed by the public.

Willkie agreed. "You write them and you hand them out to everyone except me. All I need to know is the general drift of what you'll be handing out."

Davenport was clearly not happy but he was outvoted.

Lamont turned to Tim. "You . . . ?

"I plan to intercut him with FDR."

Lamont smiled a very thin smile. "Why not? The new champ and the old. Would the studio . . . is it MGM?"

Tim nodded.

". . . Object if I got Harry Luce to use some of this film from tonight in his newsreels? You know, those *March of Time* things that he does?"

Tim told Lamont to whom he must apply for footage. Lamont made a note.

Willkie waved to Tim. "We can do an interview now," he said.

"No." Davenport was abrupt. "It's too late."

"I'm afraid my crew's gone," said Tim. "Union hours." He had now remembered where he had seen Willkie before. At Laurel House on the Potomac River, somewhat the worse for what he had drunk, while a woman—his wife?—tended to him.

"You said I could get nominated if I got out and fought for it." Willkie addressed the brothers. "Well, this is the first round."

"You won it," said John Cowles.

"But it's a big country," said Mike. "A lot more rounds."

"Roosevelt's too nervous." Willkie was still caught up in his recent performance. "That Minnesota crowd tonight is about as isolationist as you can get, but they're scared of Hitler now. They're ready to go arm real fast. I could hear them. Feel them."

"But they aren't ready to go fight in France like last time." Davenport was there to dash cold water on the newborn overheated demagogue.

"What will happen will happen. For now we've got to help England hold off Hitler and FDR is just dithering. Wish he'd been out here tonight. He's out of touch." Tim was amazed at how quickly a Wall Street public utilities lawyer could become an entire nation personified. But then, perhaps, something in him had connected with something in the audience. After all, he was closer than FDR to the average Midwesterner because he was born one while the President was always the Hudson Valley lord of the manor, speaking kindly, even wisely, but always speaking down to an electorate that needed his guidance as he, apparently, needed theirs, which he demonstrated by his reliance on polls rather more than on their official representatives in the Congress.

"They know out there. They *know* that France and England are our first line of defense. If Hitler beats them, we're next. We've got to shore up the Allies, every possible way." He drank from the bottle; seemed to get more rather than less sober. "Short of declaring war on Germany, that is." Davenport sighed his relief.

Lamont gave Tim his card. "Let's meet in New York." The others rose respectfully.

"What . . . uh, do you do, sir?" Tim saw that the card merely read "Thomas W. Lamont" with a Manhattan home address.

"I'm just another Wall Street banker." He bade them all good night; was gone.

Tim asked Willkie what primaries he planned to enter.

Willkie laughed. "None. Isn't that right, boys?"

Davenport managed his first smile of the evening. "That's right. But that's only because we have President Hoover working for us."

Plainly, this was a joke, whose point Tim was not supposed to get until Davenport explained. "Hoover's encouraging every state to nominate a favorite son who after a ballot or two will shift, he thinks, over to him."

"Only they will be coming to me now." Willkie shut his eyes; smiled pleasantly. "Did you hear the applause I got when I said . . ."

An actor, Tim decided, an actor already rather too much at home in his part. "But what about Dewey? He's beaten Vandenberg in Wisconsin and Nebraska."

Mike Cowles answered. "Those delegations don't really have to stick if they don't want to. Taft isn't going into the primaries either. He deals with the power brokers in the states, the cities." Mike gazed thoughtfully at Willkie, who appeared to be asleep, still smiling. "That's what we'll do *after* our man has had a chance to see the country and the country's had a chance to see him."

"So why not just vote for Roosevelt?" Tim asked the question that the more they talked seemed the only essential one.

Willkie's eyes opened. The mind was sharply focused. "I was a Democrat in 1932. Voted for FDR. But the New Deal wasn't on any ballot that I ever marked. Well, Mr. Farrell, I'm a businessman. Proud of it. But the New Deal has no reference or relationship to democracy. I want to drive a stake through its heart. But I will tell you one thing, I tremble for the safety of this country if Dewey or Taft or Vandenberg is nominated and elected. I'd go and vote for FDR first. I don't want a Nazi Europe. I don't want us attacked when Hitler's good and ready. The only thing he respects is strength. Well, I want us strong. Militarily. That's where a businessman is a lot more use than a Harvard man who grows Christmas trees on his Hudson River estate. I'm going to bed." He stood up; gave Tim a bone-crushing handshake, then, shedding his clothes, he moved into the bedroom and shut the door.

"Can he be nominated?" Tim asked the three advisers.

"Yes," said Davenport. "We're playing the Taft game. We're acquiring the power brokers. We've been at it since January."

Mike Cowles was on his feet. "He's got most of the press by now. He's got Harry Luce, who is shameless, if you'll forgive me, Russell, when it comes to biased reporting in favor of—or against—politicians."

"I guess your *Look* magazine must have learned all that from us." Davenport already looked like a somewhat sleepy secretary of state.

The four men parted in the lobby, now forlorn and empty.

Tim turned to Mike Cowles. "Who is this guy Lamont? He says he's a banker. What bank?"

The three men laughed. Davenport said, "Well, he told you the absolute truth. He is a banker. In fact, he is *the* banker."

"Which bank?" asked Tim.

Mike Cowles answered for his co-conspirators: "He's the head of the House of Morgan."

So, Tim duly noted to himself, it was going to be that kind of election.

THREE

I

"This was a mistake," said Harry Hopkins as Caroline and the chauffeur helped him out of her hired car.

"Your proposal of marriage to me? Or my acceptance?"

"Neither. Our coming here to Cissy Patterson's. She's a madwoman."

"But she's the only pro-Roosevelt publisher in Washington except for me, and I'm only a half, no, not even a quarter, publisher."

More or less seriously, Hopkins had proposed marriage in the car and, not seriously at all, she had promptly accepted him. "We have known each other so long," she had said, patting his hand. "At least a month."

"I think my lack of a stomach is putting you off."

They stood before Cissy's Italianate marble Stanford White palace dominating its curve of Dupont Circle. Then two footmen in livery flung open the doors and Caroline, with the fragile Harry clinging to her arm, made an entrance duly noted by those in the marble hall with its elaborate plasterwork and shining dark mahogany doors whose knobs were made of semiprecious stones. Cissy had inherited all this grandeur from her mother, whose taste she affected to deplore; yet there was no doubt that she very much enjoyed what was, after all, a proper setting for Washington's Sun Queen.

Cissy herself was still a handsome woman with hair that could well have been red in daylight but now, in the refracted crystallized light from chandeliers, seemed to be so many subtly shaded pelts of mouse intricately arranged around a dead-white face.

"Caroline!" She embraced the "pioneer" woman publisher, as the *Times-Herald* always referred to Caroline Sanford Sanford, delicately emphasizing that their own non-pioneer woman publisher was a slip of a thing by comparison.

But all eyes, including Cissy's, were on Harry Hopkins, man of mystery, the President's alter ego, seldom seen at Washington parties as opposed to those of Astors on the Hudson, Whitneys on Long Island.

"Harry! Why do you avoid me?" Cissy kissed his cheek.

"My illnesses always come first. Then you."

"Isn't he a bastard?" Cissy, well pleased with her trophies, led them into the main drawing room, where she abandoned Caroline to show off Harry, who wearily smiled at friends, acknowledged acquaintances, his sharp glittering eyes half shut as if to disguise how much he was actually taking in. Caroline had never met anyone quite so . . . sharp. Yes, "sharp" was the word. He was hardly brilliant but he was preter-naturally attentive, as he watched faces, listened to the inflection of voices, arranged and rearranged data in his mind with astonishing speed as well as, according to the President in a rare non-self-referential mood, acuity—like the perfect barometer on a sunny day at sea which surprises you with the news that there's a storm up ahead.

Since the evening that Churchill had become prime minister, Hopkins had been living at the White House in Abraham Lincoln's office–Cabinet room, now a bedroom which Eleanor, with character-istic goodwill, had made not only depressing but uncomfortable. "Really just like home," she would say contentedly, looking at the heavy dark furniture and dull wallpaper.

Cissy's onetime son-in-law, Drew Pearson, a tall humorless

Quaker, reminded Caroline that they had met before. "Years ago I tried to get a job on your brother's paper." Caroline still disliked hearing the *Tribune, her* invention, referred to as Blaise's creation. As always, when annoyed, she gave a radiant smile whose effect she could no longer gauge without, at the very least, a looking glass that magnified. "I am sure he regrets not taking you on."

"Are you going to marry Hopkins?" He asked the intimate question as if he were inquiring about the length of her stay in what local radio had recently taken to calling "the Nation's Capital."

"No. I'm much too old for marriage. Why did you and Felicia break up?"

It was his turn to be taken aback. Like all prying journalists, he treasured his privacy. He stammered something incoherent.

"Now, now," said Caroline. "Here is why." She had recognized Luvie Pearson, the second wife, who smiled and took Caroline's hand. With blond hair and equine features, Luvie was elegant in a non-Washington way. "Your husband was explaining to me how he left Felicia for you and I said that now I can see why."

Pearson's response was sharp: "I said no such thing!"

Caroline realized, happily, that she had made an enemy of a Quaker who wrote a daily column in which he mixed personal vendettas with, occasionally, actual news.

"Cissy is at it again." Mrs. Pearson addressed both husband and Caroline.

"At what?" Pearson gazed about the room, in search of ever more interesting quarry.

Luvie turned to Caroline. "Occasionally, she exercises *droit de seigneur*—or is it *madame?*"

"Tell me what *it* is and I'll try to translate."

"She picks someone—usually from the paper—someone she wants to go to bed with. Then she asks him to the party with the understanding that he's to sleep over."

Drew Pearson had moved on. Luvie pointed to a rugged young man in evening clothes; surly face flushed with drink. "*Droit de madame*, I'd say. But I'm afraid he won't be able to fulfill her rights if he drinks much more."

"She's already told him to go up to bed. That was after he pulled up his trouser leg to show us that he's wearing silk pajamas and Cissy said, 'Oh, God, my crepe-de-chine sheets are ripe peach and your pajamas are burgundy red.'"

"Will he be spared if the colors clash?"

"No. Look, he's heading for the stairs."

"I never knew Cissy had this Catherine the Great side to her." Caroline was more admiring than not.

"She's very regal. And Drew's very rude to her. They only see each other because of the child by Felicia."

"But he works for her."

Luvie shook her handsome head like a thoroughbred horse at a race's start. "He doesn't work *for* anyone."

"There are other papers . . ."

"Many other papers."

"There are also contracts." Caroline knew that Cissy would not let the "Washington Merry-Go-Round" column go without a fight.

They were joined by a large-boned pink-and-white woman in her late thirties, who said, "Mrs. Sanford?"

"Yes." Caroline was gracious. But then so few people any longer recognized her in what had once been very much her city.

"You look so well. Remember me?" A bright smile. "I'm Emma. Your daughter."

"Well!" Luvie Pearson was the one who gasped.

"So you are. So you are." For this quiet reading of lines, Caroline awarded herself an Academy Award, if only for lifetime achievement. The two women embraced formally.

"I had heard you were in town," said Emma.

"And I had heard from your Uncle Blaise that you were out of town. That you live in New York now."

Luvie excused herself, to go spread the news.

"I heard that you were staying in the White House."

"I was there for a few days. I'm at the Wardman Park now. You must come see me." There was, Caroline realized, no proper etiquette for dealing with a daughter that one hardly knew, and if she was at all the same sort of woman that she had been when they last met, nearly twenty years earlier, a renewed acquaintanceship was bound to be unpleasant.

"I should like that." Emma *seemed* quite sane. But one never knew; one moment she could charm even her mother; then, the next, she would begin a tirade worthy of Bernhardt in Racine, usually on politics, where she had passionate views about the need for total order in the lives of the common people. Caroline wondered, somewhat nervously, if Emma might have found her hero in Hitler, who seemed to sum up all the virtues that she had most extolled in the past when she was married to a conservative academic. "You know, I'm divorced," Emma contributed to Caroline's reverie.

"Oh, yes. I think you wrote me. In France. Yes. Am I to have another son-in-law soon?" Caroline hated her own kittenish tone. But then she had never played the part of a mother with a daughter; on screen she had comforted only sons, usually as they lay dying in the trenches of the First War.

"Oh, I think not. Hope not. Too busy. You have a grandson at Princeton. Aaron Burr Decker. Very brilliant. Giles—my ex-husband, remember?—got friendly custody. I'll tell A.B. to call on you. That's his nickname. Keep the name alive. You know, I'm president of Fortress America. We have ten thousand members. Growing every day. We're doing our best to keep us out of this war, which you probably want us in."

"Who do you mean by *us?*" Caroline began to focus on the face of her daughter, who had improved, in appearance at least, with age. Caroline could not recall if she had ever told Emma who her real father was. Pregnant by a married politician, Caroline had been obliged to marry John Sanford, a complaisant cousin, who had provided the child with a suitable name and place in the Sanford clan of New York. Upon arrival in Washington, Caroline had intended to tell her daughter—if she saw her—who the father was, but now she decided to withhold so fair a gift from one who would, no doubt, denounce her for this ancient adultery.

"Us! America?" Fortunately, Emma kept her voice down. "That's why it's so important that we keep your friend FDR from running again. He'll get us in, but Jim Farley won't. We're all for Farley. Byrnes will do, of course, and even Senator Day . . ."

Caroline kept a straight face as her daughter, unwittingly, named her father. As Caroline suspected, she had neglected to tell Emma that James Burden Day had been her first lover when he was a young ambitious congressman, much too happily married to the daughter of the boss of his state's Democratic Party to marry Caroline. She had only seen him once since her return. He was now like the amiable whole brother she'd never had. He was also certain that if Roosevelt did not run again, he himself could be nominated and elected. After all, he was as against the war as the rather shadowy American people, who were, with each new poll, giving even more Delphic responses to interested pollsters who asked their questions in ever more complex ways, responding to the urgencies of British agents, operating out of Rockefeller Center in New York.

"We also work with Martin Dies. I don't know where we'd be without that Un-American Activities Committee of his. You know, he single-handedly got Warner Brothers to drop that *March of Time* film about life inside Germany. We've also learned that Mr. Farrell is making a propaganda film, too."

She had always called Tim "Mr. Farrell," thus expressing her displeasure at her mother, who had lived for so long a time in sin.

"He is doing some sort of documentary." Caroline was deliberately vague. "About the election, I think."

"What are *you* doing?" Emma's gaze was direct, as befitted an informer.

"I've come home to talk to Mr. Macrae at E. P. Dutton in New York. About the publication of my grandfather Charles Schermerhorn Schuyler's reflections on the election of 1876 . . ."

"Didn't his daughter . . ."

"Yes, my mother seems to have murdered the first Mrs. Sanford. Too sad!" Caroline could not resist this tinkling drawing-room note to offset the general darkness of the first Emma now reincarnated, rather dully if what she saw was truly representative, in her own daughter. "Is your Uncle Blaise here tonight?"

"No. He's feuding with Cissy this season. She tried to steal his Sunday comic strips. How did my grandfather . . ."

"How like her!" Caroline cut her daughter off. In the middle distance Harry Hopkins' sharp predator bird's eyes were fixed, somewhat desperately, on Caroline. "You must pay me a call, Emma. I'm off." With a little wave, Caroline started across the room to be met beneath the main chandelier by a tall young man who identified himself as her nephew, Peter Sanford.

"It is," said Caroline, after he had introduced himself, "literally old home week. I was just chatting with a charming, if somewhat mature, woman who claims to be my daughter."

"So I saw. I didn't dare interrupt. Even if I could."

Caroline laughed, for the first time spontaneously. "A nephew after my own heart. Yes, Emma is a deeply serious and committed woman, with much of a disturbing nature to tell the world."

"But then these are deeply serious and committed times." Peter had charm, she decided. But then so had Blaise, in youth. But Blaise's charm had always been without ease, unlike his son's. The eyes, she noted, were blue, like his mother's. "I see you brought Mr. Hopkins."

"Have you read Saint-Simon?"

"Only about him."

"He writes in his diaries about Louis XIV and Versailles and the court, about his grievances as a beleaguered peer of France—a sort of civilized Drew Pearson—anyway, something rather similar is happening in this once small sultry African city with its dowdy court . . ."

"We grow more like Paris then?"

"We are growing more like an empire. It is exciting. I've decided Franklin is Augustus. You live here. Keep a diary."

"He'll need a war first."

"That comes." Caroline thought of France with pain. "Sad to say. You're still in school?"

"University of Virginia. But I expect to be in the Army next year. I want an early seat at the show. Have the Germans taken your house?"

"I think so. I hear nothing, of course. Ambassador Bullitt was useless before he fled, if he's fled. I do hope the Germans catch him." She changed the subject abruptly. "So what will you do with your life?"

"I must wait and see if I'm going to have one." He was serene.

"It is like that, is it?"

Peter nodded. "Just like that. When you don't know how long you've got."

"I see." Caroline stopped play-acting. Shut her eyes. Saw refracted light as so many glowworms back of the lids. "Perhaps the isolationists have a point after all." She opened dazzled eyes.

"Of course they have a point. After all, the last war . . ."

"I know all the arguments. But this time . . ." Happily, she lacked the courage to lecture someone who, any day, would be called to service in a drama where she herself was, at best, an idly redundant spectator.

"I have to go, Aunt Caroline." Then he stopped. "Father says you have some Aaron Burr papers."

She nodded. "I've also got my grandfather's journal for 1876. I've been putting the various pieces together. That's the main reason I've come back, Hitler to one side. I want to publish."

"I have a good many papers, too. Like Burr's attempt at a memoir, and so on. I've always thought I'd like to publish one day, but if you . . ."

"I shall pay you diamonds. To borrow them. That's all. You can still, one day . . ."

"If I have the time, of course."

"Yes." Caroline nodded, grandly. "If you have the time, of course. Which you will. So good a nephew must flourish."

"I'm off."

"So soon? Before Cissy's terrapin?"

"Millicent Smith Carhart is receiving next door. I said I'd come."

"She's *still* alive!" Millicent was the ancient faded daughter of a nineteenth-century president whose name no one could recall except specialists in the rich field of White House occupants. Millicent herself held a bluestocking court, very high-minded and the exact reverse of that of her only rival in Washington, the notorious Alice Longworth, daughter of the ever-notorious president, Theodore Roosevelt. Alice's running battles with her cousins Franklin and Eleanor made the small city—as opposed to ever-expanding court—a joy for the well-placed bystander and something of a minefield for ambitious courtiers.

Caroline invited Peter to come visit her at Wardman Park. "This is a sincere invitation as opposed to all the others that I scatter about as I make my getaways."

Caroline joined Harry Hopkins on a bench beneath a portrait of their hostess looking slender and decadent and wearing not a gown but shimmering bolts of material. "She looks as if she's about to play Salome."

"That's a threat." Harry was tired and pale and, as always, she had to remind herself he was only half alive, a half that was inhabited entirely by the President's will. She wondered if there was anything at all left of the original Harry Hopkins. "I shouldn't have come," he said. "Cissy really is the enemy now."

"She's for the third term."

"This week. But she's a Chicago isolationist. The worst."

"She's also very proud to be the Countess Gizycka of Poland, lost to Hitler—Poland is lost, that is. Cissy is forever at large."

A tall man of middle age and middle height and middling appearance approached and greeted Hopkins politely. He was a Mr. William Stephenson from Canada, and Harry seemed to know him well.

Mr. Stephenson was the head of the British Passport Control Office in Rockefeller Center. "A humble job," he confessed humbly.

"But fun." Harry grinned. "He gets to stamp all those passports personally."

Caroline was always amazed how, in a world where secrets were all-important, practically nothing was a secret from those few who were interested. Stephenson was thought to be in charge of all the British secret services in the United States and, personally, in charge of Mitzi Sims, who had been chosen to be the seductive Delilah who would, presently, shear Samson Vandenberg's isolationist locks. In a sense, the whole thing was a perfectly open game. Attractive ladies would service elderly senators and learn their secrets while no doubt realizing, in the process, that few senators had any secrets worth knowing. But they did have votes in the Senate. If Vandenberg and Taft and

Dewey would abandon even a degree of isolationism those martyred ladies would undergo beatification by a grateful England. Of course, in the end, it was unlikely that anyone's views would be changed by a seductress no matter how alluring, but there is always information to be gathered at the pillow's corner and, if matters should ever get entirely out of hand, blackmail was a game of some allure.

Stephenson looked about. "Is Philip here? Philip Lothian?"

"No. And neither am I." Harry got to his feet unaided. "Philip's doing a good job. The President likes him."

Caroline also liked the British ambassador, an airy aristocrat who had once been an appeaser of Hitler but was now very much Churchill's man on the spot, currently trying to get ships and planes out of the surprisingly crafty airy aristocrat in the White House. Roosevelt was driving surprisingly hard bargains with the so-called mother country, which was, as he had once mischievously pointed out, only a stepmotherly country to him, as he was a Dutchman whose ancestors had been displaced by the English when they conquered the entire American seaboard and changed the name of the provincial capital of New Amsterdam to New York. Caroline had, more than once, detected in Roosevelt a certain nonchalant animus toward England and its empire and despite his recent allegedly candid correspondence with Churchill, he still liked to tell how, in the Great War, the First Lord of the Admiralty had snubbed him because, as he was only an assistant secretary of the American navy, he was of less than Cabinet rank and so worth neither time nor attention.

"It simply goes to show," the President had pronounced with much solemnity, "you just never know who's going to be what one day, so I make it a point *always* to be the same with everyone, which is, of course, a perfectly grand thing to do."

"Well, dear," said Eleanor, "you certainly never stop no matter whom you're with."

"That is because I am truly democratic."

This conversation had taken place at the end of May, shortly after the good bad news of the successful evacuation of British and French troops from Dunkirk—over three hundred thousand men were safely transported across the English Channel. The President, Hopkins, and

Caroline were gathered in the upstairs study to celebrate. Eleanor had been late in joining them. "There has always been something odd about my blood. But the doctor says there's nothing really wrong."

As the President wheeled himself past her, he gave her a friendly slap on the bottom. "But what did he have to say about that big fat ass of yours?"

Without a pause, Eleanor had said, "I'm afraid, dear, you were never mentioned."

Even the President had laughed, with every appearance of heartiness; and Caroline had glimpsed another aspect to the Roosevelt relationship. It was the shy Eleanor who held the knife and so was the one to be feared.

Cissy tried to stop Caroline and Harry at the door. But Caroline was firm. "Harry has had a long busy day." She sounded, as she intended, like a wife.

"But busy doing what?" Cissy's malice was unremitting. "Spending and spending, electing and electing?" She quoted a famous Hopkins line.

"Yes, Cissy." Harry sounded tired. "We need ships and planes to keep you safe in Dupont Circle."

"You do bring some life to this dull town." Cissy kissed Caroline almost tenderly.

"You are kind. By the way, peach and burgundy red do not clash."

"Peach and . . . ?" Then Cissy got the point. "How I invade my own privacy! Well, you must come up and see for yourself." Cissy wickedly indicated the curving staircase.

"I've already seen them together, in a way. Those were the colors of Madame du Deffand's salon."

"I'm afraid I don't know her. But if you say so . . ."

In the car that was to take Harry back to the White House before dropping Caroline off at the Wardman Park Hotel, Harry said, "I was serious." He took her hand in his cold one. "I'm also getting a flat in New York, at the Essex House. A home for when I'm not here."

"Even without that enticement, I accepted you, didn't I?"

"You were making a joke."

"Yes. But what better way to begin a marriage?" Caroline could not find the right note to strike. She liked him. She admired him. She was flattered to be at the heart of the court of what would soon be no longer "the Nation's Capital" but the whole world's. Unfortunately he was dying and she was not, or, as the old song put it, one was taking the high road and one was taking the low and though the destination for each in the end was the same, their different roads at different times would keep them eternally apart.

They spoke no more until the car was waved through the northwest gate of the White House.

"We could," said Harry Hopkins as he kissed her cheek, breath like ammonia, "lose this war yet."

"Henry Adams says not."

"You speak to him in the grave?"

"Always. Germany is far too small, he used to say, too insignificant to wield the club."

"So was England."

"The United States wasn't really here in those days, with all our . . . magnitude. Today we are what matters, and the whole thing is ours if we want it."

"You sound like the President. Except he doesn't say 'if.' Good night." Harry entered the rectangle of light that was the opened front door; then the door shut the light back inside where it belonged, and she was driven off through the summer dark that smelled of lemony magnolia blossoms from White House trees.

2

Tim sat on the window ledge of his bedroom in the Benjamin Franklin Hotel and looked down sixteen stories to the crowded Philadelphia street below. He held the telephone receiver a half foot from his right ear, reducing in volume the rasping voice of his current employer, Louis B. Mayer, the lord of the earth's greatest ("more stars than in heaven") film studio, Metro-Goldwyn-Mayer in Culver City,

California, where, although it was eight in the morning, Mr. Mayer was at his desk, zestfully interfering in the work of the studio's employees. It was Mayer who had decided to delay Tim's picture until just before the elections on the grounds "that we got a real horse race now. Is this Wellkie of yours going to come out of nowhere like that Mr. Deeds and go to Washington like Henry Fonda—why don't you ever use Robert Taylor?—and clean up the mess or will Claude Rains stop everything with that crooked dam he wants to build?"

"Yes, L.B." Tim dreaded Mayer's tendency to outline every plot—even act out key scenes—in order to keep reminding himself what the movie under discussion was about. At any given moment he must keep an eye on a hundred productions in various states of disarray, often because of his conflicting requests and generous advice. He had been skeptical of Tim's documentary. For one thing, he disliked documentaries in general; for another, he disliked political ones in particular, ever since he had succeeded in destroying the candidacy of the novelist Upton Sinclair for governor of California. Eager to save what he believed was capitalism itself, Mayer had churned out innumerable films proving that Sinclair's quixotic desire to end poverty in California was being directed by Moscow. Sinclair was duly defeated when he might have been elected while Mayer ended up deeply despised by the very people he had saved from the Red Menace. Since then he had contented himself with making musical comedies and, of course, the Andy Hardy series that had managed to put an end to Tim's *Hometown* realism. In L. B. Mayer–land one could never be too false. Yet Tim had kept on working. One day, if only by accident, a door might open. Also, the movie business was so constituted that no one ever said never to anyone because, sooner or later, with so small a deck of cards, the same cards kept coming up, and Tim, who had once had, with Caroline, his own studio, was resigned to being, for now, an employee of L. B. Mayer, since one never knew what cards one might next be dealt from the small deck.

"The numbers I just got aren't all that good for this ten-to-one Wellkie." Mayer's racetrack parlance was at least genuine. He had a passion for horses, and more than once the head office of Loews Incorporated in New York City, where the money for the studio came from, had told him he must choose between racetrack and sound studio. Thus far, he had managed to juggle both.

"The betting in Philadelphia is that Willkie's got it on the fifth ballot next Thursday." Tim had no idea what the betting was but he knew that he was speaking L.B.'s language.

"Win or place, I think you got a picture." The shift to "you" from "we" was not a good sign. When things went well it was "my picture," when there was still optimism it was "our picture," but "your picture" . . .

Tim talked fast. "What we've got now which we didn't have before is a real horse race. Momentum's building all over the country. There are one thousand Willkie clubs. In every state. Oren Root's organizing them . . ."

"Oren what?"

"Root. His uncle or something was secretary of state. Dewey's still ahead in some of the polls *but* he's starting to slide . . ."

"He's the real dark horse and not Wellkie. He's only thirty-something. That's good casting. Look at Jim Stewart in *Mr. Smith Goes to Congress*, or whatever it's called." The one likable thing about L.B. was that he shared Tim's dislike of Frank Capra's fantasies about political life. But where Tim disliked their falsity, L.B. found them insufficiently sentimental; worse, they were made by what he regarded as a near-poverty-row studio, Columbia.

"Dewey's no Jimmy Stewart. For one thing, he's only three feet tall, with snaggle teeth."

"Cap them," ordered L.B. as if Dewey were under contract. "I've promised New York an October first opening. You'll be ready."

L.B. was off the line. Like so many of the old-guard studio heads, he did not in the least mind making a good film as long as he wasn't told about it until the box-office verdict was not only favorable but in hand.

Tim's crew was already at the Thirtieth Street station, where Willkie's train would soon be arriving from New York. Since their St. Paul meeting, Tim had observed the candidate in a number of towns, watched as the crowds got larger and larger, studied the astonishing amount of press that the candidate of the Cowles brothers, of Henry

Luce, of the New York *Herald Tribune,* was acquiring as if by divine right.

Some dozen journalists were already lined up on the underground siding. Tim had placed his crew closest to the gate and so would be able to get the busiest shot of the candidate as he made his way through the crowd, talking, talking, talking. He was like a tightly wound-up machine that simply could not run down, while his self-love was so guileless that Tim found it more contagious than repellent.

Unfamiliar cameras with the NBC logo were setting up just beyond Tim's crew.

"It's television," said his cameraman. "You know, like that closed-circuit stuff they had at the World's Fair."

"Who gets to see it?" The previous winter Tim had been intrigued when what was called "a TV demonstration" had been made for a number of technicians at Metro.

"They say some fifty thousand people in the East will be able to watch the convention at home."

"I didn't know there were that many sets in the whole country."

Several banker types came through the gate. Tim recognized Joe Pew, the elegant head of Sun Oil not to mention the Republican boss of Pennsylvania.

"I'm for Taft," he had said when Tim interviewed him. "Willkie's a New Dealer. We've already got one communist in the White House. Who needs another?"

Thus far, Tim had not been impressed by the masters of the political machinery of the republic. They thought and spoke in slogans. He had been in despair when he made his first rough cut of the footage already shot. Could one have a documentary on so grand a subject and not hear one intelligent voice? Then he realized that all these studied as well as spontaneous banalities could be arranged into an aural mosaic. The same phrase repeated in different settings by different people soon began to take on an ominous cadence, like what he imagined a Greek chorus to have sounded like: "He'll pull Britain's chestnuts out of the fire" in a dozen different accents across the country sounded as stately and as minatory as "multitudinous laughter of the waves of ocean."

Then he began to intercut footage of the bombing of London:

Troy aflame. He would soon have—or so he'd been promised—the previous week's film of the French surrendering to the Germans in the same railroad car at Compiègne in which the Germans had surrendered in 1918. Hitler now occupied all of France except for a puppet government centered on Vichy in the south.

The film's delay, thanks to Willkie's having joined the cast, had allowed history to take the leading role, or at least history in the guise of the mysterious demon-king out of Central Europe.

Although not yet an interventionist, Tim did wonder just how far Hitler planned to go, assuming that he had any plan at all, which Tim rather doubted. It would appear that world conquest and movie directing were not unlike in the sense that the best effects were often unplanned. On camera, Hitler had actually looked stunned when he realized, in Paris, that he had so quickly, even magically, conquered France. In a matter of weeks he would occupy the British Isles. Canada was now preparing to take in the royal family while Roosevelt was prepared to take over the British fleet, which alone stood between the United States and a German conquest, or so British propaganda maintained relentlessly.

"You're down here for Willkie?" Joe Pew attempted an amiable smile; and settled for a baring of his teeth. He was like a caricature of a capitalist as rendered by the old Group Theater; the sight of his portly figure made Tim nostalgic for the certitudes of the militant thirties: of us and them forever in dubious battle.

"He's the story. Right now, anyway."

Pew was thoughtful. "I hate," he said, "the way he looks."

"I thought that that was the main thing he has going for him. Man from Indiana. Simple Hoosier. Like . . ."

"Like Mr. Deeds. Or was it Mr. Smith? The problem is that for a Wall Street lawyer, he is . . ." Pew lowered his voice so that his companions could not hear his shrewd analysis of the darkest horse in the history of American politics, "He is *ill-groomed*. That hair!"

"Folksy."

"*Unkempt*. Mr. Farrell, there are only two ways that you can tell a gentleman from the way he dresses. His felt and his leather. Felt and leather," he repeated and the rosy piglet face shone in the rising sun's heat.

"Felt and leather?"

"Forget the suit, the shirt. They seldom are a giveaway now that everything's off the rack for every Tom, Dick, and Harry to look alike. I can bear—I can *just* bear—his wrinkled suits, but it is the fine felt of the hat, the imported oxblood leather of the shoes, that mark the gentleman. He fails on both counts. He looks more like an auctioneer at a county fair than a gentleman, much less a president. Even a communist like FDR never ever cheats on his felt and leather. Properly bred to it, you see."

Pew glanced at Tim; shuddered at what he saw—rubber Keds, a golf cap with visor. Then the train from New York arrived. Joe Pew and his friends made their way, slowly, past the Pathé news team, making certain that they were recognized.

Ecstatic, Tim turned to his cameraman. "You got that?"

"Yes, sir!" Tim turned to the soundman. "You got it?"

"Every wonderful word, sir."

Tim gave a rebel yell. "Orson will cut his throat when he hears all that felt and leather."

Pew and his friends met several men who looked just like them while Willkie, wearing not felt but a straw hat and high-top black shoes in need of a polishing, leapt onto the siding. Davenport followed, adequately Pew-ish. Apparently a dozen journalists had accompanied the dark horse from New York to Philadelphia.

Willkie stopped for the newsreel camera. A question was asked him which Tim could not hear. Then Willkie's voice sounded clearly in the middle distance. "As of yesterday—Friday?—Dr. Gallup had me at twenty-nine percent . . ." He indicated the journalists from the train. "Everything I know they tell me. Fact," he grinned into the camera, "if it weren't for them, I wouldn't be here. Left my wallet at home. They bought me my ticket. I guess I'm on the take now."

There was a confusion of voices. Then: "Dewey's ahead, at forty-seven percent."

"So why is everyone saying that Senator Taft is the man for me to beat when he's running third at eight percent? Anyway, it's all in the hands of the people. Now you fellows go right ahead and ask me any damn thing in the world and I'll answer it. Nothing is off the record, so shoot!"

Tim was charmed by Willkie's confidence in himself. Either he was uncommonly stupid or uncommonly shrewd or, most likely of all, an unnerving combination of the two. He held a dozen newspapers in his hands, each with his name in the headline. Every now and then he would look at a newspaper as if for inspiration. "How many delegates will I get on the first ballot? I haven't the faintest idea. Russell." He turned to Davenport. "Do you have any idea how many delegates we've got?"

"Not really. Quite a few, I'd say." This delighted the journalists, accustomed to solemn self-serving predictions and exaggerations.

"This is a wide-open convention," said Willkie. "I think we've seen to that. The country's seen to that. I know. I've been out there, up and down the states. People want a change. People want their own convention, not something run by bosses."

By accident—or was it design!—Joe Pew, boss of Pennsylvania, came into view just back of Willkie, who turned and gave him a wide smile. "Now here's Mr. Pew. I've never had the pleasure of meeting him but I know that face from photographs, and I look forward to his help come November."

A journalist shouted, "Who's your candidate, Joe?"

"Pennsylvania's seventy-two delegates will be voting for that great American Senator Robert Alphonso Taft." Pew moved on, felted head held high.

Willkie spoke in a confidential voice to the newsreel cameraman. "That's what he thinks now, but anyone who says he can deliver a certain number of delegates to a certain candidate at a certain time is just plain wrong."

On war or peace, Willkie was as adroit as the master in the White House. "England stands in imminent fear of being crushed and we should rally to her aid with everything short of war. Yes. France has fallen. But America, instead of being afraid today, should grow stronger and measure up to our true destiny!"

There was a murmur of agreement from some of the journalists. Then: "What do you think about the President's taking those two Republicans, Stimson and Knox, into his Cabinet, and the chairman of the Republican Party reads them out of your party?"

Willkie laughed. "I don't approve of anybody reading anybody out of any party. Let's read everybody in, many as we can."

"Would you include Democrats in your Cabinet?"

"I certainly would."

"Would you find a place for Mr. Roosevelt in your Cabinet?"

"What a swell idea! Never let us forget that he was a great assistant secretary of the Navy in the Great War and if, God forbid, we're ever in such a situation again, I promise—and this is a solemn commitment—to give Franklin his old job back. First-rate assistant secretaries of the Navy don't just grow on trees, you know."

On a wave of laughter, Willkie and his escort entered the station, where he was spontaneously cheered.

Tim picked up Willkie again at Broad and Chestnut Streets near City Hall. Willkie had got out of his car and was making a triumphal march along Broad Street. Tim had figured that Willkie's unerring sense of drama would take him into the Willkie Club at Locust Street. So when Willkie entered the club, to be greeted by the sharp-featured Oren Root, Tim's cameraman had a commanding view not only of Willkie at the door to the club, but of the huge crowd that had fallen in behind him as he marched forward, waving to the crowd, and acknowledging a sudden proliferation of signs that declared: "We Want Willkie." Plainly, Davenport and company were not as disorganized as they seemed.

While the crew picked up crowd shots in the street, Tim followed Willkie into the gray stone Bellevue Stratford Hotel. This was the headquarters for the convention, and the lobby was crowded with delegates all eager, it appeared, to shake the candidate's hand.

By now Tim knew where to waylay the Man from Indiana. He slipped into the Hunt Room Bar. Amidst what looked to be a celebration of ye Olde England of fox-hunting in the shires, he joined Willkie at the bar; each ordered a scotch and soda.

"Well, Brother Farrell, how's it going?"

"October first, according to L. B. Mayer. I'm also on the sixteenth floor of the Benjamin Franklin."

"Lucky to get a room. Russell thought as Taft has taken over a hundred rooms in the hotel and Dewey something like a hundred at some other hotel, we'd have only two rooms. I think he's slightly overdoing the barefoot-boy-with-cheek act . . ."

"But it's working."

"Is it?" Willkie's eyes never ceased looking about the bar as he smiled at this one, nodded to that one, all the while shaking proffered hands, and greeting strangers warmly. How he had stayed *out* of politics for so long was the real mystery.

Tim was curious. "Don't *you* think it's working?"

"The crowds tell me yes. But then I think about that old devil in the White House. There's nothing he won't do to win."

"Like declare war before November?"

"He has the power to go to war already. All this talk about just giving the British the tools and they'll do the job—that's just bull."

Tim couldn't entirely believe his ears. "But that's what you say, too."

"Well?" Then an Indiana congressman named Halleck collected the candidate and they continued on their triumphant way to the Benjamin Franklin Hotel.

As Tim emerged from the Bellevue Stratford, a large young man stopped him. "Mr. Farrell? I'm Peter Sanford."

For an instant Tim was at sea; mind concentrated on the similarities rather than the differences between Willkie and Roosevelt.

"I'm Caroline's nephew."

Tim recalled. "Sorry," he said, adding the traditional "You've grown."

"I'm working for the *Trib* this summer. Getting experience, as Father says. Though I don't know for what."

"So am I. This is my first convention, too. So I'm going through what—who—do you shoot?" Tim's crew had already moved on to the Benjamin Franklin to film Taft, whom Tim had interviewed at Laurel House the previous winter. He was easily the most dedicated isolation-

ist on offer; he was also the one that the press had picked to win the
nomination on an early ballot.

"I was just at the Walton. I saw Dewey." Peter fell in step with
Tim.

"On what ballot did he say he'd win?"

"Oh, he never talked about anything so intimate. He did assure us
that the United States is the greatest country in the world."

Tim chuckled. "Plainly a risk-taker. Where is Caroline?"

"New York, I think. She's helping Harry Hopkins fix up an apartment in the Essex House."

"Harry Hopkins?" Tim was impressed.

"They are," said Peter with a smile, "just good friends. She keeps
him company, she says."

"While he keeps FDR company. Isn't three a crowd?"

A small elephant, wearing a ribbon that said "Taft for President,"
crossed the street in front of them, giving much pleasure to pedestrians
if not to drivers. "I think he's asked her to marry him, and she's said no.
He assured her, my father says, that he wants to marry her only for her
money."

"Caroline would like that."

"She likes him."

"Maybe she can get him to do an interview for me . . ."

"No." Peter sounded certain. "He's the invisible man these days.
When he doesn't visit New York he lives in the White House. He and
the President start the day together, plotting."

"Who do *they* think will be nominated here?"

"Taft. The President's made several bets."

"Caroline?"

"She thinks it will be Willkie. She says they all laugh at her. But I
think she knows something. She also knows someone who knows quite
a lot."

"Ernest Cuneo?" Tim tried out the name but got no response.

"No. Someone called Sam Pryor. He's a committeeman from
Connecticut. He's sort of running the convention. He's working for
Willkie."

"Would he talk to me . . . to camera?"

"Ask. He's pretty busy right now. You see, he's in charge of credentials. That's who gets to sit on the floor of the convention hall and who gets to sit where in the galleries."

Tim stopped in front of the Benjamin Franklin, as did the small elephant, whose keeper led him inside. Tim hoped his team would get a shot of the elephant, preferably in a lift full of politicians. He turned to Peter. "How is it that someone who's working for Willkie gets put in charge of seating?"

"Well, the original chairman on arrangements . . ." Peter removed a notebook from his jacket pocket. "You see? I'm a real reporter." He flicked through pages of notes. "A Mr. Ralph E. Williams, aged seventy. The chairman's supposed to be neutral but everyone says he was for Taft. Anyway, at five-thirty p.m. May sixteenth, he rose to address his committee in a ballroom at the Bellevue Stratford. When he put his hand on the back of a chair, to support himself, the chair skittered away from him and he fell to the floor, dead. It was, I've been told, a very hot day and of course he was seventy years old. On the other hand he was believed to be in perfect health. Sam Pryor offered to take his place." Peter put his notebook away. "These credentials, these tickets, are all kept in a locked room next to the party chairman's office at the Bellevue. The room is guarded around the clock by Pinkerton detectives."

Jim was impressed by the blandness of Peter's recital. "You've done quite a bit of sleuthing here. Why?"

Peter smiled. "Wouldn't you?"

"No. But then I'm a movie director, not a politician. I can't imagine anyone caring enough about these clowns—that goes for every politician in the country, including the Great White Father—to kill an elderly gentleman in order to get hold of a batch of tickets."

"Well, I'm neither a politician nor a movie director but I'm very much a product of the District of Columbia. I know how much all this matters not only to the people directly involved but to foreign countries, too."

"Like Germany?"

"Yes. And like England." Tim found Peter's recital astonishingly cool. "The people out there in your hometowns are almost a hundred percent against our going into the war, but some politicians, including the Great White Father, are working to get us into the war before England folds. So, what is the life of one Ralph E. Williams as compared to the survival of the British Empire?"

" 'He Died for His Credentials'?" Tim saw black humor, as always.

" 'Credentials' is too long a word to be in a title." Peter matched blackness with blackness. "Why not 'He Died for His Tickets'?"

Tim suddenly realized that he had met Mr. Ralph E. Williams at Laurel House in September. He had said something about—or was it to?—Senator Taft. Tim turned to Peter. "You could have a great career as a scriptwriter, if you want it. And if you can stand Jack Warner. Because this story is right down his alley. Low-budget, of course. You know, the French are always praising the Rembrandt lighting of Warner Brothers films. They don't know that that's not Rembrandt, that's Jack Warner rushing from stage to stage and turning off lights to cut costs. So how about *Murder at the Bellevue Stratford*."

They went into the lobby, where they were met by Tim's cameraman, who said, "The name's Blossom."

"Whose name?"

"The pygmy elephant's. We got a great shot of her with Senator Taft trying to shove her out of his bedroom."

3

On Monday morning Peter Sanford presented his various press credentials at Gate 23 of Philadelphia's convention hall only to find the dapper Sam Pryor already on the spot, talking to several Pinkerton men. When he saw Peter, he waved cheerily. "The press entrance is further along."

"What's this one for?"

"The people of the United States." Pryor laughed. "Is your father coming?"

Peter said, truthfully, that he did not know. As he walked from guarded gate to guarded gate, he felt the morning heat damply rise. Soon Philadelphia would be like a Turkish bath.

Dutifully, Peter checked his notes. The hall could seat fifteen thousand people. The Philadelphia Orchestra would play for the delegates. The keynote address that evening would be given by Governor Harold Stassen of Minnesota. Then the next day, Tuesday, the only living former president, Herbert Hoover, would address the convention. Wednesday, the leading contenders would be put in nomination. Thursday, the balloting of the delegates from all the states would begin and the first candidate to get 501 votes would be the Republican nominee for president.

Meetings were now being held all over Philadelphia as delegates called upon Taft and Willkie in their Benjamin Franklin headquarters; on Thomas E. Dewey at the Walton; and a few, presumably, on Senator Vandenberg at the Adelphia Hotel. For reasons so far mysterious to Peter some once promising candidates were now out of the running; Vandenberg was one. But the great man seemed not to mind, as he continued to receive admirers in his suite while bright young women handed out palmetto fans with the legend "Fan for Van" on them: the ever-increasing summer heat ensured a good deal of fanning on the part of the delegates, of whom very few would cast so much as a vote of gratitude for Vandenberg. When Peter had asked the Senator why he had gone into so few primaries, the round owl eyes looked up to heaven. "Imagine killing yourself for *Vermont!*"

Peter saw glowworms as he stepped from bright sunlight into the dim arena with its huge upper-tier gallery that could seat as many people as the floor itself, according to his own dogged notes. The floor in front of the stage was marked off for the state delegations; each of the forty-eight states had a standard and beneath the state's name an elephant with an American flag in its trunk. Alongside the standard, uncomfortable folding wooden chairs were ranked, one for each delegate—seventy-two chairs for Pennsylvania, a half-dozen for tiny Delaware.

Peter circled the hall, notebook in hand. The large stage was dominated by a massive bronze eagle more suitable, Peter thought, for a Third Reich rally than for the rustic republic that gave such kindly shelter to the common man—a turkey would have been a cozier symbol. Certainly, more symbolic. From balconies to left and right of the stage the coats of arms of the states were hung, and red-white-and-blue bunting was draped everywhere. With full lighting, the effect would be cheerful but now, in the half-darkness, the effect was somewhat ominous, the circus out of season.

Peter dutifully noted that Maine and Vermont, the only two states to vote for the Republican candidate Governor Alf Landon in 1936, were given places of honor in the first row, alongside huge Michigan and Indiana. Peter sat in a Maine chair and noticed that the hall smelled a bit like the Barnum and Bailey Circus before the animals—and the people—filled the tent. Dust. Old canvas.

There was a surprising amount of activity on the floor and in the great upper tier. Numerous worried-looking police were conducting some sort of search which involved little more than marching about, looking worried. A number of members of the press were also wandering up and down, as Peter had been doing, getting the feel of the hall.

Journalism was not to be Peter's life, he decided. Blaise had always said that the *Tribune* would be his one day *if* he proved to be really interested. The "really interested" had always sounded a bit like a threat while the "proved" sounded as if he was on probation. Next year, at twenty, he would graduate from the University of Virginia; then, at twenty-one, the trust fund of his maternal grandmother would bring him untold wealth, thirty thousand dollars a year. Blaise had been furious when he saw the terms of the old lady's will but Frederika had been pleased. "He won't have to do anything he doesn't want to do."

"Suppose he does nothing at all?" Characteristically the conversation was held in Peter's presence, for maximum effect.

"Oh, that would be wonderful, wouldn't it?" Frederika's joy was intermingled with the friendly malice that she always displayed toward her husband. "Aren't too many people doing altogether too much nowadays? Imagine having a gentleman in the family."

"*A wastrel!*" Blaise was now red in the face.

Peter was thrilled. "What exactly," he had asked, "does the average wastrel do?"

"He wastes money! Produces nothing!"

"The money he wastes will be his, not yours, dear. And why should poor Peter produce anything at all? The world," Frederika proclaimed in her best gracious hostess manner, "is already crowded with useless productions."

Blaise retreated, raging. But then father and son were seldom at ease with each other. Blaise much preferred his daughter, Enid. She was older than Peter; drank too much; gave the family only trouble. Yet Blaise doted on her as well as on her ambitious young husband, Clay Overbury, a budding politician. Blaise and Clay were far more like indulgent father and grateful son than Blaise and Peter, who was more pleased than not that Blaise and Clay had found, as it were, each other, letting him off the hook. In principle, he had no great objection to Blaise as a father. Ordinarily, their relations were amiable, thanks, Peter had come to realize, to his own phlegmatic nature. He was a born observer; and to observe the world about him required not only tact but a sort of emotional neutrality unknown to his father or, indeed, to any of his family except the enigmatic Caroline, whom he observed with near-obsession: could anyone be so serenely neutral—that word again—as his aunt? Even with her appalling daughter, she never lost control; never gave away her game, whatever that game might be.

Peter daydreamed in a convention hall that would soon be the center of the American political world. He definitely had no gift for journalism, if journalism required any special gift. But then he had grown up in a newspaper family and the trade, hunting down famous people in search of secrets, did not appeal to him, nor did he want for himself to be a quarry for others. He would rather watch than himself be watched, unlike Clay, who was already scheming to be president later on in the century, with Blaise's passionate help: this meant being forever reinvented by the needs of each observer. One must entirely lack a character of one's own to submit to so many eyes. As a subject, history attracted him most, largely because there was always something wrong with it. Caroline had known Henry Adams and his circle, and although Peter found the Adams pessimism too stylized for his taste, he liked the thought of someone who never ceased to observe and ponder and formulate all through a long life only to throw up his hands at the end and say, "I never cared *what* happened, only *why* it happened. Couldn't find out. Gave it up." That was very much the right spirit. But Peter sensed a flaw in the Adams conclusion. Why assume there is a why? Why even ask why? Why not simply describe and then let the description answer all the "why" that anyone could want? Of course, Adams had had an odd, for an Adams, religious turn to his mind: the Virgin and the Dynamo. Why the one? Why the other? Why either?

"Would you like to meet your father for lunch?" The rich Rooseveltian voice emerged from a plump young man who had been, until recently, a very, very fat younger man, the quintessential insider-journalist who, with a partner, wrote a political column for the New York *Herald Tribune.* Peter got to his feet and greeted Joe Alsop. "I was thinking about history."

"About writing it or making it?"

"About what it is, if it is anything at all except different versions of something that probably never was."

"Detroit! That's the place for you, Peter. Henry Ford. 'History is bunk,' he says. And so is he. Your father's at the Union League for lunch, with the Willkie people. What they decide today might well be historical. So come along. Watch them closely. I think Willkie has a good chance of defeating Cousin Franklin. Of course, we won't allow that. But if he's the candidate, we're still safe."

"You mean England's safe."

"That's *we,* dear boy. Same boat."

"Did you know Henry Adams?"

"If he had a morbid turn of mind, it is possible that he saw me in my crib. No, Peter, I'm not that old. Ask your aunt. The old man doted on her."

They stepped out into the heat. "We shall now take a streetcar," said Joe, reveling in their plebeian adventure. "This is how you get to understand the people, up close, doing their useful sordid tasks."

With great dignity, Joe leapt onto a streetcar, followed by Peter, who soon realized that they were going in the wrong direction. "Surely they all end up passing the same places." Joe was not one to admit error.

The Union League was pleasantly old-fashioned. Blaise was holding court in a corner of the club's dining room with Thomas W. Lamont, Russell Davenport, the onetime boxer Gene Tunney, and Walter Lippmann, whose political columns read like the meditations of an unnaturally benign deity. At the next table sat the young Senator Henry Cabot Lodge of Massachusetts. He was, like his father in the Great War, a leading isolationist.

Joe and Peter were introduced by Blaise to the table. Chairs were brought. Peter had not seen his father so animated in a long time. Obviously, conventions were good for him. At first, Peter thought he should be taking notes; then quickly realized that he would be seen as a spy, which he was in the sense that the others had come together to make sure that their man was nominated while he was entirely indifferent except as a spectator.

"Cousin Alice is for Taft," Joe announced. Mention of Alice Longworth always made people smile. Possibly because they knew that a joke was on its way; and so it was. "When I told her not to be such a reactionary snob, that at last we had a true grassroots candidate, she said, 'Yes, from the grass roots of ten thousand country clubs.'" Everyone laughed, including Lamont, who said, rather mildly, "Wendell's just retired from the board of the First National Bank."

"Not a moment too soon." Blaise was brisk. "We don't want this to be a House of Morgan election like 1916."

"Then," said Lamont, "you must all deny that I was in Philadelphia today."

"I've had a long talk with Willkie about the draft." Lippmann's Chinese mandarin eyes gleamed above two large pouches. "He'll support selective service whenever the President is ready to send it to Congress."

There was a pleased murmur at the table, possibly because, of those present, only Joe Alsop and Peter Sanford were of draft age. "In fact,"

Lippmann continued, "Willkie wishes the President would move more quickly toward rearmament."

"Will he say this?" Gene Tunney was large, solid, slow; he was considered an intellectual because he had once had tea with George Bernard Shaw. Peter wondered why Shaw was interested in the world's champion heavyweight prize fighter; wondered how history could ever be written without knowing the motivations of those who appeared to be making it. How to know the unknowable obviously had been too much for Henry Adams. But suppose that personal motivations were unimportant. Peter tried to recall what Hegel had written; then realized that he'd never read Hegel but only recalled what his professor, a sort of T. S. Eliot monarchistic Anglican, had said on the subject. So much to know. So many bad teachers.

The table found it amusing that Willkie had only just switched, officially, from the Democratic to the Republican Party. Joe Alsop, as the table's know-it-all, acted as instructor, though it was clear to Peter that Lamont, plainly the leader of this enterprise, knew the full story. "He was an Ohio delegate to the 1924 convention, where he acted as a floor manager for Newton D. Baker. A sign of flawed taste." Peter had forgotten who Baker was. "Then in 1932 he was again a delegate, but this time a floor manager for—ah, you've guessed it I can see!—for Newton D. Baker."

"Thank God he wasn't for Franklin," said Lamont.

"Oh, he explains that eloquently." Joe was eating scrapple, a peculiar Philadelphia dish, not unlike tinned dog food. "When he voted for Roosevelt in 1932 the New Deal wasn't on the ballot. Had it been, he shouts, he would never have voted for a socialist."

"A born politician." Lamont tried to make this sound like a compliment.

The table then discussed the candidate's private life and whether or not it would become public. For two years Willkie had been having an affair with the book editor of the *Herald Tribune*, Irita Van Doren, once wife to a popular historian, Carl Van Doren. Willkie was eager for culture and Irita was eager to be his muse. "I don't see any great harm coming of this," said Lippmann, which sounded to Peter as if he did fear scandal.

Joe, as always, knew most. "When somebody suggested that he stop seeing her—once he's nominated next Thursday—he said, 'Oh, every newspaperman in town knows about us.'"

"I," said Russell Davenport, "was the somebody who said that, and I still think it's potentially dangerous."

"If they try that," Blaise was grim, "we'll discuss Franklin's affair with Missy Le Hand."

Lamont turned to Blaise, in mock horror. "Don't you dare. The President is our savior. Willkie is only our insurance."

Even Lippmann laughed. Suddenly it occurred to Peter that Lippmann, Alsop, and the mistress of the Hoosier candidate were all employed by the New York *Herald Tribune*. Was this a coincidence?

Blaise shrugged. "The only person we should fear in a matter like this is William Randolph Hearst. He lives for scandal."

"Happily his palace at San Simeon," said Joe, "is made of such exquisite crystal that an unkind word could shatter it."

Blaise turned to Davenport. "Do you still have your headquarters in New York?"

Davenport nodded. "We're still at the Murray Hill Hotel. We've been there since January." He gave Blaise a card.

So much, thought Peter, for the spontaneous candidacy of the grassroots candidate. He wondered if he would be allowed to write anything of interest. "Who," he asked Alsop, "is Sam Pryor?"

"From my home state of Connecticut. He's our Republican state committee man. Why?"

"I keep running into him."

"He's working hard for Wendell. He's also in charge of credentials." Joe chuckled. "The most important man in Philadelphia, this week."

"Who is Ralph E. Williams?"

"I don't know everyone, dear boy." But Peter had a definite impression that the name had indeed registered. After all, Joe did know everyone that he thought worth knowing. Peter now saw himself as a fearless investigator, making his way through the Philadelphia morgue, where he pried open a metal filing case from which he removed a yellow manila folder—this particular daydream was in full color—

containing an autopsy form with the name "Ralph E. Williams" at the top. Below the name, in bright red letters, was the word "Murder."

4

The convention hall was indeed transformed once all the lights were blazing. The noise of people talking was a constant roar as the delegates took their seats alongside their state standards.

Peter had found a corner of a press table beneath the front of the stage. Although he was not able to see what was going on above him, he had a clear view of the state delegations and of the overhanging tier at the back of the hall, where people were streaming down the aisles as they searched for their seats. Flustered attendants were having difficulty finding seats even for the irritably ticketed. Had Sam Pryor issued too many or too few tickets?

The Philadelphia Orchestra was off to one side, and the musicians were tuning their instruments loudly. In the New York delegation Peter recognized Colonel Theodore Roosevelt, Jr., who stood next to the state standard, talking to Joe Alsop, who was making the rounds. The Colonel was for Dewey.

Peter moved out from under the stage to study the rest of the press corps, all seated in a sort of pen at the back of the stage. Needless to say, the grandees of the New York *Herald Tribune* like Walter Lippmann were not to be seen rubbing shoulders with their sweaty brethren, but he did recognize, with pleased awe, H. L. Mencken of the Baltimore *Sun*, wearing a straw hat, no jacket, red suspenders. He chewed a cigar and pounded a typewriter as if it were a candidate, while from time to time he snapped his suspenders, rather as if he felt himself in need of spurring, like a horse.

Joe hailed Peter in front of the California delegation, all gloomily pledged to their favorite son, Herbert Hoover. "Out of the West, yet again," intoned Joe, "strides a giant, a leader, a man."

"Hubert Hoofer?" Peter supplied the latest line. A few days earlier, on radio, an announcer had said, "Ladies and gentlemen of the radio audience, I have the honor to introduce to you the former president of the United States, Mr. Heebert Hoobert . . . I mean Mr. Hoobert Hover . . . uh, Mr. Hubbard . . ." Mercifully, the now deranged announcer was dragged off-microphone in a swirl of static and the unlovely voice of the former president was heard in the land.

On the stage the handsome Republican national chairman, John D. M. Hamilton, was conferring with a number of henchmen. "Hamilton told us he'd like to second the nomination of Willkie but as party chairman he shouldn't take sides." Joe Alsop had an odd whinnying chuckle when he wished to express disapproval. He did so now. "He's afraid his days are numbered now."

"Why are you so certain it's going to be Willkie?"

"The polls . . ." Joe was now looking up at a balcony to which had been attached the state seal of Maine. In the balcony several important-looking personages were taking their seats. "Isn't that Rudy Vallee?"

Peter recognized the singer-bandleader who originally came from Yale and who sang nasally, but thinly, through a megaphone.

"I guess he'd have to be a Republican." Peter was actively neutral on the subject. But Joe was whinnying again, this time with pleasure. "He's priceless. He asked to have lunch with me last winter. He said that he was seriously thinking about entering the Maine primary."

"For president?"

"For president. I said that he must. The country needs him. I told Cousin Eleanor, who said she couldn't wait to tell Franklin. I hope she did. He loves that sort of thing."

Joe took a seat in the Connecticut delegation as if he belonged there, which in a sense he did; certainly, all the state's delegates greeted him. "Our secret weapon," he said to Peter, who remained standing beside the railing that contained the delegation, "is Hadley Cantrill. He works for Dr. Gallup. He helps the good doctor formulate his questions and pick his interviewees. Very important that. No Yale accents, no Rudy Vallee types to be allowed within earshot of a blue-collar worker in Berwyn, Illinois. Class speaks best to class. Hadley is a master of getting us the results we want."

What Peter had always suspected was true was true if Joe could be believed; the polls were rigged. But Joe anticipated him. "We get more or less what we want but we can't just make up majorities—so far. Cantrill's working for British intelligence and for the White House. Our current problem—other than nominating Willkie—is getting fifty elderly destroyers to England before the English starve to death. But the American people don't want Franklin to just give away any part of our fleet. So you start, unknown to Dr. Gallup, to rearrange his questions. You ask the Average American, our crafty master, 'Which of these two things do you think is more important for the United States to try to do—to keep out of war ourselves, or to help England win, even at the risk of getting into war?' Straightforward stuff, you'd think, if you're not used to thinking. Last week when the questions were asked like that, sixty percent said, in answer to question two, that they'd want to help England win, which is what we wanted to hear. On the other hand, the true isolationist will seize on question number one, which means, finally, that only forty-four percent are willing to risk war by helping England, and that isn't enough, is it?"

"The possibilities are endless?"

"For the unscrupulous, too," Joe spoke with mock piety just as the Philadelphia Orchestra began a triumphant rendering of a recent patriotic hymn, "Ballad for Americans," by what was rumored to be a young communist. The thundering music and proletarian words had taken the country by storm. Now, in a full orchestral version, it had all the emotional effect of "The Battle Hymn of the Republic." The last word was "America," and ended on a sigh like an echo.

Next a prayer from the archbishop of Philadelphia, Cardinal Dougherty. He requested divine guidance for the delegates in their selection of a candidate. Then the Boy Governor of Minnesota gave the keynote speech. He spoke for an hour, to the consternation of the delegates. His message was indomitable: "Americans must keep burning the light of liberty."

By the time he finished, Peter had found Tim and his crew at the front of the upper tier. Tim was amused. "Same speech as St. Paul. But lots more adjectives."

"Bigger audience, too."

When Stassen finally stopped talking, there was mild applause and then a group to the right of Tim's camera shouted, in unison, "We want Willkie!" This was repeated several times; and that was that.

5

The next days were a blur for Peter. He sat in a streetcar with a former vice president of the United States but could not recall his name. He went from hotel suite to hotel suite. Open house was the order of the day. Strangers came and went. Twice he visited Willkie's two-room suite down the hall from Tim's bedroom. Willkie was losing what voice he had. There was a living room off the corridor; back of this front room, double doors opened into a bedroom where two large windows were constantly open. Air conditioning had not yet come to Philadelphia.

Willkie himself stood at the center of the front room, gazing with pale blind eyes upon the parade of handshakers who came and went, each ritually grabbing the offered paw. Willkie's face was unhealthily pale; he was sweating heavily; waistcoat unbuttoned. He pretended to listen to those who wanted to tell him something. All the while, he kept repeating over and over again, "Ah'd be a lahr if ah said ah didden won be prez You Nigh Stays." Peter, after the second visit to the candidate's suite, quite believed him. How anyone could want something so badly was beyond him. But then Peter had never not known more than he had ever wanted to know about the various residents of the house on Pennsylvania Avenue; yet the city that he knew spoke rarely of that house and its occupants—the plural in Peter's case was not the long parade of presidents but, for most of his conscious life, the Roosevelt family. He just barely recalled Herbert Hoover, who, suddenly, on Tuesday evening had appeared in the convention hall as the orchestra played "California, Here I Come."

Peter had stationed himself next to Tim's crew, for whom the police had cordoned off a small section of the gallery, which had filled up the moment the doors were opened. There was again confusion over seating. Ernest Cuneo was seated within Tim's magic circle.

Peter, opera glasses in hand, looked down on the floor as the round-faced Hoover with his Humpty Dumpty starched collar marched down the center aisle, accompanied by the governor of Pennsylvania. There was genuine enthusiasm for this least charming of presidents. Every delegate was now on his feet, applauding, while a number seized their standards in order to make a ritual parade about the floor, hailing the once and future chief.

"Poor old thing," said Ernest Cuneo. "He's the only one here who doesn't know that he hasn't a chance."

"He's still popular." Peter indicated the cheering crowd of delegates below them.

"Right now. But watch what happens at the end of his speech." The mischievous face of Cuneo had a jack-o'-lantern look to it so unlike the uncarved full pale pumpkin of Herbert Hoover who was now on the stage, waving jerkily to the newsreel cameras.

Although Cuneo maintained a quiet roar in Peter's ear, he was barely audible through the shouts and screams inside the auditorium. "The isolationists are making their last stand. Hoover's their voice. He's been working on this speech since . . ." Cuneo's voice was drowned out by cheering and by the banging gavel of the minority leader of the House of Representatives, Joe Martin, permanent chairman of the convention.

Finally there was silence; and Hoover spoke. The themes were familiar. The United States was safe from any attack in any foreseeable future no matter how many countries Hitler conquered. More to the point, the militarizing of the state—the current drafting of nearly a million men—endangered the republic, whose economy had been successfully turned around in 1933, only to be undone by the New Deal of Roosevelt, which had renewed the Depression. This, Peter could tell, was the reddest of red meat for a hungry crowd of conservatives whose true majority was always for Hoover.

But the audience was not responding. Hoover's message was not getting through: literally, not getting through. Although Peter in the front row of the gallery could hear Hoover's voice, he was aware that there were dead patches all around him. People were straining to hear, hands cupped to ears.

"It's the very latest sound equipment," said Cuneo, looking more than ever like a Halloween surprise. "I can't think what's gone wrong."

Tim was only aware of his own soundman as he continued to film what was plainly an ineffective speech. The audience was now shouting, "Louder, louder!" as the droning presidential voice came to them between bursts of static. "Tragic," said Cuneo. "Hoover's last chance to be nominated. And no one can hear him."

Peter knew exactly what had happened. "I hadn't realized that Sam Pryor was also in charge of acoustics."

Cuneo gave him a sharp look. "What makes you think of him?"

"Because the mike was perfect for Stassen yesterday."

"Machinery." Cuneo was vague. "Anyway there's something a lot more serious going on than a bad mike."

Wednesday afternoon Cuneo invited Peter to join him and a special police squad. "I've known the mayor for years."

"How?"

"How does anyone know anyone?" Cuneo grinned. "I like to know things that connect with my business . . ."

"Which is?"

"Knowing things that connect." They were outside the convention hall. A hot intensely blue evening. A popcorn vendor was doing good business in front of Gate 23, guarded now by Philadelphia police. Cuneo said something to one of them: he and Peter were admitted. Just inside the hall there was what looked to be some sort of utilities room; and more police.

Cuneo was greeted as an old friend by a police captain in a windowless room. On a trestle table, two large metal containers had been taken apart and their contents—nails, nuts, bolts—were strewn across the table.

"We think—we pray we've got all of them. *No press!*" The captain had spotted Peter's badge, which he had, at Cuneo's insistence, slipped inside his breast pocket, but enough of it was visible to alarm the police.

Cuneo soothed the captain. Son of Blaise Sanford. Friend of Mayor. Of Cuneo. "We don't want any panic here, and if this story gets out . . ."

"It won't. Not from us. But who is Adolph Heller? Who is Bernard Rush?"

The captain was grim. "We hope to find out. Soon. One of our men got lucky. They hired him. He's a demolition expert. They — whoever they are—were planning to set off these bombs tonight. In the hall. To kill off the top Republicans. They also installed one at the Dewey headquarters. Anyway, this morning our man pretended he was sick. Got back to base. We arrested Heller and Rush. They showed us these two bombs already under the stage. We've defused everything."

"But who are they?"

"Ask FBI. We've done our job. It's their business now. Anyway, no word to anyone until after tomorrow."

"Does the President know?" Cuneo asked.

"That's why you're here, Ernie. Isn't it?" The chief then turned a cold eye upon Peter. "I hope you realize . . ."

"Yes. I do." What Peter had taken to be inadvertent national comedy had become very dark indeed. For the first time Peter believed that whatever malignancy had created Hitler and Stalin was now loose everywhere in the world, including, of all places, dowdy dull Philadelphia. The idea of anyone wanting to blow up Herbert Hoover was so bizarre that he wondered if, perhaps, this was actually a comic scenario awaiting its punch line so that the stately Margaret Dumont could, once again, faint dead away into the arms of the leering Groucho Marx.

Cuneo and Peter returned to Tim's high perch in the gallery.

"Why?" asked Peter.

"Why is easy." Cuneo was for once not mocking. "*Who* is the question."

"Germans? British?"

"What would either get out of something like this? Crackpots is our usual story."

"Our?"

Cuneo repeated, "Our. Yes. Remember McKinley?"

"Before my time."

"Shot and killed by an anarchist. Crazy, of course. But he'd been reading poor Emma Goldman and so she got deported to Russia, which she hated because she was an anarchist and not a communist, but our government can never tell the difference."

Peter tried not to imagine bombs filled with shrapnel going off in the convention hall and, of course, could think of nothing else but flying nails and bits of metal spraying into a screaming audience.

Dewey was nominated by a New York politician who vowed that this "lifelong Republican will keep us out of war." It was curious, thought Peter, for a moment forgetting the rain of shrapnel hurtling toward him, that everyone really knew everything. Roosevelt did intend to get the United States into war, and despite his ever more solemn public denials, no one for a moment believed him. All in all, an odd sort of nation whose true history might prove to be uncommonly interesting if one were ever able to excavate it from under so many other long-lost nations. Troy upon Troy upon Troy, some with, some without Helen, but all once afire with wrath.

The demonstration for Dewey—delegates marching about holding high various state standards—all cheering but none ecstatic, none really passionate, like the little man himself, who was, no doubt, listening to the radio in his suite at the Walton.

A vain publisher named Gannett had spent a fortune to get himself nominated and seconded. Next, Senator Robert Alphonso Taft was nominated while his mother, the widow of the largest president in American history, William Howard Taft, took a decorous bow from a balcony. Taft was also certified by his nominator to be a "lifelong Republican"; also, there would be no war if he were president, and everyone believed him. Peter suspected that, barring tricks, Taft would be the nominee, with Dewey as his vice presidential candidate. Of course, one major trick had already been played the previous month. The late Ralph E. Williams was to have served the Taftites well until his . . . How did one get a look at an autopsy report? The movies always made it look so simple. Perhaps if he got to know a son or daughter of Williams he might discover something after all. If Williams had been murdered, the family would be the first to want the story known and Sam Pryor—it had to be he—brought to justice.

Then Congressman Halleck, mildly drunk, came forward to the microphones, all in perfect working order now. Breaking with precedent, he mentioned the candidate's name in his first sentence. Peter duly wrote in his notebook, "I nominate Wendell Willkie because, better than any man I know, he can build this country back to prosperity!"

There was a howl from the delegates beneath the gallery. Then much booing. Willkie would lead them into war. Willkie was a Democrat. Willkie was Roosevelt's Trojan horse.

Then there was nothing but noise in the galleries. Peter thought he would go deaf as the roaring became a rhythmic shout: "We want Willkie!" Several thousand voices chanted in unison.

Cuneo shouted into Peter's ear: "Standing-room passes. Just people in off the street. A miracle!" He laughed but Peter only saw his shoulders heaving; he could hear nothing until the chanting stopped and Halleck got on with his speech, which was mercifully short.

The chanting began, even louder than before; then a demonstration began on the floor. Several state standards were uprooted and marched about. The New York delegation was the scene of a fight between the Deweyites and the Willkieites, who won as their floor leader was, by far, the largest man of all. The New York standard then dominated the demonstration.

Peter looked at Tim Farrell, who was directing reaction shots, particularly of the famous "passersby" from the street who were standing in the aisles of the gallery, shouting "We want Willkie."

At breakfast on Thursday in the dining room of the Benjamin Franklin, Peter found Ernest Cuneo with a stack of newspapers beside his plate. "I hope you're enjoying democracy in action." He held up the New York *Herald Tribune*. On its front page, presumably for the first time ever, there was an editorial endorsing the candidacy of Wendell Willkie.

"I don't think Father is going to go so far overboard." Peter had already seen the Washington *Tribune*; there was a mild pro-Willkie piece on the editorial page and a prediction that he would be the nominee.

Mrs. Reid, the principal force behind the New York *Herald Tri-bune*, did not, obviously, believe in understatement. Peter read aloud: "'Extraordinary times call for extraordinary abilities. By great good fortune Mr. Willkie comes before the convention uniquely suited for the hour and for the responsibility.'" Peter put down the paper. "A very balanced assessment," he said.

"I like the part where the *Trib* calls him 'heaven's gift to the nation in its time of crisis.' I detect Irita's hand in that phrase. Certainly he's been heaven's gift to her."

"If everyone knows he has a mistress is that as good as no one knowing?"

"A metaphysical point to which there is no answer but wait and see. As a rule this sort of thing doesn't get into the papers because everyone is vulnerable, with the possible exception of solemn Senator Taft, whose day is done. Read our friend Joe Alsop."

As promised, Joe had penetrated the Gallup Poll. Although Dr. Gallup had said that he would not publish his latest findings until after the candidate had been chosen, Joe had published the "latest" Gallup poll: Willkie led the poll with forty-four percent of Republican voters, followed by Dewey with twenty-nine percent and Taft with thirteen percent.

"Beautiful timing," said Cuneo. "Just beautiful. Every delegate will see this. Willkie's going to stampede the convention. Could you give me the funny papers? I've got to see 'Joe Palooka.'"

Mystified, Peter gave him the comics section from a Hearst news-paper. Cuneo immediately found "Joe Palooka," skimmed the dialogue in the balloons; and laughed out loud. "Good old Ham!"

"Ham who?"

"Ham Fisher. He draws Joe Palooka. I got to him a few months ago and told him that he'd been drawing a lot of stuffy Englishmen with monocles and as they are now our allies maybe he should start showing them as regular fellows. So he's got an RAF fighter pilot in this strip. Top hole! Though Ham doesn't have him talk like Bertie Wooster. You see, the comics are how we get to the lower orders, the average Joe, who will never read the *Trib*, or Joe Alsop."

"*You* do all this?" Peter never ceased to be amazed at the number of bases Cuneo managed to touch.

"All in the day's work."

"And what is the day's work?"

"Making sure that the light of freedom never ceases to shine from the torch of the iron lady in New York Harbor to the distant towers of Ulan Bator, if they have towers there, which I doubt."

It was after four-thirty p.m. when the convention was called to order. Peter had waved to Sam Pryor at Gate 23, where a large crowd had gathered to receive the "standing room only" passes. It was a pity that what was really happening—and had happened, perhaps, to poor Ralph E. Williams—could never be written about, at least in a newspaper.

Peter took his place with the press at the back of the stage. Of the famous journalists only Mencken was in place. Lippmann and Alsop, as befitted statesmen, were elsewhere influencing and instructing the candidates while Pearson and Winchell, as radio stars, pulsated the airwaves, heard always but seen seldom by that vast public to whom they were giving guidance.

On the first ballot Dewey led, with 360 votes, a long way from victory. Then Taft with 189 votes and Willkie with 105 votes. But this was the moment—when Willkie's name was mentioned—that the "standing room only" in the galleries boomed in unison, "We want Willkie!" The sound was deafening as it swept down from above upon the delegates and the stage. Peter saw them, all blurred in the powerful lights. He glanced at Mencken, who had dropped his cigar as his protuberant red-rimmed eyes were turned upward, as if in prayer, to the phenomenon that Sam Pryor had created. For the first time in history a convention was to be stampeded by the gallery, the audience, the extras.

Martin banged his gavel for order, which was slowly restored so that he could read out the numbers. The second roll call began. Dewey dropped to 338, which, according to an old hand in the chair next to Peter, meant "it's all over for him. No winner ever got less on the second ballot than on the first." Taft had picked up some Dewey votes: he now had 203 votes while Willkie had risen to 171. Again, at the mention of his name, the thunderous chant began, "We want Willkie!" In frustration, Martin adjourned for dinner.

Peter found his father with Russell Davenport in the lobby of the Benjamin Franklin. Peter was invited to observe history on the sixteenth floor.

The candidate sat in an armchair beside the radio, eating a steak and a baked potato. A half-dozen reporters kept him company, among them Joe Alsop. In the bedroom Peter could see the Cowles brothers, manning two telephones. On the radio, Drew Pearson was predicting that Dewey would settle for second place on the ticket with Taft.

"Not very likely," said Willkie, shaking Peter's hand with a hand that held the latest of a long series of Camel cigarettes that he had been smoking, according to the overfilled ashtray, since the balloting had begun.

Peter congratulated Alsop on his Gallup story. Joe's smile was razor-thin. "Things do fall in place, don't they."

Blaise was now talking into Willkie's ear. Peter indicated the bedroom. "What's going on in there?"

"Sam Pryor's installed a special line to the convention floor. The brothers are keeping track of our floor managers. My guess is the fifth ballot is the one when we go over the top."

But it was during the fifth ballot that Taft began to surge ahead of Willkie, who was now in second place. The Cowles were looking alarmed as they listened to their informants in the hall. Willkie was now on his feet; tie undone; waistcoat unbuttoned. He began to prowl the suite. The friends and reporters had stopped all conversation. They had also, as if obeying an unseen signal, ceased to look at the edgy candidate as he made his marches back and forth between bedroom and living room, stopping occasionally to whisper something to the brothers, who, in turn, whispered news to him. From the radio the chant "We want Willkie!" never ceased.

Joe Alsop was uneasy. "Wendell's said no to Pew. Tempting, of course. Satisfying, certainly. But if Pew gives Taft Pennsylvania he's almost certain to make it."

On the radio, the familiar flat voice of Alfred M. Landon declared that Kansas's eighteen votes were all for Willkie.

In the bedroom doorway, Willkie swung around, sweat streaming down his face. "Well, it's going to be one or the other of us." The living room applauded.

Willkie was now talking into the special line to the convention floor. "Sam, to hell with the judges. Tell him he can have them. Just get me those votes."

"This, dear boy," said Joe, again smiling, "is known as compromise."

"I felt, somehow, dirty," said Peter, in comic mood.

"So does the new earth when the first spring rain falls and the snowdrops lift their shy pale heads."

Blaise was now seated on Willkie's bed beside Davenport. Willkie was on the telephone. "Tell them no way. No adjournment now. The sixth ballot's been announced. Get to Arthur Vandenberg. Tell him . . . you know what, Sam." Willkie slammed down the receiver; his face was as pale as the cigarette ash on his suit. From the radio: "We want Willkie!"

When the roll call got to Michigan, a voice declaimed, "Senator Arthur A. Vandenberg now releases all of his delegates . . ." The rest of this sentence was drowned out by cheering.

"Here we go," muttered Willkie.

"Michigan's votes have been polled as follows. For Hoover, one. Taft, two. Willkie, thirty-five."

More cheering in the bedroom until John Cowles said, "We're still two votes short."

As if he had been heard through the radio, a voice suddenly thundered, "Pennsylvania casts seventy-two votes for Wendell Willkie."

There was silence in the suite; Willkie blinked away tears. "I'm very, very appreciative, very humble and very proud."

The special phone rang; and a voice said, "This is Senator Taft. I want to congratulate you . . ." Peter and Joe withdrew to the living room. "Now all the enraged losers will be ringing their new leader."

"Their? Or your?"

"Not mine, Peter. I shall be working for Cousin Franklin now that we have a safe Republican candidate."

"I understand," said Peter; and he did.

The next morning the miracle in Philadelphia had entered political history.

Peter joined Tim on the train to Washington. Along with news of the miracle, the newspapers reported that Churchill had been inspecting the antiaircraft batteries on the east coast of England, where the German invasion was due to begin.

"There won't be an invasion now. Roosevelt's spiked the Republican guns. We're at war."

"Will you say this in your film?"

"Never *say* anything. Just *show*." Tim chuckled. "Did you see what Mencken wrote?" He took a clipping from his pocket and read, " 'I am thoroughly convinced that the nomination of Willkie was arranged by the Holy Ghost in person, wearing a Palm Beach suit and smoking a five-cent cigar.' "

"Sam Pryor," said Peter.

"Sam Pryor," said Tim.

FOUR

I

Harry Hopkins had finally agreed to go "hiking," as he put it, on the green wooded knoll where the Wardman Park Hotel towered above Wisconsin Avenue. There were tall trees back of the hotel, as well as tennis courts; Caroline assured him that if he simply looked at them, it would be the equivalent of playing six sets.

Also, midafternoon of a weekday in July, they had the grounds to themselves. Back of them, like a stale chocolate cake, was the huge ugly dark brick main building connected by an incongruously long glass-enclosed corridor to the smaller hotel annex where all sorts of dignitaries lived in quiet seclusion, starting with Cordell Hull, the noble looking secretary of state, and Henry Wallace, the secretary of agriculture, whose mystical letters to his "guru" were certain to be published if he was nominated for vice-president at the Democratic convention, only five days away. Thus far, the White House had been unusually silent about the President's plans. It was accepted by all—by some bitterly—that Roosevelt would be the first third-term candidate in history, but on what, if any, conditions would he run and with whom?

"Peaceful," said Harry, settling on a bench near the packed red-earth tennis court where a young couple were playing a desultory game.

"It is such a beautiful city." Caroline sat in an iron chair opposite him. "And such a pity that no one ever notices it."

"Never notices it? Why, they go on and on about those dreary Roman temples, and all the marble covered with pigeon . . ."

"Well, that's the part I would tear down."

"With luck, Hitler's bombers will blow up Capitol Hill. Then we'd have some really picturesque Roman ruins. I might give him a hand there."

Only that morning a selective service bill had been sent to Congress in order to register one million men for the draft. The nays of the Senate old guard were now resounding throughout the press, not to mention in the dim green Senate chamber whose ruins Hopkins envisaged with such quiet satisfaction.

"Do you think Hitler could ever get this far from home?"

Hopkins shrugged, then belched; what was left of his stomach was irritable, and Caroline realized that if he was at all tense, as he was most of the time in the White House, he suffered. "No. I don't. On the other hand, I didn't think he could polish off France in a few weeks, or blow up London the way he's doing now." Hopkins took a swig from a medicine bottle. The gray face gained a hint, no more, of color.

"Even so, I don't see him invading England now."

"Why not?" He looked at her curiously.

"Well, I have my spies, too."

"How good are they? Ours are pretty bad."

"Bill Donovan?"

"The colonel? You know Wild Bill?"

"Everyone knows him."

"So what did I tell you? Our spies are lousy."

But Caroline knew that Donovan was uncommonly talented. A hero of the Great War and a Republican politician, he had gone to

work for President Roosevelt as a sort of roving ambassador. For the
last five years, he had been a one-man State Department, reporting
only to the President from the Balkans to beleaguered England. Caroline had met him through Léon Blum, whom Donovan had the
uncommon good sense, for an American conservative, to admire
despite Blum's socialism and his failed Popular Front government.

"Anyway, if Hitler doesn't invade in the next few weeks, he'll turn
to the east. That's his real interest. Russia. Or so my spies tell me."

Hopkins nodded. "You should share your spies with us."

Caroline smiled as mysteriously as cosmetic surgery would allow
her. Actually her only spy was, on occasion, Cissy Patterson, who got
most of her information from her former son-in-law, Drew Pearson,
who was usually more wrong than right in his predictions. Basically,
Caroline's view of the Hitler phenomenon had been shaped by Blum,
who, very early, took him seriously; very early realized that it was Eastern Europe that he wanted as "room-space" for the golden-haired,
blue-eyed Teutonic master race of which he himself was a perhaps less
than perfect example.

"Operation Sea Lion will be abandoned." Caroline used the
"secret" German code name for an invasion of Britain. "If the British
put up a strong enough air defense."

"They have so far. That's why we've got to get those ships and
planes to them. Are the boys upstairs?" Hopkins gestured vaguely
toward Caroline's rooms in the annex.

"I gave them keys."

The boys were indeed there. Sam Cohen, a White House lawyer,
and John Foster from the British Embassy were seated at the kitchen
table, a pile of books between them and pads of yellow lined legal paper
scattered about. It had been Hopkins' idea that they should meet in
secret, far from White House and embassy. Caroline's rooms were the
answer.

"You see us conspiring," said Foster.

"Welcome to the Anglo-American conspiracy." Sam Cohen, in
addition to doing legal work, sometimes helped out with presidential
speeches. Now the two men were preparing a letter to the New York

Times, requesting prompt military aid to England in the form of fifty over-age destroyers.

Hopkins went to the refrigerator and found Coca-Cola, which he had insisted that Caroline keep for him.

"Who's going to sign the letter?"

"A number of your leading constitutional lawyers." Foster stretched his great ursine frame. "Felix is assembling them now."

"We certainly don't want Felix's name on the letter." For an instant Hopkins looked troubled. The conservative Supreme Court justice had the reputation of being a Roosevelt radical; he was also a Jew. During Caroline's days as a publisher, she had always marveled at how wide of the mark were the labels pinned to public figures.

"The signers will be *sans peur et sans reproche*." Foster was blithe.

"They will also be without any collective legal sense." Cohen was moody.

Hopkins smiled approvingly. "But your letter will appear to make sense?"

"Legally, none, I should hope." Foster was cheerful. "Your Constitution is, if you'll forgive me, a somewhat airless document and aggressively flat in certain matters where true political genius requires luminous vagueness."

"The greater the challenge." Hopkins sat between the two men, glanced at their notes. "Isn't your main obstacle the various neutrality acts?"

"Yes," said Cohen. "But Congress has been changing its ground rules so often lately that we can probably fit ourselves into one of their versions."

"What legal authorization does the President need to give over those destroyers?"

Anything to do with the holy Constitution always appealed to Caroline, who found it a mystery more dense than the Trinity.

"In theory, probably none. Just an executive order. But since there's an election coming up the President needs his fig leaf." Hopkins pressed his stomach; struggled with gas.

"So here it is. Our fig leaf, courtesy of Mr. Foster." Cohen opened an old law book.

"I dote on congressional prose," said Foster.

"Luckily for us. I'd never have got as far as you have." Cohen read, " 'In 1892, Congress gave the secretary of war the right to lease military property "where, in his discretion, it will be for the common good." ' "

Hopkins frowned. "But does the secretary still have the power to . . . what's the word? To lease?"

Foster nodded. "I have read everything pertinent to this subject, and, let me confess, I have secretly reveled in your military law. Trembled at forgotten urgencies. Those Indians. That warpath, always crowded with twirling tomahawks. Anyway, the 1892 right is in perpetuity unless Congress should specifically revoke it, which they obviously forgot to do in the blind rush of history which sweeps us all before it, not to mention in and out of office."

"Sam, can the Boss get away with this?" Hopkins was blunt.

"Who will object except the isolationists? And no matter what the legal basis, they are always going to say no anyway. But, presumably, there aren't enough of them, assuming the President wins in November. Yes. This covers us."

"And," said Foster, with a demure smile, "if your Boss doesn't win, we'll still have Wendell on our team."

"Congratulations." Hopkins finished the bottle of Coca-Cola. "Now how do you go about leasing a destroyer?"

"Couldn't be simpler or more primitive," said Foster. "We barter. We have no money at all, as Lothian so tactlessly admitted the other day, but we do have an empire upon which the sun never dares to set. We'll let you lease the odd island or two from us while you lease us those ships, as well as some B-17 bombers while you're about it. In exchange we'll give you some ninety-nine-year leases on bits of the empire; jewels in the King-Emperor's crown. So for starters, how would you like Bermuda? It's close to home, lovely beaches."

"What about Nassau?" Caroline was getting into the spirit of a game not unlike Monopoly.

"I'd personally love for you to have it, Mrs. Sanford. But do you really want the Windsors? They go with it, you know."

"Tourist attraction?"

"I'll tell the Treasury."

"Newfoundland," said Hopkins. He was serious. "We need it for our defense. We're also planning to occupy Iceland now that Germany's taken over Denmark."

Foster was suddenly serious. "Meanwhile, what are you doing about the French and the Dutch colonial empires? Part of Japan's recent alliance with Germany is Hitler's concession to them of French Indochina and Dutch Java, which will give the Japs all the oil they will ever need."

Hopkins shut his eyes. "You have just mentioned our worst nightmare."

"Japan's conquest of Asia?" Caroline thought it curious that in all the worry over Europe, the ever-expanding Japanese Empire was seldom mentioned at the White House. Between the fall of France and the promised invasion of England, the President was totally involved with Europe. But Caroline's earliest imperial memory was of a morning in Kent, at the house of Lizzie Cameron, when she joined her hostess and Henry Adams and American Minister John Hay on a terrace overlooking the Weald of Kent in all its bright summer green to be told that the brief war between the United States and Spain was now at an end and Spain's colonial empire had become American property. Hay was delighted by what he had called "a splendid little war," demonstrating yet again, as Adams sardonically called it, Hay's fatal gift of phrase.

Adams saw nothing but trouble for the United States in its role as sovereign of the rebellious Philippines just off the coast of China. "What are we doing there?" he had asked, not only rhetorically but practically. But no one had ever really answered him, since empires were living expansive organisms. Caroline had had no difficulty in grasping that principle, as she helped Lizzie Cameron arrange summer—always summer for empire?—roses. Now over forty years had passed. Hay and Adams were long since dead. The Franco-German wars that had begun with Bonaparte were now in their fourth and, presumably, final act. If Hitler were to win . . . But Caroline had never forgotten Adams' crafty smile at the time of the third act in the Franco-

German war for supremacy in Europe. "Germany is too unimportant to have such pretensions. Once we've done them in for good, there will only be two powers in the world, the United States and Russia."

"No England?"

"Poor England. No. No England. Even smaller than . . . You see, at the end, there will be no Europe of any importance. Europe's our glamorous past. The Pacific is the near future. Then the northern continents. Shansi Province in China. Manchuria. Siberia. The power's all with us now. With Russia, too. More's the pity," he would always add, and Caroline would wonder, pity for whom? Arguably, for that brave pompous invention of the Enlightenment, the United States set in a wilderness, forever dreaming itself Athens reborn even as it crudely, doggedly, recreated Rome. Perhaps Adams, whose intellectual roots were so deeply set in old Europe, pitied the sudden irrelevance of his beloved Chartres Cathedral as the humming American dynamo began to turn over and over, ever more rapidly, generating as it did more and more of the powers of the sun.

Hopkins congratulated Cohen and Foster. "We shall hide behind your forgotten secretary of war, and throw our military might behind England and its empire, too, of course."

"Frankly we'd really rather have your money." Foster had a pirate's white-toothed grin. "The ambassador and I just sent on a report to Mr. Churchill. Subject: American military might. As of June 1940 how does the American army compare with other world armies?"

Hopkins sighed. "You've found a humiliating statistic."

"Thanks to your Congress—give credit where credit is due—your army ranks, as of now, number eighteen in the world, just behind Romania."

"So we'd better steer clear of Romania." But Caroline had noticed that Hopkins had winced. Then: "But next year we'll be number one . . ."

"After Russia. On the ground, that is. But it will be in the air that you will come into your own. We've already worked out a plan for you to supply us with air-cargo planes, of which you're now building a great many. You shall ferry what we lease from you, thus bringing prosper-

ity to idle plants and green or—how does your patriotic song go?—
amber waves of grain to the dust bowls."

"Congress permitting," said Hopkins.

"Roosevelt allowing," said Foster. "It is a pity your people have
always disliked us so."

"Dislike." Hopkins made the one word not a question but a neutral observation.

"The polls . . ." Cohen began.

". . . are all rigged," Foster agreed. "Often by us. Often by, it is
whispered, the White House, too. To show support for England."

Hopkins did not rise to the challenge. He stared out the kitchen
window at the hazy whiteness of the day. Then he said, "You've got
some smart people over there on Massachusetts Avenue."

"Not enough. Our propaganda mills are known as truth dispensers.
Gallant little England. Alone. Holding back Hitler so that our kith and
kin over here will not be absorbed into the Third Reich, and so on."

"And so on," Hopkins repeated. "I must meet Churchill soon. The
Boss wants me to go to London as soon as possible."

"Not possible," was Caroline's contribution. "Your health."

"If only," Hopkins went on, "to get him to stop this kith and kin
nonsense. He's a century out of date."

"We value that sort of traditionalism in our statesmen." Foster was
mild. "Even so, by a small margin, Americans whose ancestors come
from the British Isles still predominate even though Germans, unfriendly to us, and Irish, definitely unfriendly to us, form large minorities. Six million Americans were born in Germany . . ."

"A bit under two," said Hopkins. "No. You're not popular. Americans think of your snobbism, your imperialism, your reluctance to pay
your debts."

"We have made it a rule never to pay what we don't have."

"Borrow." Caroline was on her feet.

"Or lease it." Foster rose, too. "We are trying out a new kind of
propaganda. England and America together *after* Hitler. Partners in a
world without class. The working classes as one with each other; the
special relationship. Am I tempting you? Are you excited? Pulses beating hard?" He was looking at Hopkins.

Hopkins smiled, wanly. "You have made me well. The sick and the halt will rise . . ." He pulled himself up by the kitchen table. Caroline noticed the same terrible strain in his face which she had once noticed when Roosevelt, in an unguarded moment, clutched at a table and pulled the dead weight of his body from wheelchair to sofa. "I've heard of the special relationship you're cooking up. With England as senior partner."

"Well, we are so old, you know. The Raj and all that. World maps covered with pink. That's us. Surely we bring you all sorts of expertise. And real estate."

"Twenty-five percent of Americans are forever anti-British." Hopkins was, again, oddly, blankly, matter-of-fact.

"Irish . . . Germans . . . ?"

"The President's neither." Hopkins was now cold. "He's also unamused by reference to the childlike giant."

"Oh, dear. I knew that phrase should never have been put in our most secret code."

"I don't say he would disagree. He has been guiding the child for almost a decade. It's hard work. But he does not turn to you for wisdom about the future which he believes is all ours. We are in a friendly alliance. Nothing more. We'll never let Hitler invade you. But we will never accept you—with or without an empire—as an equal anywhere in the world. If we win, *we* win."

Foster no longer pretended to smile. "Churchill will never let India go or, indeed, any other bit of pink."

Hopkins shrugged. "But they will go, once the war is over. You can't afford them. We can. There are not enough of you. There are one hundred thirty million of us. Two hundred million, they say, by the end of the century."

"So, Harry, power is all, isn't it?" Foster's face was blank.

"Was it ever otherwise?"

Caroline marveled at how well two rival—even enemy—nations could collaborate so easily until . . . she could not imagine any ending other than Roosevelt alone astride all the world, seated in a kitchen chair on rollers.

2

Peter was taking his second political convention in stride. Blaise had been pleased with the stories that he had filed from Philadelphia. He had been even more pleased when Caroline arranged for Peter to work with Harry Hopkins at the Roosevelt headquarters in Chicago. Peter was kept busy writing press releases and, at Caroline's insistence, "looking after Harry," which mainly consisted of reminding him to take his medicine while seeing to it that unwanted visitors did not overstay their nonwelcome in the Blackstone Hotel's Suite 308–309, which had, twenty years earlier, been the infamous "smoke-filled room" where the Republican bosses had selected Warren G. Harding for president.

The actual Democratic National Headquarters were across the street in the Stevens Hotel. Here Postmaster General Jim Farley reigned and, it was rumored, fumed because Hopkins, as the President's man on the spot, appeared to be directing the convention. There was even, in the bathroom off Hopkins' bedroom, a special line to the White House. Yet there was something distinctly odd about Hopkins' presence. The President had already said that he himself would not make an appearance at the convention; he also denied that there was a Hopkins-led Roosevelt headquarters. Finally, Hopkins maintained a second suite at the Ambassador East Hotel. Peter wondered why.

Since Peter was allowed to listen in on all but the most secret meetings, he had been obliged to hear the various evasions that Hopkins used whenever a politician would question his status.

As he lay on his bed, wearing crumpled shirt and suspenders, he'd point to a badge pinned to a suspender: "Deputy Sergeant at Arms." He was, he said, just a guest of Mayor Kelly of Chicago.

Needless to say, everyone knew that in the bathroom there was a special telephone connected directly to the White House; needless to say, no one except Peter knew that it never rang. Nevertheless, Hopkins often visited the bathroom, giving the impression that he was reporting regularly to the President, while Peter answered the telephone that important party leaders used, carefully making notes of what they said they wanted to talk about and when they might come by. Hopkins' Washington secretaries kept an appointment book in which all was confusion. Peter feared that his father's endless complaints about the inefficiencies of the New Deal were true if Hopkins, the heart and the soul of the brave new world aborning, was the prototype. But alongside the social workers and those who worked to ameliorate society, there was the true Democratic Party of big-city machines and Southern courthouses each, in its fashion, nostalgic for the happy days of slavery. This was the party's true majority, and Jim Farley rode herd on it across the street, smoothly preparing the nomination of the President for an unheard-of third term, as he, unsmoothly, tried to keep Henry Wallace from being nominated for vice president despite the President's wishes, somewhat Delphically expressed.

Although Lorena Hickok, journalist friend and intimate of Mrs. Roosevelt's, was working across the street at Democratic headquarters, she visited Hopkins several times a day, usually to confer with him in the bathroom. On Tuesday evening, Lorena joined Hopkins, the president's sons Frank and Elliott, and a half-dozen of Hopkins' assistants from the Department of Commerce. They all sat on the dusty floor of the bedroom to listen to the keynote address of Kentucky's Senator Alben W. Barkley.

"This will be the only statement the President intends to make to the convention." Hopkins held up a yellow sheet of paper with three paragraphs written in pencil. "Here it is! In his own handwriting."

Peter noticed quite a few erasures and crossings-out. Barkley read the statement to less than rapturous applause. The President declared that as he had no wish to be a candidate for an unprecedented third term, he was releasing any votes pledged to him so that each delegate could vote his own conscience. If it should then prove to be the united will of the party . . . sacrifice . . . duty . . .

"Pa's got them over a barrel," said Frank Roosevelt. Of the sons he most resembled his father. He also, in Peter's brief glimpses of him, had much of his father's political cunning: that is, one never really knew what he meant.

As the speech ended, Hopkins said to Peter, "Tell the staff to get ready with the vice presidential stuff."

This startled even the President's sons. "Pa's made his mind up already?" Elliott frowned. "I thought he was still open to having Vice President Garner again."

"He's completely shut to that." Hopkins was coldly dismissive. "But he does want a lot of candidates out there." Hopkins bared false teeth in a smile. "The Boss wants a real horse race, he says. A Democratic horse race."

"Didn't I tell you?" Frank was always pleased to be one step ahead of his somewhat slow-witted brother.

But there was nothing for Hopkins to smile about the next day. Word was spreading throughout the convention that if Roosevelt did not get Wallace as a running mate, he himself would not be a candidate. Since a majority of the convention disliked the allegedly mystical Wallace, who was, worse for the South, a true-blue New Dealer, there was a growing rebellion in the big-city machines which Hopkins affected to disregard. "After all, a machine's a machine. It's there to drive when you're ready."

A parade of Democratic powers filed through the Blackstone suite. The secretary of labor, Miss Frances Perkins, said, "I've never experienced so poisonous an atmosphere." Then the bedroom door was closed after her, to Peter's regret because the crisis was upon them and Hopkins was now obliged to meet each of the magnates alone. There could be no witnesses to the deals that he was making as he lay back, in his suspenders, listening carefully and talking very little until he gave the signal that a deal was done.

Later, as Hopkins escorted Miss Perkins to the door to the suite, she suddenly turned on him and said, "Eleanor must come to Chicago before the vote."

"She says she won't."

"If Farley and Garner succeed in blocking Henry Wallace, the President is really going to go home to Hyde Park."

Hopkins, known as the President's other self, stared hard at Perkins. "You believe that?"

"Yes, Harry, I do. He's afraid he won't live out a third term and he knows perfectly well that neither of those two idiots could get us through a war, much less maintain his policies—our policies—which they've always been against. Anyway, send for Eleanor. Now!"

Miss Perkins left as a harassed-looking Joe Alsop arrived. "Harry, you've got to call the President. They've come up with a foreign policy plank that's isolationist . . ."

"Don't worry, Joe. It's also interventionist. I've seen to that. Anyway, who ever stands on the platform?"

"Harry, it says . . ." Joe looked at a sheet of paper: " 'We will not participate in foreign wars and we will not send our army.' "

"Well, print it in very small type except for the part about 'except in case of attack.' Hopkins always treated Joe as if he were an uncommonly neurasthenic dowager. "At the moment, we've got to cut the length of the convention by at least one day. The longer it goes on, the more trouble for everybody . . ."

"I think . . ." Joe began; but Hopkins was now in his bedroom, getting dressed. Peter was so used to him in disarray that he had failed to notice that he had, all morning, been wearing pajamas, with a raincoat for dressing gown.

"He's eager for advice." Joe was sour. "Oh, it's you," he said, now aware of Peter's presence. "Where did you come from?"

"Only from Washington."

"Is Cousin Eleanor coming?" News was traveling very fast now.

"No one knows."

"If he really wants Wallace, she's the only one who can keep these worms in their can."

That evening Peter, wearing his press credentials, sat at the back of the platform, staring into the white smoky lights trained upon the stage. So far, he had not seen Tim Farrell, who was, Aunt Caroline had told him, now cutting his film—but without Roosevelt? "United We Stand" was MGM's latest title, shrewdly calculated, in Peter's view, to put off everyone. But Tim had been excited by the title, as well as by his film. Was there a surprise of any kind left in the land? And if so, had he filmed it?

Peter stared at what was said to be fifty thousand people. How could anyone ever have sufficient nerve to get up in front of so many people and speak through microphones to those in the hall, not to mention the millions listening to the radio? At the thought, Peter suffered from acute stage fright. Yet these freakish-looking political types floated like tropical fish through the warm white-lit sea all about them, expanding contentedly whenever microphones picked up their words and cameras recorded their movements. Over the stage, a huge gray photograph of Roosevelt looked down upon them.

"These things are addictive, aren't they?" Joe Alsop was in better mood; had Hopkins said something to make him happy?

"Well, you're part Roosevelt. I'm not. I'm suffering now. From stage fright. How can anybody stand up there and have all those people watch you?"

"How can anybody, given the chance, *not* want to be up there? Anyway, I'm not that much of a Roosevelt, unlike Uncle T, who would start wasting away if there was no crowd to cheer him. The T should have been not for Theodore but for Barrie's Tinkerbell. Look!" Joe pointed to a strange-looking camera at the edge of the stage. "Television."

"Does it actually work?"

"So they tell me, but there aren't enough cables yet." Joe gave his nasal chuckle. "Someone at the *Trib* watched the Willkie convention on a television set and came to the conclusion that we'll need a whole new set of politicians, just the way we did when radio came in."

"New in what way?"

"Well, radio meant you didn't have to shout to be heard, and that was the making of Cousin Franklin, whose croon is like that of a mongoose hypnotizing a cobra . . ."

"I don't think the mongoose croons . . ."

"Whatever it does, Cousin Franklin does, too. Great voices, or interesting voices like Willkie's, are now the thing. But television will mean *faces* and God help the ugly."

"Depends on how ugly . . ."

"I'm not speaking of my sainted Cousin Eleanor, whose chinless toothy face is that of everyone's favorite aunt or every child's gym teacher. You can be plain as can be and get by with charm, but it's the tics my friend noted on his television set. The speakers are used to being miles away from the audience so they indulge in donkey grins, sinister winks of the eyes, mad furrowed brows. He said that that convention looked like a Mack Sennett silent comedy."

With unusual speed, the party's platform was adopted by the convention. Then Hopkins' hand was revealed: the chairman announced that instead of adjourning, they would proceed to the nominations for president. This energized the convention.

"Splendid move." Joe was approving. "The sooner we wrap this up the better."

"There's still tomorrow and the vice presidency."

"I'm sure Harry's got something up his sleeve."

The roll call of the states began alphabetically. From the hall came the voice of Senator Lester Hill, chairman of the Alabama delegation. He cast the state's votes for Franklin Delano Roosevelt. A band played "Happy Days Are Here Again" and a demonstration on the floor began; it lasted—Peter timed it—half an hour. On the stage the political magnates were conferring while their supporters engaged in ecstatic rites beneath them in the hall. The pale gnomelike Carter Glass, a senator from Virginia, would, presently, put in nomination James Farley, who modestly stayed out of view at the back of the stage, where the two conferred as the various states gave or withheld their votes for Roosevelt.

Peter was particularly amused by the young pockmarked senator from Florida, Claude Pepper, who gave an emotional speech not unlike the howling of some mating cat by moonlight. He also tore at the audience's heartstrings. Apparently, at the battle of Antietam, Robert E. Lee, seeing his son covered with blood on the ground, sternly ordered the lad back into battle, just as the United States would now order their weary president back into the fray.

"Gorgeous," said Joe Alsop.

"It would be better on television," Peter observed. "Pepper's scarlet face, shark's mouth . . ."

"Of course Robert E. Lee had no son. But one cannot rule out a bastard son, perhaps from the slave cabins."

At one o'clock in the morning of Thursday, July 18, 1940, Roosevelt had 950 votes; and was declared the third-term nominee of the Democratic Party.

3

The next day the convention was in a foul mood. From the stage, the fifty thousand people had begun to anthropomorphize for Peter, into a deranged giant apt to run amok.

Advised by Hopkins, Peter had stationed himself at the back of the crowded stage, shortly before the balloting for vice president was to begin. The conservative majority favored the Southern Speaker of the House; only labor truly wanted Wallace. But on orders from Roosevelt, Southern operatives were now on the floor, going from delegation to delegation, threatening and soothing their fellow Southerners.

For so tall a woman, Eleanor Roosevelt looked unobtrusive as, head down, she slipped from the back of the stage onto the stage itself, the stout sweating Lorena Hickok at her side. They quickly found seats in a corner, out of view of the delegates or, indeed, anyone else except those in their immediate vicinity, who were now entirely distracted by the boos, the jeers, the rebel yells that had begun at the mention of the hated name of Henry A. Wallace.

Peter had never properly met Mrs. Roosevelt, but as she had been in the White House most of his life, he felt, as did the rest of the population, that he knew her. Unlike at least half the population, he quite liked her. Endlessly polite, apparently shy, she had come to Chicago to master the giant in the hall. She looked uncommonly elegant, all in blue with a blue straw hat, as she sat, head cocked to one side, listening to the excited Lorena until the arrival of Ed Flynn, the boss of the Bronx, a machine politician that the Roosevelts, despite their declared passion for free and absolutely open democratic elections, relied upon to turn out large manufactured majorities for them in New York City. Mrs. Roosevelt rose to greet Flynn. Then, as if by magic, the beefy red-haired Mayor Kelly of Chicago and lugubrious Mayor Hague of Jersey City, two of the most lawless machine politicians in the land, had placed themselves protectively on either side of her. Peter was awed by the millions of votes that these three men represented; and he watched, again with awe, as Mrs. Roosevelt put her lions through their paces. She spoke to them in a low voice; they listened closely. This was brute power and she was now exerting it in order to bring the giant back of the white glare to its knees; her sons, Frank and Elliott, stood at the periphery of the power center. Peter strained but failed to hear what Mrs. Roosevelt was saying but the three bosses heard every word and were nodding, something no boss ever bestowed upon a mere mortal, since a nod was often a concession and always a commitment; yet, in the presence of absolute power, with the empress herself, they were obedient.

Finally Senator Barkley shouted at the roaring giant: "I shall now begin the roll call for the nomination for vice president." Shouts and boos while anti–Wallace slogans on sticks were held high down front.

Eleanor nodded to her liege men. An understanding had been arrived at.

Peter heard Lorena, voice cracking: "Don't you dare go up there! For God's sake! All hell's breaking loose."

"Don't worry about me, dear." Eleanor was calm. Someone had alerted Senator Barkley, who now left the podium and hurried to greet Mrs. Roosevelt; he too whispered in her ear, no doubt telling her not to speak. But she simply kept smiling as she moved onto the podium. As the tall blue figure came into view, towering above the lectern and dominating the hall, there was an absolute silence, far more unnerving in its way than the animal noises that had so abruptly stopped.

Peter again experienced stage fright as if he were the one facing the mad giant in the dark. But Eleanor Roosevelt merely smiled as she looked out across the sea of faces and waited until her presence had been fully noted. Then, by a slow count to three, there began what sounded like thunder rolling toward the stage from the balconies. The cheering had begun. She remained motionless during the ovation. Peter noticed that she had no written speech or even notes.

Finally, total authority established, there was silence and she began to speak, her high fluting voice kept very much under control. She spoke of the President and of the presidency; of how little her husband had wanted a third term but how he felt that now that men were being drafted into the Army he had a duty to go on as long as possible, even though "the strain of a third term might be too much for any man." There was an odd sound of exhalation from the audience as if, to a man, all fifty thousand had been holding their collective breath, each quite aware that the invalid in the White House was a fragile aging man.

"You must realize that whoever is our next president, he will bear a heavier responsibility, perhaps, than any man has ever faced before. So you cannot treat it as you would an ordinary nomination in an ordinary time. So each and every one of you who give him this responsibility, in giving it to him, assume for yourselves a very grave responsibility because you will have to rise above considerations which are narrow and partisan. This is a time when it is the United States we fight for.

"Whoever you now nominate for vice president is . . . very apt . . ." She paused; took a deep breath. ". . . to become himself the president and I am sure you will want that president to be the man my husband has chosen to get us through a perilous time and to a safe shore. No man who is a candidate or who is president can carry this situation alone. This is only carried by a united people who love their country."

She stopped speaking; stared gravely at the audience; then, with only the hint of a smile, she raised her right hand as if in benediction and, turning away from the light, moved swiftly to the back of the stage before any applause could begin.

Senator Barkley picked up his cue smoothly. He praised the lady for her gracious wisdom. Then: "The clerk will now call the roll of the states."

Peter was again at the back of the stage, watching with amusement as Mrs. Roosevelt made a swift arc around the three bosses. Photographers tried to catch her with this or that personage but she moved too swiftly for them, her two sons running interference for her. Peter joined Harry Hopkins, who was now shaking her hand, below the stage.

"I must say," Peter heard Mrs. Roosevelt say very clearly to Hopkins, "you young things just don't understand politics."

In due course Wallace was nominated by an unhappy convention, which was then addressed from Washington by the President, his voice echoing eerily over a loudspeaker system. With a deep sense of responsibility he accepted their nomination because "today all private plans, all private lives have been, in a sense, repealed by an overriding public danger."

Hopkins was well pleased when he met with his aides in the Blackstone suite. Joe Alsop, in Cassandra mood, said that if the British were not to get sufficient ships immediately, they could not defend the Channel should Hitler invade, as planned, in August.

Hopkins was reassuring. "The Boss is doing everything possible to get those ships to England . . ."

"Churchill asked for them over a year ago."

"Maybe Churchill should talk to Congress. The Boss is convinced that if he sends so much as a rowboat on his own without Congress's permission, he will be impeached."

Mayor Kelly had arrived in the sitting room of the suite. Hopkins poured him a drink as they conducted a postmortem of the day's work.

Peter hovered nearby. But learned very little. Professional politicians talked to each other mostly in code. Kelly did ask, "Is it true the Boss isn't going to campaign?"

"Well, he's got a lot on his plate, you know. Rearming the country. He also thinks Willkie's going to wear himself out, dashing all over the place."

"He's picking up support." Kelly looked unhappy.

"Now, Ed, you know how important it is to have a president who keeps a sharp eye on everything." Hopkins grinned. "I can guarantee you there will be a lot of inspection trips around the country where all the defense plants are, and the votes."

"Smart," said Kelly.

"But no political trips. I think, Ed, we're all agreed that the world's too serious a place for old-fashioned politics. We are all of us real statesmen now."

Joe heard this last. "By the end, Cousin Franklin will be tearing around the country like a banshee. This isn't going to be an easy election. That's why he took so long to make up his mind, about running."

"When did he make up his mind?" Peter was curious.

"Whoever knows with him? Eleanor thinks that Dunkirk did it. The thought that Hitler might actually invade England set him in motion."

"That's history, which I like."

"That's journalism, which I like," said Joe Alsop. "Anyway, there's going to be quite enough of both to go around."

Harry Hopkins said goodbye to the Mayor at the door. "To think," said Joe, "if today were two years ago he'd be here complimenting him."

"Him? Who?"

"Him, Harry Hopkins. He was the Roosevelts' choice to succeed Franklin."

"I can't believe it." Peter had come to admire Hopkins, as a brisk, brusque political manager. But this sallow unimpressive social worker out of the heartland, or wherever he hailed from, seemed no heir to the grand Hudson Valley squire.

"You didn't know him before. Before the cancer. He was wonderfully fierce and bright and even attractive as a leader. He was ideal for continuing the New Deal which Cousin Franklin is now about to bury once and for all in order to play war president like Wilson."

Peter was not surprised that war would take precedence over the New Deal, a worthy series of social enterprises that were all doomed in so reactionary a country: except for social security—a small income instead of the well-earned poorhouse for every senior citizen. But even that small victory had been a harrowing political battle; as for public works, Wendell Willkie was thoughtfully pointing out that nine million men were still out of work. "Any war president can end unemployment." Peter parroted popular opinion. "This war could complete the New Deal."

"Who cares? Because this war will give us the whole world this time. That was Uncle T's dream. I think it's Cousin Franklin's too. He pretends to revere his old boss Woodrow Wilson, but every now and then, he says what he really thinks of him."

"The man who made the world safe for democracy?"

"The man who made this bloody war inevitable." Joe gave Peter a baleful stare, as a stand-in for Wilson, or was it Hitler? "Wilson was a pompous little professor who should never have left—no, not Princeton, he was already out of his depth there—his classroom at Bryn Mawr, surrounded by the brightest of bright bluestockings. Outside that classroom of young ladies, he was a bungler, to put it politely." Joe poured himself a large glass of whiskey. "To Cousin Franklin."

Peter held up his glass. "Let us pray," said Peter, getting into the spirit that history now required of them, "that he does not bungle."

"Or," said Joe, ominously, "die on us. Before we get the world."

FIVE

Two liveried footmen somehow did not look at least one too many as they opened the door to the Dupont Circle palace so that Caroline could make her one-woman entrance to be met in the great hall by Cissy Patterson, also alone. The ladies embraced and all that Caroline could think of, as she gazed over Cissy's shoulder at the marble staircase, was the young man at the party making his way up the stairs to prepare himself as sacrificial goat upon peach-tinted crepe-de-chine sheets.

"You'll have him all to yourself." Cissy broke from their sisterly embrace. "I've got a meeting at the paper. Anyway, it's better you see your old beau alone for lunch, just the two of you in the study."

"Old beau? I thought it was to be the two of us." Caroline wondered if the old beau might be James Burden Day; wondered if, after so many years, they would have anything to talk about.

"It's a surprise for you, and a joy for him, of course, particularly if you'd talk about Harry Hopkins. I'll join you all later."

"I've nothing to tell. I hardly see him. He's busy arranging the election for a president who says he won't campaign."

"Franklin always waits until Labor Day. By which time I'm afraid poor Wendell will have lost what little voice he has." The butler had materialized beside Cissy. "Show Mrs. Sanford into the study. Serve the lunch."

"Yes, Countess."

Cissy winked at Caroline. "Ain't I grand?"

"But you *are* a countess."

"Only in Poland, which is now half German and half Russian. I would like to murder Hitler. Stalin, too."

"So you aren't an isolationist any more?"

"I don't know about that. I do know I'd like to kill my daughter. Felicia's just written a novel about how awful I am."

"But that was years ago."

"This is a new one. She's arrived back from Europe. She also says how awful Drew was in bed." Cissy laughed. "I can't say I minded that part. What about your daughter?"

"Oh. I hate her, too. But she doesn't write novels."

"Count your blessings."

Cissy was gone and the butler ceremoniously led Caroline through several grand rooms to a small book-lined study, where she found a mountainous old man standing in front of a fireplace, closely examining the underside of a Meissen plate.

William Randolph Hearst must now be seventy-eight, she calculated; and somewhat deaf, as he'd not heard her entrance. Caroline motioned to the butler to go, quietly, while she prepared herself for this unexpected encounter. Even in France, she had been able to follow the shipwreck of the Hearst empire. Personally, he was well over a hundred million dollars in debt. He had bought too many castles, too many works of art, some beyond value, some of no value at all; the palace at San Simeon above the Pacific, with its zoo and its hundreds of attendants, was constantly being added to while the dozens of newspapers and magazines that supported all this spending did less and less well in the post-Depression era. A "conservation" committee of Hearst executives was formed to curb the Chief's spending and sell off—usually at a loss—heavily mortgaged newspapers and properties, which was how Cissy Patterson had ended up leasing the Washington *Herald* from him and, as she was not shy in telling everyone, lending him one million dollars. Finally, and what probably hurt the most in Caroline's view, he had to give up the film production company that he had shared with his mistress-for-life, as it were, the film star Marion Davies. Since Caroline and Tim had been grimly obliged to do the same, she was prepared to find the ancient Hearst like King Lear upon the heath as he slowly turned to greet her.

The eaglelike face with the clear close-set eyes was certainly ravaged by his misadventures upon the heath of bankruptcy. But he was neither mad nor in the least bit defeated. He gave her a bearlike hug. She stood on tiptoe and kissed his gray dry cheek. "Chief," she said and felt like weeping to find that so much of her past was now before her, still alive, still full of energy. He had helped her become a newspaper publisher in Washington; helped her in her Hollywood career as an actress and, again, with film production. He was like some good father who was blessedly absent for all but the important moments of her life.

"Caroline. You don't change."

"You must see to your eyes." She hugged him without meaning to. "Cissy never let on it was you who wanted to see me."

"Cissy's got class." They sat on a long divan beneath yet another portrait of the lady of the house, wearing a fur hat with the steppes of Poland fleeing from her in the background.

Each occupied one end of the huge divan, covered in tapestry. Hearst stroked the material with practiced hand. "Gobelin."

"Millefleurs," said Caroline.

"I'll bet you . . . But I'm not allowed to bet or to buy, only to sell." He seemed chastened.

"Are you really so broke?" Caroline had found that plain talk was best with the genius who had discovered that the only truly credible— not to mention profitable—news was what one invented.

"On paper, I was. But then that's where money always is, isn't it? On paper. In paper. In *news*papers. I've got most of them still. I'm supporting Willkie."

"So I read."

"This means he'll lose. I never pick a winner. I can't think why."

"You're too Californian for the Easterners who own the country."

"Too American, I'd have thought. How would you like a Spanish monastery?"

"To enter? You mean a convent . . ."

"No. To own. It has a beautiful cloister."

"I don't think I want any property in Spain right now."

"Oh, it's not in Spain. It's up in the Bronx somewhere. In a warehouse. The stones are all numbered. Couldn't be easier to put it back together." He gave one of the curiously high-pitched nervous laughs that oddly punctuated his speech. "I'm not much of a salesman."

"That's because you're a buy-man."

"I'd certainly like to get my hands on that chateau of yours."

"So would I." Caroline felt a pain between her eyes. Sinus? Regret? "I think German troops are in it."

"We must stay out of the war. I write a regular column these days. Brisbane died, you know. So I took over. Couldn't be easier, writing a column."

"Except for him. You do it better than he did. I know. I read you." But then, Caroline thought, anyone wrote better than the pompous Arthur Brisbane, Hearst's prime minister, as well as viceroy at the New York *Mirror*. Caroline congratulated herself on having got out of the newspaper business. Let Blaise worry about competition from Cissy, the *Evening Star*, the newly awakened Washington *Post*, which Hearst was now studying with a professional eye.

"This one may have a chance," he said.

"Here in the cemetery of newspapers?"

"Curious place, Washington. I hated it when I was in Congress . . ."

". . . and living in New York."

Hearst looked at the front-page headline. "Wrong size type. Too small. This is the biggest news since the fall of France. But no one understands how important . . ." The voice trailed off, as Caroline took the newspaper from him. On September 27, 1940, Tokyo had joined the Berlin-Rome Axis, as it was called, a military-economic alliance involving mutual aid.

"What does your friend Harry think?"

"Harry who?"

Hearst smiled his narrow knowing shark's smile. "I publish Walter Winchell. Remember? That awful column of his is getting the syndicate back into profit, or so my guardians tell me."

"We are just . . ."

". . . good friends," Hearst completed the usual disclaimer.

"Actually he's been busy with the election. I've hardly seen him." This was not true but candor with Hearst was never wise.

"As usual, I'm not on speaking terms with the President. But I hire his sons from time to time. Particularly Elliott."

"Because he's so stupid?"

Hearst's mind did not exactly flit from subject to subject so much as take great leaps in unexpected directions, rather like Nijinsky in the Russian ballet. "Japan. That's our only real enemy. And all because we've chosen the hopeless Chinese as our sentimental allies after demonizing the Japanese."

"You speak as a Californian . . ."

"As an American with a better understanding than anyone in the White House will ever have of Asia. Japan needs to expand. Where to? To the mainland. To China, which isn't even a proper nation. Just a bunch of warlords fighting each other. Teddy Roosevelt—personally I couldn't stand him, but he was the only one that ever understood that Japan is our natural ally. When they beat the Russians in 1904—brilliant, that surprise attack on Port Arthur—TR got interested in the case. Even got himself a Nobel Peace Prize for something or other to do with them. Anyway, they scared the pants off him. And they scare me . . ."

"Yellow Peril, as you call them."

"Yes. Red Peril, too, if they ever turn Bolshevik. So don't provoke them. Taft. That's what *that* was about."

"What was what about?"

Hearst had found a small white jade dragon on a side table. He interrupted himself. "Imperial," he said. "I bought six. Han dynasty. We're talking about a sale at Gimbels. What do you think?"

"Of imperial jade?"

"Of the contents of a dozen warehouses. Since no art gallery could ever handle all my works of art, I suggested a department store. We're taking over the boys' department of Gimbels. You know, I've never *not* had money. No one ever bothered to tell me how inconvenient it is."

Caroline tried not to show her amusement. "Now you are like your readers."

"TR. picked Taft to succeed him as president because he thought Taft understood Asia. High commissioner of the Philippines and all that. But Taft was a fool. Took against the Japanese. Sided with the Chinese over Siberia. TR was furious. After all, the Japs beat the Russians once. They could do it again with our help. And the Japs are as afraid of the Russian Bolsheviks as we are. So why shouldn't they run Manchuria? That's one way of keeping the Bolsheviks out of Asia. Tom Lamont even wanted to finance this railroad for them. But the Chinese somehow persuaded Taft—no, Hoover, by then—to stop the Morgan bank from financing a railroad that would have helped seal off Siberia from the Japs. Stupid. Stupid. I wish Franklin was as bright as his cousin Teddy. But he's not. He won't recognize Japan's takeover of Manchuria, which is no different from us in Haiti. Asia should be Japan's."

Who holds Shansi Province will control the earth. Caroline could hear, in memory, the slight whistle in Henry Adams' voice on the word "Shansi."

"Franklin spends all his time conniving to get us into a war with Hitler, a lunatic but no threat to us, while he keeps the pressure on the Japs because . . ." Hearst frowned. "I can't fathom him."

"The Delanos used to trade with China. His mother . . ."

"Tell Harry. Tell Franklin, if you can ever get a word in edgewise with that talking machine, that he must let up on the Japs. Recognize Manchuria. After all, he's recognized Russia, of all places. You know, he's threatening to turn off Japan's oil supply if they don't withdraw from China."

"How do you know?"

"A letter from Joe Grew to Franklin. Last year. From Tokyo. He said if we stop the sale of oil to Japan, they'll grab the Dutch oil fields in Java. Franklin said if they tried we'd intercept their fleet before it got past the Philippines."

Caroline was astonished. If the story was true, Hearst had got his hands on a secret letter from the American ambassador in Japan to the President. "How do you get to read the President's mail?"

"The same way I got to be me." Hearst's wintry smile returned; he giggled nervously. "Anyway, you don't need anything but common sense and a knowledge of that part of the world to know Japan's on its way up and the Chinese are going even further down and out." Hearst tapped the Axis story in the *Post*. "Japan's getting ready for a war with us. So, for insurance, they join up with the Nazis and the fascists. Hitler must be praying that they'll do something to us which will take the pressure off him. Hitler doesn't want a war with us, but Franklin and his banker friends like Lamont pretend that he does. Meanwhile the Japs are getting ready to go to war with us and we're not told a word. Of course, it's an election year."

"Can you print Grew's letter?"

Hearst's sigh was closer to a groan. "I am kept on a short chain by the regency, as I call the lawyers that are running my affairs. But news will . . ."

For a moment, they sat in silence. Hearst played with the white jade dragon. Then: "Will you marry Hopkins?"

"No, thanks. Besides, he has a charming lady friend who will probably make a good wife and a good stepmother to his youngest child. Something outside my narrow human range."

"Ah, you can do anything." Caroline was deeply flattered by the offhand tone, which meant that the Chief was serious. "I'd like to do something in the war that's coming. But . . . what?" She had lost his attention. "Marion's off the sauce," he announced as butler and two footmen arranged their lunch on a table in front of the fireplace.

Caroline had always liked Hearst's longtime mistress, Marion Davies, a blond actress with a stammer and a serious drinking problem, of which the most serious aspect was how to hide her bottles from the alert eye of the Chief, whose uncanny gift of discernment was so highly developed that no suit of Elizabethan armor on the most sweeping staircase could hide, for long, her gin in its boot. But she always managed to hide enough to keep dull sobriety at bay and so increase the pleasure of her court, as fun- and gin-loving as she. A star of silent pictures, she was feared to be ruled out of talking pictures by her stammer.

Specialists had been called in. For a time, she had acted with a pebble in her mouth; then during a passionate love scene she swallowed it. Later she developed a curiously effective style of speaking that required deep breathing in the middle of words. Overnight she was acclaimed as a distinguished actress with an inimitable style. Caroline had always liked her and was pleasantly surprised that she had loyally stayed with Hearst throughout his prodigious bankruptcies.

"She loaned me a million dollars of her own money." Hearst spoke with his mouth full; his appetite was hearty. "I've got to get her another production company. Before she's too old." This was gallant, thought Caroline; herself too old for the screen, she did not in the least mind other actresses taking their allotted places in the unphotographable limbo of age.

Hearst tasted the wine but did not drink it. "We had President Coolidge at San Simeon. Forget why. He said, 'I don't drink.' I gave him some wine. 'Is this alcoholic?' he asks. I said, not so you'd notice. Drank half a bottle and said, 'I got to remember the name of this beverage.'" The word "beverage" made Caroline laugh.

"You know I'm serious." The pale eyes were turned upon her like a searchlight.

"About what?"

"That monastery. You're one of the few people with money who would appreciate it."

"But I'm living at the Wardman Park Hotel. I don't think they'd let me put it up on their grounds."

"No. No. I mean it. Blaise will let you have an acre from Laurel House, on the Chain Bridge side. I've talked to him already. . . ."

Somehow Caroline got through lunch without becoming the chatelaine of a Spanish monastery set high above the Potomac River, its luminous cloister all wreathed in poison ivy.

Not far from the MGM studio commissary there was a particularly pleasant—that is, seldom used—screening room where Tim had prepared *United We Stand*; had shown it to the studio executives and, most important, to the studio's New York exhibitors, Loews Incorporated.

L. B. Mayer preferred to watch the film in his own screening room with his invaluable secretary, who did not so much read scripts to him as act them out, scene by scene; it was rumored that her performances were better than those of the stars themselves.

On October 1, 1940, *United We Stand* had opened across the country just as the presidential election entered its final phase. The President, who had said that he would not campaign, had now taken to the stump while Willkie was openly attacking Roosevelt as a war-monger and a socialist. Nevertheless, there was still no difference between the two on the necessity of aid to England as well as the defeat, somehow never clearly spelled out by either, of Hitler, whose aerial bombardment of England was at its peak, preparatory to an invasion of the British Isles. Meanwhile, Republican leaders were urging Willkie to abandon his bipartisan foreign policy and warn the nation that if FDR was reelected, there would be war in a matter of months. All of this, though hardly good for the nation, provided an ideal audience for Tim's film. As the political debate got more and more out of control, even the President's mellifluous voice acquired a shrill edge; it was also apparent to every filmgoer that the title was wonderfully satiric and apt. If ever there was a country seriously divided it was the United States that October; and Timothy X. Farrell was suddenly hailed as the Preston Sturges of political documentaries. "Great McGinty versus Great McGinty" was *Variety*'s heading of its favorable review. All were amazed that two candidates who were basically as one on the matter of war or peace could still find so much to fulminate about.

When L. B. Mayer had said that he was satisfied with the film, Tim realized that he must somehow have failed. Essentially, he had been anti–Hitler and anti-war. Now the film was being used by both sides of the great—not debate so much as shouting match. But Tim had done his best to dramatize an election in which neither candidate dared to say what he meant to an uneasy people who realized that something was seriously wrong with their political system. Commentators were now wondering if anyone would bother to vote on November 5.

The screening room was brightly lit. Tim greeted the projectionist, an old friend. "We'll start with the latest newsreels. Then the London Blitz footage. Then the stuff Mr. Mayer wants me to see."

"Good weekend figures," said the projectionist. Everyone at the studio kept careful track of everyone else's grosses, including John Balderston, who pushed open the heavy soundproofed door as diffidently as one could perform such an operation.

"Tim! Congratulations." They shook hands. The projectionist withdrew to his booth. "L.B.'s office said I could watch the Blitz stuff, if you didn't mind."

"Are we being married?" There were rumors that Mayer wanted Tim to make another documentary about the war. So far there was no deal but the appearance of Balderston meant Gallant Little England would be the subject.

"I think this is a sort of blind date." Balderston was low-key, as always.

Since neither Tim nor Balderston was under contract to Metro, the studio could not order them to go to work; so the next best thing was to put them together for a time and then see if they would want to do whatever it was the studio had in mind, plainly something big, since the first weekend grosses had inspired agents to rub Tim's back or shoulder as they passed him in the commissary, on the deeply primitive ground that good fortune is transferable by touch. Tim was hot again.

Tim and Balderston sat at the back of the screening room, the console with its telephone to the projectionist between them.

"I never guessed when I saw you at Blaise Sanford's that you could make such an extraordinary film out of . . ." Balderston loaded a pipe. "Well, those people there."

"I'd like to say it was easy but it wasn't. An American politician is the most practiced bore on earth . . ."

"But it works, the way you string all their clichés together. I also think you're going to get quite a few votes for Roosevelt."

Tim was surprised. "I thought the Willkie footage was a lot more exciting . . ."

"Not when you intercut him with the old master. Have you heard from the White House?"

Tim shook his head. Actually, Caroline had rung him to say that Hopkins had seen the film with the President and both were pleased.

"What does the front office want?"

Tim was blunt. "If it's you, that means they want a theatrical film, like *The Prisoner of Zenda* . . ."

"No. Not this time. I think it's me leading you around England during the Blitz. You know, I was there all through the Great War, working for George Creel's Committee on Public Information."

Tim recalled the energetic Creel: President Wilson's ambassador to Hollywood and chief of propaganda. "Then you stayed on and on as a foreign correspondent for . . . what?"

"Eight years for the New York *World*. Then Hollywood."

"Where you turned every red-blooded American boy into a British Bengal Lancer."

Balderston laughed. "I did make *The Mummy*."

"Boris Karloff was British. Worse and worse!"

Tim told the projectionist to begin. Lights dimmed. Onto the screen there appeared the Pathé News logo. A voice-over explained that President Roosevelt was in Boston; and that the Gallup Poll showed Willkie was gaining on him. There was a close shot of Willkie, voice croaking, disheveled suit between a total absence of decent felt, fine leather. He accused Roosevelt for America's inability to defend itself in case of attack.

"We do not want to send our boys over there again. If you elect me president, we will not. If you elect the third-term candidate, they will be sent."

"Low blow," said Balderston.

Then the screen was filled by the large gray ovoid face of the President. Solemnly, unblinkingly, he intoned, "And while I am talking to you mothers and fathers, I give you one more assurance. I have said this before, but I shall say it again and again and again. Your boys are not going to be sent into any foreign wars."

"Except," quoted Balderston, "in case of attack."

Tim felt a sudden chill: the President had not made his usual qualification. Tim stopped the film; replayed it to see if the line had been edited out. But the second or two of applause on the soundtrack clearly marked the end of the statement. "So what does that mean?"

Balderston looked uneasy. "Well, he's always said that if we're attacked first, it's no longer a *foreign* war."

"You sound like a Jesuit. I wish I had had this in the film."

"Perhaps it's just as well you didn't."

"You want us in the war? To save the Prisoner of Zenda?"

"Well, not the mummy, certainly. But I can't think what the world would be like—what this country would be like—if Hitler wins."

"He won't, whether we go in or not."

"In the long run, the Russians will probably stop him. But are we better off with *them?*"

Tim shrugged. "We may find out soon enough." Balderston turned around to face Tim, an odd expression on his face like . . . Although Tim was a professional collector of expressions it took him an instant to analyze what he saw: they were like two Masons meeting and one has just given the sign, whatever it is, and the other has not responded.

"You know, I began the film to help the isolationists. I'm not at all sentimental about England and don't mention the word 'Irish' because I can't stand the Irish either, particularly my own family and the ones I grew up with in South Boston. No, I was all set to slant the film in Willkie's direction. I was—I am—afraid that FDR has caught the dictator flu that's going around. He's very vain. Every other major country has its homegrown dictator, so why not us? He's hugely tempted. I can tell. I study him on film. I study him in life. He wants us all to be his property. But he's crafty. If we were all Dutch, or all English or German, he would have declared martial law by now. But he's got too many different groups to outwit. One wrong move, and he's faced with a whole new set of enemies, new deals you might say. So he waits for the attack that he's sure is coming, the way Wilson did while, privately, delicately, doing his best to provoke it."

"He's not been so delicate with Germany. Lend-lease. Destroyers for England. That's an act of war. Thank God, if you'll permit me."

"I defer to the Anglophile author of *Smilin' Through.* How's it going?"

"A mess, you'll be happy to know. Due for release in '41. What changed you from America First?"

"A Marine Corps general. I have him on film but I don't dare use him yet. He's been approached twice by Wall Street types. They want to get rid of Roosevelt. By force. By military force."

Balderston dropped his pipe. "You're joking."

"I told you this bug is going around. They think Roosevelt's a communist. They prefer Hitler because they think that he'll stop the Russians. That he'll do our fighting for us."

"You know, I have my own sources . . ."

"You're British secret service. Everyone knows that."

"Does it show?"

"The pipe is the giveaway. I think you've set the carpet on fire."

Balderston retrieved his pipe. "Why haven't we heard about this?"

"Because the general has been asked not to go public just yet. He's a patriot. A patriot who actually doesn't like Wall Street. A patriot whose whole career was acting as what he calls an 'enforcer' for the New York banks, for Standard Oil. He's done their work in Mexico, Shanghai, the Dominican Republic. He says Al Capone had only three districts while he had three continents. His would-be employers are now working to elect Willkie."

"Does Willkie know?"

"I doubt it. But the President knows."

"Then why doesn't he . . . Well, my God. What's happened to the treason laws?"

"The President waits for his opportunity, as always. One of the reasons he insisted on having Wallace for vice president is that Wallace knows quite a bit about the plot and is very much on his guard."

"The United States as Zenda."

"But still smilin' through."

Tim decided he could work with Balderston; but he must keep him on the defensive. "When Roosevelt recognized the Soviet Union, the conspirators became active. Happily, they are stupid, and they went to the wrong general."

"There are right ones?"

"For a coup? Oh yes. Particularly in the Army Air Corps, of all places. Wallace knows some of their names. Anyway, you wanted to know why I shifted from Willkie to Roosevelt even though Roosevelt will get us into the war first. Because the old pro can control these rich lunatics. He's smarter than they are. After all, he's one of them. But he does a single, as they say in vaudeville. Willkie's too slow-witted, too trusting."

"So you support Roosevelt in order to prevent a coup."

"Yes."

"But you think he himself is dictator material?"

"Yes."

"Will he make himself one?"

"The war will do that for him automatically. But then . . . Well, we must wait and see what comes next. The lady. Or the tiger." Then Tim signaled the projectionist. On-screen, a siren sounded; then an explosion; followed by the black-and-white frames of London burning and then, perfectly flood-lit from below, the great dome of St. Paul's Cathedral. It was, Tim thought, very much the time of the tiger.

At the end of the bar at Romanoff's Rodeo Drive restaurant, Emma Sanford sat next to a large bearded actor named Monty Woolley who, as he glumly read a book, drank martinis and ate a chicken sandwich. Parallel to the bar, the stars held court in booths while, at the end of the bar, there was a velvet rope to keep within the restaurant proper the wide-eyed tourists, lunching in what was locally known as "Siberia," along with those whose names on the screen were idly stacked so far beneath the title as to be in a different continuum from the booth people.

Tim was amused by Emma's highly vocal contempt for tawdry subversive Hollywood being suddenly undone by her bobby-soxer fascination as Bette Davis claimed her booth, third from the main entrance. Davis nodded regally to the occupants of the other booths. As usual, she was accompanied by friends "from the East," a local expression for non-Hollywood types. Tim always marveled at how small Davis was except for the enormous breasts that had, jointly, been the despair of so many costume designers, including the one who had said, "If only Jack

Warner would give me a crowbar so that I could smash that bosom of hers to smithereens, and dress her properly."

Tim found Emma an attractive if coarser version of her mother. The affair—if that was what it could be called—had begun in Washington not long after their reunion, if that was what *that* could be called, at Laurel House. Once Emma stopped making political speeches (a pillow over her face often worked miracles) he found her a surprisingly good fit, as he had come to think of women in bed, if not in love, while her enthusiasm for him was inspired by the fact that at the time he was still making *United We Stand*, a film that she wanted to reflect her stern Fortress America views. Nevertheless, on the few occasions that they had met over the last year, he had been delighted to be with her.

Several years before, Tim had divorced his first and only wife, thus far. Although each was Catholic, they had been married in a civil ceremony on the sensible ground that should there be no children, each could go his own way. Miraculously, Caroline, in deepest France, had never known of the marriage; but then Tim was not sure that she would have been very interested. Now Mrs. Farrell was profitably employed by Travis Banton, a costume designer: she had gone her own way as had Tim. Meanwhile, Emma had developed an unexpectedly avid interest in such fan magazines as *Silver Screen*. She certainly knew far more about Hollywood marriages, divorces, reported affairs, than Tim. She was also delighted to know something about Tim that her mother did not—even more delighted, as she tactfully put it, to take "you away from her." He did not bother to tell her that no one had ever actually had enough of him worth anyone's while to take away. Curiosity and opportunity had led him from mother to daughter. As they settled into the booth next to Bette Davis, he thought what a perfect role Caroline's life would be for Davis. Although Davis was hardly a beauty, she could, if required by a script, become beautiful with magical ease.

It was Emma who pointed out the various stars on parade, of which easily the most enchanting was Joan Fontaine, all in violet, her enigmatic smile characteristically aslant.

"I was wrong about her. Wrong about Hitchcock, too. I thought they'd ruin *Rebecca*."

"I loved it!" Emma the movie fan was far more agreeable than Emma chairman of more right-wing causes than Tim could begin to count. Then they were joined by Tim's agent. Bert Allenberg was a tall slender man with a deep voice and though he looked like a vice president of the House of Morgan, he wore a too-well-cut suit of black mohair. Since for all his distinction he was still a professional agent, he kneaded Tim's left shoulder blade to make sure that his client's current success would pass to him as well. Bert was gracious to Emma, who affected shyness.

Then: "We've got a deal. Only verbal, so far. But you're getting twice the budget of *United* and you'll operate out of London or wherever you have to be."

"Oh, that will be really thrilling!" Emma sounded like a Hal Wallis starlet.

"When do I start?"

"Now. You want Balderston?"

Tim nodded. "I'll need him for London."

"But isn't he . . . ?" Emma's frown was a sudden Medusa-like tic, capable of turning even Bette Davis to stone.

"Yes," said Tim quickly, "he is."

"But *British* secret service . . ." Emma began.

"We need all the help we can get," said the agent, unaware of the enemy at the table.

Tim deflected Bert. "I've promised L.B. an interview with Hitler on camera, and the Brits say they can set it up." Fortunately, at that moment, a magnificent blond starlet from Warner Brothers made her slow, voluptuous way from the Siberia of the back dining room through the bar. The star-filled booths fell silent at so much splendor until Bette Davis declaimed, in a voice whose every neat syllable could have been heard, unamplified, from top to bottom of the Hollywood Bowl, "And there goes the good time that was had by all."

A burst of unkind laughter. The starlet fled; inside the telephone booth next to the door through which she exited, there was the sound of frantic pounding. The enormously fat Austrian writer Franz Werfel was wedged next to the telephone, apparently not for the first time, since two calm waiters, working in almost balletic concert, skillfully turned him this way and that until he tumbled out.

"Always a good time at Romanoff's," Tim observed.

Bert Allenberg rose. "You're at the Garden of Allah, Tim?

"Bungalow right next to Errol Flynn's. You can't miss the screams. The midnight splashing in the pool."

Bert waved and moved farther up the row of stars, greeting each as if he was their host at a party, as indeed a master agent tended to be.

"Noisy?" Emma's face was flushed.

"Flynn? Very."

"I must meet him." Emma was breathless.

Tim wondered if he was attracted to her only because she was Caroline's child. First the mother; then the daughter. There was some primitive instinct at work in each which made them so sexually compatible while, at best, each basically mistrusted the other, as Caroline would have intended had she been the goddess in charge of this diversion.

"You would look marvelous with blue hair." Laura Delano, the President's middle-aged cousin, turned her elegant face full upon Caroline, who took an inadvertent step backward as if to better observe the sculpted blue hair of her hostess for the night.

"I don't have the coloring to carry it off," Caroline responded smoothly, as if every day of her life she had considered whether or not to dye her hair blue. Actually, the President's spinster cousin having just missed sky-blue during her last encounter with the paint bottle had, somehow, shifted from azure-white to an aggressive dense purple that suggested eccentricity rather than the fanciful charm of international society's most glamorous figure, the first of the blue-haired ladies, Mona Williams.

"Oh, but you do. We must try before you go. Franklin thinks he's going to lose." They were seated, the two of them, in the cavernous drawing room of the Delano mansion, just north of Rhinebeck, which, in turn, was north of Hyde Park on the Hudson, where, that night, in the so-called Big House of the Roosevelts, they would join the President and listen to the election returns.

"Harry thinks . . ."

"Pay no attention to Harry. He's an optimist. That's because he's a social worker." Laura's non sequiturs had a kind of majesty.

"It's true that Willkie . . ."

"Neck and neck in the Gallup Poll. Well, for Franklin's sake, I want him to come home. Here. Where he belongs. In the valley. Home sweet home."

"Home on the range?" Wherever the President appeared, bands played this dolorous song.

"McIntire. He's the one. Dreadful song. Someone asked him—he's also tone-deaf—what the President's favorite song was and he said, 'Home on the Range,' which Franklin hates but can never say so for fear of losing the home-on-the-range vote."

"Like General Sherman and 'Marching Through Georgia.' Every time the general appeared in public, some band would play it. Finally, one day, he burst into tears."

"Serves him right. For burning down Georgia. That book with the Confederate-gray cover. You know, *Gone With the Wind*. There's also a lot to be said for not showing off all the time in public. Of course, Franklin has to. Or so he says."

With Caroline beside her, Laura drove her own car south along the River Road that had once been part of the famed Albany post road— now simply a winding lane through wooded countryside with, on their right, the estates of the so-called River Families—Chanlers, Aldriches, Delanos, Millses, Astors, Vanderbilts. Most of the houses were not visible from the road since each had been built on the high bluffs above the Hudson so that steamship passengers could marvel at the palaces of their masters, built in every style from Greek Revival to McKinley Gothic, the overall feudal effect only slightly marred by the presence, between river and estates, of the loud New York Central Railroad as it hugged the marshland at river's edge.

"This war—and we shall soon be in it—will be the end of all of us." Laura narrowly missed a turtle that had begun to cross the road at a prehistoric pace. "Such idiots, turtles. Terrapin. I can understand—to eat—at least in the South. We shall not survive, Caroline. You and I." Laura's finely chiseled face stared into Caroline's, whose eyes, consequently, seldom left the twisting road that Laura had chosen to snub.

"Hitler will bomb us?" Caroline, inadvertently, put her hand on the steering wheel. Laura pushed the hand to one side. "I can drive this road in my sleep." Narrowly a farmer's truck swerved to one side to avoid collision. "He shouldn't be driving and he knows it." Gaily, she waved to the farmer. "He's got cataracts. No, it will be the end of us because all the village boys are going to war and when they come back they won't want to be the one thing that we cannot do without—servants."

"Surely," said Caroline, "there will always be maids?"

"No such luck. Franklin says they will all be working in factories. Later, they will marry the boys who come home and one by one we—the River People—will die off in our freezing houses, with no one to so much as turn down a counterpane."

"It is a picture of horror that you paint." Caroline had always wanted to play in an Oscar Wilde comedy; now Laura was improvising one with her. Contentedly, they itemized all that would be lost when triumphant soldier boys and their factory girls fled the great estates, and Vincent Astor was obliged to cut the grass of twenty acres of lawn while his wife washed dish after dish from dawn until dusk.

"Fortunately, I'm just me," said Laura contentedly.

"How will you eat?"

"I love tinned sardines. You know, the boneless ones from Portugal? S. S. Pierce sells them. Oh, I won't starve. The rest of the time I shall simply stay in bed."

But of course, thought Caroline, Laura was, in her dotty way, absolutely right. The life that she had taken for granted in the United States—France, too—would not resume. Blum had foreseen much of the future and found it good; but then he favored *egalité* rather more than Caroline did. Even so, these were, after all, Modern Times and if

Charlie Chaplin had got it right, soulless factories would be the future while machines, not men, farmed the land.

It was nearly dark when they arrived at Eleanor's Val-Kill cottage and Laura jammed her car next to another, out of which leapt an angry state trooper. "Get that damn thing off . . ." Then he saw, in the last gold glimmer of daylight, the purple hair. "Miss Delano."

"You are an angel!" Laura cooed. "You know how rough my landings are."

The trooper opened her door while Caroline, having made herself invisible, got out the other side. Several dozen cars were parked on the driveway and on the uncut lawn; and a number of dinner guests were taking the evening air in front of the wooden cottage that was, Eleanor maintained, her only true home. Here she saw her lady friends; received her husband as a guest; and lived as private a life as she could while farther down the road, in the Big House, her mother-in-law presided in all things, including placement at the dinner table, where she always sat in the wife's place, opposite her son Franklin, while Eleanor took whatever seat was available.

The swimming pool beside the cottage had always seemed to Caroline to be more of a pond than a proper pool. Certainly it had a marshy smell but, even so, on the terrible hot days of a Hudson Valley summer, it was a refuge for all, including that occasional visitor the President.

Caroline found a number of unfamiliar faces in the sitting room, which was just off the dining room, where Mrs. Nesbitt, or one of her kitchen acolytes, had arranged mounds of creamed chicken and rice. Although there was no wine to be seen, at the very center of a round maplewood table, the work of two of Eleanor's lady friends, ardent cabinetmakers in the Early American style, stood a single bottle of whiskey, eyed longingly by a number of guests of whom not one dared do more than stare. The Roosevelt sons were all equipped with flasks, according to Harry Hopkins, who greeted Caroline by the fireplace, where a large green log smoked and hissed.

"How do you like Laura?" Hopkins was amused at the thought of two women so unlike in each other's company.

"Almost an original, I'd say, and a demon on the road. What news?"

"Connecticut returns are coming in. We're doing as well as expected."

At the far end of the room Caroline saw the giantess Helen Gahagan talking to her giantess hostess. "Mrs. Douglas is very interested in politics, isn't she?"

Hopkins nodded. "Obsessed, I'd say." He frowned. "The President's worried."

"That he'll lose?"

"I don't see how he can. But something's bothering him."

"Time's winged chariot?"

"Oh, we're all used to that old buggy. Of course, it's on its way for him. For me, too. No. He senses something wrong, something peculiar about this election. I spent most of the day with him, playing poker. He actually lost."

"Unusual?"

"Well, not exactly usual. He does like to win."

Caroline was aware that Hopkins wanted to say more but did not—dare?

Caroline asked if the President would be joining them at Val-Kill Cottage. "No. He and the dragon are dining alone in the Big House. Then, around nine, we'll join them to hear the returns. It's a regular ritual by now, like Christmas Eve."

"Will there be another one in four years?"

"If we get through tonight, who knows?"

"Get through what?" Caroline could no longer rein in her curiosity.

"There's talk of a putsch." Hopkins spoke in such a low voice that it took Caroline a moment to absorb his words.

"Here? In Hyde Park?" she asked, aware of how stupid she must sound.

"No. Here in the United States. Willkie's people are supposed to have made some sort of deal with the German government. They'll let us have the Western Hemisphere . . ."

"Which you already have."

"... if President Willkie will then force England to make peace with Germany so that Hitler can move against Russia. . . . For the good of mankind, naturally."

"To destroy communism in its nest." All through the summer Caroline had heard this line repeated over and over again by ardent members of East Coast country clubs. "But this is all . . ." For a moment she found herself thinking in French and could not think of the English for *blague*. She came up with the inadequate "bunk."

"Maybe bunk. Maybe not. But the Boss is scared of something and it's something more than the possibility of losing."

The Boss, however, to Caroline's eye, was his usual expansive self as he greeted Eleanor's supper guests in the large drawing room of the Big House. In the adjacent dining room the mahogany table was strewn with pencils and pads. In the small "smoking room" off the dining room, wire-service ticker tapes had been installed, and Secret Service men tactfully kept the guests from straying into this command post, where Missy Le Hand presided.

"Caroline!" The President took her hand in both of his. He looked both tired and full of energy, as if an unexpected source of power had been switched on. "Democracy at its messiest. Dutchess County–style."

"You seem to thrive, Mr. President, on mess."

"But sometimes I wonder if I may not be overdoing it. Three terms could be a bit much, as Mr. Willkie likes to remind us." Caroline noticed the slightest of frowns at the mention of his rival and potential—what? Putsch-maker?

Then the President was wheeled into the dining room, accompanied by Hopkins, who waved—farewell?—to Caroline as she sat beside the fire and made conversation with the President's huge, in every sense, mother. Mrs. James, as she was always called, resembled a somewhat more masculinized version of her son.

Eleanor now moved swiftly between drawing room and dining room. She had changed into a flame-colored dress and Caroline thought of her as a potential pillar of fire, and more than a match for any Mitteleuropa dictator.

Except for Mrs. James in her chair beside the fire, no one in the room was still for long: groups formed; broke up; re-formed. Eleanor would join each group briefly; answering questions. Caroline, having exhausted her small talk and not yet willing to move to larger talk for the benefit of Mrs. James, soon relinquished her privileged place beside the old lady to Daisy Suckley, another of Franklin's old maid cousins. Mrs. James seemed unaware that Caroline had been replaced, as she continued her own practiced series of observations on what it was like to be—her phrase—"a historic mother."

Harry Hopkins emerged from the dining room as Missy Le Hand entered with a pile of messages. Hopkins drew Caroline off into a corner. As he tried to light a cigarette, his hands shook. Caroline lit it for him. "He's losing," she said.

Hopkins nodded. Through the dining-room door, Caroline could see the President mopping his face; sweat gleamed in the stark light from overhead: naked electrical light bulbs on frayed wire were a Roosevelt decorating motif. As Missy Le Hand left, Roosevelt turned to a Secret Service man and said in a voice so loud that Caroline could hear him, "Get out, Mike. Shut the door. I don't want to see anybody in here."

"Not even Mrs. Roos . . ."

"I said *anybody*, Mike." The Secret Service man did as ordered, closing the doors behind him.

"Has that ever happened before?" Caroline helped the suddenly weak Hopkins into a chair. Fortunately, none of the other guests had heard the President as clearly as Caroline and Hopkins had.

"No. Never. He's . . ." Hopkins shut his eyes; then summoned a small smile. "We're getting returns from the Willkie states at the moment. It'll be another hour before we hear from our states. New York. Illinois. Ohio. Pennsylvania . . ."

"But he knows that, too. So what's really wrong?"

"Willkie's running far ahead of Landon four years ago. He's got enough going for him to cut into us badly in the big states. There's whiskey behind that photograph of the King and Queen." Caroline poured each a drink. Then she sat in the chair beside him; and they were very still for what seemed hours.

Finally, Eleanor approached the Secret Service man at the dining-room door; she was admitted. Caroline caught a glimpse of the President in his shirtsleeves; he was grinning now. "I think it has happened."

Hopkins opened his eyes; and nodded at what he saw. "We're in!"

The entire room seemed to know simultaneously. Helen Gahagan was now a self-appointed official spokesman. "Seventy-five percent of labor, Negroes, foreign-born, and all lower-income groupings are for Roosevelt." Everyone cheered. Caroline admired the professional sound of "groupings" instead of the more amateurish "groups."

The President remained at his station in the dining room but he was now smiling as he clasped his hands and raised them above his head in traditional victor's style. The guests in the drawing room applauded and Mrs. James waddled majestically into her dining room to salute her historic son.

"Come upstairs." Hopkins led Caroline to his bedroom, where they found Judge Sam Rosenman and Bob Sherwood, the President's principal speechwriters; they were listening to the returns on the radio.

"I win my bet with the Boss." Rosenman was beaming. "He didn't think he'd get more than three hundred and forty electoral votes. Now he's over four hundred and still going up."

"Bless Boss Hague, Boss Murphy, Boss Flynn," said Hopkins.

The announcer said that so far Wendell Willkie had not conceded the election but it was only a matter of time.

Then, from below, a band played "The Old Gray Mare," not a tactful song, thought Caroline, as the night sky turned red from flares. Caroline hurried to the window. Hundreds of people were converging on the house, illuminated now by the powerful lights of the newsreel cameras.

"We don't want to miss this!" Hopkins was suddenly full of energy.

Hopkins and Caroline managed to find places for themselves at the edge of the front portico. Secret Service men, looking uncommonly alert, were scattered throughout the crowd, as well as state troopers. Caroline visualized an army of brown-shirted Nazis marching upon the house.

"That must be the whole population of Hyde Park," she said to Hopkins.

He laughed. "Only local Democrats and the folks from Pough-keepsie. The rest are all home in mourning. He's never carried his hometown."

Suddenly, there was a great cheer from the crowd, as the President appeared, wearing a cloak that effectively covered the wheels of his chair; he was flanked by Eleanor and his daughter Anna.

When the cheering stopped, the President chatted with a few of his neighbors; fretted at the absence of this one or that one, which got him a great laugh, since he had named the town's leading Republicans.

Finally, he thanked them all, ending, "You will find me in the future the same Franklin Roosevelt you have known a great many years. Good night to you all." With that, he was wheeled inside and Hopkins did a little jig of triumph.

"Just like Hitler in France," Caroline could not resist reminding him.

"Every dog has his day." Hopkins was triumphant. "This is ours. Hitler's has just ended."

SIX

I

Although Peter had once thought it a good idea to go on to Harvard after graduating from the University of Virginia, he got out of bed one morning in August and realized, halfway to the bathroom, that if he were ever to learn anything of interest he must not go near a university again.

"I have been told that the winters in Boston are dreadful." Frederika had been undistressed by his unconventional decision. "I can't think why they don't hold their classes in summer."

"We are supposed to be doing our farming then. Anyway, if I'm to be a first-class wastrel, I shall need a warm climate like Washington."

"Africans, your Aunt Caroline calls us, living in tropical bliss." Frederika was swathed in what looked to be mosquito netting while a large hat shaded her face. She feared the sun's lethal rays.

"Torpor is more like it," was Blaise's contribution. But he, too, was neutral about Peter's decision as they sat beside the pool. Back of them a tall hedge of boxwood hid the shallow brick steps that meandered through a rose garden and then turned into rose-colored marble as it straightened itself out and became the formal river entrance to Laurel House on its wooded eminence.

"I *like* selling space." Peter was determined to be as good a sport as his parents.

"No one likes selling space." Blaise was authoritative. "But it gives you an idea of how a paper works. *If* that sort of thing interests you. You don't mind my prying, do you?"

Relations between father and son had been much improved since the convention summer of the previous year. Peter had a knack for making politicians sound interesting. Blaise had appreciated this peculiar gift. "Actually, I preferred your pieces to Joe Alsop's."

"But Joe knows everything."

"Yes. And then he tells you everything he thinks he knows. You know nothing. *And* you have no ideas at all. This is a blessing in a journalist."

"A relief, anyway."

Frederika seemed to enjoy the new amity between father and son. "He takes after you, Blaise."

"No ideas!" Blaise's neck, where not already sunburned, reddened. "I'm nothing but ideas. For God's sake, I'm a publisher."

"Like Cissy, yes." Frederika shut her eyes. A warm wind floated up from the Potomac. While Frederika dozed, Blaise went into the men's section of the pool house, where Peter had observed his sister, Enid, being made love to by Clay Overbury, now her husband, as well as aide to Senator James Burden Day, whose daughter, Diana, was becoming, more and more, the center of Peter's daydreams. He caught a glimpse of himself reflected in the pool. He was scowling. Why? Billy Thorne. Diana's image had been replaced by that of her unlovable husband, now a temporary employee of the *Tribune* while he tried to get financing for a *radical* political review: the adjective was his, to be taken on faith or with a grain of salt or not at all. Billy Thorne had lost a leg in Spain, fighting fascism. This loss had made him briefly a hero of the American left and so, inevitably, he wrote a book. It sold almost as well as *Why England Slept*, which had been written for the son of the American ambassador to the Court of St. James's by Arthur Krock of the New

York *Times*; Henry Luce had then written a predictable introduction. Although there was an element of overkill about the Kennedy project that Billy could hardly match, the two young authors were often coupled that season in deeply thoughtful journalistic pieces about Youth Today and could they—would they—measure up as their predecessors had so selflessly done in 1917, 1898, 1860, 1846 . . . Peter began to grin as he saw the outline of a piece in his head. Should he do it for the *Tribune* or for the first, perhaps never to be published, issue of what Billy Thorne called *The American Idea*? It would be an excuse to see more of Diana.

Frederika was suddenly wide awake. "What time did I order lunch for?"

"You never tell me," said Peter. "I never ask."

"Twelve people, including the Vichy spy." Frederika exercised her memory.

The Vichy spy was the usual designation of Gaston Henry-Haye, ambassador from the unoccupied but Nazi-controlled section of France. Morbid curiosity had made him, if not popular, ubiquitous in Washington.

"Then there's . . . if Blaise didn't forget . . . Oh, my God, there he is!" At the top of the brick steps that led down from the rose garden to the pool stood Herbert Hoover.

Peter leapt to his feet; then, in response to his mother's helpless arm-waving, he pulled her upright as the former president made his stately way toward them: a white suit was his only concession to the month of August in a city that allegedly shared the same line of latitude as Cairo. George Washington had a lot to answer for, thought Peter, as Frederika became a gracious, apologetic hostess.

Hoover was equally gracious, apologetic. "My error. I have a new secretary. I've come too early."

"No. No!" Blaise came charging out of the pool house, blue blazer, silk ascot, orange trousers all in perfect place.

Frederika fled up the stairs while Blaise introduced Hoover to Peter, who started to withdraw, but Blaise told him to stay.

"The fault's mine," said Blaise, offering Hoover a wicker chair beneath a dying elm tree. "I told your secretary a half hour early because I wanted a chance to talk to you before the others arrive. Peter's working with me on the paper . . ."

Hoover's rarely seen smile was benign. "I have no secrets, Mr. Sanford . . ."

Blaise laughed. "Perhaps I do, Mr. President. But not in the family."

Peter did his best to look reliable, an effect achieved by thinking entirely of Diana and wondering how far things might yet develop between them. From the oblique hint or half-stated criticism, she was no longer as thrilled by the hero of the Lincoln Brigade as she had been when they first met and had startled everyone by a late-night visit to a justice of the peace in Maryland. It was well known that Senator Day could not abide his new son-in-law while Diana's mother, Kitty, was totally preoccupied with the wildlife of Rock Creek Park. She spoke intimately to certain birds, lectured squirrels, gave material advice to possums while largely ignoring the one-legged stranger in her attic. Actually, as Peter knew, it was Diana's unexpected interest in Billy's as yet unsponsored magazine that had brought together this most unlikely couple. She had done her best to interest Peter in *The American Idea;* thus, interesting him in herself. They sometimes had lunch near the *Tribune,* usually when Billy was elsewhere, searching for sponsors in a city that regarded itself as embodying the sole American idea: the winning of elections and the subsequent division of spoils among the victors.

"What do you think, Mr. Sanford?" The President was now looking at Peter with what appeared to be interest.

Peter tried to play back the last few words. One was Philadelphia. The convention?

"I told President Hoover what you told me," Blaise cued him, "about those altered microphones."

"Oh, yes!" Peter generated a degree of what he hoped might be mistaken for boyish enthusiasm. "*I* could hear you. But I was at the front of the gallery. I could also tell that there were a lot of dead spots all around me. I think I know who switched the mikes." Why not feed presidential paranoia? Go all out.

"The Willkie people, of course." Hoover was now leaning forward in his chair, right ear cocked toward Peter.

"Yes, sir, and I'm pretty sure the person in charge was Samuel Pryor."

Hoover sat back in his chair. "From Connecticut? I see. Yes. If I could prevail upon you to prepare a private memorandum . . ."

"We'd be delighted," Blaise answered a bit too quickly for both. "Now, sir, may I tempt you once more with a platform . . ."

Hoover shook his head. "I always thought that President Roosevelt—the *real* President Roosevelt, Theodore—made a great error in writing a column for that Kansas newspaper after he left office. I think we are at our most useful when we speak softly to those who follow us. Although even a whisper from me to that chameleon in the White House would be hardly welcome. Yet I have no personal animosity toward him. None!" Hoover could at least lie with as much apparent sincerity as his blithe successor. "Mr. Sanford, I don't rule out the occasional interview. Written questions. Written answers, of course. But I won't write a column. Even so, should I have something on my mind . . ."

Peter was relieved that he would not be assigned to the great man, who apparently did have something on his mind. "Everyone knows that I don't care for the President's foreign policy. He wants us in the war. But so far Congress has been able to keep him on a short leash with no help from our recent candidate, Mr. Willkie."

"Remember when Wendell said that if FDR was elected, we'd be at war by April? Well, that was five months ago."

"Speeches," Hoover sighed. "Mr. Willkie will *say* anything. In fact, I happen to know what he said when he and the President had lunch at the White House a few weeks ago. They discussed the creation of a new political party. An interventionist party. A socialist party. Imagine!"

Blaise nodded. "I've heard the gossip."

"Mr. Willkie also paid me a call at the Waldorf Towers." A bleak smile. "A dis-courtesy call you might say: I took some pleasure in reminding him that despite his large vote, he ran behind several governors." Hoover interrupted himself; turned to Peter. "You said—about the microphones—that it was Sam Pryor who gave the order to switch them?"

"So we think, sir."

"Curious. After the election I tried to get in touch with Mr. Willkie. He was in seclusion, I was told. With Sam Pryor. In Hobe Sound, Florida. Interesting." Hoover turned back to Blaise. "I might write a single piece for you and your syndicate. Or, perhaps, an interview might be better. We'll see. Anyway, I want to do something along the lines of the Willkie–Roosevelt lunch last July. On the possible breakup of the two parties. I would make the case that it is already beginning to happen at the highest level, which is why I regard my former secretary of state, Henry L. Stimson, as the second most dangerous man in the United States." A dragonfly—in shock?—stopped in mid-flight, just over Hoover's rosy head.

"I agree with you about the number one dangerous man." Blaise was suddenly a Republican clubman, ready to denounce that man in the White House as a traitor to his class. "But why Stimson, for second place?"

"When Roosevelt made him secretary of war just before the Philadelphia convention, he said he wanted a bipartisan Cabinet. Actually, he wanted, and now he's got, a War Cabinet. Colonel Stimson, as he likes to be called, is even more eager for war than the President."

This, thought Peter, was *The American Idea* in action, who was for—who was against—what?

The "what" came quickly. "In 1931 I discovered that Henry was using the State Department to make policy of his own. He deplored, as I did, what the Japanese were doing in China. But unlike his president, Henry wanted us to invoke economic sanctions against the Japanese. He was, he confessed in his modest way, evolving a 'Stimson Doctrine,' presumably to compete with the Monroe Doctrine." Hoover's sarcasm was heavy. He waved the dragonfly away. "He wanted to make all Asia our responsibility. That means if the Japanese would not let go of Manchuria, we would go to war with them. When I realized what he was up to, I called a Cabinet meeting and read Henry the riot act. I agreed that although Japanese behavior on the mainland of Asia was deplorable, we were in no way threatened, economically or morally. I have the impression that he thinks of himself as a stern moralist, appointed by heaven to force people to be good, even if he must shoot them first. I then said that I would never sacrifice any American life anywhere unless we ourselves were directly threatened. Oh, I stared him down—he was seated just to my right at Cabinet. I also reminded him that to go to war on the mainland of Asia at a time when our civilization was unusually fragile, to say the least, would be absolute folly. I know Asia firsthand. He doesn't. I know we'd be obliged to arm and train a million Chinese soldiers. This would involve us with China in a fashion that would excite the suspicions of the whole world." He chuckled, "Oh, I took some pleasure in tearing up Colonel Stimson's blueprint for a war in Asia."

Deliberately, Hoover took a handkerchief; mopped his forehead; and continued. "I am told that men of great imagination can often foresee what wars are like and so will have nothing to do with them. The Colonel, of course, has no imagination at all, and as I am an engineer, I'm not supposed to have one either. But I do have something Roosevelt and Stimson will never have. Experience. Franklin goes on and on about how he hates war because he has seen war. As usual, he lies. He toured a battlefield or two after Germany had surrendered. And that was that. He saw no war. Does he hate what he has never experienced? Who knows? But I had to feed the victims of that war and I don't want anything like that to happen ever again. But Stimson does. Roosevelt does. I find them unfathomable. You know, Roosevelt tells this tall tale about when he was in the Navy Department, and the Marines were occupying Haiti—Professor Wilson's contribution to their welfare. Anyway, Franklin claims to have written the Haitian constitution. As if he's ever read ours! People forget that when I was elected president, we were occupying most of Central America and the Caribbean. I pulled the Marines out of Haiti, out of Nicaragua, and then when our war-lovers insisted that we invade Cuba and Panama and Honduras, I said no. They invoked the Monroe Doctrine. I invited them to read it. We should never possess more military strength than is needed to make sure that no one will ever dare invade us. But then after the . . . uh, debacle of 1932"—Peter saw a look of real pain in that round innocent-eyed bejowled face—"Stimson, still in my cabinet, sneaks up to Hyde Park to sell himself to the President-elect. Obviously, the price was right. Those two are made for each other."

"Mr. President, you must write all this for the *Tribune*." Blaise was excited, to Peter's surprise. Peter had not expected his unimaginative father to get the point to Hoover's originality so perfectly disguised for so long from his countrymen by his forbidding and consummately dull persona.

The butler was now at the top of the brick steps. "Mrs. Sanford is ready, sir."

Hoover stood up. "Naturally, a fallen statesman is always willing to mount whatever pedestal he can find. I'll make some analysis of our elderly secretary of war's peculiar view of the world, and his alliance with that mysterious presence in the White House." Flanked by Blaise and Peter, Hoover moved with firm tread up the steps, where rambling roses grew to left and right.

"I am anti-war as you may have guessed but not because, as some deep thinkers believe, I am a Quaker, born and bred. I'm perfectly willing for us to fight if we have to. But I see something worse than war on the horizon. I am certain that the next war will absolutely transform us. I see more power to the great corporations. More power to the government. Less power to the people. That's what I fear. Because once this starts, it is irreversible. You see, I want to live in a community that governs itself. Well, you can't extend the mastery of the government over the daily life of a people without making government the master of those people's souls and thoughts, the way the fascists and the Bolsheviks have done. In his serpentine way, Franklin is going in the very same direction that they have gone in, and I think he knows exactly what he's doing while Stimson is simply stupid, a common condition."

"Why, sir, did you make him your secretary of state?" Peter was bold.

They were now at the lawn facing Laurel House. The lunch guests were gathering on the terrace. "Well, I could say that I, too, suffer at times from the common condition. I, too, can be stupid."

Blaise scowled at Peter's impertinence. But Hoover was matter-of-fact. "Perhaps I was, in Stimson's case. I suppose I didn't think I needed any help with foreign affairs. Most of my professional life was spent abroad, working with foreign governments. I suspect I just wanted to have Stimson around so that I could keep my eye on him, and all the other Wall Street boys."

The guests on the terrace were now applauding Hoover. He gave them a mock-Rooseveltian wave.

"See how they admire you, Mr. President."

Hoover was now examining the guests as they saluted him. "I think every last one of them gave money to Willkie."

"They had no choice, sir . . ." Blaise began.

But Peter broke in on his father. "Sir, did you really say that line about the poem?"

Hoover actually laughed, something generally thought impossible. "Yes, I did. When the Depression was at its worst, everyone wanted to know what we should do. General Electric even offered to take over the government and run it for me like—well, General Electric, I suppose. Oh, I was given a great deal of advice. Finally, I was inspired to say, what this country really needs is a great poem. Something to lift people out of fear and selfishness."

"Do you still think so?"

"Of course."

"You should have written it, sir."

"I am no poet. And there is still no poem by anyone—yet."

2

Senator James Burden Day was standing in a leafy homemade pergola, pruning grape vines. Even in shirtsleeves the old man looked distinguished, thought Peter, who had known him all his life. "It is my theory," said Burden Day, "that grapes pruned in August turn out to be the best. No one agrees with me, of course."

"That should not stop you, Senator."

"It never seems to, does it? Diana's in the house. Billy is *not*." The Senator's dislike of his son-in-law was simply taken for granted by everyone, and never remarked upon.

Peter entered the house through a door just back of the pergola. The stone house was cool even on the hottest of days. In the shadowy living room, Kitty Day was bandaging what looked to be a large brown rat; on closer inspection, it was a wounded squirrel. "I found him in a hydrangea bush. Shot. He's all right now. The bleeding's stopped. Filthy bastards." It was Kitty's peculiarity to say exactly what she was thinking while remaining blissfully unaware that she was often surprisingly, certainly bluntly, informative.

Diana appeared in the doorway. "Mother, are you sure that thing isn't rabid?"

"Of course I'm not sure. But then you went and married *him* of all people." Kitty bore the wounded squirrel away.

"Mother." Diana was aware that Peter knew the family's secret.

"Why *did* you marry him, of all people?"

"The American Idea." She stammered slightly on the "m" in "American." "He now thinks Irene Bloch will come up with the money if she gets an invitation to dinner at Laurel House." Irene was married to the owner of Washington's largest department store. Since she lusted for social dominance, Billy had made Peter an associate editor of the review with the understanding that he would work on Irene. "Invite her to lunch at Laurel House. Impress her." Peter had done as asked, Irene proved to be quick-witted, and Frederika now tolerated her. When Peter explained the plot to his father, Blaise was perversely amused. "We'll ask Sam next time." Samuel I. Bloch of Bloch's Department Store was a major *Tribune* advertiser. "Then *you* can sell him some more space."

"Oh, Billy's clever." Diana sounded almost disapproving. "But then he has to be."

"He really is if he's hooked Irene. She'll never interfere with the magazine." Peter sat on a comfortably frayed sofa. "I think I'll write a defense of Herbert Hoover. If Billy would print it."

Diana was absently straightening cushions. "Why not? You're one of the editors." She stopped. "Did you say Herbert Hoover?"

Peter described his encounter with the former president. Diana agreed that the bit about the poem was nice.

Burden came into the room just as a car moved up to the house.

"Shall we go?" Diana was on her feet.

"Stay. Senator Gore's bringing over a cousin."

"I think I'd better go," said Peter. "I told Irene I'd take her to Cissy Patterson's."

"This might be more interesting. The cousin is Admiral Richardson." There had been a good deal of conjecture in Washington's whispering gallery about the summary dismissal by the President of the commander in chief of the United States Fleet. Burden Day's Subcommittee on Naval Affairs had wanted to investigate but party unity had suddenly been invoked. Now Peter wondered what the cousins were up to. Senator Gore had lost his seat in the Senate after a falling-out with Roosevelt. Now Admiral Richardson had been abruptly retired. Although Burden Day was usually an ally of the President, he had very much wanted to be the Democratic candidate for president in 1940 until Roosevelt had chosen to succeed himself. Even though Burden was looking ahead to the 1944 elections he was quite aware of the ticking of that clock which would, more soon than late, erase any hope of the presidency. But a clash with the President might revive a fading career. "It is like some incurable disease," Diana had suddenly said one day over ice cream at Huyler's. "This passion to be president has ruined Father's life."

"Well," Peter was mild, "it has done wonders for Roosevelt. Saved *his* life you might say."

Blind Senator Gore arrived on the arm of the Admiral, who wore civilian clothes; each stood very straight, otherwise there was no family resemblance. As always, the blind Senator said to Peter, "Nice to see you again."

Diana went for iced tea. The visitors did not appear to mind the presence of the young.

"Mr. Day." Senator Gore was always formal, even with friends. "We felt in need of your wisdom this afternoon."

"What there is isn't much, Mr. Gore, but I'm always ready to lend an ear."

"Admiral Richardson, as you know, left his command of our fleet last February . . ."

The Admiral chuckled. "I was fired by the President himself. Quite an honor."

"This means that you dared to disagree with him." Burden was to the point.

Senator Gore turned to the Admiral as if he could see him. "Didn't I tell you? Mr. Day is the wisest man in the Senate, now that I'm gone."

"Because you also disagreed with him," said Richardson.

"The family resemblance," intoned Senator Gore, "grows closer and closer."

"I assume, Admiral," Burden's pale blue eyes were concentrated now on Richardson, "that your disagreement wasn't over the gold standard."

"Nothing so mysterious, sir. We disagreed about life and death."

Diana returned with iced tea. Kitty waved at them through the window; a scarlet bird, perching on her shoulder, pecked at her hair. Diana served tea; and left them.

"Last October, just before the election, I was asked for lunch at the White House. The President was his usual happy self. We discussed the recent maneuvers of the Pacific Fleet."

"Was Harry Hopkins at lunch?" Burden stirred ice with his forefinger.

"No, sir. Just the two of us. Upstairs. It soon became apparent to me that the President has a plan, even some sort of timetable. 'Sooner or later,' he said, 'the Japanese will commit an overt act against the United States and the nation will then be willing to enter the war.'"

Burden put down his glass hard. "He said that? In those words?"

"Yes, sir. He also said he was convinced that sooner or later they would make a mistake—he used that word, too—and then we would be in the war because Germany and Italy would have to honor their military treaty with Japan."

"He's like a magician," said Gore. "He keeps us occupied with England and the Atlantic and Lend-lease and then while he's doing tricks with his European hand, the other is provoking Japan into attacking us so he can live up to his campaign promise that, if elected, no sons of yours will ever fight in a foreign war—unless, of course, we are attacked."

Peter was alarmed and excited. Were these three men just ordinary Roosevelt-haters who tended to say anything? Or was the Admiral's story true? And if it was true, and if Japan were to make a "mistake," couldn't Roosevelt be impeached and removed from office?

"Specifically, Admiral . . ." Burden began.

"Specifically," Richardson answered, "the President wanted to put one of our cruisers in Japanese waters, to just 'pop up,' as he put it, to intimidate them. He was willing, he said, to lose one or two cruisers but not five or six."

"Dear God!" Burden shook his head.

"And then *you* said . . ." Gore prompted Richardson.

"I was angry enough to tell him the truth. I said, 'I should warn you, Mr. President, that the senior officers of the Navy do not have the trust and confidence in the civilian leadership of this country that is essential for the successful prosecution of a war in the Pacific.'" Richardson laughed. "Yes. I memorized what I said in case, one day, I am invited to repeat it for the record."

"That could be soon." Burden looked grim.

"Let's hope not," said Richardson. "For now, I'm officially silent. But, privately, I've told a number of my fellow officers, and now I've let you gentlemen in on this dangerous game that Mr. Roosevelt is playing."

Peter did his best to appear invisible. Plainly he was not one of the gentlemen that the Admiral intended to warn.

"It's a very clever game." Gore's one glass eye had strayed northward while the blind eye was half shut. "Eighty percent of our people don't want us to go back to Europe for a second world war and nothing will ever persuade them, no matter how many of our ships the Germans sink. So we at least learned that lesson from last time. But to get the Japanese to strike first is true genius—wicked genius."

"Certainly, it's the way Hitler works. Accuse your victim of aggression. Then," Burden struck the arm of his chair, "attack him."

"Secretary of the Navy Knox tells me that the President's been considering a naval blockade of Japan. He wants two lines of light ships. One from Hawaii to the Philippines. The other from Samoa to Singapore. The President collects stamps, you know, and he loves looking at maps, and daydreaming. I said it would never work even if our fleet was in first-class condition, which it isn't. Mr. Knox told me, very sadly, that my bluntness had hurt the President's feelings. So now you know how I earned my gold watch, and Admiral Stark got promoted."

They discussed the politics of the matter. The secretaries of war and treasury, Stimson and Morgenthau, were eager for a showdown with Japan. Two weeks earlier, Morgenthau had responded to the Japanese move into Indochina by freezing Japan's assets in the United States as well as cutting back on oil sales even though the Navy, perhaps due to the influence of Admiral Richardson, had warned him that with the United States engaged in the Altantic supplying Britain with arms and in the Pacific with preparations for war, the newly inaugurated two-fleet Navy needed time to make itself battleworthy. Certainly, the day the Japanese could not buy oil from the United States, they would go to war with the Dutch and seize the oil fields at Java. "Then," said Richardson, "according to some sort of agreement Roosevelt made with Churchill on one of their yachting trips in the North Atlantic, the British, the Dutch, and the United States will go to war with Japan."

"*Secret* agreement?" Burden shook his head. "He can't make such an agreement. Only the Senate makes treaties."

"Perhaps," said Gore, "we've gone and made one without knowing it. One curious detail, Admiral. It's plain that the President wants the Japanese to attack us first. But if he does, why is he allowing them to keep right on buying oil at this very moment from—if memory serves—the Associated Oil Company at Porta Costa, California?"

Burden frowned. "To postpone the attack on Java?"

Richardson shook his head. "Our Pacific Fleet won't be ready for war until at least mid-December. Our Philippine air defenses won't be ready until February or March, next year, thanks to MacArthur's majestic slowness. It's my theory that the Administration will go on selling them a minimum amount of oil so that they won't attack us until we're finally ready for them. When we are, we'll deliver our ultimatum whatever it is. We want them to have sufficient fuel for a major strike but not for a major war. This leaves the timing up to the President."

"You make it sound as if there is some sort of a . . . a . . ." Burden was, to Peter's eye, unnaturally pale.

"A master plan. Yes, sir. I'm convinced of it. We've got some diabolically bright young officers."

"Thank God for that." Gore smiled. "Usually the enemy has all the clever devils and we have all the dim-witted angels."

"There are a number of hidden-away offices at our Eighteenth and Constitution headquarters. Some are supposed to be highly restricted. But there is always a lot of leakage, this being Washington. Last October one of our brightest young devils came up with an eight-point plan, carefully designed to force Japan, in the most plausible way, to attack us. I don't know the full details. But then as commander of the United States Fleet, I was not supposed to know anything at all. The young devil in question had assumed—remember this was almost a year ago— that the British were done for and that we should, at their request, put Singapore and so on under our protection. The same with the Dutch East Indies. Then we should beef up our Chinese warlord, Chiang Kai-shek. Send divisions of cruisers and submarines that we don't yet have to the Asian mainland while keeping the bulk of our fleet in Hawaii. Finally, after first persuading the Dutch to stop selling oil to Japan, we will, together with the British, stop all trade, particularly oil, to Japan. And wait for them to attack."

There was a long silence in the room. Gore rested his chin on the curve of his wooden cane. The Admiral sat as if at a Senate hearing, which, in a sense, he was.

Finally, Burden spoke. "How good is your intelligence?"

"Mine, sir? Or the Navy's?"

"They were as one, until recently."

"I should say that our intelligence is much further advanced than our fleet."

"I understand," said Burden. Peter wondered what it was that each did not need to say.

"Shortly before I was relieved of my command, our ambassador to Tokyo sent a message to the Secretary of State. This was late last January. I've read the message. The Peruvian minister to Japan warned our ambassador that in the event of 'trouble' with the United States, Japan would launch an all-out surprise attack on our fleet at Pearl Harbor."

"I don't believe it." Burden shook his head.

"The first duty of a naval commander is to see to the safety of his men, not to mention his fleet. Even the President, a naval genius in his own mind, knows that. Yet he's deliberately setting our fleet in harm's way. Since I objected, I had to be got rid of."

Burden rubbed his eyes. "Do you really think they'd ever dare attack Hawaii?"

"Driven to the wall, as we are driving them, why not? But Pearl Harbor does seem to me to be a bit far afield, unlike Manila, Singapore, Hong Kong, Java. The obvious targets."

"Once they attack, they will be destroyed just as we Southerners were destroyed when we attacked the Union." Gore was grim.

"At least our common cousins, the Hawkinses, were Unionists, even in Mississippi." Richardson's starched collar was beginning to crumple in the heat.

"True," said Gore, "but that didn't stop us from fighting alongside our kin even though we knew we'd be on the losing side. Admiral, there is a peace party in Japan. In fact, Prime Minister Konoye is eager to sit down with our side and come to terms, or so he says."

Richardson nodded. "Politically we have good intelligence out of Tokyo because Konoye is desperate to make a settlement in the Pacific. Unfortunately, the President does not want a settlement. He won't meet him."

"As simple as that?" Burden stared out the window.

"As simple as that, sir. The hawks in Tokyo—practically the entire military—are praying for Konoye to fail so that they can replace him with a military government." Admiral Richardson rose; as did Senator Gore, who took his arm. "I've been speaking to you today for the future record. Originally, I was tempted to go before your subcommittee, but I'm afraid we are already in so deep that anything that I might say could jeopardize the fleet."

"Mischief is afoot." Gore sighed. "I saw this coming in 1916. I saw it coming, again, in 1936. I can think of no worse fate than being an unheeded ancestral voice."

"A ghost," said James Burden Day, "is probably worse."

Peter slipped away, unnoticed. In the woods above the house, Diana was seated on a log beside a bright clear spring, bubbling out of fine brown sand. Here salamanders lived; this spot was always cool even on the hottest August day since thick-leaved trees met in a dark green canopy overhead. Peter sat next to her on the log. She smelled of lavender.

"I think I knew what was coming," she said.

"Well, if they are right, it's coming very fast. Scotty is enlisting in the Marines. This week." Scotty and Peter had grown up together in Washington.

"Can he get a commission?"

"He graduated from Virginia Polytechnic. Whatever that is. Yes, I'm sure he can. And so can I."

She looked him straight in the face, something she seldom did with anyone, eyes always aslant; Peter thought of Emily Dickinson's odd word. "You'll go in before they draft you?"

"I have a plan, too, which means using influence. Mercilessly. I've got to find out what's actually going on."

"Then go into intelligence. Safer." She looked away. "I can't see how this war is worth the life of any of us."

"You mean you don't get misty-eyed at Roosevelt's Four Freedoms?"

"So like Mr. Wilson's Twelve Commandments."

"Points, wasn't it? Anyway, who keeps score? What matters is that our leaders have always been so marvelously good."

Diana nodded. "And, best of all, they truly love us. Love us so much that there are times when I feel wickedly unworthy of them."

Peter put his arm around her, something he'd never done before with Billy Thorne's wife. "Don't worry. When we make the supreme sacrifice for them, they'll know then that we were truly worthy of them. I can't wait to get into my hole at Arlington."

"I shall tend your grave."

Then each burst out laughing and Peter said, "We shall be the first cynical . . . no, the first realistic generation of Americans ever to go to war because we know that if we don't go our masters will either kill us or lock us up."

"The American Idea . . . at its purest." Then Diana kissed him, missing his lips and making contact with his earlobe. In an instant, each broke from the other, preparing, for now at least, laughter at the trap that had sprung.

3

Since the Mrs. Auchincloss who lived not far from Laurel House was divorcing her husband, Caroline had, through the subtle intricacies of the various servants' halls of Washington and neighboring Virginia, got her hands on the departing Mrs. A's personal maid, who came, as did the mythical Emma Traxler, from Alsace-Lorraine. Marie-Louise was fifty and preferred French to English as well as a small flat at Wardman Park to an airy mansion ever vibrant with the sounds of slamming doors, of sobbing—often masculine—and of numerous shrieking children being constantly packed off in different directions. Did they ever get them all back? Caroline sometimes wondered but never dared ask Marie-Louise.

Meanwhile, as Caroline worked on her grandfather's memoir of the first national centennial, Marie-Louise was packing an overnight bag for her. The hotel was uncommonly silent. It was the last day of October and the end of what had proved to be an uncommonly anxious summer.

A new letter from Timothy described the start of his film in London. "I'm afraid we're either too early or too late for anything interesting here. Hitler was supposed to be in Moscow last week or next week or whenever. But wherever it is he is going to be, he won't be scaling the white cliffs of Dover. The invasion has been called off but the bombs still keep falling, presumably to depress the people, who seem to be having a pretty riotous time, particularly during the blackouts when couples couple in every doorway. Rumors are that we are already in the war but no one can mention it, least of all your friend Harry Hopkins, who is regarded as the Archangel Gabriel in these parts, the source of trumpet blasts and dispenser of Lend-lease. But until Congress declares war, everyone here is in limbo. Last week, L. B. Mayer asked me to screen-test a local songbird called Vera Lynn. I have done so. In a diabetic coma . . ."

Marie-Louise came into the living room from the hallway.

"A Mr. Elliott Macrae, Madame."

Caroline was startled. "The front doorbell just rang?"

"Yes. And I just answered it. I hope I didn't . . ."

"No. No. It's just that I didn't *hear* it ring. This means I am now quite deaf. Tell him to come in."

Caroline fixed her hair in a console mirror; rubbed straight eyebrows that had been plucked for so long that only the shadow—the merest essence of eyebrow—was left.

Mr. Macrae was a short, bouncy gentleman. He had inherited from his father the old publishing house of E. P. Dutton in New York City. He had been preparing for some time the two books of Charles Schermerhorn Schuyler. "I was just passing through town . . ."

"Quite all right." Caroline motioned for Marie-Louise to bring coffee.

Macrae sat down; opened a briefcase; withdrew a duplicate of the manuscript on Caroline's desk. "We've been working simultaneously," he said.

"Well, perhaps." Then Caroline thanked him for a book that he had recently published by Van Wyck Brooks. "If I were not so French I should dare to say he's perfectly captured the United States of the eighteen-seventies."

"He returns the compliment about Mr. Schermerhorn's work, *and* your editing. He plans to write a preface for us, about 1876, the centennial year."

"But not about the other book?"

Macrae looked uncomfortable. "You know, Mrs. Sanford, I'm from Virginia originally."

"That must be nice for you." Caroline had yet to find a way of striking the right note with the noteless.

"Yes it is. Fact, I'm off to visit relatives this weekend. The problem is not the centennial year story."

"Even American schools must admit that the Republicans stole the election. My grandfather and my mother witnessed the whole thing."

"Oh, that's perfectly all right. This is the age of debunking, you know."

"A valuable word, 'debunking.' A valuable activity, I should think.

Of course, I'm basically so foreign." Caroline realized that she was overdoing this particular number but she felt obliged to fill in notes—cadenzas—where he offered only resonant monotony. The dread Pearl of Alsace-Lorraine was suddenly beginning to fill up the Wardman Park Annex.

"Have you heard of Dumas Malone?"

"No. But I love the name. The wonderful juxtaposition *and* the possibilities. Goncourt O'Reilly, Maupassant Murphy."

"Yes." Macrae had missed the point. "You know, Mr. Malone is—well, no, you couldn't know—but he is writing a five-volume life of Thomas Jefferson which I hope to publish one day."

Caroline did her best to look both fascinated and benign. "Well, Jesus's life appeared in only four volumes. So why not Mr. Jefferson's in five?"

"I took the liberty of showing him your grandfather's work on Aaron Burr. I hope you don't mind?"

"Why not? This seems to be my answer to everything today. You see how agreeable I am, as a writer?" Caroline noted happily that Macrae was starting to sweat.

"The fact is, Mrs. Sanford, that Mr. Malone found your grandfather's portrait of Jefferson—ah, well—the word he used was certainly extreme . . ."

" 'Judicious'?"

"No. 'Treasonous.' "

"What nation is my grandfather supposed to have betrayed?"

"Well, his subject committed treason against the United States . . ."

"That was Mr. Jefferson's invention. Aaron Burr was found not guilty in a trial presided over by Chief Justice John Marshall. Surely, Charles Schermerhorn Schuyler's personal knowledge of Burr, not to mention years of research, can now set things straight even with a patriotic Virginian."

Macrae shook his head, looking very miserable indeed. "Mr. Malone also objects to Burr's observations that some of Jefferson's slaves were his own children."

"Who doesn't object? Of course, Mr. Jefferson should have freed them. But my grandfather thought he needed the money."

As Caroline spoke, Elliott Macrae seemed to be having trouble breathing. She paused. "Are you all right?"

"Well. I . . . As I told you, I'm a Virginian and we can't . . . that is, accept as fact that Mr. Jefferson ever had a child by a slave girl."

"I admit it was more like a brood. And why not? After all, he was disseminating his genius throughout what is thought of in some quarters as an inferior race."

"Mrs. Sanford, Mr. Jefferson was a gentleman! No gentleman could ever have had relations with a slave."

"If that is the case, Mr. Jefferson's father-in-law was definitely no gentleman, since it was his black daughter, as my grandfather pointed out, who bore his son-in-law—the widower Jefferson—all those children."

"What *he* was is not the point. What Mr. Jefferson was means a lot to us . . . and we reject this story."

Caroline fixed him with a cold eye.

"Mr. Macrae. When I first bought the *Tribune,* it was owned by an octoroon, I should guess, who was in direct descent of Jefferson, and, as if to prove his blood, he was every bit as bad a businessman as his famous ancestor."

Marie-Louise came in from the small dining room; she was carrying the overnight bag. "The White House car is waiting for you."

Caroline rose. "We shall all go down together."

The White House had suddenly concentrated Macrae. The red face paled. "You are going to see Mr. Roosevelt?"

"He is an old friend, from my publisher days."

In the long walk from the front door of the Annex to the driver at the car door, Caroline made it clear that if Mr. Macrae was not happy publishing her book . . .

She was greeted with a series of no's, followed by a plaintive "I wish you'd reconsider, but, of course, if you must you must. I should warn you that you will get many, many outraged notices in the press."

"I certainly hope so. I can't think of anything that my grandfa-ther—wherever he is—and I would like better." Caroline shook Macrae's hand with undue warmth. "You must get Balzac O'Toole to review us."

Caroline found the presidential boat—"yacht" was too elegant a word for the *Potomac*—completely comfortable, while the river from which it took its name was looking-glass-still as they headed toward Mount Vernon on the far side. The sun was beginning to set and the lights in the salon had been turned up as Filipino stewards in white jackets set out an elaborate curry dinner. The President had not yet emerged from his cabin; a half-dozen aides and assistants were either below or in the bow. For the moment, Caroline and Hopkins shared the cushions at the ship's stern. The air off the water was hotter than the breeze from the ship's wake, and Caroline, with her hand, tried to discern the dividing line. Hopkins looked more dead than asleep as he slouched alongside her. But, as always, he could see through what looked to be shut lids.

"What are you doing?"

"At *this* point," Caroline's outstretched hand was two feet above the stern, "the air from the river, very hot, starts to fall back and the evening air replaces it, like a layer of water. But then, the air is our ocean, isn't it? I am partial to the natural sciences."

"You wrote Monday's editorial, didn't you?"

Caroline had been wondering when—and if—Hopkins would notice her handiwork. "Yes. With help. I seem to have lost the knack. But Blaise sent me a good rewrite man."

"The Boss says the *Tribune's* much improved since you came home."

"I'm not home." But even as she spoke, she wondered where, if anywhere, was home now.

"If you should want something from the Boss—a story first, anything—we'll let you have it. He's never forgotten you in that movie, *Huns from Hell.*"

"Then tell him that the first thing I shall want is for him to forget *Huns from Hell.*" She suddenly got the scent of curry. "Dinner smells grand."

"The Filipinos feed him curry and between that and being on the water, he is as happy as a man conducting two wars can be."

"Two undeclared wars."

There was a silence. The stewards were giggling as they carried onto the deck a small table with familiar-looking bottles. Hopkins sat up. "The sovereign approaches. You know, I'm going into the Naval Hospital November fifth."

Caroline wondered if this was to be the end. At her age, friends, so hard to come by, were altogether too easily lost. "What do they say?"

"Some repair work is needed. I'm having trouble walking. You'll come see me?"

"Of course."

"I've alerted my children." At the end of the salon, two sailors appeared, carrying the President in the chair on rollers; then his physician rolled him out onto the stern, followed by a half-dozen men. Caroline recognized Judge Sam Rosenman, who, along with the playwright Robert Sherwood, wrote the President's speeches under Hopkins' alert eye. Caroline had once been allowed to watch the process, which reminded her of the young Hearst putting together a front page, inventing and disinventing news as he worked. Caroline once asked Hopkins, "You never disagree with the President, do you?"

"I agree nine times out of ten. That's because the tenth time I want him to agree with me." Thus, the social worker traded with the emerging Augustus.

"Caroline!" Roosevelt's chair was now in place back of his bar. "I've brought Grace Tully so you won't feel trapped at a stag party." The President's secretary had been for years "Missy" Le Hand's assistant until, earlier in the summer, that paragon had suffered what was said to be a mild stroke and had gone on leave. Characteristically, Hopkins feared the worst and Roosevelt assumed the best. But then, as Eleanor had once confided to Caroline, "Franklin has taught himself optimism about everything. He still thinks he will walk one day. I wish," she had added, wistfully, "I could be like that."

"You," decreed the President, looking at Caroline, "will have the Roosevelt special martini." As he mixed this lethal concoction, he was suddenly reminded of Huey Long, the assassinated Kingfish of Louisiana politics. A mysteriously motiveless doctor had shot down Huey in the state capitol at Baton Rouge just as he was about to contest the 1936 presidential election with Roosevelt. The Long family and their supporters were convinced that Roosevelt was behind the assassination. Since the mysterious doctor was himself promptly slaughtered by Huey's bodyguards, it was unlikely that anyone would ever know why the doctor did what he did—if he did it.

But Roosevelt had cheerier recollections. "I just saw an old newsreel of Huey. He's back of the bar at the Roosevelt Hotel in New Orleans. What a comedian that fellow was! He's standing next to this colored waiter who makes, so Huey says, the world's greatest Sazeracs. Huey then gives us the recipe while the bartender is shaking up this foamy drink. When he's done, Huey says, "Now, George, you better let me check that one out. Got to make sure you haven't lost your magic touch." So Huey gulps it down and says, maybe just a dash more grenadine. Well, they just let the camera run and after four Sazeracs, old Huey was carried out, feet first." Roosevelt laughed loudest of all, as he continued his bartender duties. Although the others seemed to prefer straight bourbon, their host made them Manhattans anyway. Then, labors done, he sat in the center of the stern between Caroline and Hopkins.

"I thought T. V. Soong very eloquent today."

Roosevelt looked at Hopkins, who nodded: "I'll get the ships to him as soon as I can."

"The poor Chinese are always overlooked." Roosevelt turned to Caroline. A swaying overhead light made his features look unusually sharp. "I was tickled pink by that editorial of yours."

"I'm glad. I did it, of course, to curry favor with you."

"Naturally. You're angling for a job with Eleanor in civilian defense and you think that if you play your cards right I'll be able to make an appointment for you to see her. But I simply can't promise to deliver her. She is inhumanly busy."

"I think I'll let the civilians look to their own defense. No, I was really trying to do poor Harry justice. He gets only attacks. Yet he's rearming the country and though it's still a secret from the public, the New Deal's winning. The Depression's almost over."

"You are good, you know. I clipped your line about how Dr. Win-the-war has now taken the place of Dr. New Deal. It's in my speech file and should we ever by some . . . ah, terrible misadventure be at war, you can count on me to plagiarize you, without credit, of course."

"Of course."

Everyone was now in festive mood and the conversation became general, which meant that the President would now start telling tall stories and indulging in what seemed like exciting candor until one realized that even as he was blurting out some dark secret he was carefully dismantling it as he continued to elaborate, with much head-tossing for emphasis.

"We saw T. V. Soong today, Harry and I. Madame Chiang's brother. I told him how we Roosevelts are old China hands. Why, as a child my mother lived in Hong Kong for several years. Loved it. Spoke perfect Mandarin."

When Eleanor had heard this familiar story yet again, she had said to Caroline, "Mrs. James never learned a word of Chinese, because they were afraid that she'd talk to the servants, the sort of thing *I* would have done but Sara Delano, never, ever."

The President was now in full flood. "Our Chinese connection goes back to the clipper ships. My grandfather, Warren Delano, made a fortune running opium to the poor Chinese." There was an appreciative murmur at this. "The Republicans are still trying to find a way of using that one. Grandfather Delano went up to Swatow and Canton— this was 1829—and even up to Hang Kow. All the while he was doing what many red-blooded Americans were eager to do back then—make a million dollars. Then he came home, put everything into Western railroads, and in just eight years, he had lost every dollar!"

The court laughed on cue. Harry's eyes appeared to be shut. But he smiled.

"Then in 1856 he went out to China again and stayed there all through the Civil War—with my mother—and made another million. This time he decided to be clever. He put everything into coal mines. And guess what? They didn't pay a dividend until two years after he died!"

At dinner Caroline was placed on the President's right, Hopkins to her right. The curry was elaborate and the President ate like what he was, a starving fugitive from Mrs. Nesbitt's kitchen. Tomorrow he and Harry would go to Hyde Park for a few days. Then Harry would enter the Naval Hospital. . . . "How *do* you feel?" she asked as she helped him to chutney.

"The way a clock must feel when you take out half its springs."

"I'm counting on you to live. For selfish reasons."

The large protuberant eyes turned toward her. "Why selfish?"

"I'm old. I have few—if any—friends now. I need you to keep me interested."

"In what?"

"Life."

"Life? I thought you'd say *me*."

"That's because you've been psychoanalyzed so many times. You think too much of me—you. Think of keeping *me* interested. After the President, that should be easy for you and bliss for me."

"You two are somewhat alike."

"Because we look to you for reflection?"

The President had now turned to Caroline. "Madam Publisher. Explain to me why the press has made so little fuss over the sinking of one of our destroyers today. One hundred and fifteen dead is the first report."

"I think it's because we take it for granted that we're already at war. You have given orders to shoot enemy vessels on sight. So this is no longer news—sensational news, that is."

"Not exactly. It's true I can make war. But I cannot declare war." He adjusted his pince-nez. "Only Congress can do that. Even so, I find it curious how little is being made of Germany's crimes against us in the press. What are you waiting for?"

"We're waiting for Hitler to defeat Russia . . ."

"You may have a long wait. The Russians are putting up a splendid defense at Leningrad. Then, very soon, it will be winter . . ."

"General Winter takes to the field, as Napoleon said, and Holy Russia is saved!"

The President covered his rice with shredded coconut. "You know, I have made it a rule never to try to influence a publisher."

"A rule which you are now planning to break."

Roosevelt laughed. "They call me the inscrutable sphinx, but for you I'm just a pane of glass."

"No, Mr. President, a series of panes of glass, set at angles."

Roosevelt accepted another serving of chicken curry. "Eugene Meyer has just come back from London. You know him?"

Caroline had met the banker who had bought the Washington *Post*, to the annoyance of Blaise and the fury of Cissy Patterson. "Hearst thinks his paper has a chance."

"Then that means it's done for." Hearst was not a name to be dropped lightly in Roosevelt's presence. "You yourself want us in the war, don't you? I mean you're not maybe yes but then maybe no like your brother."

"I am yes, with no maybe." Caroline had become an interventionist on the day that Hitler had driven through the streets of Paris.

"People think that I have all sorts of power that I really don't. I can maneuver at times. Help out. Lend-lease. That sort of thing. But if you ever want me to do something that I can't or won't do—that I'm not able to do—you must force me."

"How is that done?"

"A constant barrage in the press from those papers not thought to be pro-British, like yours. Insist that I do more. Indicate steps that I must take in order to save civilization, like—oh, direct military aid to Russia, that sort of thing. Accuse me of cowardice in the face of Nazi evil."

"Surely, that's more the Hearst style?"

"Well, perhaps it's a bit lurid for the *Tribune*. Then describe me as . . ." He chewed a moment; swallowed. "I have just the word. *Pusil-lanimous*. I've always loved that word but no one ever uses it anymore and it's absolutely perfect for a powerful editorial in a paper like yours."

Thus, Caroline got her orders.

When the dinner table was cleared, the men settled down to a poker game while Caroline and Grace Tully sat in the stern and watched the dark rounded hills of Virginia glide slowly past. The air had suddenly cooled; heat no longer rose from the river. "It's autumn now," said Grace. "Just like that. Summer's gone."

"I shouldn't think you ever get to see much of the seasons in the White House."

"He works us hard."

"How is Missy?" Caroline had got to like the unofficial wife of the President, whose stroke in June had paralyzed her right leg and arm and so affected her throat that she could hardly speak.

"Warm Springs is helping her. They say she'll be walking soon, with a brace. She is—most people don't know it—a very emotional person. She takes things hard."

"And that brought on the stroke?"

"Combined with too many sleeping pills. I used to warn her, but . . ." Grace put her hand over the boat's railing. "The river's cooling off."

Caroline, who had vowed never to betray curiosity, now betrayed her own vow. "Crown Princess Martha was considered, perhaps, an opiate too many for Missy?"

Grace turned to face Caroline. "What a time the gossips have had with that! Of course Missy was jealous. For years she'd sit beside the President when they went for drives in the country. Now the Princess sits next to him." Caroline had found Martha both charming and transparent. After the Norwegian royal family had been driven into exile by the Nazis, the handsome Martha, with her young children, was sent to the United States while her husband and his father, the King, remained in London. Roosevelt had let her stay in the Rose Suite of the White House. He was besotted with her, to Missy's grief and Eleanor's judicious disdain. "Franklin must always have a beautiful woman nearby, to tell him how marvelous he is." Eleanor shook her head. "Well, *she* is just his type. And, oh, how she simpers and does her little-girl performance for her dear kindly 'Godfather,' as she calls him. Too sickening."

Like everyone, Caroline wondered if polio had rendered the President impotent. Some thought yes; others no. The President's talkative son, Elliott, had told her, "Pa's still active, particularly down at Warm Springs."

"We hope Missy will be able to come back to her old room in the White House. She's very lonely away from here. You know, there was a time when we all hoped that she and Harry Hopkins would marry but, thank heaven, they didn't. Two invalids instead of one. Oh, dear."

Grace stopped herself as she recalled Caroline's somewhat equivocal relationship with Hopkins.

Caroline was happy to set the record straight. "I'm just a—pal." This was the first time Caroline could recall ever having used the word. "But he does need a wife. And very soon I should think."

"Missy really married the President and now that she's no use to him, she realizes that life's simply passed her by. No husband, no children, and now she's past the age."

"Princess Martha must have been the last straw." Caroline loathed herself for betraying such overt curiosity; on the other hand, this was court history. Saint-Simon would have asked the same questions.

"I can't think why she takes it so personally. She certainly knows better. Years ago she told me that the President is incapable of a personal relationship."

"I can understand that. It is the nature of power. Perhaps it is the secret of power. Indifference to everyone."

Grace sat up straight. "I shouldn't have said that."

"Why not? I am very worldly and very old. I can figure this sort of thing out on my own. Anyway, he will always need people no matter what he may or may not feel for them. He'll certainly always need you."

"What makes you so certain?"

"The tooth."

"What tooth?"

"The one he must wear over his front two teeth when he gives a radio speech, to keep from whistling into the microphone."

Grace laughed. "He told you that! Now you know everything. Yes, he keeps his dental bridge in a romantic heart-shaped box in his bedroom. Then he forgets all about it until he's in front of the microphone, ready to go on, and I have to rush upstairs to get it." Grace rose. "I'm to bed. Or berth. Or whatever it's called." She was replaced a moment later by Hopkins, who fell onto the seat beside Caroline.

"I have been given my orders by the President," she said.

Hopkins had shut his eyes. "An editorial about Russia?"

"How did you . . . ?" Caroline stopped. "You really are his other self."

"Or maybe he's mine. That's not for publication. The President cabled Stalin yesterday. Shipments of up to one billion dollars' worth of materials are to be sent under Lend-lease."

"Only the Russians aren't covered by it, are they?"

"Once your voice is heard in the *Tribune*, Congress will replace Old Glory with the hammer and sickle. You might mention, in exchange, we'll be getting all sorts of things from the Soviet Union."

"Like what?"

"Caviar, I suppose. I'm sure you'll think of something. Certainly we'll think of something. Maybe coals to Newcastle. Don't worry. Actually, the Russians have been covered by Lend-lease for the last two or three weeks."

"Who did that?"

"Well, if it wasn't ordered by what you call my other self, it was me."

Caroline wondered how best to win over Blaise, who had, that summer, come under the unlikely spell of Herbert Hoover.

Hopkins smiled. "I'll find you some Vatican quotes, to ease the pain of your Catholic readers."

"Can Russia survive?"

"Not if there should be a mild winter."

"There never is."

"So that's your answer. Hitler's overextended. He must keep an army in the west. And another in the east, moving on Moscow."

"We are in the same situation."

Hopkins turned his head and opened his eyes. "How?"

"The German fleet in the east. The Japanese fleet in the west. Blaise's new friend—don't laugh—Herbert Hoover . . ." Hopkins laughed. ". . . is convinced that we are deliberately provoking a war with Japan."

Hopkins looked away. "We don't have that much control over events, sad to say."

"Hoover thinks that Prince Konoye was our last chance to make some sort of settlement with the Japanese but the President refused to meet him."

"August was a bad time for a meeting with the Japanese. The Boss had to meet Churchill in Newfoundland. Then he was sick . . ."

"He was stalling? Why?"

Hopkins stared through the open salon door at the back of the President's head, which its owner tended to use like a conductor's baton to provide the tempo for those about him. "This wasn't the best of times for him. Old Sara died. Then Eleanor's alcoholic wreck of a brother died in Poughkeepsie. I've never seen either one of them so upset before."

"Then he does have feelings for others?"

Hopkins gave her a somewhat suspicious sidelong glance. "Grace?"

"Grace? Innocent. Me. Caroline. Observation of Eleanor, really. She will suddenly blurt out something startling. Even—bitter."

"I know. Anyway, one good thing. With the old lady gone, Eleanor will finally start to feel at home in Hyde Park." Hopkins' smile was crooked. "After only thirty-six years. Funny, the Boss and Eleanor are closer now than I've ever seen them before. The wicked witch is dead. Witch." He repeated the word. "You know, the day the old lady died, the tallest oak on the property just fell over. And there wasn't a breath of wind. No repayment for five years."

"No what for five years?"

"No repayment of the loan to the Soviet Union. And no interest. We rely on your skill to indicate that this is a desirable form of book-keeping." On the shore closest to them, a number of shadowy figures could be seen dancing about a bonfire.

"What's that?"

"Halloween," said Hopkins. "It's tonight."

"So it is!" Caroline shuddered with—what? Nostalgia? "The night of all souls. In France they believe that for this one night the dead are abroad among the living."

"Have you ever seen a ghost?" The question was serious.

"How could I? I've not been analyzed."

"Low blow."

"I always thought in my movie days that the shadow of oneself on the screen is the true ghost preserved forever, at least in theory."

"I believe ghosts come to us in dreams."

"That's because you sleep in Mr. Lincoln's office."

"Well, I've never seen *him*. But one does feel trouble in that room. Almost as much as one feels it in the Boss's bedroom down the hall when he's having his breakfast in bed and looking at newspapers and cables and endless bad news."

"He's lucky to have you."

"Lucky for me to have him. For the country, too." A match blazed as Hopkins lit a cigarette. "For the record, Prince Konoye was no prince of peace. He was simply the most civilized of the Japanese politicians. The Boss saw no point in meeting someone who would soon be gone, which is what he was, two weeks ago, when General Tojo formed the military cabinet."

"Had the President bothered to meet Konoye, he might still be in power."

Hopkins coughed through the cigarette smoke. "Or maybe not. Anyway, for once, we have good information. They are finally ready for a war with us. But we won't be ready for several months. So that's why *we* stall for time."

Caroline realized then that, as was so often the case at this imperial court, the truth was often a mirror reflection of reality, an obverse image intended both to mislead and signal.

She looked into the salon at the cardplayers. Each must know something of what was to come but only the President, in his shirt-sleeves, understood the entire web that he was spinning all across the earth.

Caroline looked over the dark slow-moving water at the fires on the shore. What spirits, she wondered, were abroad tonight? "You know, it was on All Souls' Eve, twenty years ago, that I turned over most of my shares in the paper to Blaise and moved home to France."

"Home?"

"Yes. Home." She allowed herself to frown in the dark. "Home that was, anyway. Now I'm a ghost abroad, too, for this one night at least." The light from the bonfire on the Potomac shore illuminated Hopkins' face, like a cheerful goblin's.

"We are waiting," he said, with what Caroline took to be a gob-

lin's Delphic gravity, not to mention his own special gnomic eloquence—if gnomes were ever eloquent, "for the other shoe to drop."

Caroline recalled the prayer that her nurse had taught her. *"Com-
memoratio omnium fidelium defunctorum . . ."* she began.

"Defunctorum are the dead?"

"Yes."

"There will be plenty of new ones soon enough."

"I don't doubt it. You should have put out some food in your
room for Mr. Lincoln. The dead like it when they come home on this
night."

"I'm sure he's in Springfield, Illinois, tonight."

The bonfire suddenly flared and so lit up the boat that for a
moment it looked to Caroline like a painting in which they were, all of
them, forever fixed on canvas, and dead.

SEVEN

Blaise seemed more pleased than not for Caroline to be once again co-publisher of the *Tribune* on condition, of course, that her name would not appear on the newspaper's masthead. "Your Roosevelt connection is purest gold," he had observed as he welcomed her to the old office, unchanged in twenty years except for war maps covering one wall.

"The connection is fragile." Sooner or later, she would be asked to write or do something that she could not or would not do and that would be the end of the gilded connection. The nation was littered with former Roosevelt intimates who had been found unusable.

"Speaking of fragile, how is Hopkins?"

"He moves back into the White House next week." All through November she had visited Harry regularly at the Naval Hospital. She had gracefully, she thought, handled the inconvenience of having to leave the room whenever the President rang on the specially installed telephone. Since the conversations lasted longer and longer, Caroline had become a familiar figure as she paced up and down the hospital corridors, trying to recall how she had once played a wartime nurse.

The Japanese had sent two special envoys to Washington; one was a diplomat, the other an admiral. The noble-looking white-haired secretary of state, Cordell Hull, was dealing with them as best he could, which was apparently none too well according to Hopkins. "Of course, it's not his fault we don't have a policy at the moment."

"Stalling is a policy, isn't it?"

"But for how long? We need five months to be ready for them." The eyes were glistening now but he was skeletally thin while the parchmentlike skin of his face was whiter than the sheet pulled up to his chin. He complained of the cold.

"If I may criticize the regime . . ." Caroline began.

"That is your function."

"Accepted. Isn't it always wisest to strike the first blow?"

"Wisest for whom?" He lit a forbidden cigarette.

"Wisest for the side that means to win the war."

"You sound just like Churchill."

"I had not noticed the resemblance. He wants us to strike first?"

Hopkins nodded. "But we won't because it is wisest for the President to let them make the first move. We think they'll attack Manila, and if by some miracle they should manage to blow up that horse's ass MacArthur, our cup will truly runneth over."

"All this because of a campaign promise? No sons of yours will . . ."

". . . ever fight in a foreign war, *unless attacked*."

Caroline blinked. "This is all very daring."

"Fate decides what must be done. I'm convinced of that. Anyway, there's no going to war unless all your people are united behind you. Well, they are nowhere near united even though we keep losing ship after ship to the Nazis and no one blinks an eye. So we must take one great blow and then . . ." He stopped.

"Then what?"

"Then we go for it. All of it. And get it."

"What is *it*?"

"The world. What else is there for us to have?"

Caroline was properly chilled. "One hears that Hitler's table talk is somewhat like yours."

Hopkins grinned. "*Was*, I suspect. You have to change your tense when you start something you can't finish. And he can't. Joe Stalin's got him stopped. Then, when we join in, the whole world gets a New Deal."

Mentally, Caroline replayed Hopkins' speech as the late edition of the November 26, 1941, front page was placed on her desk. She had never heard an American speak like Harry since the turn of the century when Adams and his circle used to discuss the possibilities of an American world hegemony that had, thus far, not come to pass, for which she had always been grateful. At the time, she had agreed with the ever-wise, always droll Henry James that where the acquisition of an empire had been the making of the British it would be the ruin of the Americans, who would simply export their Tammany Halls all around the globe. "Imagine," said the master, taking a deep breath as he prepared to unfurl one of his elaborate sentences, "the sight somewhere in—would it be a luxuriant green jungle? loud with the cries of strange scarlet birds, all dominated by the minatory presence of an elaborate wigwam, so called by the sachems, as I believe the masters of Tammany are known to their faithful followers, themselves so many avatars of the savage Americans whose preferred edifice was not actually a tent or wigwam but a cabin fashioned from huge rude logs, not unlike the very first residences of those bold Europeans who settled the island of Manhattan, so gloriously celebrated—the island not the immigrants—by the good Walt Whitman. In any case, either in some island wilderness or, now, in the Spanish city of Manila, all whitewashed and ablaze beneath a tropic sun, we have enlarged our domain to include half a watery world whilst bringing its residents all the arts of political corruption as demonstrated by numerous—countless—ceaseless elections, wringing vote after vote from the poor immigrants or, in this case, the former joyous clients of Spain's flowery archipelago, now so many American wards huddled together beneath Old Glory, their plaintive cries for freedom unheard by the Great White Patriarch—sachem—call him what you will—at Washington . . ."

"Mrs. Sanford?" It was Harold Griffiths.

"I was daydreaming," she said.

"Of France?"

"No, of Henry James."

"You knew him?"

"We all did, back then. He liked—at least he said he liked—to come to Washington and stay with Henry Adams and laugh at all of us, in a kindly way. He took great pleasure in watching the cows trying to graze on the Capitol steps. So like the statesman within. What are you wearing?" Harold was dressed as an Army officer but without insignia.

"I'm a war correspondent."

"To what war?"

"Moscow. For the *Tribune*."

"Blaise has influence." Caroline was mildly distressed that her superior influence had not been put to use. Plainly, Blaise had his own ways. "What will happen to the movies while you are gone?"

"They are on their own."

"Your four-part series on—who was it?"

"Ida Lupino. Postponed until Hitler is defeated. Last things last."

Blaise joined them. "You look very convincing, Harold!" He gave the new correspondent a War Department envelope. "You're being routed through the Azores. It's all in there. Of course, they can't guarantee that you'll ever get to Moscow . . ."

"How Chekhovian," was Caroline's absentminded contribution: she was now reading the front page of the *Tribune*, still smelling of fresh ink.

Harold withdrew, leaving his employers to their joint creation. "Blaise, where did this story come from?" The headline: *Hull's Message to Japanese Envoys.*

"United Press. The Associated Press is hopeless. They simply parrot the State Department line. We thought that this might be authentic."

"I wonder how the UP got a look at Hull's message."

Blaise shrugged. "We were all hoping you'd get the word from Hopkins."

"He tells me no secrets that I haven't already worked out for myself. You realize, Blaise, that . . ." Caroline put on her seldom-used glasses; the mock-up front page had started to go in and out of focus: expanding and contracting glowworms adorned the page. Was she about to faint?

"Are you all right?"

"No. Not really. I feel—it's like morning sickness. Am I pregnant?"

"That doesn't seem possible." Blaise looked over her shoulder. "I can't say I read this story all that carefully . . ."

"Read it now."

Blaise read aloud. " 'The United States handed Japan a blunt statement of policy which informed quarters said . . .' Those informed quarters sound like Laughlin Currie."

Caroline liked the bright youthful Currie, one of the President's administrative assistants. Currie's principal task was to act as liaison with the Chinese; isolationists thought him to be a communist in thrall to Stalin. Actually, Currie was a shrewd observer of the world, loyal only to the President and somewhat overenchanted, like so many men, by the beautiful imperious Madame Chiang Kai-shek.

Blaise continued. " '. . . virtually ended all chances of an agreement between the two countries on the explosive Far Eastern issues. The United States government is reported to be demanding, as the price of any concessions it grants, that Japan abandon plans for future aggression, pull her armies out of China and French Indochina, restore the Open Door policy in China, and substitute peaceful negotiations for the sword in achieving her so-called Co-Prosperity Sphere.' "

Neither spoke for a moment. Caroline listened to the rattling of streetcars in Ninth Street, to the noise of horns being sounded despite every sort of city ordinance limiting their use. Then she said, for her own edification if not Blaise's, "The other shoe has dropped."

"The what?"

"Oh, something someone said was about to happen." A young newsman entered the room on diffident tiptoe. "Mrs. Sanford . . . sir. I have Hulen's story. He's just filed it to the New York *Times*." Caroline took the proof sheet, scanned it quickly as she tended to do with the predictable *Times*: Hulen was a company man in every sense, serving both his newspaper and the Administration. "He's peddling the official line. 'Facts' about Chinese pressure on our government. Oh!" She laughed. "He has inside information that Japan will back down in China *if* we cancel our economic restrictions." Caroline gave the proof back to the young man, who tiptoed from the joint Sanford presence.

"I can't see how any sovereign country would accept such an ultimatum." Blaise seemed more bewildered than alarmed while Caroline was simply alarmed. The scenario of the falling shoes was now in play.

"What is our editorial?" Caroline asked.

"Admonition." Blaise had been obviously preparing the word. "We ignore the AP and the State Department. We respond to the UP's report. We warn that the nation is not yet ready for a Pacific war."

Caroline agreed. Blaise went into the office next to hers. Caroline rang Currie at the White House. He was in a conference with something the operator referred to as "the War Cabinet." Then Caroline called in her secretary and dictated the next day's editorial. Later, she and Blaise would compare notes with the chief editorial writer, who would mandarinize their efforts. Curiously, he had taken well to her recent use of the word "pusillanimous," never suspecting its lofty origin.

As agreed, Senator James Burden Day arrived at exactly three in the afternoon. Caroline was, at first, somewhat dismayed by his appearance. He was unmistakably old. But then, on close examination, he was still handsome and the blue eyes shone much as they had when she seduced him, or had it been the other way around? In any case, she had fallen into his arms a virgin and arose, later, a woman fulfilled, *totally* fulfilled as it later proved, for she gave birth to Emma within the year, obliging her to persuade a dim but fortunately impoverished cousin named John Sanford to marry her, thus giving legitimacy to Emma and respectability to herself. During that period of planning and scheming and the deployment of troops, as she thought of her campaign to maintain an affair with Burden while creating a fairly convincing appearance of marriage with John, she had felt all-powerful if somewhat nervous, like Napoleon on that raft at . . . where was it? In Prussia . . .

"Tilsit," she whispered softly into Burden's ear as he embraced her with a surprising degree of warmth, considering the age of each.

"What?" They separated.

"I was trying to think of the place in Prussia where Napoleon . . . Oh, it's not important. I'm writing an editorial."

"You haven't started talking to yourself, like Kitty." He looked mildly alarmed.

"Nothing so . . . endearing." That was the *mot juste,* she thought; then she motioned for him to sit on the leather sofa while she sat in a straight chair, back erect, chin high but not high enough to reveal her neck in all its latest imperfections.

"Do you ever see our daughter?" he asked.

"Not for months. Do you?"

"No. But then she still doesn't know about me. I do keep an eye out for her. She's almost exactly Diana's age."

"Do they get on?"

"Different interests. Emma seemed happy at the FBI. But when Hoover got involved with the British secret service, she quit." He smiled. "She's a passionate isolationist. Like me."

"You are too sensible to be passionate."

"Only if we are attacked."

Caroline felt as if she had been suddenly administered an electric shock. There it was again, the phrase that would precipitate a war that she very much wanted if it meant the liberation of France but that, simultaneously, she did not want at all when she thought of the horrors that had befallen Europe during the Great War. In a sort of mindless daydream she had drifted through the past months, listening to Hopkins while hoping that, somehow, Hitler would be destroyed by Russia and the sorcerer's spell broken. Burden continued to talk while she flitted in and out of her fantasy. Finally, she tuned him in, as he was saying, "Yesterday the President told the War Cabinet . . ."

"A War Cabinet without a proper war."

"Not for long. I thought, as a responsible publisher . . ."

"I wonder if I am responsible. I am too much at court."

"Then perhaps it won't come as a shock to you to hear that FDR said, yesterday, that the Japanese are apt to attack us by next Monday."

"Then, today, he delivers his ultimatum which he knows will make an attack inevitable. Yes, the master plan is working nicely."

"Master plan?" Burden was tense. "But that's exactly why I'm here. I have proof he's been planning this all along."

Caroline was torn between loyalty to Hopkins and a not entirely extinct affection for her ancient lover and father to her admittedly unloved and unlovable child. "I think FDR has been *preparing* for this, which isn't quite the same thing as bringing it on." She had forgotten how quickly and easily and, she hoped, plausibly she could lie. A season at court had honed her skills. "No. From what I've seen of him I'm surprised that he hasn't attacked the Japanese first." This was first-rate. She commended herself.

"Wilson. Remember? He was reelected, barely, in 1916 'because he kept us out of war.' Then, once elected, he promptly got us into the war and the people punished him. Turned down his League of Nations. Turned against him. Roosevelt also lied to get himself reelected. But he was cleverer than Wilson. He kept saying again and again and again, no foreign wars *unless we are attacked.*" Burden tapped the UP story on the *Tribune's* front page. "Today, he has made sure that we will be attacked, perhaps next Monday, and then the country unites behind him and he'll be ready for a fourth and then a fifth term—why not a dictatorship for life?"

"That's a bit extreme," said Caroline, who tended to agree with Burden. She also did not in the least mind a Roosevelt dictatorship. She had never much liked what passed for a republic in her homeland. Why not try something else? She thought of her native land, France. In two hundred years, the French had tried two or three monarchies, a directory, a consulate, a couple of empires, several republics. She had lost count.

"I have a friend in the Navy. An admiral who knows a great deal about what the President's been up to. He thinks this ultimatum will lead to an immediate attack upon us. If it does, a number of us in the Senate will call upon the House of Representatives to bring an act of impeachment against the President."

"You are extreme," Caroline weakly reprised herself.

"War is extreme and he has started one, all on his own."

Caroline held her chin even higher. "Will your admiral tell what he knows?"

"It depends on events."

"When and where does he think the attack will come?"

Burden walked over to the map of the Pacific. "I have one of these in my office, too." He pointed to the North Pacific. "Since July much of the Japanese fleet has been in this area. This means that they will probably strike at Wake Island and Midway or Guam down here." He touched three specks in the pale blue paper vastness. "Since July they have been assembling their forces over here." His hand moved west to the main islands of Japan. "This is the Kure Naval Base, where Admiral Yamamoto's flagship is."

"Is it true that we have broken their codes?" On this subject, the War Department had been both peremptory and nervous. Thus far, with the threat of total censorship hanging over the press, no newspaper had yet done more than obliquely speculate.

"If I knew, I wouldn't say. But I don't really know. I do know we have excellent intelligence. We even have someone who reports to us directly from what they call the Throne. That is, from the center of everything where the Emperor receives his prime minister and the chiefs of staff and they decide on war or peace."

"They have already decided, haven't they?"

Burden nodded. "Their ambassadors have come here with two proposals. The first plan was for a mutual peaceful settlement. That was scuttled today by Hull with his ten-point ultimatum. The second plan, which they will be prosecuting in a week or so, in response to Hull, will be a declaration of war."

Caroline thought of Hopkins' almost casual admission that the United States was not ready to fight a war in the Pacific. Why, she wondered, had the President's shrewd stalling for time been so suddenly abandoned?

"Yesterday, the main Japanese fleet began to move east, in our direction. My naval friend is concerned about the lack of intelligence Washington has made available to the Pacific Fleet. Everything is filtered through the White House and the War Department. Before my friend left the Navy, he set up his own naval intelligence center in the Pacific and out of Washington's reach. He's been tracking Yamamoto. He's also tracking the Navy Department. They have done nothing except for an order from Admiral Stark—just this morning—to the naval commander at Pearl Harbor, telling him to send his two newest aircraft carriers, along with twenty-one other new ships, west toward Midway and Wake . . .”

“Where, presumably, they will meet Admiral Yamamoto on his eastern cruise.”

“Yes. It is . . . diabolic.”

“Or, maybe, very . . . complicated. There is something uncanny about Mr. Roosevelt, other than diabolism, of course. He leads so many lives. Last night he dined alone upstairs with Princess Martha. Eleanor had conveniently gone off to New York earlier to stay with lady friends and so . . . *What* do you want, Burden?”

Burden sat heavily on the leather sofa. “To talk. To talk to you. To talk to someone who knows far more than I do about Mr. Roosevelt and Mr. Hopkins.”

“I know character, perhaps, but I don’t know their war plans, if they have any. I get the sense that they are just drifting, waiting for something terrible to happen.”

“My naval friend thinks that we should bomb the Japanese fleet. Now.”

“So does Mr. Stimson. ‘It’s not too difficult,’ he told Hopkins, ‘maneuvering them into firing the first shot without them doing us a lot of damage in the process.’ ”

Burden nodded. “The first sensible thing I’ve ever heard attributed to Stimson. All right, what do I want? I’ll see to it that the *Tribune* gets the full story of what the President did and did not do. I’m holding sub-committee hearings in mid-December. All I want from you is fair coverage, something we’re not apt to get in the rest of the mainline press.”

“Oh, you can count on me, up to a certain point.”

“France?”

“France. But I think you’ve delayed too long. If there’s a war by Monday, there will be censorship on Tuesday. Also, I can’t see your other senators indicting—or whatever it is they do—the Commander in Chief in a time of peril.”

Burden shrugged. “We shall see what form the peril takes.” He smiled; shifted a gear. “I think about you—often.”

"I return the compliment."

"If I'd been free to marry . . ."

"I was never designed for marriage, other than the one of peculiar inconvenience that I was obliged to make, thanks to our . . ." She laughed at the phrase: ". . . love child."

As Caroline led him to the door, she tried to recall exactly what it was that she had once felt for him. Lust, she finally decided, giving herself moderately high marks for inner truthfulness. They embraced at the door. She felt in full control of herself not only now in the present but in the turbulent past tense as well.

"I gather that our offspring is in London," said Burden.

"Oh?" Caroline had no idea where Emma was.

"Yes. She's working on a film with your old friend Farrell. I assume you got him to hire her. Keep it all in the family, as they say." And with this unexpected haymaker, James Burden Day was gone, leaving the ever-cool, superbly well-balanced Caroline trembling with unanticipated rage.

Hopkins returned to the White House on December 3. The next day, at his invitation, Caroline went straight to his sitting room in the Lincoln suite. He was seated in an armchair, reading what looked to be War Department memoranda. "There you are!" He waved at her. "I had intended to leap boyishly to my feet but . . ."

"Don't." She kissed the top of his head. "Did they find out why you were having trouble walking?"

"Of course not. But whatever they did, I don't totter as much as before. Your paper is beginning to sound suspicious of us."

"That's only because we are. Because I am." Caroline sat opposite him, deliberately facing away from the portrait of a brooding Lincoln, the bad-luck, in her eyes, president. "I don't understand Hull's infamous ten points. You say you stall for time and then you order the Japanese out of China, out of everywhere, and expect them to obey you."

"Hull's given up. Hull . . ."

"It's not Hull. It's the President. Why?"

Hopkins placed the War Department documents facedown on a table beside him. "Hull should have waited one more day, because we had just come up with a brand-new series of delays. But this may all be for the best. We'll soon have the Japanese response to Hull."

"This morning General Tojo said that the United States will be driven from East Asia by a great wind."

Hopkins pulled himself out of his usual slouch. "A great wind?"

Caroline repeated Tokyo's cryptic message to the fleet that morning. "East wind rain."

Hopkins shook his head. "False alarm, I think. Most of their fleet is still in home waters."

"Except for six or seven aircraft carriers."

"Who tells you these things?"

"In the Washington whispering gallery all things are told."

"All things false as well as true. Senator Burden Day, I'll bet."

Caroline made a little speech on the sacredness of the relationship between a journalist and his sources; neither of them listened to her.

"Tell your spy in the Navy Department that much of the Japanese fleet is now heading south, toward Saigon. That's the area where they will take us on, and the British and the Dutch."

"Not the mid-Pacific? Not Wake Island?"

"Unlikely. They're close to home in the South Pacific. They're too close to us at Wake or Midway, too close to San Diego. We should have their answer to Hull by the weekend."

"How is the President?"

"He is well, thank you."

Caroline laughed. "I expected no more, in the way of information."

"You are asked to lunch on Sunday. Judge for yourself."

"Is Eleanor back?"

"Oh yes. And the Crown Princess of Norway has gone into purdah at her Bethesda, Maryland, castle."

"Young love will find a way," said Caroline and left Hopkins to his papers.

James Burden Day rang Caroline in her office at the Tribune. "For your private information, Admiral Stark cabled, on November twenty-eighth, all the Pacific Coast naval commanders, from Alaska down to Panama and over to Hawaii. Here's his message: 'If hostilities cannot repeat cannot be avoided the United States desires that Japan commit the first overt act.' My friend tells me that otherwise no information is getting through from the War Department to the Pacific." With that, Burden hung up.

Caroline went into Blaise's office. The ticker tape was clattering beside his desk: United Press—after November 26—was currently the news provider of choice. "All the Japanese embassies around the world are destroying their codes."

Caroline told Blaise what Burden had told her. "On the other hand, I think Harry really believes the danger to us is in the Philippines."

Blaise shuffled papers on his desk. "A garbled report's come in from Singapore. They are expecting a Jap attack at any moment. There is also a reference to some sort of secret mutual defense deal between the U.S. and England . . ."

"You mean between Roosevelt and Churchill?"

"Which isn't exactly the same thing, is it? I can't find the damned thing."

He rang for his secretary, an excited young man who said, "It's started coming through."

"That's very interesting. But what I want from you is that copy of . . ."

"*What* is coming through?" Caroline spoke now as the true founder-publisher of the modern *Tribune*.

"The answer to Mr. Hull's ten points. The Japanese Embassy is busy decoding it. There are fourteen parts. Thirteen are coming through now. The fourteenth, for some reason, won't come until tomorrow, just after noon."

Blaise dismissed his secretary. "So now we'll know."

"If we don't already," said Caroline. "I suspect that the war is already under way." She picked up the latest poll from Dr. Gallup. "I hope for Franklin's sake—well, for the war's sake—that the blow when it falls is decisive, because," she held up the latest poll, "over eighty percent of the unconsulted people of this model democratic republic are still against any foreign war."

"Unless," Blaise was uncharacteristically sardonic, "we suffer a surprise attack from a foreign power."

Eleanor Roosevelt embraced Caroline in a spontaneous outburst of affection. "I'm so glad you could come! We need cheering up." The lines about her eyes were deeper than ever, and though she smiled her great toothy Rooseveltian grin she kept frowning at the same time, an unnerving effect.

They were in the Red Room. The guest of honor at lunch was a British naval officer along with a number of Roosevelt cousins.

"You must be exhausted!" Caroline suddenly realized how fond she had become of Eleanor over the many years that they had known each other. "Since we can't get your column, we print your schedule. It's like the Court Circular. Her Majesty, accompanied by His Honor Mayor La Guardia of New York, inspected the nation's civil defense."

"Her Majesty also discovered that there is no civil defense of any kind on the West Coast." Eleanor completed the Circular. "Her Majesty disguised her ill pleasure as best she could while His Honor screamed epithets at every official in the state, including the heads of the fire departments. They are, he says, crucial. And, oh, how Fiorello can scream!"

"You are unlikely partners to be in charge of Civilian Defense."

"Perhaps too unlikely." Eleanor moved away as Hopkins came limping in from the adjacent Blue Room. He came straight up to Caroline.

"The President's not coming down to lunch, so I'm going up to lunch with him."

"The news is that bad?"

Hopkins nodded. "They have broken off all relations."

"Part fourteen?"

"Yes. It won't arrive officially until one p.m." He looked at his watch. "Now. But we got an advance look at it. Come upstairs. *After* lunch."

The lunch was no different from any other. Eleanor made dutiful conversation; and betrayed no anxiety. Caroline knew that she ought not to go upstairs on such a day, but as the invitation had been made, she also knew that nothing short of the Marine Guard could stop her. In the east-west corridor several military aides were hurrying in and out of the oval study. No one paid the slightest attention to her. The White House staff recognized her while the aides knew that, at any given moment, all sorts of ladies were apt to be staying with the Roosevelts. She did her best to look like a cousin, preferably Laura Delano; fiercely, she concentrated on turning her hair blue, in sculptured waves. She also concentrated on invisibility as she passed the study where Hopkins was slowly pacing up and down, papers in one hand. The President was at his desk, bent over the telephone, an untouched lunch in front of him. On another telephone an admiral was giving orders. Without permission or acknowledgment, military aides came and went, depositing cables on the President's desk.

Caroline slipped, unobserved, she thought, past the door en route to Hopkins' sitting room. But he had seen her. He led her to the Lincoln study. "Stay here in my room. Read this." He handed her what was the entire Japanese response, including the fourteenth part.

"Why did they delay sending it?"

Hopkins showed her into his study. "They delayed because, at one o'clock our time, just as we were enjoying their prose, they bombed our fleet at Pearl Harbor."

"It's not possible."

"That was my reaction. But the Boss has taken it all like a glacier. I was with him last night. He read the fourteenth part first. He gave it to me and he said, 'This means war.' Oh, we had a busy night."

"But where was naval intelligence in all this? The Japanese must have had an enormous fleet. Why no warning?"

Hopkins turned away. "We'll know soon enough."

"But you knew last night they would attack . . ."

"Attack, yes. But not Pearl Harbor. Somewhere. In the southwestern Pacific was my theory. But I did change my tune last night. I said, 'We ought to hit them first,' but the Boss said, 'No, we can't do that. We're a democracy.' This means that Congress would blame a first strike on him. 'We're a peaceful people,' he said. 'But we have a good record.'"

"What does that mean?"

Caroline knew that every word her friend was telling her was being said for the record, for history—for the defense?

"A good record of winning virtuous wars, I suppose. Anyway, we tried to get Admiral Stark but he was at the National Theatre, at a performance of, God help us, *The Student Prince*. The Boss knew it would cause a panic if he were paged so he talked to him later."

A military aide appeared in the doorway. "Sir . . ."

"I'm coming." Hopkins vanished into the busy corridor.

"May I?" Mrs. Roosevelt looked into the room. Caroline rose to her feet. "Please." Eleanor half-shut the door behind her. She looked exhausted. "I've come for a moment's peace, if you don't mind."

"It is your house."

"No. It is the nation's house." She sat down in a heavy wood mission rocking chair. "One tends to forget that until . . . something happens." She shut her eyes and rocked back and forth. From the corridor, many hushed voices could be heard. Military aides, secretaries, cabinet members were assembling—like ants when their hill has been kicked over.

Caroline had a thousand questions that she wanted to ask and so asked none. "I have four sons." Eleanor spoke with a degree of wonder. "They are all in the military or will be. What are the odds, with four?"

"I should think good."

"The last time there were all of Uncle T's boys, and one was killed. Franklin was eager to go, too, until Mr. Wilson ordered him to stay at the Navy Department. But one's own sons are different, aren't they?" Eleanor's eyes were moist. Caroline wished for Eleanor's sake that she would weep, let go. But instead she simply shut her eyes, as if she wanted, suddenly, in the midst of so much disaster to sleep her way out of it. "You have no son, do you?" This was Eleanor's spontaneous politeness. To include the other.

"Only a daughter."

"I remember—she must be married by now."

"Married. Divorced."

"The usual story these days." Eleanor opened her eyes; *they* were as usual. "I saw Mr. Farrell's film about England. We liked it very much. Mr. Churchill was delighted, of course. But then Mr. Farrell let him overact outrageously. What is Mr. Farrell doing now?"

Eleanor was obviously determined to put out of her mind the ships, sunken and aflame in Pearl Harbor.

"Tim will probably want to cover the war in the Pacific." Thus, Caroline mentioned the unmentionable. Quickly, she created a diversion. Chose drama. "Only I haven't heard from Tim in some time. You see, Emma, my daughter, is with him now."

"Wasn't she working in his film?"

"Yes. But they are also . . . they are now a couple, I am told. I suppose there are precedents for a mother to be replaced by her daughter but I've never actually known of one. But then, to be precise, Tim and I parted for good twenty years ago, in the most friendly way, and so I am no longer a part of the story."

"This," said Eleanor, "is rather the sort of thing that happens along the River." The River Families were, mostly, all related to each other and so given to complicated marital and extramarital arrangements. "I am sorry."

"No. No. Please. I am well out of it. I am only sorry for poor Tim. He is stuck with Emma, a fate one would not wish on an enemy much less an old friend."

Mrs. Roosevelt was now thoroughly distracted, the object of Caroline's exercise. In general, Eleanor seemed immune to gossip, but now, rather like a great psychoanalyst or whatever witch doctors were currently called, she wanted more and more details about Emma's general character, details which her mother was happy to provide, including her work with Fortress America, which brought a frown to Eleanor's pale brow. Then Caroline concluded with a revelation. "To my surprise, I think I am something that I have never been before—jealous."

"Never before? Oh, you *are* lucky! I'm afraid that I've always been jealous of those I care about, and since they are so very few, one's apt to become ridiculously jealous. Sooner or later, I always blame myself. I always try to forgive. And I think I do. Only . . ." The mouth was suddenly compressed to a straight line. "I never forget." She took a deep breath. "It is sad we never know where we have gone wrong as parents until it is far too late. My late mother-in-law felt that I had made every mistake one could make as a mother while I *knew* that she had made, deliberately, every mistake a grandmother can make, spoiling the children when I was away and undoing all my efforts to bring them up as they should be brought up or so I, perhaps wrongly, thought. This house has been no help." She went over to the window where Lincoln's desk had been so placed that he might get the southern—Confederate?—light. She stared a moment at the monument to Washington. "It is a terrible place to bring up children. With everyone flattering them because they want something from Franklin. There are times when I think there must be some sort of curse on this house."

"There is a curse on power."

"Not when used for others, or so I like to think."

"Where does one's own self leave off and that of others begin?"

"There are . . ." Suddenly, the great grin. ". . . markers, I believe, like no-trespassing signs. I keep running up against them all the time." She rose. "Now I must go write my radio broadcast. You've done me a world of good, Caroline."

"You do us all good."

"Now. Now. I am just an old politician of the wrong sex or the right sex but born at the wrong time." She was gone.

A moment later Hopkins limped into the room and stretched out on the sofa. "Eleanor . . ." He stopped.

"We talked about sons and daughters."

"She's ringing all her children now."

"How much damage did the Japanese do?"

"No one knows. But just about every ship in the harbor was hit.

They've also attacked Hong Kong, Malaya, Guam, the Philippines, Wake, Midway. He'll address Congress tomorrow." Hopkins sighed. "It's an awful thing to say but this is a terrible weight off all of us. No more waiting. No more stalling. Everything plain."

"Did you expect so many shoes to fall at once?"

"Shoes? Oh, yes. Well, now, we're a bit worried about the West Coast. Without Pearl Harbor, we're vulnerable to air attack. Even invasion. The Boss thinks we can certainly turn them back by the time they get to Chicago."

"You're joking."

"He's only thinking ahead, which is what he is paid to do."

Caroline restrained herself from remarking that if the President had been seriously thinking ahead in the last year the United States might still possess its Pacific Fleet.

Hopkins was on another tack. "I think we should find a job for Wendell Willkie. He's eager. The Boss likes him. They've become sort of pen pals." Hopkins appeared to be talking to himself rather than to Caroline. "What a ticket that would be in '44. Roosevelt and Willkie."

"A *fourth* term?"

"Why not? Unless the war is won by then. In which case, we can all go home."

"Politics never stops, does it?"

Hopkins made no answer.

Caroline rose. "I'll be covering the Capitol tomorrow. For the paper." Hopkins nodded; his eyes were shut again. "Oh?" She stopped at the door. "What ever happened to Hitler?"

Hopkins chuckled. "Don't worry. We never lose track of him. He went into winter quarters yesterday. He's been bluffing the Japanese. He had them convinced that Moscow and Leningrad were about to surrender any day now, which meant that this was the best time for them to hit us. Now Adolf's taking a well-deserved rest. Moscow and Leningrad are safe, and the Japanese are busy committing suicide. In a few days, Hitler will do something very unusual for him, he'll actually honor a treaty. The one with Japan. He'll declare war on us. Is Mrs. Woodrow Wilson still alive?"

"Yes. Why?"

"I think history requires for Eleanor to sit with her tomorrow when the Boss makes his speech."

Eleanor did sit with Mrs. Woodrow Wilson while Caroline was squeezed into a corner of the press gallery. The President struck all the right notes. The face that had yesterday been gaunt and gray was now its usual ruddy color. The voice was resonant and firm as he looked out over the combined houses of Congress, Cabinet, Supreme Court. He spoke of the "surprise" attack as a day that would "live in infamy," yet, thought Caroline, it came as no surprise to anyone except the American people, as always kept in the dark. Nevertheless, he made his case; then, almost graciously, he said, "We may acknowledge that our enemies have performed a brilliant feat of deception, perfectly timed and executed with great skill." Thus, most eloquently, he described his own tactics that had got him the war that he had so dearly wanted for reasons which Caroline hoped were virtuous because if they were not . . .

In the crowd, after the official declaration of war, Caroline found James Burden Day and Arthur Vandenberg standing in front of the glass swing doors that led into the Senate chamber. Vandenberg was owl-solemn; Burden was grim.

Caroline congratulated Vandenberg on his blessedly brief speech to the Senate before the vote was taken.

"Unity is all-important." Vandenberg shook his jowls menacingly. "When the war's been won, we can argue about how the Administration might have avoided it."

"Or, worse, might have provoked the attack," said Burden.

"All that's for later. We mustn't seem to be playing politics, particularly not now with all the dead and the dying in Hawaii."

Caroline asked if any figures had come through.

Burden nodded. "Something like three thousand men are thought to be lost aboard the ships."

Vandenberg slipped away. Burden was bitter. "We were all set to investigate this whole matter but now Arthur is too busy playing at being statesman to be one."

"Were you at the White House yesterday, with the other congressional leaders?"

"No. I was the one leader *not* asked. Roosevelt knows that I am on to his game. He also knows that now, with all the panic building, he's home free."

As if on cue, a reporter from the *Tribune* hurried over to Caroline to tell her that San Francisco had just been bombed.

Caroline turned to James Burden Day. "How long a war will it be?"

"The last one was only a year for us. Four years for the Europeans."

Caroline was suddenly struck with what was, for her, an entirely new thought. "Why, if this war should be profitable for us, shouldn't it go on forever? Particularly if," she thought of Hopkins' line, "we gain the world."

"Countries wear out."

"Countries also change. Like people. In fact, most of us tend to become what we have always hated."

"What have you always hated?"

Caroline remembered to smile. "Old age. And the weakening of the mind."

"You are in no immediate danger of either." Then, gallantly, he led her across the rotunda with its numerous crude statues of forgotten American statesmen. As they walked, admirers shook Burden's hand. "Little do they know that I have now become what *I* have always hated."

"What is that?"

"Powerless," he said.

E I G H T

|

Caroline stepped through the open French window onto the rose brick terrace and into the full heat of the day. Opposite her, Frederika cowered in the shade of a striped umbrella, weakly fanning herself with the society section of the family newspaper. "This is *not* October weather." Caroline kissed her sister-in-law's cheek, redolent of eau de cologne.

"It is unseasonable," Frederika whispered as a one-eyed butler placed a tea tray in front of her. "Thank you, Lionel," she smiled vaguely.

"It's George, Mrs. Sanford."

"I know, Lionel."

Lionel-George withdrew.

"He lost an eye in North Africa. Before that he worked for Vincent Astor. Between the two, I must say I'd prefer North Africa . . . with both eyes, of course. Poor Lionel was the last butler on offer at the agency. He couldn't be nicer except that he lost his depth perception along with the eye. He pours wine straight onto your lap."

"We must make some small sacrifice for the war effort." Caroline mopped her upper lip with a muslin sleeve. "Laura Delano has warned us that the servant class will not survive the war. They will simply wither away."

"Too sad." Frederika seemed unperturbed as she poured them tea. Caroline ate a star-shaped cucumber sandwich, a specialty of Laurel House. "Blaise thinks we should sell the place."

"Will anyone want so large a place, with no servants?"

"Oh, there are always embassies. And schools for disturbed girls. You know, the usual sort of buyers. Of course, we still have the Massachusetts Avenue house, though that's also far too big. I shouldn't in the least mind crawling into one of those hideous brick ovens in Georgetown, like Joe Alsop."

"I think you'd mind very much. At least here you're cool indoors. Harry Hopkins says the White House is an inferno now."

"I thought all the windows were blacked out after Pearl Harbor. That should cool things."

"Just the opposite. And since Franklin won't permit air-conditioning the house is as musty and depressing as Tutankhamen's tomb." What was it she had intended to say? With failing memory, Caroline had taken to making mental lists. Tombs? "Oh, yes! Speaking of tombs, Wendell Willkie died last night. In New York. Heart."

"So young! How lucky for Franklin that poor Wendell wasn't his running mate this year. For the fourth term!" Frederika let the newspaper drop to the terrace. "A *fourth* term? Who would ever have imagined such a thing?"

I would, thought Caroline. Between the victories of the Russian army on the ground in Europe and the American victories at sea and in the air against Japan, it had been clear since the Allied invasion of Europe that each half of the global war was drawing to a close. As a result, every Democratic politician, including Burden, had been positioning himself to succeed Roosevelt in the election of 1944. But Caroline had known, instinctively, that FDR meant to reign and to rule for all his life and so he would run for a fourth term and, as a matter of course, win. Although there were many disturbing stories about the President's health—some no doubt true—she rather doubted that the sixty-one-year-old Roosevelt would forgo so great a triumph as a lifetime presidency during which the United States would, in effect, govern most of Europe and Asia. He must also rule long enough in order to accomplish what his mentor, Woodrow Wilson, had so dramatically failed to do—create a world organization in order to maintain a permanent American peace.

After a quiet summer, the President was now on the move across the Midwest, addressing huge crowds, while the Republican candidate, Thomas E. Dewey, having taken to heart the criticism that his carefully studied statesmanlike campaign of four years earlier had lost him the election, had metamorphosed into a prosecuting attorney, attacking the President with all the fury of a terrier tightly leashed by wartime censorship, not to mention by the aura of a president grown mythical to an electorate hardly able to recall any other sovereign.

Caroline opened her handbag; withdrew a United Press report. "He should be in Chicago today. He's going to promise sixty million new jobs after the war. And no depression."

"Bad luck to count your eggs before they are even laid." Frederika clung uneasily to folk wisdom; then she asked the butler for Dubonnet and ice. "Caroline?"

"Nothing, thank you . . . George." George smiled his gratitude at Caroline and went inside. She continued, "You know, I was actually in the Cabinet room when Wendell Willkie came to pay a call on the President. It was the morning that Harry and the President were going over the third inaugural address . . ."

"*Third!* I still can't get used to any of this. It makes our country seem like . . . like Santo Domingo, without the loud music."

"With no music at all. Anyway, Grace Tully came rushing in to say that Mr. Willkie had arrived to pay his respects to the President, who had forgotten all about him. So Franklin rolled his own chair to the door. When I offered to help him, he said, 'No, we would both be compromised.' He was gleeful that day."

"Old goat . . . in *his* day, anyway."

"Young goat, then. Anyway, he'd got as far as the door when he said to Harry, 'Hand me some papers.' Well, the Cabinet table was piled high with every sort of paper. 'Which ones?' Harry asked, and Franklin said, 'Just grab anything. I want to spread them all over my desk so that Willkie can see just how busy I am, and what a killing job the presidency is.'"

Frederika took the Dubonnet and soda from the butler. "Thank you, Lionel."

"Actually, the two of them were already planning on 1948, Roosevelt and Willkie . . ."

"Not a *fifth* term." Softly, Frederika moaned.

"No. No. A first term for Wendell at the head of a new party. With Franklin up at Hyde Park, writing his memoirs and pulling the strings. They were planning to spend the next four years joining the liberal wing of the Democratic Party to the liberal wing of the Republican Party."

"Nonsense!" Frederika was obscurely firm. Frederika was also not so interested in what might have been as in what was: "Franklin had a heart attack last week. From his angina."

At that moment a handsome young woman with a sun-flushed face appeared on the terrace; she was carrying a small girl. Behind them, a nurse in white uniform kept watch over both.

"Enid." Frederika motioned for her daughter to join them while her granddaughter climbed onto her lap in order to inspect the sandwiches. "I thought you'd gone back to . . . uh, back to . . ."

"To prison?" Enid's smile was pretty. "My parole has been extended. Hello, Aunt Caroline . . ."

"I never see you," said Caroline, somewhat inanely since Enid was more often than not in the care of one Dr. Paulus, whose home-away-from-home clinic in the Virginia woods was not only a refuge for those whose nerves had been unduly frayed by life's exigencies but, if one also followed Dr. Paulus's special regimen long enough, the need for unnatural stimuli would gradually cease and one would be "made whole again," as he put it in his gentle evangelical way, so at variance with Enid's brisk "He means he'll get you off the sauce and out of the way."

On Caroline's only visit to the sanitarium, she had been inhibited by Blaise's presence. She had sat in the parlor while father and daughter made stilted conversation. In fact, so much was *not* said between them that Caroline, in the car on the way back to Laurel House, bluntly asked, "Why on earth is she in that ridiculous place?"

Blaise put up the window between them and the chauffeur. "She tried to kill herself."

"Since you've always found her a problem, why didn't you encourage her?"

"I am sure that sounds very witty in French . . ."

"It doesn't sound too bad to me in English. What are you up to, Blaise?"

"She is an alcoholic. She also takes morphine when she can get it."

"Who doesn't? Morphine, that is. I certainly did when I was younger, in Hollywood. But never alcohol! Ruins your looks. You wanted her out of the way. Why?"

Blaise was getting red in the face. "She has a child . . ."

"Who has an excellent, dedicated nurse. . . . No. It's Clay Over-bury, isn't it? Her man-of-destiny husband. She is an embarrassment, isn't she?" Caroline had been as impressed as everyone else by Clay's leonine beauty. For years an invaluable secretary to James Burden Day, he had also been, everyone agreed, a congressman soon-to-be until the war claimed him. Now he was on duty in the Pacific, where his recent exploits during the reconquest of the Philippines had been featured not only in the *Tribune* but also nationally in Harry Luce's *Life* magazine, ever eager for a photogenic conservative hero.

"Clay could have a great political career . . ."

"What is that to you, if I may pry?" Caroline had always thought her brother overly susceptible to his son-in-law's . . . what? It couldn't be simply beauty. "The son you never had? Is that the not so dusty answer?"

Blaise turned away from her and looked out the window at Virginia's state capitol, so like the national one in miniature. "Perhaps."

"I prefer Peter."

"Because he's like you. He'll say anything. You know, he's joined up with Burden's son-in-law. The communist with the wooden leg. They want to start a magazine and they want me to pay for it. A *liberal* magazine."

"I assume you said no."

"Peter's clever." Blaise was always oddly grudging about his son. "He'll do well. Without me. While . . ."

"Clay Overbury needs you." That was the end of their discussion.

Now on the terrace, Caroline took Enid by the arm. "Let's take a stroll. I have been neglecting my duties as an aunt, lately."

"Lately?"

"At my age, thirty years is like thirty minutes, and all of it is always lately."

Frederika warned: "Stay out of the sun. Both of you. It makes your hair grow."

Caroline patted her head. "Good. I am getting dangerously thin on top."

"I mean," said Frederika, feeding a small cake to her granddaughter, "the hairs on your body. Modern girls on the beach look like monkeys, with horrid long hairs on their arms and legs . . ." She shuddered and pulled a lace shawl close about her.

Caroline and Enid descended the pink marble steps edged with boxwood. "Mother gets these strange notions." Enid sounded tranquil. The swimming pool was now in view.

"Like that sanitarium for alcoholics?"

"Well, that's not so strange. I am what's known as an alcoholic, I think. At least I do get very drunk and sometimes . . . I paint, you know."

"I didn't. But until you cut off an ear . . ."

"Oh, I'm not that good. Not that bad, either." They stopped at the pool's edge. A cool breeze suddenly stirred the woods back of the connecting cabins that served as a pool house. Enid pointed to the cabin on the left. "That's for the boys. The other's for the girls. It was in the boys' changing room, one hot summer night, during a storm, while there was a party up at the house, that I was deflowered, on the floor, on a pile of men's Jantzen bathing suits."

"It sounds a bit soggy."

"Actually, I thought it was quite romantic. I still get a bit of a shiver when I smell chlorine . . ."

"And Clay Overbury's wet Jantzen?"

Enid laughed. "Actually, we started out in dinner clothes. It was some sort of celebration for old Burden Day . . ."

Caroline winced at the adjective. "Old" Burden. "Old" Caroline. Were they slipping offstage so noticeably? "I must have been in Hollywood then."

"It was the year you played Mary Stuart. I liked that picture. Where you had your head chopped off. Just as they are going to chop off mine." Enid began, noiselessly, to weep. Caroline, who had never before played the scene of kindly old aunt comforting young—mad?—niece, embraced Enid, whose tears, with surprising rapidity, passed. "I'm sorry." Enid took Caroline's proffered handkerchief and blew her nose.

"Why?"

"Why what?"

"All this nonsense. That peculiar doctor in the woods when you can be . . . looked after just as well at home. Why have they put you away?"

"Because my father wants Clay all to himself."

Caroline was unsurprised. "That's obvious."

"Oh, it's not what you think."

"How do you know what I think?"

"You are French." Enid smiled. "A movie star . . ."

"Neither the French nor movie stars take sex as seriously as Americans who live in Washington do. As I see it—or part of it—Blaise wants a son who will have a great political career. He has selected Clay. So if you . . . make scenes, are difficult, you must be kept out of sight. Simple as that."

Enid's frown made her very much as Caroline imagined her own mother to have looked when bent upon some murderous task. Beautiful, hard, dark. "Nothing that gets in my path can ever be simple. Particularly for me." This was followed by a radiant smile. "Peter's my ally, you know."

"May I join the . . . unpopular front?"

"You can certainly be a fellow traveler."

At the terrace, Enid dutifully kissed Frederika and Caroline farewell; and then she led her child into the house, where the nurse was waiting. Presently, doors shut; a car could be heard driving away.

Frederika looked at Caroline. "What do you think?"

"She seems no crazier than anyone else in this city."

"She terrifies me." Frederika's voice quavered. "She is so menacing."

Caroline could not believe what she was hearing. "Are you sure that 'menacing' is the right word?"

"When she is drinking or on drugs, she is quite another person. . . ."

Caroline was less than impressed. "Surely, that is *why* she drinks. That's why we all do—or did, in my case, long, long ago—to be a different person. For a time. Why not?"

"She is . . . violent."

"I suspect she will only turn it upon herself. The real question is, what have you and Blaise and Clay done to get her to this state?"

"Lionel!" The butler arrived with another Dubonnet. "Thank you, George. Caroline?"

Caroline ordered a Tom Collins. "To ward off the heat." Except that she was actually somewhat chilly.

"I can never forget that book of yours about your grandfather, and about how Blaise's mother killed your mother. These things so often run in families, you know."

For the hundredth time, Caroline explained that it was her mother's neglect that had led to the death of Blaise's mother. "If there is a killer trait, I—not Blaise—inherited it, which means that my daughter, Emma, not your Enid, is the one to avoid in the dark."

Frederika changed the subject. "How is Emma?"

"She is still with Timothy Farrell . . ."

"That name sounds familiar. Wasn't he . . . ?"

"Yes, Frederika, he was." A bit of Frederika went an astonishingly long way—a way along which Caroline was suddenly too weary to travel further. She rose to go. "You must let Enid come home to her own house and to the child."

"Of course." Frederika's gracious hostess voice meant that she had stopped listening. "I'll see you to your car. We must all write that nice Mrs. Willkie. She was so good about Wendell's mistress."

"A model Republican wife."

"You are cynical, dear." As they passed the library, Caroline inhaled the nostalgic smell of old wood smoke and summer's last roses. "Does one write the mistress too?"

"Of course," said Caroline, enjoying the consternation such a letter would cause Mrs. Willkie, particularly from a stranger. Happily, Frederika would forget all about it. At the door, Frederika said, "When does Franklin think the war will end?"

"He says not until 1947."

"Oh, no! I don't think I can take three more years of this." She frowned. "How does he know it won't be until 1947?"

"Because that's what a highly respected astrologist has predicted. He was much impressed."

"Really?" Frederika was somewhat awed. "I hadn't thought Franklin was so . . . so very sensitive. I mean, reading nothing but detective stories and the Gallup Poll, the way he does, I wouldn't have thought . . . Even so, three more years . . ."

2

Peter had very early found a place for himself in Army Air Corps Intelligence, known as A-2 at the Pentagon. Although officially classified as a lowly "clerk nontypist," Peter found that his connection with the *Tribune* was of considerable use to the Air Corps publicity machine while his connection with A-2 was equally useful to the *Tribune*. As a wise assistant secretary of war—an old acquaintance of Blaise's—had explained to him, the principal task of Air Corps Intelligence was to glorify the American air force in the world press.

Peter's section was a most unmilitary collection of former newspapermen, professional writers, and schoolteachers. Despite their uniforms, they performed few military duties; instead they transmitted, or even invented if necessary, astonishing victories in the air over Europe and Asia. Happily, as of the first Tuesday in November of 1944, their creative talents were no longer so urgently needed. The Philippines had been reconquered. In a firestorm of publicity, General MacArthur had waded ashore, corncob pipe clenched between his teeth; all cameras were upon him as he declared, "I have returned." Meanwhile, the Germans were preparing a counteroffensive on their western front. At this point, Peter thought that honest reporting might be enough but for some—aesthetic?—reason, it seldom was; his section chief, Warrant Officer Aeneas Duncan, thought that this was due to the lead set them by such privileged journalists as Drew Pearson and Walter Winchell. Peter knew (and Aeneas did not) of Ernest Cuneo's highly privileged sources, duly vetted by the White House.

Prewar, Aeneas had been a lecturer at something called the New School for Social Research in New York. He wrote on philosophy in scholarly journals. He was also fascinated by American political history, a bond with Peter. Recently divorced from his wife, Aeneas was now seeing a child psychologist with a practice in Manhattan. Since she was pregnant, he intended to marry her once he was free of the Army.

Meanwhile, he wrote, as did Peter, for *The American Idea*. Since members of the armed services were under tight censorship, they published, somewhat nervously, under pseudonyms.

A serial smoker, Aeneas had fore and center fingers stained dark yellow. Comfortably, he coughed on his own smoke. "The first study I'm going to write once we've been liberated from the Pentagon is on the absolute failure of airpower. What we've been selling the public is just a variation on the Lindbergh syndrome. The Lone Eagle. High in the sky. Remote from earth. Prey only to gravity as he drops his bombs, usually on the wrong targets, while the real victories are being fought, as always, by infantry, by Marines on land. They take back—along with sea power—Pacific islands. They reconquer France, occupy Italy, all on the land, where the dying's done. Basically, we do fireworks. Frighten off demons. Like Chinese New Year. And, of course, kill civilians."

Peter and Aeneas worked in an office for four. Since the omnipotent bureaucratic table of organization had never got around to providing them with two missing helpers, they were able to assemble stories that would then be passed up the line to an energetic colonel who pretended that their work was his work, which he, in turn, submitted to a conclave of intelligence cardinals whose imprimatur transformed the art of Peter and Aeneas into world news and the primary stuff of history.

Aeneas seldom strayed far from their office while Peter liked nothing better than to explore the miles of antiseptic Pentagon corridors where, it was said, if you walked far enough and long enough you were bound to meet yourself coming from the opposite direction, a nice metaphysical exercise in quantum physics, a subject that they had recently, mysteriously, been ordered to read up on. Aeneas had thought that this probably had something to do with the much-whispered-about secret bomb that had been in the works since the start of the war. "Hitler's got that last-minute buzz bomb of his so now we must come up with something even more exciting." Aeneas was skeptical about doomsday weapons. "It's all a bit late in the game."

"Late in the game or not, Hitler's bomb is doing an awful lot of damage. And it's airpower, too."

"But it's not *our* sort of airpower. How can we glorify a bomb without a pilot? Without a hero? Forget it." Aeneas opened his desk drawer and removed the latest issue of *The American Idea*. "Some good stuff on the postwar world, if there is one."

Peter was edgy. "Keep it in the drawer. We could be court-martialed."

"Why? We divulge no secrets . . ."

"But we question what our own office divulges." For over a year the review, printed on ugly wartime pulp paper, had been slowly gaining an audience. Irene Bloch had financed them in exchange for an introduction to Frederika, while Billy Thorne openly acted as editor even though he was a civilian employee of the War Department. For reasons obscure to Peter, Billy was being unofficially encouraged by intelligence to edit *The American Idea*. Aeneas suspected that elements within the government were deliberately, secretly, supporting a publication highly critical of government policies in Europe.

Aeneas tended to take a Jesuitical line. "If they *are* giving Billy money and they really understand what the paper is doing, then some uncharacteristically intelligent people have infiltrated intelligence." The telephone on Aeneas's desk rang. He was all attention. "Yes, Colonel. The B-29? Yes, sir. I've seen one. Never seen a plane so large, like . . . like a skyscraper lying on its side." Thriftily, Aeneas made a note of his own phrase. The colonel's voice kept talking and Aeneas responded with numerous "Yes, sirs." Then he hung up. "They want a big B-29 story. The superplane story for . . . what?"

"The superweapon?"

"I'll believe it when I see it." For two years there had been wild rumors of an astonishing new bomb that was guaranteed to sink, one by one, Japan's imperial islands but, thus far, the bomb was myth.

The rest of the day was spent assembling the first of a series of stories on the B-29 bomber and its legendary range, capable of abolishing the Pacific's vast distances in order to avenge Pearl Harbor—at last.

Peter and Aeneas joined Diana and Billy Thorne at the Flying Tiger, a Chinese restaurant that was a favorite of military men more at home in offices than foxholes or cockpits. As always in wartime, women outnumbered men three to one, much as men had outnumbered women during the last century when mostly single men had swept from east to west in pursuit of California gold. Now, during the war years, a reverse tide of adventurous young women had abandoned village or country life for whatever work they could find in the capital. Failing that, there were a million jobs available in the factories of less glamorous cities.

The heavy perfume from aromatic joss sticks set in brass candle-holders mingled with the smell of beer and sealike soy sauce. Clouds of blue cigarette smoke gave an indistinct infernal look to the diners in their booths.

Just back of Peter's table, a radio had been set on the bar. Although the presidential election was underway, hardly anyone in the Flying Tiger paid the slightest attention to the predictable results. Everyone knew that the haggard old wizard could not lose. Had he not always been president? That was simply the order of things.

Peter ordered dinner.

"FDR wins larger than last time." Billy's voice was gravelly, authoritative. "That's the word from our office."

"What *is* your office?" Aeneas was mild. "Other than totally secret. And where is it?"

"We're all over the place. Nothing very exciting. We're information mostly. Nonmilitary. My end, anyway. Economic reporting. Very useful for *The American Idea.*"

"They don't even mind that Billy was once a communist," said Diana sweetly, delighting Peter, who never ceased to look for proofs of Diana's serene nonlove for the husband that she had so thoughtlessly married.

"The fact I'd once been a communist got me the job. Fact, our office is a sort of comintern of ex-Reds. The chief's also been very good about the review. Of course, I'm only a *civilian* employee. I'm not under the military code."

"Will we ever know who your chief is?" Peter suspected that it was someone high up in the Office of Strategic Services, the invention of one Wild Bill Donovan, a New York lawyer, politician, adventurer, who had created an international spy service for the President. As far as Peter could tell, General Donovan spent most of his time in Europe while the core of his staff was hidden away, according to fantasists, back of the aquarium in the basement of the Commerce Building. But whether or not Billy's supervisor was in or out of the aquarium, he seemed to be both patient and civilized from the hints, many of them broad, that Billy let fall from time to time. "You'd be surprised if you knew who he was." One of Billy's eyes was a sincere brown; the other a bright liar's blue. He blinked the brown one at Peter, who wondered, as always, if either of Billy's eyes could ever be believed.

"I would be surprised," said Peter, "I'd ever heard of him. After all, we're not supposed to know who's a spy and who isn't."

"Actually, he isn't a spy. He's an intelligence analyst."

"What's being analyzed at the moment?" Aeneas poured Chinese beer into a glass.

"Can't say."

"Why not?" murmured Diana. "Sooner or later you always do."

"Cover stories." But Billy was plainly stung by Diana's offhandedness. This was not, Peter decided happily, going to be a long marriage. "I'll tell you what's on the Chief's mind. And should be on ours, too. A year ago November, our military production peaked. Last month it started to fall off. During the last German offensive we were so short of ammunition that Hitler nearly sent us back across the Rhine." Billy narrowed both eyes. "Something's gone wrong. We aren't making enough war matériel. And we aren't making enough refrigerators either."

This caught Aeneas's attention. "We still haven't started to convert to peacetime?"

"No," said Billy.

Opposite them, a group of Nationalist Chinese soldiers were singing, in off-key falsetto, the German army's favorite song, "Lili Marlene."

"For some reason, the Pentagon's doing its best to keep us permanently on a wartime footing while . . ."

"At war with whom?"

Billy shrugged. "It's hardly a secret. A lot of the military brass want an all-out war with Russia just as soon as Hitler's got rid of."

Peter and Aeneas exchanged a glance. Hardly a day passed that someone at the Pentagon didn't say what a shame it was that we weren't on Hitler's side against the true enemy, Stalin. Whenever one of these geopoliticians was encouraged to explore the matter more deeply, he would invariably say that Franklin and Eleanor Roosevelt were a pair of communists who had got us into a world war on the wrong side. Peter was constantly amazed at the boldness with which certain officers expressed themselves. Although Aeneas took none of them seriously, Peter was sufficiently alarmed to suggest that perhaps the best way to avert a possible military coup would be to muster everyone out the instant the war was won. Simply send them all home.

"I don't think," said Diana mildly, "that the American people are ready for another world war."

"But they may not be ready for peace either." Billy opened a fortune cookie; read the fortune; tore it up with a frown. "Fourteen million men are in the military. We have full employment for the first time ever. But if we just stop. Send everyone home. Will the Depression come back? That's what terrifies the Administration."

"You really think things are going so fast?" Aeneas seemed unconvinced. "I have a hunch there are a lot of surprises up ahead."

Diana promptly provided them with one. "It seems—according to Father—that Governor Dewey knows all about what really happened at Pearl Harbor."

"Why hasn't he used it?" Aeneas had not yet grown accustomed to the Byzantine way that Washington went about the careful planting, nurturing, and gathering of rumors in every season.

"Because General Marshall got to Dewey." With time's passage, Peter had become more and more pro-Roosevelt despite—because of?—the President's inspired and inspiring lies, while Diana—out of love for her father—grew more and more impatient with FDR's high-handed imperial ways.

Peter addressed Aeneas, the only innocent at the table. "I know how hard it is to believe that so righteous a good soldier as Marshall would insist that Dewey lie about what only a few of us know really happened and—worse—didn't happen that Sunday December morning, still living on contentedly in infamy, but just as there is a time to live in infamy there is a time to cover ass . . ."

"Father says Marshall went to Dewey entirely on his own and warned him how this story would tear the country apart and, if it did, Dewey, not FDR, would be the villain."

"For telling the truth?" Aeneas's surprise was genuine. "And Dewey backed down?"

"Of course." Diana was matter-of-fact. "In the middle of a terrible war that we are winning the President's opponent is not about to blame him for all those hundreds of thousands of men lost through a . . . deadly provocation."

"No one tears down Old Glory by dawn's early light." Peter had now grasped Marshall's actual motive. "Marshall is the one man everyone trusts. If Dewey were to reveal that Marshall had an active role in the Japanese attack—how he knew that the attack was on its way but refused to alert Pearl Harbor—then General Marshall could take his place in our history alongside Benedict Arnold."

"FDR too," said Billy, who had not, Peter was pleased to note, entirely grasped the subtlety of the play.

"No." Peter was firm. "The Artful Dodger always gets out of scrapes like this. Dewey and the truth are no match for such extrahuman skills. Had Dewey dared attack, it would have been the noble Marshall who would have fallen upon his sword." Peter turned to Diana. "And so, as a patriot, Marshall talked patriot Dewey out of doing *his* patriotic duty."

Diana nodded. "That's what Father thinks. But how can we ever be sure?"

"FDR's being elected for a fourth term tonight, isn't he? And tomorrow Dewey will be returning to his lucrative New York practice. What more proof is required?"

The Chinese Nationalists were now singing in atonal mode—still in varying degrees of falsetto—"Besame Mucho," complete with authentic Mexican accent. On a hearty round of applause for their Chinese allies, Peter and Diana left, followed by Billy and Aeneas. The radio on the bar still continued to report election returns but no one was listening. Soon, Peter thought, with a great leap of his imagination, we will be in the post-Roosevelt world. Meanwhile, the old man was good for at least another four years.

3

On Saturday, January 20, 1945, Caroline was shown into the White House. Unescorted, she made her way up the stairs to the study where the inaugural guests were gathering. For the first time since the early days of the republic there was to be no parade and no celebration of any kind, while a mere five thousand members of the public fulfilled their choric duty by standing in the freezing slush of the South Lawn, eyes raised to the South Portico, where the President would take his oath of office.

Caroline knew very few of the guests personally; but she knew almost every face. These were the now historic figures of the New

Deal: members of the Cabinet, heads of bureaus, justices of the Supreme Court, as well as congressional figures, among whom the Republican Vandenberg took up his usual considerable space. Plainly, Roosevelt was not about to make Wilson's mistake of ignoring the opposition party when it came to creating a world peace organization.

There were also a great many children on hand as well as a number of unlikely-looking figures that could only be eccentric Roosevelt relatives—Delano, too. Laura's blue head was held high as she sailed toward Caroline; as always, Laura was talking. ". . . and now it's war at last. Did you see the papers?"

"Which war at last?"

"Mrs. Nesbitt and Franklin. He solemnly vowed that this time, if he won reelection, he was finally going to fire Mrs. Nesbitt. Well, look!"

Laura showed Caroline a copy of Cissy's newspaper. In bold headlines, *Mrs. Nesbitt Rejects President's Ultimatum of Chicken à la King for Inaugural.* " 'You can't serve two thousand people a hot dish like that in January,' says Mrs. Nesbitt. 'He's getting chicken salad.' "

Caroline sympathized. "Will he ever be able to get rid of her?"

"Only if he divorces Eleanor first. Anyway, those White House guests who really matter know enough to get something to eat *before* coming to a meal here. Have you seen Franklin lately?"

Caroline shook her head. "He's been somewhat busy. And I've been busy, too. Winding up things."

Laura found a glass of sweet California sauterne, the Roosevelt staple wine. To Caroline's horror, she dropped two tablets of saccharine into the wine and waited for them to dissolve. "I can't say I care for the way he's looking." Laura sipped her enhanced wine. "He's too thin. Cadaverous, really. Between him and Harry Hopkins it's like a hospital ward." Laura moved on to a group of relatives clustered by the fire.

Caroline sat beside Hopkins on the sofa nearest the door. "Where's your wife?"

"Mingling with Roosevelts. This is family day."

Hopkins' face was so white that his eyes looked black. "We're traveling soon."

"Tomorrow, they say. Together?"

Hopkins did not answer. "He's still insisting on unconditional surrender."

"Doesn't that prolong the war?"

Hopkins shrugged. "There are always special conditions for an unconditional surrender. Anyway, it has a nice sound of finality. And, of course, it's what Lincoln and General Grant insisted on, back in the Civil War. Why do we never see you?"

"You are a couple. A family. In Georgetown. I am only a widow. And not so merry."

"When I come back, try to stop in . . ."

"In Georgetown?" Since Caroline and Harry's wife, Louise, had nothing at all in common except Harry and as he proved to be far too much for just one or the other, Caroline had properly left the field to the wife.

"Of course not in Georgetown." Harry's smile was sardonic. "I meant here. The White House. I've never seen the Boss so lonely. Eleanor has taken to the open road. Missy's dead. And I'm hardly here anymore."

"Health?"

Hopkins waved to friends across the room. Presently, Caroline would lose him to the great world. "Partly health. Partly fatigue. I'm viewed with suspicion. Too many people think I'm pro-British. Pro-Russian. Pro-communist . . ."

"Does that make the President nervous?"

"Hard to tell with him. He must deal so often with the appearances of things that you never know what actually matters to him as opposed to what *looks* to matter."

"Surely they are the same thing. You must seem to get along with Stalin for the President's sake, which means you must actually get along with him, I should think."

The gnomelike sharp-tongued secretary of the interior, Harold Ickes, joined them. He gave Caroline a perfunctory greeting; then, "What sort of speech did you write him?"

Hopkins shook his head. "I wasn't asked. Sam's on the case. It'll be short. That's all I know. Short because he wants to stand the whole time."

"Oh, God!" Ickes looked concerned. "I thought he couldn't get up on those braces anymore."

Ickes looked suspiciously at Caroline, who said, "I'm a fellow conspirator, too."

Across the room, Eleanor was standing with a group of lady friends; she beamed and waved when she saw Caroline, who joined her.

"You're here to cheer us up on this dismal day." They embraced. "When they asked Franklin why he didn't want a parade, he said, 'There's no one left in town to march.' I'm afraid it's going to be fearfully gloomy."

"I'm sure the President will liven things up."

Eleanor's smile never faded, just as her eyes never ceased to watch the guests. Then a familiar figure approached. It was Caroline's neighbor in the Wardman Park Hotel, the outgoing vice president, Henry Wallace, a tall, somewhat Lincolnesque figure who had been sacrificed to the party's Southern conservatives.

"Dear Henry," said Eleanor; she was known genuinely to like and admire this reputedly mystical, definitely intellectual figure, so out of place, Caroline had always thought, in American political life. Caroline asked after his black dog, whom she often met in the elevator.

"He hates the cold. I'm trying to invent some sort of slippers for him. I'm experimenting with rubber. From a tire inner tube. But so far they keep slipping off." Wallace turned to Eleanor. "I've just been told that I'm to swear in the new vice president."

Eleanor giggled. "You do have your priestly side, Henry. And think what a good start it will be for Mr. Truman. Oh!" she looked toward the fireplace, where the small, gray, thickly bespectacled Senator Truman was standing, unnoticed, with his very large wife. "There he is. There *they* are. I must say hello. I don't think they've ever been up here before." She crossed to the fireplace.

Caroline said, "Will you be leaving Wardman Park now?"

Wallace shook his head. "No. I'm supposed to stay on. In the Cabinet. Or so the President tells me. He tends sometimes to vagueness."

The guests were now being guided inexorably to the chilly South Portico.

Caroline paused just inside the doorway; beside her stood the President's eldest son, Jimmy, a tall man in uniform, going bald. "We're almost ready for Pa," he said. He and Caroline were old acquaintances.

Caroline was prepared to make idle conversation with Jimmy Roosevelt but, to her surprise, he had a good deal to say, all the while watching the closed door between the President's bedroom and the oval study. "It's going to be a nightmare when this war's over. Because we're going to have millions of hillbilly boys on our hands who don't know how to do anything except to kill people."

"Isn't—wasn't that—true after every war?"

"Not on this scale. Anyway, look what happened last time. When the veterans got hit by the Depression, they marched on Washington to ask for a bonus and General MacArthur shot at them. Pa also says it was even worse after the Civil War when the country was full of all these men with no work, riding the rails . . . hobos they called them. Well, this time we could have millions of hobos on our hands. And I know these boys. I've served with them. I know that if we don't find something for them to do, all hell is going to break loose."

Quietly, a valet appeared at the bedroom door. Slowly, he pushed the President's chair into the now empty study. Roosevelt wore a lightweight suit and no overcoat. The outline of his heavy metal braces was visible through thin trouser material. In the year since Caroline had last seen him, he had lost weight and his shirt collar was loose. Most alarming, the head was so bowed that his chin rested on his breast, as if he were unconscious.

Jimmy heard Caroline's sudden intake of breath. "Don't worry," he said. "The old warhorse is ready." Within a yard of Caroline, the great head was slowly raised at the sight of her and the eyes came into focus. A blue-lipped smile was abruptly switched on. "Caroline!" The voice sounded strong.

"Mr. President." Caroline shook his hand and then, to her own amazement, she did a full court curtsy.

"Bravo!" he said. "The same curtsy you did for Queen Elizabeth in *Mary Stuart*. Even so, I still prefer you in *Huns from Hell*."

"I was certainly never nobler."

When Caroline saw that valet and son were now preparing to lift the President from his chair, she started to slip out the door, but FDR said, "Stay. The more the merrier. Actually, since I'm going to walk, I'm going to need as much window dressing as possible. So you stay close to my side, next to Jimmy."

The two men lifted the President a foot in the air: then, plainly a dead weight, he dropped back into the chair with a bump.

Caroline reached for a carafe of whiskey and filled half a tumbler. With shaking hand, the President took the glass and drank the contents as if it were water. Color returned to his face. "You can say what you will about the new ways in medicine but the old are still the best. Yet Eleanor never stops complaining about how bad it is for me to stay up at night with Winston drinking. Finally, I had to tell her, 'The problem with drink is on *your* side of the family, dear, not mine.'"

Once again the two men, very carefully, tugged the President upright; and the valet locked his braces. FDR stood, swaying a moment. Then he said: "In my end is my beginning." He smiled at Caroline. "I still remember your last words."

Aided now by a Secret Service man, the President swung first one leg then the next, back and forth from hip to brace, like some sort of absurd toy.

As they appeared on the portico, the band played "Hail to the Chief": the crowd below on the lawn cheered. Caroline stayed near the President, who was not so much standing on braces as being held in place all during the national anthem, a prayer, the swearing in of the vice president. Then the chief justice of the United States, Bible in hand, stood back of a lectern which the President now clutched and, in full view of crowd and cameras, Franklin Delano Roosevelt, for the fourth time, swore to preserve, protect, and defend the Constitution of the United States, "so help me God."

A short speech was on the lectern in front of him. The voice was hesitant at first; then it grew clearer as he held himself upright with two never very steady hands. Caroline was reminded of the Pope when he spoke to the city—Rome—and to all the world beyond. *Ad urbe et orbi.* "Things will not always run smoothly," he warned. The paper made a sound as it brushed the microphones; he pulled back. "The great fact to remember is that the trend of civilization is forever upward . . ." This ought to have been true in a Darwinian world but Caroline was agnostic on the subject. He did concede that "our own Constitution of 1787 was not a perfect instrument; it is not perfect yet. But it provided a firm base . . ." A cold stillness seemed to envelop all the world; his voice alone sounding as, delicately, he alluded to the next task: "We cannot live alone at peace . . . our well-being is dependent on the well-being of other nations far away . . ."

Caroline could hear a woman behind her softly sobbing. Who? Why? "We have learned to be citizens of the world, members of the human community . . ." He quoted Emerson. " 'The only way to have a friend is to be one.' " How odd, thought Caroline, that the one thing that earth's new master could never himself be to anyone, he now proposed that his nation be—or appear to be—to everyone, a friend.

At the end, there was a great burst of applause from the South Lawn below: strong applause from those on the portico. Simultaneously, Caroline and Jimmy met like two sides of a curtain coming together in order to shield the President from the view of the crowd. Then, once the valet knew that they were out of public view, he unlocked the braces and the President fell into his chair.

Caroline turned to the source of the sobbing. All in black stood the widow of Woodrow Wilson, confronted for a second time in her life with the pale horse that marks the death of kings. Caroline crossed herself; and shuddered in the cold.

NINE

Caroline had first known Lady Mendl when she was Elsie de Wolfe and, if not the first, certainly the most successful of the early century's interior decorators. She was also one of the first professional women to live with another woman in a relationship that neither bothered to euphemize; there was no nonsense about a white or Boston marriage. They were, simply, a delightful couple who entertained interesting people in New York and Paris, always in small perfect rooms. Caroline thought of their settings as essentially dollhouses. Elsie's friend was a literary agent and Elsie herself had literary inclinations. The never easily pleased Henry Adams himself delighted in their company during that long bright unbroken summer before the First World War. Then, in readiness for a new world, Elsie had married some sort of English civil servant called Sir Charles Mendl; as he was neither rich nor decorative, the marriage was an ongoing mystery that none bothered to solve. People came to Elsie for the other people that she had cast to decorate her rooms. During the Hollywood of the war years, she was counted among such distinguished European émigrés as Stravinsky, Mann, Huxley, Schoenberg, and, like them, she was—though American—expected to go "back" to Europe now that, as of this morning, May 8, 1945, Germany had surrendered. Since most of the islands of the Pacific had been occupied by American forces and a huge new bomber called the B-29 had made rubble of much of Tokyo, it was assumed that Japan would soon collapse.

A joyous day, thought Caroline, walking up the dark red-brick path to Elsie's latest dollhouse, a white frame building set among flower beds and exotic trees that produced Technicolor blossoms. The effect was like MGM's notion of a humble cottage in the English countryside, no longer menaced by Hitler, who had killed himself the previous month just after President Roosevelt's abrupt death at Warm Springs, Georgia. As the world stage was being emptied of the great players, what looked to be ill-rehearsed understudies were taking their places in the ruins of Berlin, the chaos of Rome, the echoing White House where a dim former senator with thick glasses seemed altogether too aware that he ought not to be there but, as he was there, he doggedly soldiered on.

"We must chat a moment *before* the others come." Elsie had been firm on the telephone.

In the living room, banked with flowers, Elsie sat in a straight-back chair. In the ten years since they had last met, Elsie had acquired a smooth pink-and-white enamel face and, as if to fit more easily into her latest dollhouse, she had, startlingly, shrunk in the process; yet her energy was undiminished. She hurried forward to embrace Caroline. "*You* don't change!" she said, almost accusingly.

"Neither do you." Thus ladies lie, thought Caroline, reassured, even comforted, that the somewhat reduced Elsie was actually so little changed. There were not many left at that certain age which each of them had got to at her own pace and in her own way; able, at last, temporarily perched, to look about in some surprise at those who had made it, too, almost always—if not the wrong—the unexpected ones.

Caroline sat beside her hostess; took orange juice from a waiter. Elsie's nose seemed to have got more arched and sharp with age; it was now like that of an early Roman emperor or, perhaps, a paper knife.

"How did you know to plan a party for today?"

"For today? Well, it was the only free day. There's so much going on out here. Then, of course, the negotiations took forever. Was it on? Was it off?"

"I thought the surrender was handled very briskly."

"Briskly? Negotiations dragged on and on. Why, February was to have been the start date and here we are in May."

Caroline realized that Elsie was deaf. "Well, it's over, anyway."

"Indeed it is. Cary signed his contract last week and Cole's delighted, of course. Some Hungarian will direct. But then some Hungarian always does nowadays."

Caroline wondered if she were going mad. Who was Cary, who was Cole? What she had thought would be a party for the Allied victory in Europe seemed to be some sort of movie party.

"Caroline Sanford! This is a joy!" It was Sir Charles. He was dressed like a stage Englishman with a gray waistcoat and a chain about his neck to which, Caroline feared, a monocle had been attached.

"Charles dear, we're having a private chat."

"Sorry to barge in. But the war's over in Europe. Thought you'd like to know."

"Caroline!" Elsie looked stricken. "Is *that* what you were talking about?"

Caroline nodded.

"But why did no one tell me?"

"But I just did." Charles was reasonable. "You were so busy with the party all morning, I didn't get a chance to break the news."

"Oh, dear." Elsie was like some great general arrived, all flags flying, to the wrong battle.

"You will simply turn this into a V-E celebration," was Caroline's contribution.

"V-D?" Elsie looked faint.

"No, dear." Charles was soothing. "V-*E*. For victory in Europe. V-E is what they call it. V-J is next, I suppose."

"That may be." Elsie was now rallying. "But everyone is coming because Cary Grant finally signed his contract to play Cole Porter in Jack Warner's movie *Night and Day*, the story of dear Cole's life, such a powerful story, and now this has to happen."

"Dear Elsie, you can have three guests of honor—Cole and Cary and Ike."

"Ike who?"

"Nickname, dear. Of General Eisenhower." Charles enjoyed being the Answer Man.

"Surely, General Eisenhower's not in Beverly Hills today?" Elsie was starting to panic.

"No," said Caroline, enjoying herself. "But *pretend* he's at your party, in spirit, and that the war is over after only forty months. I made a bet with someone on how long it would take to win. But I can't remember who it was."

A butler drew Charles into a corner. The sound from the street of car doors opening and slamming announced the arrival of guests.

"Why didn't you marry Harry Hopkins?" This was the old Elsie at last.

"He needed a nurse, not a wife, and I'm no good at that."

"Hire a nurse. We were so pleased by all those stories about you and him. To live at the center of history." Quite lost was the hostess of the *Night and Day* launch party. "You must have felt like our dear old Henry Adams, living across the street from the White House."

"Only he hated his President Roosevelt and I quite liked my President Roosevelt. Now gone."

"They do go, don't they? What's to become of Eleanor?"

"She has the cottage at Hyde Park, a place in New York . . ."

"With two lady friends of mine." For a moment, Elsie let slip the Sapphic mask of *omertà;* thus giving Caroline inordinate pleasure. "But she will want to keep busy."

"I think President Truman . . . how odd to call him, anybody *else,* that . . . is going to make her something at the United Nations."

The front door was now being opened. Elsie leapt to her feet as befitted one who stood on her head half an hour a day.

"Is it true," she spoke quickly, "that his old girlfriend, Lucy Rutherford, was with him when he died?"

"Yes. That is why Eleanor was playing Medea at the grave."

"Well, adultery is apt to take the edge off one's grief. Here come the guests. Even so, I'm surprised that Eleanor would have been jealous after so many years." Elsie moved across the room to greet Ann Warner, queen of that Sapphic Hollywood which so sternly governed the film "industry," the word their complaisant husbands used when referring to the chaos of moviemaking.

"She was very jealous," Caroline said to Elsie's back, "unto the very end, I should think."

Caroline was greeted by elderly strangers who turned out to be old friends and acquaintances from her days as Emma Traxler. Facial surgery was boldly presented as if for her approval; generally, it looked as if someone had stapled onto an old friend someone else's young face; happily, voices still provoked memories. By and large, men had lost their inhibition about what was now universally known as face-lifting even though Richard Barthelmess, an early victim of a bad surgeon's knife, had eyelids that could not properly close, the lower lids seemingly glued to his cheekbones while glazed eyes constantly filled up with tears. Caroline greeted him fondly as well as his wife, Jessica, if that was her name.

The younger set were ridiculously young; or so they appeared to Caroline, whose youthful myopia, guaranteed to become farsighted with age, had, in her case, got worse. Rather than wear glasses, she used a lorgnette to get a quick look at those about her; then, if they approached her, she shut it with what she took to be a wry smile intended to mean: why on earth am I holding this?

Fortunately, Cary Grant looked like himself. He also looked to be in a bad temper. "Back in Bristol, where I was born, every time you came on the screen the pianist, those were silent days, of course . . ."

"Of course, I found my voice too late."

"Oh, you certainly didn't need to speak with that painist in your corner. He had a crush on you. Every time you appeared on screen, he'd play the *Hungarian Rhapsody*."

"Even during the love scenes?"

"Particularly during the love scenes. It was splendid. Of course I was only thirteen."

He need not, Caroline thought, have given his age so assertively. "I was an old twenty-five."

Grant flushed. "I do put my foot in it, don't I. Is Cole here?"

"I haven't seen him. How are you going to play him?"

"With my hand over my face. I've got a scene where I play Cole as a twenty-year-old boy at Yale. And here I am forty-two. I must also sing. But I can't sing. And then, there's the wardrobe. I've just had one fitting."

"As a college boy? Argyle socks?"

"No. As the king of musical comedy. Mirror of fashion and all that." Grant's face was a mask of pain. Then, slowly, for dramatic effect, in a voice more suitable for Richard III than Cole Porter, he whispered, "The cuffs of my shirtsleeves go *a quarter of an inch* beyond the sleeve. I thought I'd have a stroke. Only a cad would show that much cuff. No gentleman ever exposes more than *one eighth* of an inch of cuff. Maximum."

"Use it!" Caroline was getting into the spirit of wardrobe: the dressing-up part of movies that had always so appealed to her. "Play him as a cad!"

"Cole? Poor dear Cole, a cad? Oh, I couldn't." But Grant was smiling mischievously. "Of course, *I'm* a cad . . ."

"Never."

"I was an acrobat when I started out at thirteen . . ."

"Inspired by the *Hungarian Rhapsody* in Bristol . . ."

"How did you guess?"

"I'm sure you will have great love scenes, to the melodic *drip drip of the clock* or whatever it is."

The mischievous face became somber. "The script is deeply boring. Nothing happens except a horse falls on him and he breaks his legs. After that, he spends a lot of time in hospitals. Cheery stuff."

There was a murmur of excitement at the door as the crippled Cole Porter hobbled in. He was small, elflike, with a sweet cold smile and large spaniel eyes.

"Is Lynda with him?" asked Caroline. She quite liked the edgy lady that Cole had married in order to present to the world a somewhat sequined façade of everyday marriage.

"No." Grant sighed. "I must say hello to my fellow guest of honor."

"Who directs?"

"Mike Curtiz." Grant's eyebrows moved, briefly, upwards. Curtiz, Caroline knew from experience, was a bad director who, occasionally, inexplicably, made a good film; he was only slightly handicapped by the fact that English was not a language that he ever intended to master.

"A Hungarian!" Caroline was cheerful. "Then you'll think of me while anything goes."

A blond pretty woman put down what looked to be a glass of gin and embraced Caroline. "The Chief's in the sunroom. He's longing to see you. So am I. Come stay at the beach house before we sell it, which is any second now. He's finally got most of his money back. But even so, it's too much to keep up—all those servants."

Then Marion Davies led Caroline to a bright room with a view of a rose garden. The gray-haired, gray-faced, gray-suited Hearst greeted her affectionately. "Never guessed you'd be here." He gave his nervous giggle.

"Aren't you glad now I got you to get out of the house?" Marion retied his tie.

"No," said Hearst. "I'm going to miss the beach."

"I've found us a nice place in Beverly Hills. Only I keep forgetting where it is. It's either on North Beverly Drive or up Coldwater Canyon. Anyway, the driver always knows." She was gone.

Caroline sat beside the now truly ancient Hearst. Other guests looked into the room; then quickly withdrew, as if he were somehow otherworldly like history itself come to call on V-E Day.

"Well, it's about over. Japan's trying to surrender, I hear, but Truman's dragging his feet. Why?"

"I am no longer at court," said Caroline.

Hearst's smile was wintry. "Changing of the guard. Yes. How is Hopkins?"

"Not well. He was in bed most of the time during Yalta. Then, when they finally came home, the President died."

"How much did he give away at Yalta?" Hearst's pale eagle eyes blazed out of the dead gray face.

"Surely," said Caroline in a voice that she could not prevent from trembling with anger, "you don't believe what you read in your papers?"

Hearst shrugged. "I don't believe the sob sisters, no, but . . ."

"They argued over Poland. One of the last letters the President was working on was a complaint about Stalin's high-handed way with the Polish government in exile . . ."

"So what about Latvia, Lithuania, and Estonia? FDR left them in Russian hands without a peep."

"You sound," said Caroline, her sudden flash of unexpected partisanship under control, "like Mrs. Roosevelt."

"That's a definite first." Hearst was good-natured.

"She told me that after Franklin came back from Yalta, one of the first things she asked him was what about those three countries and he said, 'The only way they can be freed would be if we were to go to war with Russia. You might want such a war—I might—but the American people are fed up with Europe. We must get used to the fact that wherever the Red Army is is Russian and a thousand Yaltas can't change that fact.' Eleanor said she found her husband's argument unanswerable."

"Do the Russians really want Germany to hand over ten billion dollars?"

"Yes. They suffered the most from Hitler. They also got to Berlin first."

"I wonder why we let that happen. I must find out," he added ominously. Then he said, in the same high urgent voice, preceded by a nervous chuckle, "You should have married Harry Hopkins."

"I never suspected that you, of all people, would think so highly of matrimony." Hearst's gray face became ever so slightly pink. Caroline found it touching that it still worried him that he was living in sin with Marion Davies, a devout Catholic. "Anyway, Harry found Miss Right, one Louise Macy. She moved into the White House three years ago. I was delighted for Harry. Less so for myself. When I told her that my role in his life had been simply that of caretaker, she looked rather angry and confused, a common condition with her, I should think. Anyway, she'll be a good stepmother. They think he has cirrhosis of the liver."

"Did he drink all that much?"

"No. 'To have the consequences without the vice is unfair,' he says. Mr. Truman is sending him to Moscow soon. I wish he wouldn't go but I no longer see him. He is too ill to see much of anyone."

"Like FDR, in the last years."

"Don't exaggerate. I must fly."

At the front door, Caroline stepped straight into a tall Air Force major. In her most convincing American voice, inspired by the nearness of what resembled and probably was Ginger Rogers chewing gum, she said, "Long time no see," to Timothy X. Farrell.

2

Peter's brother-in-law, Clay Overbury, sat in Blaise's study at Laurel House. He wore ribbon after ribbon on his chest over the heart where Peter had nothing at all on his uniform except one ribbon for "Good Conduct" and another that confessed to service exclusively in the United States.

Blaise sat at his desk, piles of clippings in front of him; he was a proud, even ecstatic father of a son who was not the well-conducted Peter but the hero Clay. All in all, Peter was delighted for them. Blaise was always a somewhat implausible father for him but a dream come true for Clay.

"You signed the commitment papers?"

Clay nodded. "Wasn't easy." He blinked his blue eyes, to denote strong emotion.

"Best thing, all around. Burden tells me things are going well back home in the district."

"So I hear. Should I go see Enid?"

Blaise shook his head. "The doctors say no. Not now. Not yet."

The eyes of all three men were now on the portrait of Aaron Burr over the fireplace. In the middle of the left eye there was a small round hole where Enid, aiming unsteadily at her father with a pistol, had managed to do what Alexander Hamilton had failed to do so many years ago at Weehawken, New Jersey—shoot Burr, if only in effigy, dead. Peter, who preferred his sister, when sober, to the rest of the family, had not been present. If he had . . . Anyway, this was, as Blaise had said, "the last straw." Now he and Clay could put Enid away; lock the door to the sanitarium and throw away the key. Then, unencumbered, Clay would be elected to the House of Representatives in the fall and so continue a rise that now seemed to many to be inevitable. Thanks entirely to Harold Griffiths, he was a national figure, "the Hero of Lingayen Gulf Airfield" in the Philippines, where he had gone into a burning hangar and saved a wounded marine from the flames and then, practically sin-gle-handed, captured the airfield, all witnessed by Harold Griffiths, for whom Clay was like a figure out of legend, "like a knight in a tapestry of jungle green."

Newsreel cameras, arranged by Blaise, had greeted the knight at Union Station when he stepped off the train to take his place in the Capitoline frieze of gods and heroes. He would be president in a dozen years, thought Peter, staring with open distaste at his admittedly deco-rative as well as decorated brother-in-law, soon not to be related to him in or out of law. Could Clay and his father actually be lovers? So Enid had charged the night that she shot Aaron Burr instead of Blaise, or had Clay been her target? Peter could never determine which of the two had been the chosen victim or even if she had made her selection as she denounced them and then, for fatal emphasis, fired her pistol at drunken random.

Peter stood up, holding in his stomach. Clay's lean body was visi-ble reproach to a less-disciplined contemporary. "You two seem to have business . . ."

"No. No." Blaise waved him back into his seat. "Clay and I are fin-ished. I want to talk to you, Peter." In a flash of golden light, white teeth, blue eyes, Clay firmly, sincerely, shook Peter's hand, allowing—deliberately?—the essence of his own persona like a surge of electricity to flood Peter's somewhat weaker system. Then Clay was gone, and Blaise was again his usual self. What, Peter wondered, idly, did Enid really know?

"How is *The American Idea* doing?"

"The real thing or the paper?"

"I doubt if there is a real thing. We're stuck with too many ideas as it is. No. The paper."

Peter told him, more or less accurately, the unglamorous circulation figures. Blaise understood all this better than he did. Then, "How's your ex-communist working out?"

"I doubt if he ever had the nerve to be one." Tension between the two was on the rise. Billy Thorne had interpreted the Yalta meeting of Roosevelt, Churchill, and Stalin as the beginning of a partnership that would stabilize and restore all of Europe, while Peter was certain that everything would fall apart with Roosevelt dead and the American military on so many simultaneous warpaths. There were other quarrels, including the implicit one over Diana. Although Billy could hardly be said to be in love with his wife, he was not about to give up so shining a capitalist trophy, while, simultaneously, Peter was not about to dissolve into thin air. "We've also got Aeneas Duncan. He was with me at the Pentagon. In A-2. Intelligence. He's basically a philosopher."

"Heavy stuff. I've tried to read him. Do you think you'll ever break even?"

"Yes. There's nothing else really. Nothing that treats Washington today as if it were already history."

"Well, I'm sure you know better than I about that sort of thing." Blaise's humor, never light, was now oppressively heavy. "I've always thought history doesn't really begin until it's over."

"Well, when it's over—when you're absolutely certain it's over—I hope you'll let me know." Peter meant to infuriate; and failed.

Blaise was bland. "Have you thought about the paper?"

"Yes. And . . . no."

"I have no heir, except you."

"There's Aunt Caroline."

"She'll vanish into the French countryside any day now."

"Her daughter?"

Blaise shuddered. "Emma has gone back to fighting the menace of communism."

"Is she still with Tim Farrell?" Peter had been as amazed as everyone else in the family when Emma Sanford had, with such aplomb, collected her mother's old lover and gone off to join him during his filming of the war in Europe.

"I'm not in touch with Emma. Or with your Aunt Caroline, who's on the West Coast this week. Anyway, you're perfect, now, for the *Tribune* once I'm . . ." Blaise paused.

"You'll never let it go, which would make me highly imperfect for your purpose."

"I could die." This was said with some effort—superstition?

"So can anyone. Even I. But you won't for a long time. Train Harold Griffiths."

"Tiresome pansy." Blaise seemed to have turned a page in his head. He opened a manila folder. "This mysterious weapon . . ."

"It's almost ready to be tested."

"*What* is it?"

"It has greater power than anything man-made. It is supposed to be able to disintegrate the planet."

"In that case, hardly an ideal weapon. On the other hand, for our country's greatest secret, what's known already is too much."

"At the Pentagon, we assumed that the Nazis, now defeated, and the Japs, on their way to the exit, knew about it all along because the science—which has something to do with breaking up atoms—is known to everyone in the physics business, but apparently only we had the technology and the money to build it. Aeneas is my expert, at the moment. He has good sources . . ."

"You wouldn't . . . ?"

"I don't see how I could."

"When do you get out of the Army?"

"I am out. As of last week. Didn't I tell you? But since I don't have any clothes that fit, I still wear my uniform and sleep in the office."

"In the Union Trust Building?" Blaise chuckled. "Well, you're at the center of power."

"Why?"

"The law firm of Covington and Burling is located there. You must see them from time to time."

"They dress very well. At least that's how they look in the elevator where I see them."

"Dean Acheson is back with them. But not for long. The President wants him at the State Department. To keep an eye on Jimmy Byrnes."

Like most of Washington, Peter had hardly been surprised when Truman selected his old Senate crony South Carolina senator Jimmy Byrnes, to be secretary of state. Peter's last memory of Byrnes had been during the 1940 Chicago convention, where the sharp conceited little man had, for a moment, thought himself the next vice president only to lose to Wallace, who had then been cast aside in 1944 for Harry S— the S was for nothing—Truman, a senator not only Byrnes's junior but, in the eyes of Washington as well as of Byrnes, his inferior. The relationship had already begun to go badly or, as Blaise put it: " 'A president,' Acheson said to me, 'can be his own secretary of state, but a secretary of state cannot be his own president.' "

"Words of wisdom . . ."

"Do you want to see them all in action at Potsdam, with Churchill and Stalin?"

"As a *Tribune* reporter?"

"Correspondent."

"I've too much to do here."

The two-room office suite in the Union Trust Building contained not one but two chief editors in almost perpetual conflict. Billy Thorne's assistants had taken on Billy's harsh contrarian style, while Peter's team responded with polite contempt which, in the case of Aeneas Duncan, took the form of cold disapproving silence. Aeneas was again a civilian, with a child-psychologist wife in New York, which obliged him to commute between the two cities twice a week, writing book reviews in the club car of the Pennsylvania Railroad's Capital Express. In order to see as little as possible of her estranged husband, Diana worked at home in Rock Creek Park and only came to the office when Billy was not there, which was a good deal of the time, since he was now in some demand as a lecturer on the evils of communism as observed at first hand in the Spanish Civil War. Precisely how his eyes had been opened to the menace was never entirely clear to Peter, who had yet to attend one of Billy's excited and exciting lectures.

Peter shared a partners' desk with Aeneas. They faced each other at the center of a room lined with bookcases and filing cabinets as well as a woman secretary whose typing was so rapid on an Underwood so old that its staccato sound was like an unceasing firing squad. On the walls there was a mock-up of the next issue of *The American Idea*. One entire blank sheet was headed "Potsdam."

"All I've got in the way of news is hearsay." Peter was having trouble sorting out his impression of the surreal meeting in the Berlin suburb where he had been a part of the world's press, kept to a most unworldly minimum. In fact, it was only as Blaise's son that he was able to be billeted in the appropriately named Babelsburg, the seat of what had once been the German film industry. The conference itself was held at the Cecilienhof Palace, located in the relatively unruined suburb of Potsdam. Armed with passes, Peter did his best to look invisible as he drifted from hall to hall.

Although the Russian military were very much in charge of the palace, they plainly had orders not to disturb the American and English visitors; that is, the few actually accredited to the conference. Of perhaps two hundred journalists assembled in Potsdam and Berlin, Peter was one of the few allowed inside the palace, thanks to Blaise's friendship with the President's military chief of staff. Admiral Leahy had been Roosevelt's principal adviser; now he performed the same task for Truman.

One of Leahy's aides, an amiable lieutenant commander Peter's age, took charge of him and let him look into the totally off-limits conference hall, whose large round table was covered with a dark red cloth. "The red's a bit tactless of the Russians," whispered Peter. Everyone tended to whisper in the vast halls, as if terrified of awakening the slumbering gods of war.

"Well, it is their city. For now. Actually, they're pretty easy to get on with. So far."

From a distance, Peter duly noted Churchill's small fat figure as he lumbered into the anteroom with its somber wrought-iron chandeliers. He moved as if he were, physically, a giant; muscle-bound with power. He was usually accompanied by his sad-looking doctor, Lord Moran. Stalin was as small as Churchill but not as plump. He had a genial expression somewhat undone by pale yellow eyes more suitable for the lion house at the Rock Creek Park zoo than a peace conference. Truman wore a gray suit; his breast-pocket handkerchief was arranged in four structured peaks of equal size.

The lieutenant commander gave Truman high marks. "He's on the spot and he knows it. Not only does he have to prove he's up to Roosevelt's standards, which he isn't, but he's got to ride herd on Jimmy Byrnes, who thinks he's Metternich at the Council of Vienna, except he wouldn't know who Metternich was."

That was one obvious theme, Peter had thought at the time. A wily South Carolina senator with no knowledge of foreign affairs and a president who affected a profound knowledge of history although whenever he made an allusion to the historic past he unerringly got it wrong. Apparently, FDR had had neither the time nor the inclination to educate Truman during the weeks of his vice presidency. This now looked to be a real-life version of a Capra movie: honest little American guy, up against both the sinister smooth English and the bloody barbarian Asiatics. Peter had a lot to write about, only . . .

Peter put down the draft of his piece; looked across the desk at Aeneas, who was looking at him. "Problems?" Aeneas wheezed; always a signal for him to light another cigarette, which he did, careful to blow the smoke in Peter's direction.

"Yes. I've written a mystery story—a murder mystery, really—but I don't know who did the murder or why."

"Obviously, we can't accept the New York *Times* view of Potsdam, where the conquerors met in perfect harmony, the future of Poland and reparations only mild amusements."

"Something happened on—" Peter checked the date—"July 16. Up until then Stalin had twice reassured Truman that by mid-August the Soviet Union would enter the war against Japan. He also said he'd do nothing to help the Chinese communists. Yet later that day—no, the next day—I was with Leahy and my lieutenant commander at the lunch break. They were looking grim. They kept referring to 'the message.' Leahy said, 'I pray the damned thing won't work.' The aide said, 'But, sir, the message sounds like it does.' Then Leahy said, 'For what it's worth, Eisenhower's against using it.' That was all I heard. I couldn't ask either of them what they were talking about. I'd already heard too much. But the whole mood of the conference suddenly changed. Oh, everyone was still friendly and Truman kept boasting about how well he was getting on with 'Uncle Joe.' He seemed to think he was back in Kansas City with Boss Prendergast."

"It's obvious they were talking about that project I've been researching for years now. But all I really know is top-secret hearsay." Aeneas was strict in matters of ethics. If one could not absolutely verify a story, it was not to be used. Hence, his low-key but quite genuine loathing of Billy Thorne.

"Maybe." Peter looked at his typescript for inspiration. There was none. "Actually, I had stopped believing that there was such a weapon. Seemed too much like the sort of thing we were hired to peddle at the Pentagon. But after I eavesdropped on Leahy's comments, I could tell there was a definite change in mood at Potsdam. Nothing more was said about Russia entering the Pacific war, which means . . ." Peter shut the folder. "Truman's decided to use *it*, whatever it is, and so he feels that we don't need Russia's help in defeating Japan. All our show now."

"Guesswork."

"Yes."

"Then you can't use it, can you?"

Peter sighed. "No." He put the Potsdam story in the top drawer of his desk.

Two weeks later, he opened the drawer. On August 6, 1945, the United States Twentieth Army Air Force had dropped an "atomic bomb" on the Japanese city of Hiroshima, killing an estimated 130,000 people. The world was duly stunned. Peter began to type, vigorously, with two fingers. He finished his piece on August 9, just after the news came that another atomic—now called nuclear—bomb had been dropped on Nagasaki, killing some 70,000 people. Five days later, Japan, which had been trying for some months to surrender, surrendered. Peter had now solved the mystery—literally a mass-murder mystery set in secret motion at Potsdam to intimidate the Russians and keep them out of the war in the Pacific. Meanwhile, Peter was now the first of many to ask, in print, why a dramatic demonstration would not have been as effective as the incineration of so many innocent citizens. Why not transform the snowy top of holy Mount Fujiyama into a deep crater-lake whose radioactive waters would be guaranteed to heal a myriad of skin diseases? Why not . . . ? With this one issue *The American Idea* was well and truly launched; and the day it was on the streets, Peter, in a complex move worthy of Stalin in his glory days, fired Billy Thorne.

3

Caroline and Marie-Louise had now moved into a bungalow at the Beverly Hills Hotel not far from Marie-Louise's old employer, Mrs. Auchincloss.

Timothy X. Farrell had his own raffish bungalow at the Garden of Allah, where the serious actor-playboys tested their systems in competitive drinking and drug contests. Here the girls were, to Caroline's bleak eye, perilously young as they made their way along palm-tree- or hibiscus-lined paths that led to crumbling bungalows which smelled of gin and mold.

The day after Elsie Mendl's V-E Cole Porter celebration, Tim had picked up Caroline at the Beverly Hills Hotel, a vast clammy barn of a building that Caroline could have bought for two hundred thousand dollars from the discouraged woman who owned it. But the last thing that she wanted, even at a bargain price, was property in a country she was planning soon to abandon.

"By the first of next year," she said to Tim, "the State Department says, I'll be able to go back to France. But that's only because I have property there. Tourists are being kept away now. No fuel. No food. Pretty grim." She looked about Tim's living room, dark from the thick leaves of unpruned trees that grew so close to the bungalow that they threatened to break through flimsy walls. "What a dreadful place. And what is that funny smell? The lobby of the Beverly Hills smells the same way."

"Damp. It's the smell of Hollywood. Don't you remember?"

"It's been twenty years." She put her feet on the coffee table; since Caroline was wearing slacks, it seemed the correct thing to do. But then even "old" Hollywood had tended to bring out the boy in girls.

"Why did you come out?"

"Why not? With the Roosevelts gone and poor Harry busy dying in New York, Washington is pretty empty." She changed the subject. On a wall there was the movie poster: "Timothy X. Farrell's *Winter War*." This was his last documentary; and Caroline thought it his best. He had assembled captured German footage of the original invasion of Russia; then he followed the ragtag Russian army as it swept across Eastern Europe and into Berlin, where a forlorn Hitler was last seen handing out autographed photographs of himself to child soldiers in the ruins of the capital of what was to have been a thousand-year empire and had lasted not too many more days. The film had been released in May, too late for the Academy Awards, which something called *Fighting Lady* had won.

Tim was philosophic. "You can't time these things for awards. Anyway, we're doing fair business. But I expect peace will be something of a downer for me."

"There's always *Hometown*—to go home to."

"Would I recognize it?" He picked up a pile of glossy stills from *Winter War*. He gave several to Caroline. Russian troops in silhouette crossing a white frozen river.

"*Alexander Nevsky*," she said, impressed.

"Right the first time. I stole and stole. Did you like Stalin's joke?"

"Did he make one?"

"Not in the film." He gave her a picture of Stalin standing at the center of a long table, smiling and holding up a glass to propose a toast. "This is the Kremlin. Everyone's celebrating the fall of Berlin. Stalin's laid on a party for the Kremlin's staff. One of them is a clerk called Ivan Ivanov who works down the hall from Stalin's office. One day when the Germans were only a few miles from Moscow, Stalin starts down the hall just as Ivan comes out of his office. 'What?' Stalin roars. 'You still alive!' Ivan nearly faints. Stalin moves on. Ivan goes home. Tells his wife that this is the end. He'll be dead by morning. Sits up all night. No arrest. Finally, goes back to work. A year later Stalin sees him in the hall. This time Stalin is beside himself. 'I still can't believe it! I'd hoped never to see you again,' and so on. Ivan knows that this is really the end. Goes home. Waits. Nothing happens. Now it's the victory dinner in the Kremlin. Stalin makes a patriotic speech. 'We have been through terrible times together. We have known terrible defeats. We have known hunger, pain. But never once did we lose heart. Never once did we falter and, best of all, never once did we lose our sense of humor.' He turns to Ivan Ivanov, and roars, 'Did we, Ivan Ivanov?'"

Caroline laughed. "You make Stalin seem almost inhuman."

"Inhuman is a step towards the human, I guess. I wonder if he was as cruel as Roosevelt."

Caroline was startled. "Roosevelt, cruel?"

"In a different way. Obviously, our Siberia is a lot nicer than theirs. But Siberia is still Siberia for those you send there."

"I suppose," said Caroline, "the temperament of one man of power may be very like that of another. Churchill's a great bully, you know, constantly clawing at those who don't dare claw back."

"And Roosevelt held endless grudges. Deliberately ruined careers."

"Perhaps that's how you have to govern. Frighten everyone, particularly your rivals." Caroline came to the point. "I've talked to your John Balderston."

"*My* John Balderston?"

"The world's John Balderston."

"I haven't seen him since England and the Blitz. Isn't he trying to do a remake of *Berkeley Square*?"

"He has other notions, too. He came to me in Washington about one of them. I told him I was long since retired, as a producer. But when he told me what he had in mind, I thought of you. What happens to the veteran when he comes back to his hometown after the war? Has the town changed? Has he changed? What does he want?"

Tim shook into place a broken venetian blind, not quite hiding a candy-bright hibiscus intent on occupying the bungalow.

"Everybody's doing that one. I'm sure Capra will get there first and ruin it for the rest of us."

"What about your doing it? With Balderston."

"What about you doing it? With me?"

Caroline realized that for two or three beats she had neglected to inhale or exhale. She gave a great cough to restart her lungs. "Dust," she said.

"That's because every maid slinks about in terror of being raped by the likes of Errol Flynn, not now in residence. You've got a director. Get a script. Maybe from Balderston. Interest a studio."

"A Sanford-Farrell production? Or Farrell-Sanford?"

"It makes no difference. Anyway, for postwar Hollywood, we're probably out of date . . ."

"I doubt it. At worst, historic."

"Like D. W. Griffith? He's only two or three years older than you and no one will hire him. His last job was with Hal Roach ten years ago. Then look at Orson."

"I'd rather not. But you're at your peak . . ."

"No offers except for documentaries, and now with no war . . ."

Caroline picked up the shot of Stalin making his toast. "Ivan Ivanov the Terrible. The story of a clerk in the Kremlin. We could make it in Paris. For very little."

"I didn't pitch you the story as a picture."

"But that's how I . . . caught it."

Neither spoke for a moment. Caroline stared at the smiling Stalin as Tim stared at her. Then he said, "You haven't asked me about Emma."

"No." She put down the photograph.

"You don't want to hear about her and me?"

"No. You have my sympathy, of course. You always will."

"You'll never like her." This was more statement than question.

"If I never see her again, I might come to appreciate her . . . her . . . her energy, more than I do."

Tim walked over to a pinewood sideboard. A framed photograph lay facedown. He set it upright. Emma had been photographed by a studio photographer. Blond hair, with which she had not been born, made a heavenly nimbus about a heart-shaped face from which all lines had been removed by exquisite lighting rather than by the retoucher's art.

Caroline took a long look at her daughter's face. "She photographs well, doesn't she? She is—with the dyed hair—very like her father."

"Who was not your husband, Mr. Sanford?"

"No. No. I was pregnant by someone else. I married Sanford for respectability. He married me to settle his debts. He was a good man, though I never really got to know him. I was too busy with work."

"Who was the father?"

"Do you care?"

"I'm just curious. She cares, of course."

"James Burden Day."

"The senator?"

Caroline nodded. "He knows that Emma's his. He also keeps an eye on her. I used to when she was young. But now she's grown up. Middle-aged, in fact. How I hate that phrase! Middle of *what* age? The stone age or the age of reason? She must be—what?—forty-five now."

"Forty-two."

"Did she really tell you?"

"She had no choice. She had to produce a birth certificate when we married." He laughed. "She knew I liked older women, obviously."

"Obviously." Caroline remembered to keep her voice light, offhand. "Did you marry her in the church?"

Tim nodded. "The war brought me back to my awful roots in South Boston. I've lapsed back, partway, to the church. Emma's an eager convert."

Caroline rose. "I must congratulate you on having found God again." She kissed him lightly on the cheek. "I had hoped we might meet again—in films, that is—but you have made me a mother-in-law instead, and Mother-in-law Productions doesn't sound right."

"Emma's here. In town."

"Congratulate her for me. Tell her how much I admire—what was it I said? Oh yes. Her energy. I'm going back East. Then France. Good-bye."

As Caroline stepped out into the too bright sun she had a sense of having lived through this scene before. In a film? But she had never had a daughter in a film, only doomed sons. Then she remembered Emma's long-ago denunciation of her because she was living in sin with a communist. But then that was to be expected, because Caroline was a fellow traveler. Emma could tell. After all, had she not worked with a tenured professor who was doing a study of communism in the universities? When Caroline saw fit to criticize Professor Becker . . . Decker? . . . Emma said that she had, the previous day, married him, thus sparing Caroline her daughter's company for a decade or two. Now, thanks to another surprise marriage, Caroline would never again see Emma; never see her grandson, perhaps a pity. In any case, to be rid of Emma nearly compensated for the permanent loss of Tim, not that, to be fair, he was hers to lose except in memory, a faculty that time could be relied on to dim—cool—erase.

Caroline was now at the entrance to the Garden of Allah. An out-of-work actor was playing the part of doorman to the shady Garden of Allah. He was convincingly seedy. Caroline asked him to order a taxi. He blew a whistle. She murmured to herself, "If I had a heart, it would be marble by now." She had said that line in one of her first talkies. The actor-doorman opened the door for what he plainly took to be a great star of yesteryear.

"You're an actor," said Caroline with the shards of a broken smile. "How did you . . . ?"

Caroline was now into the taxi. "What do you think of the title 'Ivan Ivanov the Terrible'?"

"What does it mean? Who's Yvonne?" Caroline had imitated Tim's Russian pronunciation of Ivan.

"A woman with a past. The Beverly Hills Hotel," Caroline told the driver, who then made the perilous turn on Sunset Boulevard up to the Chateau Marmont driveway; then an abrupt right to the hotel, the sunset, the sea. "And no discernible present," she added to herself, not quite able to feel much sympathy, as yet, for the terrible Yvonne.

T E N

I

The first thing that Caroline saw as she entered the hospital room was a small bright Renoir propped up on a table beside the iron hospital bed where Harry Hopkins had been cranked almost to sitting position. He was as bright-eyed as ever but his eyes were now set in a face that had fallen back into its skull. Awkwardly, she embraced him. The room smelled of disinfectant and chrysanthemums, a flower no European would allow in a sickroom since it was thought to be the flower of the dead and not to be displayed until the funeral.

"Renoir." She indicated the picture as if she were passing an examination. "You have become an art collector."

"It's only on loan. I've been looking at pictures for the first time in my life."

"When you're out of here, and the weather's better, come to France. My pictures are safe, or so I'm told." She sat in a chair, the painting between them.

"If I get out. I'm back at death's door, they tell me."

"It must be a quite comforting place by now to be. . . . How long has it been? Ten years' attendance at the familiar door?"

"The last trip to Moscow finally did the trick. Have you seen Eleanor?"

"Only once since the President died. She's busy with the United Nations. Something to do with human affairs. It was good of Truman to put her back to work."

Hopkins shut his eyes; and sighed; then he stopped breathing. For an instant Caroline thought she had witnessed the end. But, eyes shut, he started to speak—from beyond death's door? "Things went wrong between us, you know."

"I didn't know. I don't know." Caroline could not imagine so great a partnership ever foundering.

"It started when I married. Or just before I married Louise. Eleanor accused me of spending all my time with the President—and the war—and forgetting about what truly matters, the New Deal."

"First things first."

"That was my answer. She was—she became—hard to believe, hysterical. She said I'd only pretended to be her best friend in order to get closer to the President and once there I had dropped her and all our work together and saw only him, which is true up to a point, but he had no one else and, finally, neither did I."

"She should have understood that." Caroline was quite aware that no one in—whatever love should be called in this case—was ever entirely sane much less reasonable.

"I had thought she liked Louise. 'So pleased you're getting married at last. Someone to look after you.'" He opened his eyes to look not at Caroline but at the Renoir. He smiled with, she hoped, pleasure. "Then we made the mistake of staying on, in the White House. Eleanor was away almost all the time and the Boss's jokes about her constant gallivanting suddenly stopped. A bad sign. He was also seeing Lucy Mercer again. You know who I mean?"

"Yes. An improvement, I'd say, on the ice princess from the Aurora Borealis."

Hopkins chuckled. "How you girls all took against Her Nordic Majesty! Anyway, there was a White House lunch for some of Eleanor's lame ducks. But Eleanor was in New York that morning and the staff didn't know how to arrange the seating, so Louise did it. Then Eleanor arrived just before the guests. Blew up at Louise for meddling. Redid the seating while Louise and I made arrangements to take a place in Georgetown."

"She is simply jealous?"

"Of Louise?"

"Of you." Caroline recalled Eleanor's confession to her. "Jealous of all the people that she loves, or so she told me once. I'm surprised that never occurred to you."

"How could it? I never counted on anyone loving me, which is why I've always made myself so useful . . ."

"For which you were ever so greatly loved. At least by the Roosevelts."

There was a long pause. The bulging eyes nearly filled their dark sockets. "I'm glad you came. Actually, if I weren't so busy dying, I'd be bored to death. Here I am back in New York, seeing the same social workers and trade union people that I escaped from thirty years ago. Full circle." He sighed. "Full circles make zeroes, don't they? And zero's nothing."

Caroline put her hands on his cold bony one and steered the conversation away from those dark waters where monsters lurked. "Do you see much of Truman?"

Hopkins shrugged. "A nice little man. Way out of his league. I wanted Wallace or Douglas but the Boss had to be reelected and Truman made the old-line Democrats happy."

"Surely Roosevelt knew he was picking the next president."

"No one believes he's really dying. Oh, you accept the possibility while you're alive and you live with it until you're dead because waiting isn't really your problem anymore. But I do think the Boss might have given him a course in foreign affairs. Harry knows nothing. Nothing at all. He didn't know about the atomic bomb until the day he became president."

"Do you think Franklin would have used it the way Truman did?"

Hopkins shrugged. "Who knows? Probably not. After all, the Japanese were ready to surrender—unconditionally. Of course, the Boss was secretly working on a special condition to their unconditional surrender. He was willing to keep the Emperor on, to stabilize the country."

"The left hand never knew what the right was up to."

"He was a master. Harry's a muddler. Henry Wallace says Harry will agree with you before you've actually said what you mean. Then he'll go around telling everyone he gave you hell. Now it looks like he wants to give Stalin hell. That's bad news. The Boss was always willing to treat Stalin in a normal way. As the head of the other great world power. That's why Stalin trusted him, to the extent Russians ever trust anybody. Then Harry goes off to Potsdam and starts to renege on every agreement we made at Yalta. All because he's got the atomic bomb and they don't. So we're going to have a very expensive arms race and trouble everywhere."

A nurse came into the room with several newspapers. "Mrs. Hopkins gave me orders you were not to see the papers today . . ."

"And you disobeyed her! Good girl."

"Oh dear," said the nurse and left the room.

"What shouldn't you see?"

Hopkins held up the New York *Times*. Caroline saw the headline: *Pearl Harbor Inquiry*.

"The shoes keep on falling, don't they?"

Hopkins grunted, glanced at the front page. "Congress has been at this since November. I've offered to testify. But . . ." He pointed, somewhat incongruously, at the Renoir. "The doctors won't let me up, much less out."

"We're covering it at the *Tribune*."

"I know." He held up the *Tribune*. "It's a pity so many of us aren't able to tell our side of the story. The Boss is dead . . ."

"And Grace Tully won't hand over the files."

"Why should she? And Knox is dead. Stimson's ill. And I'm living it up here in Memorial Hospital."

"Stimson refused to be cross-examined."

"Happily, he was born senile."

"What would he have to fear? Three Democrats, who will say that the attack was a total surprise, and two Republicans who disagree."

"That's the advantage of our controlling Congress." He let the newspapers drop. "The only problem might come from some maverick in our own party."

"Why not just tell the truth?" Caroline hadn't meant to be so blunt.

"I think we have, more or less. The Boss is guilty of only one thing. He kept saying *they* must strike the first blow. That was his order because he knew that if we hit first, our isolationists would say *he* had started the war. So in spite of all the information we had about their plans, he held back, and waited and waited until . . ." Hopkins was out of breath.

"I'm sure that *is* a truth. But there are other truths—aren't there?"

"The only truth that matters is we won the war. If we win the peace, whatever that means, we'll have all the cards including the nuclear one, so who cares why it took fifteen hours for General Marshall to warn the commanders in Hawaii. Anyway, the General's a saint in khaki, according to the *Tribune*."

"That was Blaise. But why did Marshall wait so long? And then why did he send his warning by commercial Western Union and not by scrambler telephone?"

"For want of a nail a shoe was lost." Hopkins was suddenly in better mood. "Anyway, Marshall hates politics. So he won't have to worry about what people will say when he's busy *not* running for president in '48."

"Who will run?"

"Harry, if he can get through the next couple of years. If he doesn't, Ike will. He's a Republican, by the way. He told me that he voted against Roosevelt the first three times but . . ." Hopkins shut his eyes; gathered his strength. Eyes shut, he said, "Funny thing. When I got back this time from Moscow, I reported, like always, to the President. I said Stalin was in friendly mood, which he was. Truman was suspicious, of course. He only sees hawks like Acheson and Marshall. Particularly Acheson, who wants to go to war as soon as possible. So I said, 'Mr. President, you must learn to see things from the other side's point of view.' Truman stood up, took my hand, and said, 'I want to thank you, Harry, for everything you've done for me and for the country for so long.'" Hopkins' voice broke. "I had to go into that little room off the office, to pull myself together. When I came back, he said, 'What's wrong?' And I said, 'In all these years no president of the United States has ever said thank you to me.'" Hopkins opened red eyes, filled with tears.

"Caroline!" It was the handsome Louise Hopkins at the door.

"Dear Harry." Caroline patted Hopkins' hand and turned to greet Mrs. Hopkins at the door. "I hope I didn't tire him out. We were talking about the Pearl Harbor Investigation."

Mrs. Hopkins frowned. "That should get his blood pressure up."

"Good thing since I don't have any." Hopkins waved, merrily, at Caroline. "Remember what Harry Truman said: 'The country is as much to blame as any individual for what happened at Pearl Harbor.'"

"You wrote that for him?"

"Ask me no questions and I'll tell you no more lies."

Mrs. Hopkins glared at Caroline, who smiled—compassionately, she hoped—and went. It was not until she was in the corridor following an anesthetized body on a rolling trolley that she started to wonder how on earth the American people, in their carefully nurtured ignorance, could have been responsible for an attack provoked by a governing class whose first principle was never to inform them of anything that might have to do with their welfare.

2

Peter and Aeneas Duncan were met at the door by James Burden Day, more than ever like an Old Testament prophet save for his still winning public man's smile.

"You could come, after all," he said. "I'm glad you found the time." He led them into the garden room. Grapes from the adjoining loggia had begun to ferment on the ground.

"It smells like a brewery in here. Kitty's upset about the birds eating the grapes. It seems they're drunk all the time."

They sat, with a view of the Senator's woods, leaves bright red and yellow in October light.

Peter felt obliged to make some comment about Clay. "He seems to have a good lead in what looks like a Republican year."

Burden nodded, "I'm going out for a two-week swing of the state. Might do him some good." Peter wondered what it was in Clay that made him everyone's ideal son or, as he put it another way to himself, why was it that *he* himself was no one's son? No father figure, ever, in his life, starting with Blaise. When he had remarked on this to Diana, she had said, with her patented smile aslant, "Maybe you're like Napoleon. When he was asked if he was descended from the noble Buonaparte family of Florence he said, 'I am not a descendant. I am an ancestor.'"

"I read your magazine faithfully," said Burden. "You always come up with something no one else dares print."

"We are not very popular in a lot of places." Aeneas Duncan was now opening his briefcase.

"That's all to the good, I'd say. We've got far too many secrets these days."

Peter's face was suddenly hot. One secret—if true—was that Burden Day might have taken a bribe from an oil company. "We'll leave this one to Drew Pearson," he had told Aeneas. "Don't tell Diana."

"You say, sir, you have new material on what happened at Pearl Harbor?" Aeneas withdrew a sheaf of papers from the briefcase.

Burden nodded. "We should have started our own Senate investigation the day after Pearl Harbor but FDR was too quick for us, setting up his own board of inquiry with all their whitewash."

Aeneas carefully arranged documents side by side on a coffee table: each equidistant from the other just like, Peter thought, morbidly, the sunken ships that had been berthed all in a row at Pearl Harbor. "He— or they, to be exact, have had a lot of time to suppress evidence." Aeneas tapped a folder. "A rear admiral named Leigh Noyes was ordered to hide or destroy all the coded Japanese diplomatic and military intercepts. Ostensibly, we didn't want the enemy to know that we had broken their codes. But it is my theory, in dealing with our government, that the enemy invariably knows all our secrets—like the making of the nuclear bomb—while it is the American people who must be kept in the dark."

Aeneas picked up another document. "As soon as Japan had surrendered, the Senate, quite rightly, set in motion the present investigation. You will see here," Aeneas held up a somewhat smeared mimeographed sheet, "an order from Admiral King, placing every relevant document out of the Senate's reach by describing it as top-secret. Any naval person, if he reveals any one of a million top secrets, is subject to imprisonment, loss of veterans' benefits, and so on. They must honor, presumably until death, a secrecy oath that each has been obliged to take."

"But the joint committee has already been shown all sorts of Japanese coded messages—intercepts."

Aeneas replaced his blurred glasses with an even thicker pair. "What has been shown the committee are transcripts from what is called Code Purple. This was the diplomatic code used between Tokyo and its embassies in Washington and London and so on."

"So that's what Owen meant!" Burden sat back in his chair.

"Sir?" Aeneas was very much the respectful graduate student faced with an oral examination.

"Senator Owen Brewster—a Republican but my only friend on the committee—told me that the War Department won't produce anything to do with Pearl Harbor or with those . . . those . . ."

"Intercepts from the Japanese fleet as they were preparing for war. Yes. Most of them are either destroyed or hidden away."

"How do we get our hands on what's left?"

"Sir, I am not the legislative arm of the republic. You are. The war is over. The Executive has no authority to withhold anything from the Legislative. After all, constitutionally, you financed the war. It's your business if negligence is being covered up. Not to mention a policy of provocation."

Burden nodded. "That's what we're really after, isn't it? I have been told that there exists the original Navy plan, to force Japan into attacking us."

"And then to blame the disaster on the Pearl Harbor commanders, who were kept in total ignorance of Washington's game."

"Proof?"

"There is so much." Aeneas sounded weary, but then, as Peter knew, he had been working for more than a year with his various sources. Washington's famed whispering gallery was always full of rumors, mostly conflicting, since different players want to disguise the nature of the games they play but, sooner or later, all things are revealed if one knows how to assemble the puzzle.

"One indirect proof—a negative proof—is that the Navy has made unavailable to everyone, including Senator Brewster, *anything* to do with what actually happened at Pearl Harbor. Everything is under lock and key until 1995, by order of Admiral Noyes."

"A bit late for Owen and me."

"A bit late," said Peter, "for the truth to make us free."

"The truth, more likely," said Aeneas, "would get us imprisoned for treason or whatever they decide to trump up against the first whistle-blower."

There was a silence as all three stared at Aeneas's "evidence," spread out on the coffee table. Then Burden spoke, as if for the prosecution. "Every time Owen and the others speak of codes, the War Department refers only to the diplomatic codes. Is that right?"

"Code Purple. Yes, sir. By October 1940, our cryptographers had broken that code. Simultaneously, we broke what is called the Kaigun Ango codes . twenty-nine naval codes. Every time the committee gets close to a naval code, the Navy produces Code Purple. For instance, we broke the Japanese Code Book D. This made our victory at Midway possible. Now, the Navy pretends it was actually the Purple Code that told us all we needed to know, which is nonsense."

"The President . . ."

"As early as January 1941, Mr. Roosevelt was receiving full reports of Japanese naval movements in the Pacific. He continued to be kept informed right up until Pearl Harbor. I'm still working on the chronology. The Administration has already admitted that they expected a Japanese attack but not at Pearl Harbor, which is why they now say that they didn't warn the local commanders. Yet at least twenty-four hours before the attack they knew that a large Japanese fleet was coming down from the North Pacific. It is also possible that they had known this for some weeks before. But I can't penetrate the vaults of the Navy any more than the Senate can. Worse, my informants are terrified of being found out."

"Why then," asked Burden, "do they inform?"

"Why," Aeneas was sharp, "did those German officers get themselves hanged for trying to kill Hitler?"

Burden smiled bleakly. "Not an analogy that would have appealed to Franklin. Now I ask for no names." Burden began to pace slowly up and down, past a series of paintings of his dry cactus-studded state. "I have a naval friend."

"I know," said Aeneas. "Admiral Richardson."

"You said the name, not I." Burden did not seem surprised.

"It is my impression, Senator, that Richardson opposed the President's policy of provocation and so was relieved as commander in chief of the United States Fleet."

"Your analysis, sir, not mine." Burden was formal. "In the course of your investigation, Mr. Duncan, which is plainly considerably more thorough than that of Justice Roberts or Congress, have you come across a young officer who might have drawn up a plan? Of provocation?"

"Yes, sir. I even worked with him, briefly, in Naval Intelligence. He was head of the Far Eastern Desk. I was on loan from Air Forces Intelligence. His name is Arthur McCollum." Aeneas handed Burden a folder. "The plan of what you call 'provocation' is here, with some other relevant information."

Burden opened the folder. "Annapolis. Regular Navy. Born 1898 in Nagasaki, Japan. That's ironic, I suppose."

"Parents were Baptist missionaries. McCollum speaks perfect Japanese. He says he taught the Crown Prince, now Emperor Hirohito, how to dance the Charleston. In due course Lieutenant Commander McCollum ended up here in Naval Intelligence as an authority on Japan. It would seem that his principal task, other than using his own first-rate intelligence for the service, was to act as liaison between the Navy and President Roosevelt. He did this from the beginning of 1940 up to Pearl Harbor. The President liked him. They also seemed to have come to an agreement since each believed the war with Japan was inevitable, why not provoke it at a time convenient to us."

Burden sighed. "Convenient!"

"Well, sir, it is *in*convenience that undoes Machiavelli."

"Nice," said Peter.

"I just made it up." Aeneas smiled wanly. "It's probably not true."

"If this is the same young man that my naval friend was referring to, did he ever draw up a   program for the President?"

"Yes, sir. Eight points of provocation in a memo dated October seventh, 1940. The same month that we were breaking the Japanese codes. As far as I can tell, all copies—and there couldn't have been many—have disappeared."

"Grace Tully must have one."

"So has McCollum, I should think. I worked out the contents from other documents currently missing from the open files."

Burden was looking at a page in the folder. "These eight points. From A to H . . ."

"If acted upon, would require the Japanese to respond with an act of war." Aeneas took back the folder; began to read.

" 'A. Make an arrangement with Britain to use their Pacific bases, particularly Singapore. B. The same arrangement with the Dutch for the East Indies C. Then more and more aid to Chiang Kai-shek on the mainland of Asia. D. Send a division of long-range heavy cruisers to the Philippines. E. Send two divisions of submarines to the same area, possibly based at Singapore. F'—this is what upset your naval friend— 'Keep the main Pacific fleet at Pearl Harbor instead of San Diego.' In order to tempt them—as I read it—to try for a knockout blow. When Admiral Richardson objected, the President fired him. 'G. Oblige the Dutch to stop all sale of oil or anything else to Japan.' Finally, H., which produced Mr. Hull's memo of November twenty-ninth, 1941. We would embargo all trade with Japan if they did not withdraw from China, Manchuria, and so on. That did the trick. Since they could not accept this ultimatum, they blew up our fleet. So the eight-point plan did the trick."

"They actually thought they could win a war against us?" Burden was incredulous.

"Not win. Buy time." Aeneas began, slowly, to twirl his wedding ring, a sign of—for some reason that Peter had not worked out—

uncertainty. "They figured it would take us a year to recover, by which time they would have occupied southern Asia and we would never be able to dislodge them. They also knew enough about the President to figure that his only real interest was Europe. They also didn't think we had the means or the power to fight two major wars on two hemispheres. So they took a calculated risk that proved to be *mis*calculated."

Burden started to pace the room again. "Will McCollum testify to the Senate?"

"He must, if ordered to. Will he tell you about his program? No. He has sworn a military oath of secrecy."

"No military oath takes precedence over the Constitution."

"The military, sir, have the guns."

Burden stopped in his tracks. "They would overthrow the government?"

"I think—this is only a guess, sir—that if they were driven into a corner by Congress or the new President, they would . . . well, let's say be mutinous. After all, it's their view that they have just won two great wars despite the politicians."

"And it is our view that we won despite the generals and admirals." Burden's sarcasm was genuine. Peter knew that the Senator had always been suspicious of the military, particularly at appropriation time. "Is there proof, Mr. Duncan, that the President ever said or gave the go-ahead to these acts of provocation?"

"Only circumstantial. Commander Arthur McCollum himself often made deliveries of intercepts to the President, but usually they were routed through his naval aide."

"Who is what my naval friend calls one of the military kowtowers at the White House."

"Admiral Richardson is already on record as saying that the chief kowtower, Admiral Stark, is the most culpable of anyone for Pearl Harbor because he deliberately refused to inform the Hawaiian commanders of the coming attack."

"Why didn't he, Mr. Duncan?"

"Surely the Senate must find the answer." The wedding ring no longer twirled.

"No." Burden shook his head. "Not this Senate. Brewster will complain. The Democrats will paper everything over. Then in—when did you say?"

"1995."

"When we're all gone, the story will come out. Frustrating."

Peter had caught a glimpse of Diana coming out of the woods above the house. Peter rose. Aeneas retrieved his various folders. "I think," said Peter, "that we can put together a sort of hypothetical story, without running the risk of prison. 'Unanswered questions' we might call it."

"You're very brave, Peter." Burden seemed to mean what he said. "I'll do what I can . . ."

"Put our unanswered questions into the *Congressional Record*. That would be a help."

"Hardly a great blow for liberty. But the trend toward liberty is hardly noticeable these days. Too much has been done in unconstitutional secret, too many crimes covered up."

"The cost," said Peter, as blithely as he could, "of empire."

They parted. Aeneas drove back to the Union Trust Building while Peter asked Diana for a ride. "Where to?"

"Laurel House. Unless you object?"

"No. I like your parents, as parents go." Mostly in silence they drove along the canal that paralleled the Potomac. The early morning's light snow was turning to slush. "They've taken in Alice, haven't they?"

Peter, at first, had no idea whom she was talking about. "Alice who?"

"Your niece, Enid's child. By Clay. We assume."

"Oh, yes. I suppose so. How did you know?"

"Clay told me. After Enid was put away . . ." She did not finish

"And Clay is now a legal resident of the Sunflower Hotel in that state of his, until November at least." Peter turned onto Chain Bridge, a splendid relic of the Civil War, all chains and skeletal girders flung in what looked to be a haphazard way across the Potomac, now darkly aswirl with icy winter currents. The bridge was doubly symbolic: the last thing for him to cross after leaving home on the Virginia side of the river, the first thing that he crossed when he left the District of Columbia for Laurel House. He noted how comparatively placid the river was for this season. Usually it had risen dramatically by January, twisting and turning and roaring. Were there floods to come? As a boy, he had watched with awe sheets of water strike the bridge which would then writhe and sway and threaten to break into pieces and fall, full fathom five to the dark mud bottom. Threaten but never had. So far.

"Do you see her?" Diana was frowning. Peter wondered why.

"See Alice?"

"See Enid."

"Yes. From time to time. Dr. Paulus thinks it may take a year or two to dry her out and deal with her demons . . ." Peter glanced at Diana's profile; the jaw was set, concentrating on the road. "Have you been out to the sanitarium?"

"No. But she did ring me not long ago. To warn me against Clay." Diana turned onto the river road, made dangerous by black ice; she drove in second gear. The road was narrow, two lanes that, at points, particularly on curves, could not properly accommodate two cars as they passed each other. One would have to skid to a halt. Peter tried, as he often had in the past, to visualize the Washington dignitaries in their carriages, on a warm summery day, driving out to see the Union Army suffer its first major defeat at Manassas Court House. A former slave, allowed to live for nothing in his cabin on the Laurel House grounds, enjoyed recounting the events of that fateful day, and though the Union Army eventually took credit for freeing him, he himself favored the white Confederates whom he knew as opposed to the Yankees of whom he had never heard a good word. Peter assumed he was no longer alive.

A mirage of low-slung coaches containing smart congressmen and be-bustled ladies faded into the snowy woods on either side of the river road. "Warned you of what?" The thought of Enid and Diana even knowing each other well enough to talk on the telephone seemed somehow wrong.

"She is convinced that Clay will run against Father in 1950."

"Isn't this a little too soon to be plotting? Clay won't be elected to the House until November, if he's elected, which he can't be without your father's help. Then, if he is, 1950 is still four years away."

"I know. It makes no sense to me. I just wondered if Enid had said anything to you."

"No. But I'll bring it up when I see her next week. I've never trusted Clay."

"I know." Diana swung the car onto the driveway leading through woods to Laurel House; then she stopped, engine running. "He's in a great hurry."

"Is that the excuse for what he's done—does?"

"I think it probably is. Of course, he's used Father mercilessly."

"He's also used my father—but mercifully." Peter was rather pleased with that highly fraught adverb. "I've always suspected a wide streak of lavender, as Blaise would say, in Blaise. Clay brings it out."

Diana stopped frowning and smiled. "He flirts."

"He's catnip, obviously, to powerful old men."

"Women, too."

"To you?" Would what had been unspoken between them for so many years now be said?

"Yes."

Peter stared out the car window. A red-brick wing to Laurel House was visible through the rows of thin trees neatly set in fresh snow the way department-store Christmas trees are set in fiberglass. "They used to say that during the fighting here at Fort Marcey, all the trees were knocked down, and that the new ones never again grew to their old height. You should have told me."

"I never thought you'd be really interested."

"What splendid antennae you have! No emotion goes undetected; no matter how delicate." Irony was an easy option at such a time. But then Peter had never before encountered such a time as this. He was cool in most relationships and easily satisfied with brief encounters in those parts of town where he was not apt to find anyone that he knew except, of course, those also on the prowl, in which case mutual discretion was the rule. Also, in wartime, the ratio of women to men in the city had been so skewed that between working women and military men serious emotions need be neither tapped nor affected. But with Diana that day beside the spring in Rock Creek Park, he had experienced a sense of total familiarity, if not of lust—friends, for him, were exempt from so predatory an emotion. Rather, a powerful desire simply to be with her was, in his view, a far deeper emotion than the mere sexual, particularly because he had assumed that it was exactly the way she herself had felt when she hastily, mistakenly, kissed his earlobe.

"Clay was the first," she said.

"And Billy Thorne the second."

"Yes."

"No one can accuse you of having a type."

"Each made the weather, in his way."

"Each used you." That was brutal.

"I'm not vain. Why not be used? Or be of use. Of course, Billy turned out to be ridiculous and so did I, for marrying him."

"And Clay?"

Diana turned and faced him. "We plan to be married after the election."

"Even if he's not elected?" This was most brutal of all.

"That's below the belt. Anyway, if he's not, which is unlikely, I admit that he probably will not renew his offer to me. He will need a rich wife. Of course, he needs one now, but I serve his purpose in other ways. I'm Burden's daughter. That will help him in the state. In Congress, too, only . . ." She stopped; again, the frown. "Father thinks he can beat Truman. In the 1948 primary. He thinks Dewey will be easy to beat in the general election."

"In which case, President Day's daughter gets her man."

"To put it bluntly. But Father's too old now. He'll settle for reelection in 1950. I think Clay may try to . . ." She stopped.

"I can't imagine him running against his own father-in-law."

"I'm not so sure. If he did, he would be obliged to run as a divorced man. Twice divorced. First from Enid. Then from me."

"It would seem that you hold all the cards."

"No. Only what I've been dealt. But I'm not sure if I want to play them. I think when my father was young he must have been very like Clay. Ruthless. In a hurry. That excites Electra, you know."

"How would I know? I'm only what's his name? Her brother? Orestes. Pursued by Furies."

"I think Father must have been involved with many women."

"Including my Aunt Caroline. He's supposed to be the father of the unspeakable Emma."

"Good God! What an awful thought." She started the car, and began the descent to the house. "Emma, the toast of the FBI, is my half sister?"

"So Blaise once told me. In his cups, of course."

"Does Burden know?"

"I'm sure Aunt Caroline confides in him the occasional sentimental secret."

Diana parked in the driveway. Peter took her arm and led her across a sheet of ice, glittering with large rough grains of salt.

Blaise and Frederika were in the drawing room, staring at the bedraggled Christmas tree, whose needles were gently falling off. The room had the exciting—to Peter still—Christmas smell of pine and peppermint.

"We are beginning to think about having it taken down." Absently, Frederika kissed Diana and rather formally shook her son's hand.

"Alice wants us to keep it here for the rest of the year." Blaise turned to Frederika. "I've stopped thinking about it. Let's get it out of here before she's finished her nap." Blaise led Peter and Diana into his library. "People are still talking about your Potsdam piece. I hear the White House is fit to be tied. That's always the bull's-eye. Why don't you come work for me?"

"Oh, I like having my own little paper."

"You'll have mine one day." He turned to Diana. "What's happened to that husband of yours?"

"I have no idea. Someone said he may have gone to work for the *Wall Street Journal*."

"A man of total principle." Blaise chuckled.

"He left his coat and hat in the office," said Peter, angling his chair so that Aaron Burr was not in his line of sight. "We may raffle them off." Then he realized that he had so arranged his chair that immediately in front of him, on a side table, he could enjoy the silver-framed portrait of Enid and Clay on their wedding day. He tried not to look at Clay and, of course, could not look at anything else as he envisaged the preposterously handsome face and body entwined with Diana on a bed—but where? When? How often?

"Your sponsor, Mrs. Samuel I. Bloch, paid me a call." Blaise was in a good mood.

"My ideal sponsor. When I wanted to get rid of Billy Thorne, she discovered, quite on her own, a loophole in our agreement with him, and that was that."

"Practical woman. She wants to buy the house."

"Laurel House?" Diana sounded astonished.

"The very same. When I told her how much I wanted for it, she didn't bat an eye."

It was Peter's turn to be astonished. "You'd really sell?"

"For the right price. Why not? We're too far out of town. Your mother likes the idea of being able to walk to Woodward and Lothrop's."

"She'll never walk there, or anywhere else." Like so many indolent people, Frederika never ceased to celebrate the virtues of exercise, which, in her case, meant, once a week, a stately dog paddle across— never the length of—the pool.

"Where will you live?" Peter felt suddenly ejected from what had been for so long his home.

"There's no hurry. Georgetown maybe. Or back to Massachusetts Avenue. Our old house is only rented for another year. Anyway, we must adjust to postwar America. We must simplify. We've always had trouble getting servants to work so far out of town. Now we won't be able to get any. Besides, it appears that all the servants were killed in the war."

"That means another monument at Arlington." Peter had just done a piece celebrating Washington as the great necropolis of a nation so furiously dedicated to peace that it was almost never not at war to ensure ultimate peace for all time. "President Truman will dedicate it to the Unknown Upstairs Maid, sunk at Pearl Harbor, while polishing the brass."

"What are you going to do about Pearl Harbor?" Blaise had lately shown more than a polite interest in Peter's projects. Peter wondered if, perhaps, his father might not be poaching his ideas for the *Tribune*.

"It depends on what *your* father does."

Peter turned to Diana, who simply shook her head and said, "He can't hold hearings because hearings are being held. He could release his . . ." Diana paused, in search of a word. ". . . his findings. But who would testify in his favor?"

"What . . . findings?" Blaise was now the alert publisher of the capital's finest morning newspaper.

But Peter was not about to give his father so potentially sensational a story. "It's something that may or may not be relevant—the higher hearsay."

"So I'll have to wait until I read what you write?" Blaise's attempt at a jolly smile vanished beneath disappointed jowls.

"If I write about it. How is Enid?" Peter changed the subject.

"We're still trying to find a way for her to divorce Clay."

"I thought it was going to be the other way around." Diana was bold.

Blaise seemed surprised that she would be interested. "Well, yes, that's been discussed, too. Which is worse for a young man in politics? To divorce a wife in a sanitarium or have her divorce him? Neither's apt to be very desirable."

"Particularly," said Diana, "back home in the ultraconservative Second District."

"Burden! Of course. Yes, he'll be concerned, won't he? He's handling Clay's campaign."

"Very concerned," Diana reprised, glancing at Peter, who looked away. He had still not absorbed the fact that she was back within Clay's orbit. But then he had not believed the rumors—admittedly, before he knew her well—that she had been in love with Clay, who had then left her to marry Enid for the sake of his career while she had married Billy Thorne to show that her judgment in these matters could be as misguided as his. After all, Clay had finally lost Enid to alcohol and a lover in the Navy, but, in the process, he had obtained custody of Blaise Sanford and, presently, he would be free, one way or another, to return to

Diana, daughter of his mentor and campaign manager. Idly, Peter tried to hate Clay and was pleased to note that even a second-best effort was more than enough to start his blood pressure to rise.

"I'm going to New York," Peter announced, somewhat to his own surprise.

"To live?" Blaise was politely neutral.

"No. To stay with Aeneas. Meet some of our contributors."

"That's *always* a mistake," said the senior publisher. "They'll ask you for more money which you don't have."

E L E V E N

Mr. and Mrs. Aeneas Duncan and three-year-old Master Duncan lived five floors up in an old gray—for some reason—brownstone in Thirteenth Street west of Sixth Avenue. "We have a guest room," Aeneas had admitted when Peter said he'd probably stay at the Gotham Hotel where Sanfords always stayed.

"Petesie!" Rosalind Duncan threw her arms around him. She, alone in the world, called him Petesie, but then she had pet names for everyone; indeed, she had a tendency, thanks to her profession as a child psychologist, to chatter away in baby talk, which no doubt delighted tiny patients but unnerved her contemporaries. "Isn't him a bit porky-worky?" She patted Peter's stomach, which he promptly drew in.

"Actually, I've lost four pounds. I play squash three times a week," he added, defensively.

"Of course Petesie does."

While Aeneas made them a drink, Rosalind showed Peter his room, which looked out on a windowless cement wall. Well, this was the New York of the intellectuals and Peter must get to know it since he had finally raised enough money for *The American Idea* to increase its coverage of the arts. Although Peter had thought of Aeneas as a philosopher with a polemical bent, he was now discovering that that diligent sleuth, who had pretty much solved the Pearl Harbor mystery, was addicted to poetry; Aeneas had published his master's dissertation on Pope's *Dunciad*; he was now excited by a young poet, Robert Lowell, whose collection *Lord Weary's Castle* was far too Roman Catholic for Peter's taste. Aeneas was reviewing it at length in the magazine, thus launching the new arts section.

"It would be a lot easier to publish out of New York," said Aeneas, not for the first time. In the next room Rosalind was now tending to Master Duncan, with many a coo and hoot from overbonded mother and child.

"We can't. Every America idea is political. That means Washington."

"Lowell . . . political?" Aeneas shook his head.

"A young Boston Puritan from that solemn clan becomes a conscientious objector in the war and then turns Roman Catholic. What could be more political? More weirdly American?"

"What a Marxist critic you would have made!" Aeneas chuckled and coughed on cigarette smoke. "Speaking of Marxists, there's one who wants to meet you. He's a fan of the magazine. Lives at the Chelsea Hotel. Stays up all night in nightclubs. Writes songs. Been married but there is always a young man around."

"I have heard of the love that dares not whisper its name. Mother says it's more of a New York sort of thing than a Washington one."

"Mother's not just, as we used to say in the Army, beating her gums." Aeneas blew smoke at a Léger poster set in a somber bookcase crowded with review copies of recent novels and books of poetry. Peter saw to it that history and politics were sent to the Union Trust Building office, already too small for their increased circulation.

Peter had never before seen the Chelsea Hotel, an old building that had once given shelter to Mark Twain and Thomas Wolfe. A suspicious man at a desk in one corner of the lobby shouted, "Where you going?" Aeneas told him. The man barked a number as they entered what looked to be one of the first elevators in the city: a wire cage with a scarred wood floor, precariously set within a vast dark staircase that filled the center of the building.

"Grim," said Peter.

"There are those who love it."

At the end of a long corridor, Aeneas knocked on a door, which opened to the sound of an entire orchestra reverberating off high-ceilinged rooms. The voice of Paul Robeson was thundering the plangent question "Who am I?" then answering himself, in thunder: *"America!"*

"Come in," said John Latouche, a short barrel-chested, barrel-stomached man with a large head, bushy dark hair, bright blue eyes. "No one's here yet. Except Paul Robeson. He often drops by to sing for me: it's the acoustics in the Chelsea, he says. Better than the Ear of Dionysos in Syracuse, the one in Sicily not New York. I've never been to Sicily. But I know upstate New York like the back of my hand. Utica in the spring is why there were all those bloody footprints in the snow at Valley Forge. Why we fought!" During this, Latouche switched off Paul Robeson, who was currently inhabiting an old scratched record.

Latouche shouted, "Don!" A lanky young man came in from a bedroom that looked as if a tornado had been rehearsing among the bedclothes. "This is Don. He's a poet from St. John's College in Maryland. Currently, he's my secretary. He also drives a taxi, for the sheer adventure of meeting exciting people outside his usual ken."

"We've got whiskey or rum," said Don. Peter and Aeneas asked for whiskey. Don went to the bar, which was a large tray uneasily balanced on the back of a life-size llama made out of innumerable bits of coiled plaster of Paris. "I call this," said Latouche, "my llama in sheep's clothing. The sculptor does only one work every five years. Like clockwork. He rolls what he calls his worms of plaster of Paris with his own hands and then, slowly, builds up his figures. This llama took him most of the thirties to complete. As you can see, very prewar in feeling. Better than Brancusi. For me, he is the Donatello of Macon, Georgia."

Peter found the room somewhat hard to take in. There were posters advertising musical comedies and ballets. Apparently, Latouche had written a film called *Cabin in the Sky*. A piano covered with sheet music was set in an alcove. Books were piled everywhere. He had the latest of everything, including every issue of *The American Idea*.

"I read your paper from start to finish. It's perfect for the toilet if you have colitis which I do and so plenty of time to concentrate. Do you really think that the old gentleman who was for Taft was killed in Philadelphia?"

"You do read everything!" Peter was startled. "Yes, I do. But I could never follow up."

"Don, is that friend of yours who works for Pinkerton still in town?"

"If he isn't in jail."

"Give him a call. We'll get him on the case." Don went into the bedroom and shut the door.

"Did you know," Peter felt obliged to compete in the omniscient league, "that on the first day of the 1940 convention . . ."

"The Philadelphia Philharmonic played my 'Ballad for Americans.' Yes. I heard it on the radio. I'm sick of it. Here's something new." He sat at the piano and played a melodic tune and sang, "It's the coming home together when the day is through, something, something boom and then to do, and the dah dah duh-duh that's always you . . ."

He struck a great chord. "It will sound better when it's actually written. Most pieces don't. Schubert was on the right track. Of course, what's never begun is always best. Like 'The Madonna of the Future.'"

"The what?" Peter was being left far behind.

"A story by Henry James." Aeneas was smug.

"James is coming back, according to my publisher friend Eileen Garrett. She was Conan Doyle's last medium. What a good title." He struck more keys while improvising a duet between Sherlock Holmes in the spirit world and the mysterious Eileen Garrett in Murray Hill.

Then the room began to fill up.

"Contributors, or contributors-to-be," said Aeneas to Peter, who knew only a few of their names. One was a tall languid young man who could, at the drop of a hat, according to Latouche, sing all of Gertrude Stein's opera *Four Saints in Three Acts*, playing all the parts. "But," said Latouche ominously, "no hat will be dropped this night."

In due course, the composer of the opera, Virgil Thomson, appeared. A fussy precise-voiced little man with a pink bald head, he introduced himself to Peter. "I live in the Chelsea, too. Touche provides us with twenty-four-hour entertainment. Amazing that they haven't thrown him out yet. He never pays rent. It's a principle with him. What do you do?"

Peter gave him a brief report on his few attainments. "I'm not reading about politics this season." Thomson was crisp. "There's been too much history lately. Hate it. Not good for the arts. That's why I'm so glad you're giving more pages to the arts. Who will you get for music?"

"You?"

"No, baby. I'm taken. *Herald Tribune* forever. What about Paul Bowles?"

Peter had not heard the name before. Fortunately, Thomson liked to answer his own questions. "He spells me at the *Trib* when I've got a concert. He's a real critic. Knows what *not* to write about. Rare gift. Also, *never* gives his opinion. Who, outside maybe your mother, wants to know what you think about Mahler? Just describe for the reader exactly what you hear. That's the trick of it. Paul and Jane—his wife— are staying up at Libby's in the country. You know—Libby Holman. She killed her husband, the Reynolds tobacco man. Singer. Good Singer, Libby. She's hired Paul to make an opera of *Yerma*. Paul and Jane have a dowsing rod for money. But then you have to, if you're a serious composer. Anyway, when they come back to town, you must meet them. You do pay?" Thomson's eyes were suddenly very sharp.

"Oh yes."

"Baby, you only get what you pay for in this world, as I always tell Mrs. Reid at the *Trib*."

Latouche brought over a Dracula-pale man with eyes that seemed to be permanently half shut. "Here's your film critic. Parker Tyler. There's no one like him."

"Is it true that you are the nephew of Emma Traxler?" The voice was pansy-eager with an ironic intermittent base—bass?—to it that captured Peter's full attention. He confessed that he was.

"Someone—Julian Sawyer over there, I think—said he saw her in the lobby of the St. Regis the other day. He does the lobbies of all the grand hotels, hoping to see stars. He saw her, obviously."

"She was in town for Harry Hopkins' funeral."

"I've seen twenty-seven of her films, including the one she made in Tunisia with René Clément, a mistake because he's not in her class. I regard *Mary Queen of Scots* as a touchstone for film criticism. A sort of high mark never to be reached again by any actress with such primitive lighting and dentistry."

"I must tell her. She did say that that film ended her career in Hollywood."

"*Two-Faced Woman* did the same for Garbo, and that was a negative masterpiece, too. I wrote about it in *View*."

Peter wondered what *View* was. There was, obviously, a vast intricate world in New York, as distant from Washington as moon from earth. Were the two compatible? Aeneas thought so but then Aeneas belonged to both and Peter was at sea with Parker Tyler if not with the merry Latouche, who introduced him to a round little woman with squirrel-bright eyes.

"Peter. This is Dawn Powell. The economist. She's longing to write for your magazine."

"It's been my dream ever since your first issue. But I warn you, I'm a post-Keynesian. I'm also postmenopausal as of last September at Doctor's Hospital. I've got the scars to prove it. So I'm giving a party to celebrate. A carnival. Carne-vale, dear. That's Latin for . . ."

"Flesh farewell."

"Go to the head of the class." She turned to Latouche. "Yesterday Mary McCarthy paid a call on Bunny Wilson." To Peter: "Her exhusband. And when he locked himself in his study to escape her, she set fire to a wastebasket and tried to smoke him out. It was a metal wire basket, by the way. Always get details like that right. Otherwise your listeners start to wonder why the house didn't burn down."

"I'll make a note of that," said Latouche, moving away.

"Why smoke him out?" asked Peter.

"Because he's made so much money out of *Memoirs of Hecate County* and, of course, Mary's envious. In fact, envy's sort of a religion with her, which really makes *her* to be envied as someone with some-

thing to believe in. To cling to in the bad times when the living isn't—
'ain't,' I should say—easy. All my friends are communists. But then so
am I. And all of them are eaten up by envy, too. The Golden Calf is
their god. Of course, I'd love to make money, too. No. Not make it. I'd
love to be *given* a lot of money."

"Are you really an economist?"

"Oh, no, child." Suddenly, she became a gracious grandmotherly
crone, presiding over a cookie jar. "Not poor old Dawn, trying to get
that ole debil checkbook in order. No. I'm simply a purveyor of home
truths, the more devastating the better. A mere teller of tales. About
exotic places that make the reader's heart—hearts—pound. 'I' before
'E' except after 'C'—oh, there is nothing about the literary art that
your old granny don't know in her bones."

"What exotic places?"

"Ohio, you silly-billy. That's where everyone in Greenwich Village comes from. I'll write you a monthly 'Letter from Ohio.' About
real folks who sit on front porches, incest and depravity forever on their
narrow minds. I can't think how Faulkner gets away with it and I don't.
Of course, he doesn't make any money either except when he prosti-
tutes himself by writing for the movies. He sold out years ago to Hollywood. Now, God knows, I'm perfectly willing to sell out, but I can't
find a buyer. Just top the rum, Touche, and be quick about it. Auntie
Dawn is parched." She gave Peter a lascivious wink. "So tell me exactly
what it is about George Sand you *don't* like. And tell me exactly how
you finally fell out with her. Oh, her promiscuity is a given. You must
have known that going in. Even so, I want *all* the details. And remember this—you can trust me, dear," she added with a Satanic leer.
"Mum's the word, cross my heart and hope to die. Your secrets are my
secrets. The word 'mongoloid' will never pass my lips. That is a solemn
promise."

By midnight, Aeneas and Peter were running out of money as they
followed Latouche from nightclubs in the Village all the way up to
those on the East Side. Wherever he went, at his entrance, musicians
would play "Taking a Chance on Love." He also acquired, along the

way, a train of admirers, some actually known to him, and like a Pied Piper he led them from dark place to dark place until he arrived at the elegant door to the Blue Angel in Fifty-fifth Street. When Latouche shouted, "Cover charge!" he lost most of his entourage.

As the smiling doormen held the door open, Touche said to Peter, "I've got a surprise for you."

The Blue Angel occupied a thin brownstone. The front part of the ground floor contained a bar on the left and shiny black plastic booths on the right. The back part was full of round tables set before a small stage where comedians practiced their desperate art and musicians played, all in an onyx-black room with hanging plaster angels backlit in pink. "It's just like Juliet's tomb," said Touche as the tall pale green manager, Herbert Jacoby, a Frenchman who had once been secretary to Léon Blum, greeted Touche and his party, to which had been added a beautiful black singer who had joined them at some point in the Village along with a stout banker named Reg Newton, "A veritable Midas, aren't you, Reg?" Touche was exuberant. "Give him an apple and it turns to twenty-four-karat gold. So, Reg, we'll let you pick up the bill. But just this once. Mustn't spoil you." Reg beamed.

The surprise was at a booth opposite the bar. Peter's first cousin Emma Sanford and her husband, Timothy X. Farrell, were greeting Touche, who introduced Peter to Emma. "I just know you two will have a lot in common."

Two parties now became one. The lugubrious Jacoby suggested supper for the newcomers. Sadly, he told them his menu. Glumly, he gave their orders to a maître d'. Despairingly, he moaned, "I must go introduce Alice Pearce. She is," he gasped, "funny." He left them for the crowded back room

"Herbert missed his calling," said Touche. "He's a born funeral director. *Pompes funèbres* grow out of his ears like celery. He has all the joie de vivre of an open grave. Yet he gets the funniest people in the business to play the room for next to nothing." Touche finished a large snifter of brandy; then cleared his throat. "Now I suppose you're all wondering why I asked you here tonight. Tim Farrell and I are doing a movie together. A musical, actually. The story of Ulysses—except this

Ulysses is an American farm boy who goes off to the Spanish-American War and gets lost on his way back home . . ."

At a pause in the ongoing monologue, Peter turned to Emma. "I suppose I should congratulate you on your marriage."

"It was sudden, I think." Emma, the new blonde, was handsomer than Emma, the old brunette. "I do know that I was just bowled over by Tim when we first met."

"But that," said Peter in the interest of major mischief, "was years and years ago when he was with the Black Pearl of the Baltic."

"Alsace-Lorraine," said Emma. "Yes, I knew him as a child when he and Mother . . . You know? Then I met him again years later, after they had broken up, and he was a different person. I was a different person." The waiter asked her what she wanted on the supper menu. "Oh, the lobster Newburg! I love it! But instead of the Newburg sauce, I'll have it with just plain mayonnaise. Hellman's, if you have it. Though I despise Lillian's politics. I'll start with the onion soup. Really thick, if you have it. And could I have a glass of dry white wine with ice on the side? Not *in* it but *on* the side. And some butter right now."

While Peter ordered a minute steak, his cousin proved not to be much changed since she had headed Fortress America. She was now in full flow while Latouche and her husband conferred, Aeneas and the spectacular black girl—could she be Thelma Carpenter?—laughed together, something Aeneas rarely did with anyone; Reg smiled happily, wallet at the ready.

"Tim and I are both interested in the *Hometown* series." Emma sliced the butter squares into triangles; and ignored the bread.

"Aunt Caroline's dream."

"Well, it was Tim who made the pictures. We're looking for something offbeat. But with the right sort of message, you know?"

"No, I don't," said Peter, who did know what she meant. When he had heard of the surprise marriage between Emma and Tim, he had decided that either she had changed for the better or Tim for the worse. He had no way of judging the weather of Tim's soul, but Emma was as wildly overwrought as she had been in her prewar campaign against the Russian Bolsheviks, only now her fight had shifted to the menace of communism within the United States itself.

"We're safe from the Russians. For the moment. We have the atomic bomb. By the time they have it, we'll have the hydrogen bomb and then, one day—when they go too far—we'll drop it. Pow! No more Moscow." Methodically, she broke the crust of her onion soup and, voluptuously, stirred the contents of the bowl clockwise, inhaling the steam with distaste. "It's all so clear. They want to conquer the world. Just the way Hitler did. It's also clear—now, anyway—that we should have let Hitler destroy them first. Then we could have dealt with him. But my mother's Red friends like Harry Hopkins were too busy working for Stalin. Now the life-and-death struggle for Iran's begun. Stalin's on the march in Azerbaijan. We must stop him. By force. And we will. This year, anyway." Now the spoon which had been going clockwise was going counterclockwise. Was this some coded message American patriots used to identify one another?

"You and Tim," Peter was tentative, "will make a film about Stalin?" Was this the right response to the onion soup code?

"No. No. We wouldn't dare. I mean, tell the truth. Hollywood is honeycombed with communists."

"Like L. B. Mayer?"

"Not the studio heads. Except, in a way, they are the worst. They only want to make money. They turn a blind eye on communists like Capra and Myrna Loy because they are box-office. Mother's friend Eleanor Roosevelt gives them their orders—directly. I've heard Mother on the telephone with Eleanor. Thick as thieves." The waiter asked if Emma was through with her now well-exercised soup. "Yes, thank you. It was delicious. Could I have *more* ice. And white wine?"

The butter, untouched, was melting on its chaste plate.

"Our plan is to do a *Hometown* film with what look to be true-blue Americans who turn out to be secret Reds. They take over the schools. At least one classroom, anyway, where they subtly question capitalism."

"It hardly seems possible!"

Peter was rewarded with an angry glance. "Don't think your magazine isn't being thoroughly examined by the Justice Department."

"For typos?"

"No. For un-American ideas. We've been lobbying President Truman and he's promised to set up a Loyalty Review Board in the next few months. Everyone in government must swear a special oath of allegiance to the country and vow to fight communism in all its forms."

"That's what Hitler made the Germans do. It's not very American, Emma."

"Well, it's going to be Thank heaven. You have to fight fire with fire. Besides, why should a loyal American fear a loyalty oath?"

Peter was amused. "Why should a *dis*loyal one fear an oath?"

"Perjury. Three years in prison." Emma was prompt.

Peter saw that her powerful emotions had swept her far past mere common sense. Had it swept the President too? If so . . . "Dewey may well be elected in '48 as the freedom candidate."

"This is bipartisan. Everybody's aboard. We've got them all."

"Who's 'we'?"

"That would be telling." Emma giggled as she scraped the mayonnaise off her lobster and onto the edge of the plate. "I'll give you one clue. Senator Bingham's with us. He may be heading up the whole thing. Look! We have to do it. We've no choice. The propaganda is so heavy on the communist side. So weak on ours. That's how I convinced L.B. that our picture has to be made if we're to win this war against the Reds."

"And Myrna Loy?"

"You should take those matters more seriously, Peter. When they break up the great fortunes, that will be the end of *you*. Go ahead, laugh. You won't when it happens. The IRS is in the hands of a cell of dedicated Marxists." Delicately she removed a lobster claw from its shell and placed it neatly on the side of the plate opposite to the mayonnaise. It was then that Peter realized that she was not going to eat anything. As a sign of her specialness, the most expensive items must be brought her; then as a sign of her . . . of her what? Ascetic character? . . . everything she'd ordered would be thrown out. Since she was on the verge of plumpness, she obviously nourished herself plentifully when not on view.

The rest of the evening was something of a haze. Peter and the beautiful black singer ended up not in romantic Harlem as he had hoped with Cab Calloway's hi-de-hi's and hi-de-ho's echoing in the streets, but in a comfortable Murray Hill flat where the young singer, daughter of a prosperous orthodontist, lived with a roommate, currently home with her folks in Oklahoma. As always, at the moment of climax, Peter felt that the rest of his life must be spent doing just this with so uniquely perfect a girl, even as he rode wave after wave of ever-diminishing passion until sleep abruptly engulfed him. When morning came, passion spent, he was ready for his usual getaway; even so, he was hurt that she, the soul of easy amiability, was quite as eager as he that he be gone.

"Could I have your number?" he asked, wondering what had happened to that dream of the eternity he had wanted to spend with her. He got the number. Eternity, presumably, could look after itself.

Aeneas was relieved when Peter returned. Rosalind had gone to her office.

"There's a Tudor ballet at the Ballet Theatre . . ."

"Except for *Nutcracker Suite,* I've never seen a ballet. I don't think anyone in Washington has, either—at least not in the city. The National Theatre just does comedies like *Three Men on a Horse.*"

That evening, Rosalind stayed home with a feverish child while Peter and Aeneas watched an extraordinary actress who was billed as a ballerina perform Antony Tudor's *Pillar of Fire.* Peter had never seen anything like it and, apparently, neither had the rest of the world until the war's end and classical ballet, with "psychological" variations, had conquered New York. For Peter, the result was revelatory.

Later, in the bleak Russian Tea Room in Fifty-seventh Street, Peter ate pressed caviar and drank hot tea from a glass; while Aeneas poked at beef Stroganoff, Peter quizzed Aeneas about ballet—what it had been, what it was becoming.

"The fact is that the war froze every one of the arts. Particularly the performing arts. The best young men were gone. Now they're back. But instead of the androgynous types that used to go in for ballet we've got what look to be American high school athletes up on stage, and they make their British and French counterparts seem much too fragile by comparison."

Peter was looking through a stack of Ballet Theatre playbills. There were photographs of a ballet about three young sailors on leave in wartime Manhattan. *Fancy Free* was the title. Not a swan in sight. The music was by the young Leonard Bernstein, who was talked of—if not listened to—even in Washington.

"Bernstein?" Peter looked at Aeneas, suddenly become his guide to Parnassus.

"Late twenties. Does everything. Composes symphonies. That musical comedy *On the Town*. Conducts . . ."

"And young. Everyone's as young as we are," Peter marveled. "Is that the sign of a new cycle? Or arrested development, arrested by war?"

"I have no idea. Probably both."

Peter was thoughtful. "Young. American. The American idea. Something new. But only for us? Or is the same thing happening in Europe?"

Aeneas shook his head. "They're too busy trying to survive this winter. Certainly, we're inventing the new ballet. We're far ahead of the French *and* the British, who don't know it yet. Our poets . . ."

"Lowell. Yes. I know. Prose? Painting?"

Aeneas shrugged. "I don't read novels. Don't look at pictures. Peggy Guggenheim's in charge of modern art. At least here in Manhattan, She will know."

Peter was beginning to feel a—what? Want or desire? Like the first stage of sex that he'd experienced the night before? Except he knew that this sensation was not about to fade away, stage by diminishing stage, because there would never be a climax to what would be for him—or any interested contemporary—an endless process of engulfment by a newborn civilization in a traditionally artless land. An *American* ballet! The concept had not existed before the war. Now if all the other arts were suddenly to be airborne . . .

"Could it be that . . ." he started; then stopped.

Aeneas said, "It's bad manners to begin a rhetorical question and then not finish it. Could it be that—what?"

"I don't know. That is, I don't know what it could be."

"Start by telling me what it is." Aeneas had shifted into ontological gear.

"That ballet where the dancer I like so much . . . the one who acts."

"Nora Kaye."

"Gives birth onstage . . ."

"*Undertow* by Antony Tudor. Giving birth to the very large Hugh Laing."

"Well, that's the 'it.'" Something very large is being born now."

"In ballet?"

"In the United States. Given half a chance, of course. Depression's over. War's over. Europe's our dependency. Japan's our colony. Russia's freezing and starving this winter while we have *Undertow*."

"A renaissance? *Here?*" Aeneas was skeptical.

"I'll settle for naissance. We've never had a high culture or anything close . . ."

"New England Indian summer?"

"What was new? What was English? What was Indian? That was also far too chilly a season for summer. A handful of eccentrics in Boston with old Walt Whitman down in New Jersey singing the body general electric." Peter was now in full imaginative flight. "Think of all the energy we put into these two wars. Into breaking the atom. And now the education—or what passes for education—of the veterans, a whole class, millions of them, freed from the virtues of the family farm and the assembly line, are going to go to Harvard . . ."

"Surely Detroit is the true home of our genius and Cambridge, Mass, our school for dunces."

Peter, unable to sit still, went over to the window and looked out at the plain cement wall of the next building. "This is classic," he said. "Literally. Think of Rome when Augustus made peace in all the world that he and Rome had conquered."

"Romans still celebrate his birthday, two millennia later. August fifteenth. But," Aeneas was dour, "his peace didn't last all that long . . ."

"It lasted four hundred years. That was when all the arts flourished. When something new was born . . ."

"Like Hugh Laing in *Undertow?*"

"Except he is born onstage at the Ballet Theatre and not in a manger. If it wasn't too late, I'd change *American Idea* to something like *American Civilization*."

Aeneas laughed. "A thin paper but there will be those who love it."

Peter was in no way deflated. "We start from scratch. Take me to Peggy Guggenheim's."

Peter was pleased that many of the assembled artists and patrons in Guggenheim's low-ceilinged flat—more like a small house than a Manhattan apartment—had heard of his paper if not of him. The hostess was dressed as a peasant girl in a frilly skirt, wooden beads, close-cut gray hair; she had a large rosy nose not unlike that of the congenial W. C. Fields. She squinted at Aeneas. "Oh, it's you. So this is Peter Sanford!" Peter shook her hand. "The Sanfords are very rich so you can buy all sorts of things in the gallery. There's Léger." Peter turned to look at what even he could tell was not a painting by Léger.

"No, Peter, not the picture. The painter." She introduced him to Léger, a tall burly Frenchman in workman's clothes. Then she vanished. Since he had nothing to talk to Léger about, Peter wandered about the room. The editor of *View* introduced himself. He had three names. He identified various poets and painters. "Peggy scoops them all up." Peter was now more than ever at sea.

Aeneas was sardonically aware that Peter's first plunge into postwar American civilization was not quite what he had expected. The two of them drank cheap red wine at the edge of a group surrounding their hostess's husband, Laurence Vail—or ex-husband—with Peggy such formalities were seldom spelled out. Vail was demonstrating how to put a model ship inside an opalescent bottle.

"Everybody's foreign," Peter muttered to Aeneas.

"Not everybody. There's James Agee. He writes about movies for *Time*. He thinks a lot of junk movies are high art . . ."

"That's part of the changeover." Peter was beginning to recover his enthusiasm. "The line between high art and popular . . ."

". . . has been fading away for some time now. But this isn't really New York. It's a displaced Paris. Soon everyone here will be going home."

"Peter!" A blond girl with slightly hyperthyroid gray eyes greeted him.

"Cornelia." They had known each other from the years that they had served together at Mrs. Shippen's dancing school, where the young of Washington were sent at puberty and then, year after year, were expected to ascend life's social ladder together until marriage within the dancing class and the prompt replication of themselves in order to repeat the process until, presumably, the Day of Judgment, when prizes would be awarded to the best waltzer, best Lambeth Walker, most enthusiastic interpreter of the Big Apple.

Cornelia Claiborne had taken up with several young academics who believed that the country urgently needed yet another academic quarterly review. Somewhat jealously, he quizzed her; was relieved to discover that the review they were planning would be mostly literary with a classical bias. Nothing new need apply. Then she introduced him to a lean young man with a blond crewcut like Clay's, not a recommendation in Peter's current mood. But then Peter realized that they knew each other from Washington. Gene Vidal was several years younger than Peter. Each had been at St. Alban's; each had attended Mrs. Shippen's; then war had taken Vidal to the Pacific and Peter to the far more perilous corridors of the Pentagon. Now, to Peter's bemusement, Vidal had dropped his Christian name and as Gore Vidal had published a first novel; a second novel was on the way. Although Peter would have preferred death to reading a book by a Washington contemporary even younger than himself, he had not realized that the book he had read about—some kind of war novel—was by the boy that he had known prewar.

"My mother insists that Gore writes just like Shakespeare," said Cornelia, causing the young—twenty? twenty-one?—author to blush.

Peter nodded gravely. "With our new civilization we'll certainly need a Shakespeare sooner or later. Why not you?"

Vidal shook his head sadly. "I could never manage those rhyming couplets at the end of scenes."

"I could do those for you," said Cornelia. She turned to Peter. "Gore almost married Rosalind Rust."

"It was her mother that nearly married me." Peter now remembered hearing about Vidal from friends in common. After three years in the Army he had refused to go on to college. Instead, he had left Washington for New York, published his first novel, and taken a job with a publisher. Plainly a reckless optimist.

Aeneas had joined them. Peter made introductions. Then he said, "We've just decided that the United States is going to have a civilization at last. We've been auditioning Shakespeares."

"Do we really want a civilization? Isn't it sort of nice, the mess we've got?" Was Vidal mocking them? He seemed too young and bland to have that sort of humor. "I mean, we've done awfully well as the hayseeds of the Western world. Why spoil it? Certainly we don't want to be like these jokers." Vidal indicated Peggy's version of Comus's *rout*. "And do nothing but speak French all day long and in our sleep, too. No, we've got to stay dumb. We owe it to our forefathers. To Plymouth Rock. That great rock we landed on. That really thick rock. Dense, too. Our foundation and our emblem. In the sign of that clueless rock, we're bound to conquer the world."

Aeneas was not amused but Peter was. "You should go in for satire. For us. In *The American Idea*."

Vidal laughed. "I mostly do storms at sea. The ones Conrad didn't bother with."

There was a round of applause for Laurence Vail, who had finally raised the sails of a miniature ship inside a bottle. "That's my sort of ship," said the young war novelist.

"I intend for us to create—we'll include you and Cornelia if you want to come along for the ride—America's Golden Age." Peter was overwhelmed not only by his own megalomania but by the new world empire's untapped resources.

He was promptly deflated by Vidal. "How can you have a golden age after Roosevelt took us off the gold standard?"

"Uranium," said Aeneas, "will do just as well."

TWELVE

|

The new offices of *The American Idea* were located in a nineteenth-century red-brick building to the east of the Capitol. The neighborhood was middle-class Negro and a ten-minute walk from the Capitol. Peter had made a flat for himself on the third floor, and so, at last, he had a home of his own on his own.

The new arts pages had magically increased circulation in New York City and Boston and not harmed it too much in the District of Columbia, where the arts were regarded at best with indifference, at worst with active dislike or, as Representative Smith of Virginia said, when yet another doomed bill came before Congress requesting some sort of minimal funding for the arts, "I have always regarded poker as a peculiarly American art form, and so I must respectfully propose that this magnificent card game be federally subsidized along with your symphony orchestras and picture paintings, thus acknowledging the native creativity of the true American."

Peter had written an editorial expressing wonder how it was possible that the world's political capital should have only one theater, no opera house, no symphony hall, and no museum of art had it not been for the Mellon family, who had built for the city an imperial marble building of Augustan splendor to house their great collection. Since this palace was begun pre–world empire, it was, Peter wrote, somewhat recklessly, a premonition of what was sure to come. Thus far, of course, only a mock subsidy for poker had been proposed by the Capitoline geese.

In February, after they had got back from the conquest of New York—conquest in the sense that they, not New York, had been conquered—Aeneas had begun to cultivate a smooth young Missouri lawyer called Clark Clifford who was now very close to the Missouri president. Clifford had come to the White House as a naval aide. Then he had become the President's legal counsel, the same job that Sam Rosenman had performed for Roosevelt. It was Clifford who had written the speech that Truman had delivered to Congress during the great railroad strike in which the President, by some sort of executive decree, drafted all the railroad workers into the Army; then he ordered them, as soldiers, back to work. Fortunately, for what was left of the republic, the strike was settled while Truman was addressing Congress; later the Senate rejected the dictatorship that he had so temptingly put on offer.

Peter called for a symposium on the subject. Most of the worthies who participated affected alarm at the thought that the vast wartime powers Roosevelt had armed himself with might somehow have become permanent. Aeneas had then interviewed Clifford, found him charming if evasive. "I suspect," Aeneas had summed up, "that they are not very thoughtful over at the White House. Everything's calculated for short-term political advantage. During the strike, Truman was accused of being weak. So he does something that looks to be strong."

"Dangerous," said Peter.

"Irresistible," said Aeneas. "Wartime powers are the dream of every peacetime president, even the meek and mild Harry."

"Why don't we print the Bill of Rights on the front page of the magazine?" Peter made the suggestion casually. Aeneas could be scathing.

"Every issue?"

"Why not?"

"Wouldn't it be too radical?" Aeneas was not joking.

"Perhaps un-American." Peter was now tempted to act upon his sudden seditious impulse. Curious things were happening in the city and, presumably, in the country as well. A series of strikes by militant labor unions had caused considerable unease. Yet why was anyone surprised? The wage and price controls made necessary by war could not be maintained indefinitely in a so-called free economy. Then a serious shortage of housing affected everyone, while the election of 1946 had been called "the beefsteak election," thanks to a mysterious shortage of beef. At the center of the turmoil was the timid nearsighted little President eager to be farsighted and formidably strong, particularly with the Russians, who were now being blamed for whatever was wrong in a world where nothing seemed to be going right for the triumphant new world empire whose mock Roman and Greek temples looked more than ever out of place beside the homely Potomac River where once wigwams had housed an earlier, less busy race.

Peter and Aeneas disagreed on Truman's character. Peter thought him ignorant and hopelessly ineffective. Aeneas thought him almost as decisive as he pretended to be in his odd outbursts at the Russians, not to mention at political rivals like Henry Wallace, whose sensible speech in Madison Square Garden the previous fall had lost him his Cabinet seat. Although Wallace had cleared the speech in advance with Truman, the President had not grasped its hardly complex message: "We have no more business in the political affairs of Eastern Europe than Russia has in the political affairs of Latin America, Western Europe, and the United States." When faced with this attack on his Administration's tendency to meddle everywhere, Truman had told the press that he had not approved the contents of the speech, only the Secretary of Commerce's right to make it. Even the most ardent Red-baiter found Truman's lie unhelpfully crude, as was his furious letter to Wallace firing him from the Cabinet, a letter which, upon uneasy second thought, Truman asked Wallace to return to him. Wallace gracefully gave back the letter; then quit the Cabinet, to begin a race for the presidency in

1948. The Wallace business had finally convinced Aeneas that Truman was simply too inept for the office that Roosevelt had so absently placed him in line for.

The two editors then chose as their "Fool of the Week" the favorite Christian divine of the reactionary liberals, one Reinhold Niebuhr, *Life* magazine's resident saint, who had declared war on the Soviet in the name of Henry Luce: "Russian truculence cannot be mitigated by further concessions. Russia hopes to conquer the whole of Europe strategically and ideologically." This did not seem to be possible, wrote Aeneas at his most reasonable, since the United States had already established itself as the master of Europe. Meanwhile, he noted that Neibuhr's analysis was very close to that of Clark Clifford's memorandum to the President in September of 1946 entitled "American Relations with the Soviet Union." Clifford had "proved" that the Soviet Union was aiming, like Nazi Germany before it, for eventual world domination. Since the President had insisted that all copies of the report be kept under lock and key, Aeneas had only been able to ferret out key passages, copied by others before the top-secret memorandum was withdrawn. But it was known that Soviet military power had been greatly exaggerated in order to justify an American military buildup. "It's pretty much the usual stuff," said Aeneas. He handed Peter a page of quotations. "Red Flag over the Tower of London. The Kremlin's flag, not the Labour Party's. It's very alarmist."

Peter's eye had caught one line at the end of the page. He read aloud. " 'The United States should support and assist all democratic countries which are in any way menaced by the USSR.' Isn't that a bit broad?"

"Mr. Clifford's strokes are very broad indeed. He can only mean that we have the right—in fact, the God-given duty—to interfere in any country anywhere."

"Has Truman really bought this?"

"We'll know when he speaks to Congress. On Greece and Turkey."

Aeneas promptly read: " 'Two freedom-loving democracies are now threatened by monolithic communism,' except that they aren't enthusiasts for freedom nor are they democracies, and now with Tito and Mao off on their own, communism isn't monolithic. Curious how nothing our government says ever means anything at all."

"More curious how no one notices, except us." But Peter had been impressed by the Administration's ability to manipulate the crisis brought on by England's financial inability to support a thuggish Greek government faced with an internal communist threat. Although Stalin had agreed at Yalta that Greece was within England's sphere of influence, he was now faced with a communist Greek party eager to overthrow the newly restored monarchy with, it was said, the aid of Yugoslavia, whose leader, Tito, had recently broken with Moscow. Stalin, Peter had written, was in a no-win situation. If he helped the Greek communists, the United States would be certain to intervene at a time, to put it minimally, of considerable inconvenience for him. But if he did not aid the Greeks, acting in his name, the apostate Tito would help them, thus expanding a dangerous new Slav hegemony in Southeast Europe. Into this complex situation the bold certitudes and misrepresentations of Clark Clifford had, suddenly and forcibly, been reinforced by the new under secretary of state from the Union Trust Building, the polished Groton-Yale lawyer Dean Acheson.

Happily for *The American Idea*, Senator James Burden Day had attended a high council of state chaired by the President himself and consisting of the new secretary of state, General George Marshall, and leading congressional figures. Although Marshall was still unable to recall the events leading up to Pearl Harbor, he was, otherwise, a respected and respectable figure in an Administration that was more and more coming to resemble a Mississippi River gambling boat on a Saturday night.

Senator Day had prepared a memorandum immediately after the meeting; he had sent Peter a copy, not for attribution.

February 27, 1947. The White House.

We met in the Cabinet room. The President was in a low-key mood. He had nicked his cheek shaving and a piece of Kleenex clung to the forming scab. On his right sat General Marshall with a State Department folder in front of him. Next to Marshall was Dean Acheson, looking more than ever like a British colonel with his bristling *moustache and clear hawk's eye and what I suppose to be an authentic English accent, or is it just that prep school where he and FDR went? School's name beginning with "G"? On the President's left was Speaker of the House Martin; then Vandenberg, very much the chairman of the Senate Foreign Relations Committee; then Styles Bridges, looking mighty sleek as chairman of the Senate Appropriations Committee; finally, Tom Connally and myself for the Democrats' minority in the Senate. The presence of Bridges meant that the substance of this meeting was to be—what else?—money. The week before the House had cut $6 billion from the President's budget. This made it impossible, said the Secretary of War, for us to maintain our occupation of Germany and Japan.*

General Marshall in civilian clothes is somewhat unimpressive. Like a small-town bank president trying to persuade his board of directors to lend money to an undesirable client. A Southern small-town bank, for the accents of the great-eared Tom Connally of Texas and the bullet-bald Rayburn, also of Texas, set the tone of the entire congressional leadership while the Virginian Marshall and the Missouri President made me think the Civil War might just as well not have been fought. Incidentally, the Southern senators have their offices all in a row in the Senate Office Building—Rebellion Row we call it. I digress.

Marshall gave us an overview of the current crisis in Greece and Turkey. Apparently on Monday the British ambassador presented him with what is called a "blue paper." This means not only "urgent" but "crisis." The British are out of money again and can no longer sustain the Greek government. They feel that if we do not step in, Greece would soon have a communist government and Turkey, everyone's traditional enemy, would be at risk, thus weakening Britain's position in the Middle East, all-important to us because of the Arab oil reserves.

I have never understood the public's reverence for professional military men nor their habit of electing them, from time to time, to the presidency, usually with disastrous results. Admittedly, Marshall's executive talents are of the highest order, or so everyone says. Certainly Roosevelt thought so and kept him on in Washington and out of the war, leaving all martial glory to MacArthur and Eisenhower, the first a master of publicity and the second another chairman of the board, like Marshall himself.

But my objection to Marshall, not least as of last Thursday, is his inability to show us where the danger really lies. We are, all of us, professional politicians, with a tendency to speak in a special code known only to each other and incomprehensible, thank God, to the public. But on an occasion like this where the issue could well be a war with the Soviet Union over Greece and Turkey and our competing spheres of influence, Marshall sounded as if he wanted us to appropriate more money for the acquisition of cavalry horses or military bands. During his recital, I watched Truman, who was beginning to fidget. Was he thinking that he had made a mistake in exchanging sly Jimmy Byrnes for this sea-green incorruptible but slow-witted Army officer? I also could see that Dean Acheson was less than happy with his boss's presentation. Marshall ended with a request that the military budget not be cut; rather it should be increased. "We must act with energy," he said, "or lose by default." He did not say what we would lose.

Truman, plainly unhappy with Marshall, asked for questions.

Bridges, in charge of appropriations, wanted to know just how much this somewhat ill-defined operation would cost.

Connally boomed on about unforeseen consequences. Were we ready for a third world war just to save face for the British, who are forever running out of money just when their presence is actually needed somewhere? The Speaker wanted a price tag. Vandenberg wanted to know if it was true that Stalin was not helping the Greek communists since he was too busy disciplining Tito. In which case this is more of an embarrassment for Stalin—as well as the British government of the day—and hardly a world crisis for the United States.

Acheson was now whispering loudly into Marshall's ear. Marshall nodded and asked the President if the Under Secretary could speak.

I guess Acheson has to be a really sharp lawyer. Also, unlike Marshall, he has mastered his brief—perhaps too well.

He began with an overall look at developments during the last *eighteen months. Apparently, unnoticed by us, the Soviet is conquering the entire world.*

Acheson's aristocratic dislike of our Southern Congress is always apparent. Up to a point, I can sympathize with him. He thinks in great historical terms. He says that our world is now as polarized as it once was between Rome and Carthago—though he hasn't yet repeated Cato's insistent cry "Carthage"—the Soviet Union, that is—"must be destroyed."

For most of our Congress, Carthage is a dull town set in Tennessee's chigger belt. On the other hand, for all their hickish ways, our congressmen are not interested in replacing the European colonial empires with one of our own or making everyone on earth a believer in Dale Carnegie's gospel. This is difficult for a no doubt bookish and delicate lad like Acheson at that school beginning with "G" to grasp.

Those rich boys daydream about vast armies and navies conquering all the seas and lands while we humble folk think of boys that we know—sons even—dying in a process that benefits no one but the international banks and their lawyer-lobbyists, like Mr. Acheson himself. The real political struggle in the United States, since the Civil War, has been between the peaceful inhabitants of the nation with their generally representative Congresses and a small professional elite totally split off from the nation, pursuing wealth through wars that they invent and justify and resonate for others to die in.

Acheson resonated. Currently, the Soviet is putting pressure on the Dardanelles, Iran, and northern Greece, where the local communist firebrand (begins with a Z) is an agent of the Soviet; there is, as usual, no evidence. My subcommittee held hearings on the matter. Man's name is Zahariadis. In a trembling voice, Acheson told us that practically any day now Soviet armies—tanks pulled by horses?—will break through into the Balkans, putting at risk three continents. Since he didn't name them I assume he means Europe, Africa, and North America. Russian troops in Carthage, Tennessee: I see it now—the blood of the Reds will be a rich diet for our homegrown chiggers and mosquitoes.

Acheson, in a hurry to start the next war, abandoned his usual Gibbonian eloquence for some down-home rhetoric calculated to excite us yokels. Yes, the one rotten apple in the barrel was his metaphor of choice. Before our eyes he demonstrated how that one spoiled apple would infect Iran and everything to the east as far as—he didn't say but one knew he feared for the health of Mikado MacArthur. Then the same busy apple would infect Africa by way of Asia Minor and Egypt, where Marc Antony died in Cleopatra's arms—or was it Martha Washington's stout arms? One can get carried away by the sheer poetic beauty of Acheson's internationalistic vision for all us plain folks who've just become, practically overnight, heirs to the Roman Empire, to the Macedonian Empire, to the Aztecs . . . But I write too soon: that infected apple has not yet finished its terrible work. Acheson completed his tragedy with the warning that Europe was already at risk thanks to Italy and France, two frivolous nations that, in the interest of suicidal democracies, had allowed powerful domestic communist parties to turn the entire barrel into potential poison. "America has no choice," he cried. "We must act now to protect our own security, to protect freedom itself!"

It is always amazing to watch the discomfort of professional politicians outplayed at their own game by what they take to be— mistakenly in this case—an amateur. We are a bit like ministers or priests when a member of the congregation claims to have seen a vision. We don't quite know where to look. What to say. Truman was nodding his large rosy head, whose glasses these days now magnify his eyes to Cyclopean proportions. As usual, it was Vandenberg who leaped upon the caboose just as the train, Freedom, was leaving the station. "Mr. President, if you will say that to the Congress and the country, I will support you and I believe that most of Congress will do the same. But, Mr. President, the only way you are ever going to get what you want is to make a speech and scare the hell out of the country."

If Herbert Hoover said, "What this country needs is a great poem," I'd like to say that what I think it really needs is another Mark Twain, to record "The Administration of Colonel Sellers" or "More Deadly Innocents Abroad."

Peter made his way on foot to the Capitol. For March the day was unpleasantly warm and humid, and he himself was both warm and humid when he got to the Diplomats' Gallery, already full up while the floor of the House of Representatives was crowded with senators as they, irritably, tried to find places for themselves on the fringes of the House. The front row had been reserved for Supreme Court and Cabinet.

Peter ended up on the steps of the Diplomats' Gallery with one half of the *Herald Tribune*'s Washington column "Matter of Fact," Joe Alsop himself. After an active war, attempting single-handedly to defeat the Chinese communists, Joe had resumed his political column in tandem with his brother Stewart.

"*The American Idea* made flesh," said Joe, merrily malicious as Peter lowered his heavy self onto the step beside him.

Seated nearby, Joe's cousin Alice Longworth waved at Peter—to annoy Joe?—"Come to lunch Sunday." Peter said that he would. Although he had served a good deal of time at Laurel House lunches and dinners where the grandees of national politics were to be observed, exchanging information for publicity, only recently had he begun to exist in his own right as a guest in demand. *The American Idea* was not much read by the reigning hostesses, except for Virginia Bacon, who read everything, doggedly. But Pauline Davis, the grandest of all hostesses now that Frederika had cut back on her entertaining, quite liked him, or so she said, "because you are the balance of power to Joe—at least at table." Peter feared that they were doomed to become a clown act, Joe with his Achesonian warnings of the noxious apple of communism and Peter with his unfashionable view that nations were nations and did not change identity despite revolutions and invasions. Czarist Russia and even Roman Scythia had seemed to him more worthy of study than Lenin, Trotsky, and Stalin, recent phenomena only to be understood in the light of what had preceded them for a millennium or two.

"I suppose," said Joe, "that you will take the view that today we are crossing the Rubicon."

"With Harry Truman—your little gray man—as Julius Caesar?" Peter knew that Joe much regretted his first summing-up of his great kinsman's heir. "No. We're not dealing in clichés except for your neighbor in P Street, who has compared our rivalry with Russia over Greece as the greatest conflict since the Punic Wars."

Joe swiveled on the step until his bloodshot eyes had Peter's in full focus. "Where did you get that from?"

"Acheson's rhetoric is still echoing throughout the whispering gallery of our city. He took the floor when Marshall proved to be less than inspiring. Acheson spoke powerfully of that one rotten apple which spoils a barrel . . ."

"*When* was this?" Joe did not enjoy the needling of those who did not feel as he did about the manifest destiny of the United States.

"At the White House. The President called in . . ."

". . . the congressional leaders. I know. To ask for money, to support the Greek democracy . . ."

"Resting comfortably in peace ever since Philip of Macedon came to town."

"You tend to overdo the history, dear boy."

"Mr. Acheson is overdoing the history. Not since Rome and Carthage, he says, has the world been so polarized, which is nonsense. We're no Rome, while landlocked Russia is no maritime empire like Carthage or even Britain . . ."

"Don't niggle. We stand at Armageddon."

"Theodore Roosevelt? Oh, God, not now."

"Why not Uncle T when we need him, in spirit at least?"

"My Aunt Caroline quotes your Cousin Eleanor as saying that your Uncle T's love of war killed dead all attempts at progressive reform in this country."

Joe gave his most disagreeable snort, causing Bess Truman, First Lady of the Land, to turn around in her place to identify the snort's source.

Fortunately, the doorkeeper's roar brought silence to the chamber. "The Cabinet of the President of the United States." Peter looked at his watch—almost one o'clock. History was in the making, as the Cabinet came down the aisle and took their places in the front row. Acheson sat in for Marshall, who was in Moscow—or should one say Carthage now? Next, the doorkeeper announced, "The President of the United

States of America . . ." The entire chamber stood, including Peter and Joe Alsop. To Peter's amazement, there was as much of a roar of applause from the Republicans as from the Democratic side of the House. History was flinging the dice. For war.

Truman took his place at the clerk's desk beneath the speaker's rostrum; opened a black folder; waited for the applause to stop. Then he began to read in a high-pitched nasal voice. Peter made a few notes. Although he would soon have the entire text, he liked to test himself against it, liked to test the speaker against the speech. What were the key lines? The declaration of war, if there was to be one.

Peter and history did not have long to wait. The President not only briskly assumed for the United States global primacy but made it clear that from this moment forward the United States could and would interfere in the political arrangements of any nation on earth because "I believe that it must be the policy of the United States to support free peoples who are resisting attempted subjugation by armed minorities or by outside pressures." There it was: *droit de seigneur*. Peter waited for an analysis of what constituted "attempted subjugation by armed minorities or by outside pressure." After all, the United States itself was both armed and outside Greece and Turkey. But no further explanation was given other than "I believe that we must assist free peoples to work out their own destinies in their own way."

What, Peter wondered, was a free people? Had Americans ever been free of a governing class that often acted against that majority rule which was supposed to be the source of all political legitimacy? If the Canadians had the military and economic power, might they not have had an equal right to save their southern neighbors from two European world wars on the ground that an American minority, armed with great wealth, could so subjugate the American political process as to oblige the many to go glumly to war for the benefit of the few?

Peter suddenly realized, as the little President recited his Achesonian message, why it had been so necessary for Roosevelt to provoke the thunderbolts at Pearl Harbor and then, even more necessary, for the excluded majority never to know what he had done to them. The few always knew best; the many must always follow their lead. This was the "democratic" way in the United States.

Suddenly, everyone was on his feet except for Peter, who remained seated, scribbling in his notebook. Standing ovation. Loud applause. Raw imperialism? Or simply a tribute to a plucky actor whom no one thought capable of pulling off such a role.

"I suppose you'll object?" Joe smiled his lupine smile, somewhat disconcerting viewed from below.

"Are we to aid every country?"

"Why not?"

Peter wondered if Joe was serious; if Truman was serious; if the current "crisis" was serious. But if what had already been billed in advance as the Truman Doctrine were to take effect, would a total world empire ever be in anyone's interest? The war industries, now languishing, would profit. But would the general economy improve? Would . . . ?

Back, alone, in his office, Peter began to fit together—and find a pattern for—Truman's various statements, starting with the news that Hiroshima had been destroyed. "This is the greatest thing in history," he had said. It was not recorded whether he smiled or wept when told that Europe had lost thirty million people in the war while the United States had lost a "mere" three hundred thousand military men. Where Roosevelt saw four world spheres of power—American, British, Russian, and Chinese—with the United Nations as their joint police depot, Truman saw only two great powers, which, as of today, were in open conflict: Rome versus Carthage. In this context, Acheson had pretended that the Soviet Union was on the march everywhere in Eastern Europe, which, true or not, could hardly put them on an imperial par with the American acquisition of three-fourths of Germany, soon to be an American province, and of militarily occupied Japan, an American dependency. Then, of course, there was all of Latin America, most of the Pacific islands, while in Africa . . .

How had Acheson and Truman got away with so much misrepresentation, leading to so many false conclusions, without anyone seriously questioning their hectic and hectoring analyses? It reminded Peter of British intelligence before the war—White Cliffs of Dover rolling over and over Mrs. Miniver and her parched rose, awaiting FDR's legendary life-saving garden hose. But what was the American equivalent of England's well-motivated propagandists? In just eighteen minutes at the Capitol, the President had arbitrarily divided the entire world into two "alternative ways of life," when the truth was that if the United States was not so eager for war, there were many alternative ways of life from the fragmented Chinese and the turbulent Indians to the Soviet Union which had already "lost" Yugoslavia while never getting much of a grip on the Chinese communist leader, Mao Tse-tung, a positively celestial figure in his self-absorption.

Nevertheless, a deliberately leaked cable from General Lucius Clay in Berlin suggested that war with the Soviet Union was imminent. It was hard to take seriously the cries of Truman and Acheson that the skies were falling in when, as of 1947, the United States was responsible for half the world's industrial output. Clipped to this fact sheet, Peter found a Truman quotation from August 1945: "We must continue to be a military nation if we are to maintain leadership among other nations." This had been said in Cabinet shortly after the two nuclear bombs had fallen upon Japan. The enemy appeared to be something Truman called "totalitarian states." Apparently, he had said, "There isn't any difference between them. . . ." Except the ones that were treasured allies like Iran and South Africa.

In the file that contained a number of Truman quotations, he found a memo from the Joint Chiefs of Staff dated 1946:

"Experience in the recent war demonstrated conclusively that the defense of a nation, if it is to be effective, must begin beyond its frontiers." Aeneas must have collected this. When a senator had asked the secretary of the Navy, James Forrestal, if he meant for American ships to be based everywhere, Forrestal had replied, "Wherever there is a sea." Aeneas had also found a copy of some twenty places where the United States would maintain air bases or air transit flights. They girdled the earth from Indochina to Guatemala, Canada, Peru, Karachi, New Zealand, while most of the Pacific's islands had been more or less officially annexed. All in the name of "security" against an enemy or enemies unknown except for the nonatomic and fleetless Soviet Union.

When Truman was asked in 1945 if the United States would now become the world's policeman, he said, of course it would have to. After all, "in order to carry out a just decision the courts must have marshals. . . . To collect moneys for county governments, it has been found necessary to employ a sheriff." In the vigorous effort to make a case that must at times be, in Dean Acheson's own exquisite phrase, "clearer than truth," only the United States had the power "to grab hold of history and make it conform"—to what Acheson did not say.

So there it was. The grab was in. On March 21, nine days after Truman declared his "doctrine" to Congress, he created a Loyalty Review Board before which several million government workers would each be forced to swear that never, ever, deep in his heart of hearts, had he for an instant lusted after the evil, the godless, the monolithic, the world-conquering doctrine of communism, whose Vatican was the Kremlin and whose dupes were everywhere in the government, in the classrooms, and even, it was whispered, in the churches of God's last best hope of earth. Aeneas and Peter had fought over the text of their editorial deploring this astonishing restraint on a "free" people. Their compromised result was hardly Miltonian and, sadly, Peter agreed with Aeneas that his own inspired heading, *Ein Reich Ein Volk Ein Truman*, was perhaps almost as excessive as the Loyalty Board itself.

It came as no surprise to Peter that *The American Idea* was promptly included by the attorney general in a list of subversive periodicals and organizations while FBI agents wondered, in the course of a long visit, why—and to what end—the paper was published in a Negro neighborhood. In due course, when Aeneas applied for a passport, he was warned by the State Department that journalists critical of America's foreign policy could—and would—be denied the right to travel abroad. But, as Peter wrote, there were also intermittent joys in the course of that remarkable year, 1947. The Office of Education had created a program to nurture patriotism in the schools; it was called "Zest for American Democracy!" This soon became a regular feature in *The American Idea* while, for the editors, "Zest" became the adjective of choice to describe the latest hyperbole from the Administration and its thundering chorus of approval in the press, whose Heldentenor was Henry Luce with his surging aria "American Century," all rights unreserved, as Aeneas had noted.

2

Miss Perrine showed Peter into James Burden Day's office, whose great windows and long view of white marble and green lawn was visual proof of his seniority in the Senate. Over the fireplace hung a painting of Jefferson. One wall displayed the obligatory political photographs of the Senator with the likes of William Jennings Bryan as well as, unexpectedly, the late Huey Long. "I was always drawn to the larger-than-life losers."

"So unlike the smaller-than-life winner in the White House."

"Isn't he a ring-tailed wonder!"

"A born leader."

The Senator laughed and motioned for Peter to sit on the black leather sofa while he himself sat just opposite in a rocking chair. "On the other hand, Harry's not so bad at following orders. I guess he learned that from Tom Prendergast. When Van told him last February that he'd have to scare the hell out of the country to get all that money for Europe, he did a bang-up job but, as old Mark Twain used to say, 'There were things which he stretched.' Anyway, we gave him everything he asked for. Twelve and a half billion dollars that we certainly could have used a lot better here at home." The Senator stopped his rocking. "I hope you've kept my tactless unsigned memo locked up."

"Only Aeneas and I have ever seen it. Of course its message has been shared with our shocked readers."

"Funny how *un*shocked people are by what's going on. Harry and Acheson have gone to war with our tax money and no one's dared blow the whistle on them—at least in Congress, which includes me, I'm afraid, along with the rest of the stout hearts. You know, the other day Dean came up to the Hill to lecture us on the facts of life. We can never, he solemnly testified, sit down with the Russians and solve problems. In which case, I asked, why not fold the State Department? But what's really so peculiar is that we've never been richer or more powerful, yet all we do is wring our hands and tremble at the thought of the bankrupt Russians conquering Europe. Then us."

"Do you think the President really believes this nonsense?"

The Senator was amused. "Never forget that politicians are not like other people. We don't really believe in anything except getting reelected. The Red Menace is a wonderful way to scare the folks into voting for you. As for Harry . . ." He frowned. "He's ignorant. He reads one history book and thinks he understands history. Everything's like a cartoon to him. Stalin equals Hitler. We tried to deal with Hitler at Munich. Mistake. War. Treaty with the Russians equals Munich. No treaty. But, just in case, prepare for war. He hasn't yet read a book that will tell him how history *never* repeats itself."

Peter withdrew the National Security Act from his heat-crumpled seersucker jacket. The Senator duly noted Congress's latest handiwork. "What line do you take?" he asked.

"I don't know if we're going to have a line or not, because . . ." Peter took a deep breath and plunged into what he took to be the heart of history. "It's possible that for all the wrong reasons they—Truman, Acheson, Marshall—are right."

The Senator's smile was wintry for so bright a day in July. He rocked slowly in his chair. "Go on," he said.

"If we're not destroyed by the Russians or the Chinese or—who knows?—enraged Panamanians, then everyone will agree that the total militarizing of the country was a very good thing and history always marries the winner . . ."

"Because he is the only one left standing?"

"Because he's the only one willing to pay her price. But the big question is: will this world empire end up bankrupting us, as it's done the British? Or will it make us even richer, as it did the Spanish once upon a time?"

Burden opened his copy of the National Security Act. "What we have now in our wisdom done is create . . ." He rifled the pages. "What did we call it? Oh, yes. The National Military Establishment. We're putting the Army, the Navy, and our newly independent and vainglorious air corps that won the war all alone to hear them tell it into a single department. We're shutting down the War Department. Much too provocative a word, 'war.' Henceforth, we shall speak only of our desperate need to defend ourselves against what's rapidly turning out to be everyone on earth."

Burden turned more pages. "We have also created a National Security Council. That's the president, plus secretaries of state, defense, and so on. They will form a high command, no doubt on the Prussian model. To be kept informed by a new agency, dedicated to spying not only on our eternal enemy the Soviet but also, far more important, on our unreliable European allies . . ."

Peter was startled. "Is that in there? In the act?"

"Good Lord, no. That was in one of our closed-session briefings. Our security requires that we do everything possible to prevent a left-wing party from ever coming to power anywhere in Europe. This new agency with its bland name," he glanced at the text, "Central Intelligence Agency, tells us that next spring the Italian communists are expected to win Italy's first free election. The CIA has sworn that they can see to it that the communists will lose *if* they are adequately funded."

"Who are they?"

"The old OSS. Cloak-and-dagger types from the war. Colonel Wild Bill Donovan and his merry men."

"Is there no congressional control over them?"

"I believe a joint committee will be tolerated but, basically, this is a White House show. We are on the sidelines from now on. Vandenberg sold out the Republicans in order to get his name in the paper, while most Democrats around here believe there will be a Republican president next year so why not let Harry Truman go hang himself alone?"

"It's easy enough to get rid of him." Peter put the fateful document away. "But how do you get rid of this act?"

There was a long pause. Burden Day stared at a bust of Cicero, who was staring at another empire, being born, as it turned out, over *his* dead body. Since Burden Day could have no answer to this, Peter asked, abruptly, "Is Diana going to marry Clay?"

"What?" The Senator had been daydreaming. "Oh, Diana. Well, there was an understanding that after the '46 election he would marry her. There was also an understanding that Enid be got rid of. Sorry. Your sister. I forget. I'm tactless."

"That's all right. She's put away. For good, I suspect. But she won't divorce him."

"And Clay can't divorce an invalid wife, which is how the state sees this matter. So Diana is in limbo."

"She's left the paper."

"So I gather. I wish she would . . . go on with it. You are a good couple."

"I thought so. Think so. She's been seeing Billy Thorne in New York." Peter attempted a smile. "Only professionally. He's as interested as we are in what happened at Pearl Harbor."

"You must all wait until—when was it? 1995—when the papers are unsealed. You'll get to see them. I won't. Though I reckon I might be available through Ouija board." Suddenly, the Senator's mood darkened. "What has gone wrong with the people that they can't see what is happening to them?"

"What is wrong with *us* that we can't get through to them?"

The old man stopped his rocking and sat up straight. "Perhaps they know something we don't. Perhaps they really want something that we don't."

"High taxes? A peacetime military draft? Loyalty oaths? Censorship? And it's only two years since the war was over."

"But perhaps all this fits their mood even though it overthrows two centuries of rhetoric." Burden Day got to his feet; the trousers of his white linen suit were stuck to the back of his thighs. He switched on a fan and cooled himself in front of it. "I confess that I, too, have sometimes thought that we were meant to govern the earth. Well, if *I* thought that—and I'm a populist, a mind-your-own-business sort of person who knows from experience whatever is good for the banks is bad for the people if . . . Where was I? Oh. If *I* often think that way, what must all the others think? Brought up on manifest destiny and TR's nonsense about the glories of war. It is no accident that for three hundred years our people willingly, I believe—maybe even joyously—slaughtered their way across this continent, enslaved Negroes, drove out Mexicans, broke more Indian treaties than Hitler ever bothered to make. Then, for the last half century, we've made the countries of the Caribbean and Central America our property while occupying most of the islands of the Pacific including, after due incineration, our only Asian rival, Japan. Who are we to say that this was the work of a few war-lovers like TR?"

"Say that in the Senate."

"And return to private life in Lewisburg Federal Penitentiary?" The Senator laughed. "Such a speech would not be considered loyal. Even so, three hundred years of bloody expansion cannot be accomplished entirely against the will of the people who do the fighting."

"Are you suggesting there's something demonic in our highly mixed race?"

Burden Day's face was now as white as that of the marble Cicero. "I don't know. How could I? Or anyone. But if at some deep level that's what they truly want, I must stop short and confess that I am not representative."

"They also wanted slavery."

"Some did. Some did not." Burden Day sighed. "But does anyone really want to give up so much freedom and so much money to allow an American general to play Mikado in Tokyo and another one play Kaiser in Berlin? I doubt it."

"Probably not if it was explained to them. But the Few dominate the Many . . ."

The Senator completed Hume's incontrovertible law. ". . . through Opinion. We have our work cut out for us."

Peter prepared to go; shook Burden Day's papery old hand. "Let's hope it does some good."

"It does us good, and that is all that matters. The end will be what it will be."

3

With considerable fanfare, John Latouche got Peter and Aeneas tickets to New York's most successful new play, which had opened at the Ethel Barrymore Theatre on December 3, 1947: Aeneas was unusually precise about such things when he was serious, and he was very serious, "because it's time we took a close look at the American theater, to see what's happening . . ."

"And why?" Peter added automatically.

Their cab had been obliged to park a block away from the theater because of the many cabs and limousines inching past the marquee, where, spelled out in white electric lightbulbs, were the names of director Elia Kazan, and of playwright Tennessee Williams. Of the two names, Kazan's was the larger in lights. The play's title had immediately intrigued the world: *A Streetcar Named Desire*. In the three weeks since the play had opened, radio comedians and newspaper columnists had made a thousand jokes about streetcars and lust.

The lobby was crowded. The aisles were crowded. Peter had not seen many plays in New York and he had never attended a recently opened "hit." As a result, he was hardly prepared for the tension in the audience as he and Aeneas slowly moved towards their seats at the center of the third row. "It's like what an audience must be for a public execution," he muttered to Aeneas.

"Latouche is a friend of Irene Selznick, the producer." Aeneas had not heard Peter. He was too busy with his notebook, pen, miniature flashlight, for which, he now discovered, he had forgotten to buy batteries. "Touche has invited us to a party after the show. . . ."

Curtain up. The play irradiated the theater. The color of everything beneath the proscenium arch was brown, either viewed starkly, head on, or dreamlike through a shadowy scrim; there was a murmur of New Orleans voices speaking Spanish (why not French?) in the street beyond the tenement where the characters Stanley and Stella lived. From left to right, a blank space for a sort of foyer, and an iron staircase spiraling up against a begauzed view of sidewalk. Then, in a row, living room, kitchen, bedroom, with a door to the bathroom. Mysteriously placed lights flared and dimmed, came and went. Enter Blanche Du Bois. Pale. Slender. Deliberately out of her place, *place*. In flight. From Belle Rêve. Her house. Stella's house, too. Upriver. The home has been lost. Stella's husband, a sweaty, muscular youth in a T-shirt, played by a young actor, literally famous overnight—Marlon Brando. Peter could see now what the fuss was about. Hear it, too. No male had ever seemed quite so nude on the stage before. Nor quite so entirely at home with his sex not to mention that of the audience, too. A mild speech defect was used artfully. To hold attention—make suspense? Could he ever say an "R" properly? Did it matter? The audience looked only at him when he spoke. Stared even more intensely at him when he was silent. Peter felt sorry for the somewhat manic actress who played Blanche. She was being excluded from what, surely, was supposed to be her play.

When she was taken away at the end, barbarism—"the apes" as Blanche had called the Stanleys of this world—had triumphed. Was this a warning or a prophecy? What on earth was this most vivid play about?

"What is Chekhov about?" was Aeneas's answer as they made their way up the aisle while the rest of the audience stood, shouting bravos, applauding the somewhat bewildered-looking cast. Brando tugged idly at his crotch. A signal? Or merely his way of saying "Until next time."

Latouche met them in the lobby. "Don has his taxi across the street."

As they drove to the party in East Thirty-sixth Street, Touche described the opening of the play. "Everyone knew that the theater was never going to be the same again. Brando's changed the whole idea of what an actor is—the way Barrymore did before the war."

"An *actor?*" Aeneas was scribbling fast as the cab rattled down Sixth Avenue. "Surely what he's changed is the notion of what a man is."

"You mean a sexual object?" This was very much Touche's territory. Amateur anthropology.

"Object. Subject, too. A man's not just a suit anymore." Aeneas was talking as he wrote. "Dim background for the erotic woman. Dim partner to glittering ballerina. Black velvet foil for diamond."

"Too much," warned Peter, the austere editor.

But Aeneas and Touche were both excited by what each seemed to believe was a total realignment of the sexes as demonstrated onstage at the Ethel Barrymore Theatre one winter's night two years after the war, two years into a fermenting new world.

They were met at the door to a modest sublet flat by its current if somewhat, to hear him tell it, fugitive tenant.

"Oh, Touche. Come on in." Absently, Tennessee Williams shook hands with Aeneas and Peter. "There seems to be a party going on."

There was. Two dozen theatrical people were helping themselves to drink arranged on a long table. "I seem to have had a permanent party going since the opening." Williams put a cigarette into a long holder; he lit up, producing a smoke screen about his head. His eyes were cloudy-cataract blue. A moustache emphasized full lips.

"Were you at the play?" he asked his new guests. He squinted at them suspiciously. Enemies?

Aeneas began what promised to be a panegyric laced with practical suggestions about staging in order to clarify meanings.

Williams cut him short. "I am finished with the theater. You have seen my last play, the very last. You must understand that my heart has been affected by far too many illnesses, not *all* of them venereal-related." His high heh-heh-heh laugh was like someone imitating a barnyard resident, just as his voice, though pleasantly Southern, could suddenly become extremely precise, with all sorts of single and double quotation marks as well as italics which he used to put forward, as if for exhibit, certain words that were not usually given such emphasis. "I shall be dead before the *end of this year*. It is a miracle that I lived long enough to undergo the rehearsals, not to mention the *tender mercies* of Dame Selznick. On the other hand, Gadge is merciless. But a *genius* at directing me." Williams drifted off.

Touche brought Peter whiskey while Aeneas stalked the dying playwright. When Peter asked if Williams was really in a terminal condition, Touche laughed. "He's a total hypochondriac. On the other hand, to steady his nerves, he munches Nembutals with vodka as a chaser. This is not healthy. He's off to Europe at the end of December. What's become of your uncle or whatever Tim Farrell is to you?"

"I thought you'd know. Weren't you doing a film together . . ."

"It was often a rich subject of conversation at three in the morning in Harlem. But rich subjects of conversation seldom end up on screen. I'm doing it as a musical for Broadway. Oh, here's Paul. Virgil says you need a music critic."

"I'm a composer, actually." Bowles was slender, small, blond; he could have been any age that was not young.

"He's now becoming a writer." Touche moved away.

Bowles seemed mildly annoyed. "How do you *become* a writer?"

"I suppose by writing something."

"My wife, Jane, is a writer and she never writes *something*. In fact, she writes practically nothing." He seemed approving. "Which is what Gertrude Stein told me to do when she read my poems in Paris. 'You're not a poet, go on with music.' So I did. Until now, perhaps."

"You did the music for the play tonight." Peter recalled the playbill.

"You've just come from *Streetcar*?"

"Yes." Peter was not about to use an adjective which would then be examined and assayed for value.

Bowles seemed disappointed that there was no hyperbole to dissect. "I also did the music for *The Glass Menagerie*. Tennessee thinks music enhances his plays."

"You don't?"

"I don't think I could tell. I only hear the music. He sees and hears the play. Whose American Idea?"

Peter gave a brief report: news as history, history as news.

"I've never seen any connection between the way the world works and what is written of it."

"And I don't see how there can *not* be. The writer's in history, like it or not."

"The composer's part of the play but he listens for the music not the words."

"Try," said Peter, succumbing to his worst didactic instincts, "to do both."

"One should, of course, always *try*." Bowles's solemnity plainly disguised a certain watchful glee. "But, of course, I do listen to the words, up to a point."

"Which is?"

"One *stopping* point is Tennessee's unerring misuse of foreign languages."

"Spanish instead of French in New Orleans?"

"The wrong Spanish instead of the right. I've given up correcting him. He doesn't hear."

Leonard Bernstein made a movie star's entrance. Darkly handsome, he wore on his shoulders a coat with a mink collar. All eyes were upon him as he embraced Tennessee.

Bowles sighed. "It must be a terrific burden to be the whole of American music at twenty-nine. To have it all and still want more?"

"What more could there be?"

"He says that he would like to be a man of fashion like me." There was a cheerful glint in Bowles's eyes; and Peter noted that Bowles was indeed elegantly turned out in a prewar school-of-Paris gray suit, pinched in at the waist. "Not long after his musical comedy, *On the Town*, he offered me a job as his valet."

"Valet?" Peter was astonished.

"He was serious. I suppose because I'd lived in Europe before the wars. He wants to have a European style like the other great conductors. But, of course, they *are* European and he's from Lawrence, Massachusetts. Even so, I might have helped him with French and Spanish and tactfully talked him out of that mink collar. I see astrakhan as being more Lenny's style."

"Why didn't you take the job?"

"The salary wasn't much more than what I'm getting at the *Herald Tribune*. Besides, Jane and I expect to be living in Morocco . . ."

Bowles turned away to greet friends. Peter suspected that either his leg had been pulled or it was actually Bowles's nature to be flatly literal and precise in all things and what he said he simply said and he always meant exactly what he had said like his mentor in Paris, Gertrude Stein. At the other end of the room, Bernstein was discussing himself with all the passionate zest of a professor enthralled by his subject. "I've never seen anything like it! The crowds on the sides of the hill. All the leaders of the country were there to hear me conduct. I felt like weeping. I was home. In Israel. They said my success was the biggest thing in their history! Yes, the old history as well as the new. They said I was a bigger hit than Jesus Christ!"

"But, Lenny," said Touche, sweetly, "are you sure that was a compliment? I mean, look at what the Jews did to Jesus."

"Oh, Touche. Stop trying to be witty. You know what I mean."

"Of course, *I* do. I was just wondering what *they* meant." Latouche's round.

Later, walking in the cold to Aeneas's flat, they compared notes on the evening. "Bernstein's basing a symphony on Auden's *Age of Anxiety.*"

"The pieces are starting to come together."

"One interesting bit of gossip," said Aeneas, who never gossiped. "Williams is interested in an Italo-American who was in the Navy."

"Curious the number of homosexuals there are in the arts now. Or has it always been the same and we just didn't know?"

"Probably the same. Anyway, this former sailor lived awhile with Touche. Then, before that, you'll never guess who he was with."

"Aeneas, I don't care what men and women are doing, much less men and sailors."

"Then I won't tell you that the sailor lived with Joe Alsop."

Peter stopped in front of a Sixth Avenue bar. "I don't believe it. Joe's too . . . too . . ."

"Too what?"

"Careful. No. Too snobbish."

"It adds depth to his character, doesn't it? The Baron de Charlus of Georgetown."

Peter shuddered as a cold wind came down the street from the north. "This is a new world, isn't it?"

"Or the old world, better understood."

THIRTEEN

|

In June of 1948, Caroline returned to Laurel House. For nearly a year she had been in France restoring Saint-Cloud-le-Duc to what it had been before the comparatively mild German occupation.

Frederika had insisted that she launch Caroline's Aaron Burr book with a garden party which, she said, ominously, would doubtless be the last before Irene Bloch took possession.

"But that," said Caroline, "is two years from now."

"Even so, the way things are going . . ." Frederika's voice trailed off. They were seated on the red-brick terrace that overlooked the Potomac, for the most part, at this season, screened by tall trees and thick-growing laurel.

"I love the roar of the river," said Caroline.

"Don't tell me you can actually hear it?" The one-eyed butler brought them iced tea. The other guests had not yet arrived.

"I *think* I hear it, which is almost the same." Caroline's hearing had been gradually fading, a condition which she had learned to accept as she had fading vision, various arthritic pains, and a memory no longer reliable. "My bones are turning to sand," Caroline observed with what she hoped was sufficient cheerfulness. "What about yours?"

Frederika shook both arms, thoughtfully. "I don't think I have any left. At least nothing aches. We're really much too old to be up and around."

"Up from what? Around what?"

"The grave." Frederika maintained her cool hostess voice. "Oh, I've got some copies of your book." On a coffee table there were a half-dozen copies of *Memories of Aaron Burr* by Charles Schermerhorn Schuyler, edited by Caroline Sanford. Absently, Frederika picked the price tag off the black-and-gold dust jacket. "Five dollars for a book. Imagine. Weren't they all two dollars and fifty cents before the war?"

"Novels. Not works of history."

"Curious to think that your mother killed Blaise's mother. Or was it the other way round?"

Caroline treated this lightly. "She did not exactly kill her. She let her die."

"Surely it's the same thing."

"Not in court. And when all's said and done, history's court."

Blaise came out of the house. "The authoress. First in the family. They say Cissy Patterson's dying out at the Dower House."

"Such a pretty place," said Frederika, always more interested in the state of houses than that of their occupants. "I wonder who will inherit?"

"The grandchild," said Blaise. "Drew Pearson's daughter. It's the *Times-Herald* that I want to get my hands on."

"Doesn't it still belong to Hearst?" Caroline tended to rise above age and decrepitude at the mention of newspapers.

Blaise shook his head. "No. Cissy's got it all now, and the paper's making money for a change. She wanted it to go to her—what is it?— niece, Alicia Patterson, who's started a newspaper out on Long Island."

"Long Island? That's not a real place." Frederika was firm. "What a perverse thing to do, to put a newspaper there." She went inside to make final arrangements for the buffet.

"Should we take it on?" Blaise turned to Caroline. It was like the old days when they were working publishers and partners.

"Aren't we . . . Oh, I swore I'd make no reference to time's wingèd wastebasket, but we're old, Blaise."

"I don't feel it. You don't either."

"I'm also French again. Even so, it is tempting."

"If we don't take it on Eugene Meyer will merge it with the Washington *Post*, and that will be the end of the paper."

"A good thing for Meyer. And probably a good thing for us, too. Anyway, the city's far too small for three morning papers."

Blaise gazed thoughtfully at the boxwood hedge that had grown so enormously during his reign.

"You're really going to sell the place?"

Blaise nodded. "Too much trouble to run. Irene's got the energy. And she'll pay my price."

"How is my nephew?"

"Obstinate. Prefers his little magazine to the paper. I've always thought a publisher should be able to write and even, if necessary, think, which neither of us could really do but Peter can."

"Speak for yourself. I do nothing but think. Only now I promptly forget whatever it is I was thinking. Isn't this the day Dewey is to be nominated?"

"And elected in November. Yes. He's about to be nominated. In Philadelphia. I should've gone but he's such a bore. Even so, I'll be glad to see the end of this gang. What's happened to Tim Farrell?"

"Other than my daughter Emma?" Caroline could not even simulate malice, so tired was she of the idea of her daughter as opposed to the reality, which she was cunningly able to avoid.

"The picture Tim hoped to make was promptly made two years ago. *The Best Years of Our Lives* was the optimistic title. Harry Hopkins' friend Robert Sherwood wrote it."

"Bad luck. For Tim." Blaise went inside.

"Bad luck," she repeated to herself. Some relationships simply broke off, rather as if one of the two had died; others continued to flourish even after death, in memory. The affair with Tim had been erased while the affair with James Burden Day was a permanent part of her life in the present as well as the past; at least as long as she could recall herself at all, which might not be too much longer; promptly, she recited to herself, in a whisper, the speech of Mary Queen of Scots to Queen Elizabeth. This was her touchstone: the day she could no longer remember the "Cousin speech," as she always thought of it, she would be gone. Today she remembered it all, including the last line that American censors had not allowed her to say: "A bastard sits upon the throne of England."

Caroline had her lunch in Blaise's study with Burden Day, demonstrating to herself the depth and nature of her fidelity to what should have been her husband had she ever actually wanted one. Now he seemed old to her but the charm was still present. "I see your nephew from time to time. We agree on most things, a sign of premature wisdom in one so young."

"Surely you've not become a socialist in your golden years?"

Burden laughed. "No. Peter isn't one either. But Aeneas Duncan can occasionally raise my blood pressure."

"I like him when he tells us about American culture. Apparently the musical comedy is our unique art form, and Cole Porter is our Phidias." Caroline had quite enjoyed herself for a week in New York, going to the theater. She had even dined with Cole Porter in his Waldorf-Astoria Tower suite; and she had betrayed no surprise when a manservant carried the one-legged Porter into the drawing room and placed him carefully on a sofa as if he were a rare porcelain vase. "Caroline." He took her hand; she kissed his cheek; he smiled his chilly gentle smile. He drank martinis as they spoke of the dead. Then the manservant asked her to step out of the room, which she did while Cole relieved himself.

At dinner they were joined by the ancient but lively Elsie Woodward, who lived on another floor in the Tower with Van Dyck's triptych of King Charles the First, which Caroline had always coveted. Elsie had reigned over New York's society for so many generations that she had taken to exclaiming apologetically whenever she saw an old friend after any passage of time, "God seems to have forgotten me!" So she greeted Caroline, who replied, "At last we have something to be grateful to Him for."

"You are quite as bad as old Mrs. Wharton." Elsie was reproving.

"Isn't it nice," said Porter, "all of us being in the Tower together."

"So very hometown." Elsie nodded at Caroline to show that she still kept up with the world.

"I can't think why Tim and I didn't make those films here in the Waldorf. I'm sure that if we had, we'd still be making them. This is the real America, after all."

"What a good idea!" When Elsie smiled her face was crisscrossed with a thousand lines. "Make one now. And get what's his name . . . Arnold Edward? . . . to play Herbert Hoover, who's also in the Tower and actually rather fun! Of course, I'm a Republican."

"Edward Arnold." It was Cole Porter who corrected Elsie. Movies now absorbed everyone, Caroline noted, with a pang at what she'd once taken for granted, and lost.

Blaise entered the study and switched on a mysterious box which turned out to be a new television set. "One of the editors just rang. They're showing Harry Truman on that train tour of his. Here he is a week or so ago."

On the gray screen a blizzard swirled. A voice sounded. "President Truman arrived in Los Angeles on June fourteenth. He was driven from Union Station to the Ambassador Hotel." The blizzard had begun to arrange itself into an open car, a waving president, and Wilshire Boulevard lined with cheering people. "A crowd of over one million people came out to greet the President."

"One million!" Burden was astonished.

Blaise nodded. "I didn't believe it either."

"This means," said Caroline, "that he'll be reelected in November."

Blaise and Burden laughed at her; rather rudely, she thought. "No chance. Dewey's got it. He's too far ahead." Blaise switched to another channel. A convention hall. Dewey banners. Band music.

A commentator looked the camera disconcertingly in the lens. "It seems that what was supposed to be Governor Dewey's day here in Philadelphia has been preempted by the President and the Russians. The Soviet military has cut off all access to the American sector of Berlin on the ground that with the recent formation by the United States of a West German state, the city of Berlin, being within the

Soviet zone of Germany, is rightfully an integral part of the communist German state. If the Americans can, unilaterally, create a West German republic, so can the Soviet. The question everyone is asking each other at this convention is—is this the start of an armed conflict?"

Blaise switched off the set. "Well, Senator?"

"It depends on how badly Truman wants to win. A war before November will certainly keep him in office."

Caroline did her best to appear unshaken by this appalling news. "It's hard to believe that we would begin the third world war so soon after the second."

Blaise shook his head. "Stalin's not ready—yet. He's just bluffing. Testing us."

"Laboratory tests," Caroline observed, "often explode, even in the best-run laboratories."

"It's a curious—coincidence, I suppose," said Burden, "that this morning Truman signed the Selective Service Act. All men eighteen to twenty-five must promptly register and then some two million of them will be drafted into the armed services, *in peacetime,* something unheard-of in a country like ours. At least, as ours was."

"Could Truman have known the blockade was coming?" Blaise was making notes at his desk.

"Probably. Politicians like generals always fight the last war. Roosevelt began drafting troops while Willkie was being nominated in 1940, now Truman does the same to Dewey."

"Actors call it upstaging," said Caroline.

Blaise was on the telephone to his managing editor, who had a great deal to say while Blaise simply made noises of affirmation. Then he put down the receiver. "The President says that we're staying in Berlin, according to the terms of the Yalta-Potsdam agreements."

"Terms we broke when we set up the West German government." Burden shook his head. "The four powers were supposed to govern an undivided Germany jointly. Now we've gone and split the country in two. We keep the rich part. We leave them the poor part. We act. Stalin reacts. Who can be surprised?"

"Poor Mr. Dewey," said Caroline. "This is not really his day, after all."

"It might be no one's day." Burden was glum.

Blaise was grim: "We are preparing to fight our way into Berlin."

"Suppose we fail?" Caroline could only think of Russian soldiers looting Saint-Cloud-le-Duc.

"It might encourage us to change our form of government." Blaise was very red in the face. "To make sure that crazed haberdashers are not given the power of life and death over all the world."

Caroline rose. "Now we know what 'mad as a hatter' really means."

Burden rose too. "This hatter may be mad. But he's sly."

Caroline circled the drawing room, responding graciously to the grandees of what had been for so long her city. Although only Alice Longworth had read her book, all had read the review of it in the New York *Times*, where the reviewer, one Wilbur or was it Orville something—Wright?—had been horrified by her repetition of the canard about Jefferson's children by his slave Sally Hemings, so magisterially disproved by no less an authority than Balzac O'Toole. Worse, Wilbur found deeply offensive Burr's letters describing his sexual exploits to his daughter, confirming the reviewer's suspicion that Burr had been neither a moral nor a good man, the only sort worthy of a sympathetic biography.

Alice was delighted to be able to console Caroline, who was delighted by this attention. "Actually," she told Alice's broad-brimmed hat, which hid her face from those taller, "Orville or Wilbur or whatever he's called helped sell the book, according to Dutton's."

"Curious how so many books get written by the likes of us in this place but no real writer has ever appeared until you."

"We did produce Henry Adams."

"He's Boston." Alice was precise.

"Anyway, I'm only my grandfather's editor. . . . But what about your father? All those books he wrote. All those copies sold." Caroline laid it on. Actually, she had never been able to read anything by Theodore Roosevelt.

But Alice was grateful for the praise. "Actually, I never think of father really being a Washingtonian. He's the Wild West."

"Of Long Island?"

Alice ignored the gentle mockery of the greatest American president of all. "Did you hear my line about Dewey?"

Washington phrasemakers were like radio comedians or the newspaper wits who met regularly at the Algonquin Hotel in New York to exchange jokes. "That he is like the groom on the wedding cake? Yes. But in New York, Clare Luce is given credit for it."

The gray eyes looked like polished granite. "Clare claims everything. She even has the nerve to say that she actually writes her own plays."

"She will stop at nothing. But I did like what she said about your Cousin Franklin. 'He lied us into war when he should have led us into it.'"

"Not bad. But, of course, he should have done neither." Alice was sharp. "So devious, the poor feather duster, while Eleanor is now so incredibly noble." Alice bared her teeth, pulled in her chin; and looked exactly like her first cousin. Then: "I'm for Taft." She allowed her features to reassemble.

"But Dewey's got the nomination."

"Republicans have a death wish. I should be in Philadelphia today but I'd rather talk to you about Aaron Burr. He seems so much closer to us than poor Harry Truman. But Bess is a joy. You know, she's almost as large as Eleanor but then, unlike slothful Eleanor, she was a champion basketball player in high school. I hope she still finds time to play. To at least—what do they call it?—shoot a basket. Of course there will be all the time in the world when they go home to Independence next year."

2

Alone in the train to Philadelphia, Peter enjoyed his solitude by reading Evelyn Waugh's *The Loved One*, an entire novella printed in *Life* magazine. Hollywood funerary practices as viewed by the plump pop-eyed little Englishman who joyously lampooned the residents of movieland while himself embodying, inadvertently *and* advertently, every known cliché about the English. Doubtless it took a fraud to detect in such detail the fraudulent. Aeneas had wondered why no one had noticed how much Waugh had lifted from Aldous Huxley. Peter was then able to one-up Aeneas with Dawn Powell's *The Happy Island,* in which a concert pianist, in need of money, had been hired by a Bronx mortician to guard the bodies and, if he chose, paint them prettily, for which useful service he could sleep on his own slab and, in the still watches of the night, practice on the funeral parlor organ.

The taxi driver who drove Peter to the Benjamin Franklin said, "You've never seen such sour-looking delegates. They don't need taxis. What they need is hearses."

Plainly, the Democratic Party was not in an optimistic mood. The Roosevelt sons, headed by James, had come out for General Eisenhower to replace Truman. But Eisenhower had, finally, said no. Considerable pressures must have been brought to bear on Eisenhower to force him to release a Shermanesque statement declining any nomination for president from any party. The whispering gallery's rumor of choice was that during the war he had written, as military protocol required, a letter to Chief of Staff Marshall asking for permission to divorce his wife in order to marry the English woman that British intelligence had thoughtfully provided to spy on him as his personal driver. Marshall graciously gave permission for the divorce, with the offhand postscript that should this marital drama be enacted, Ike would be not only relieved of his supreme command of all Allied forces in Europe but he would also be granted early retirement in order to enjoy a second youth with the British Mata Hari. It was said, by some, that Truman had obtained a copy of the Eisenhower letter to Marshall. It was said by admirers of the sternly virtuous Marshall that he had destroyed the document. In any case, Truman had had no challengers of consequence. Today, he would accept the nomination of his party for president—a reluctant, no, a *despairing* nomination—and Peter was now trying out adjectives to describe what he expected would be one of the grimmest occasions in American political history, the nomination of an unelected but incumbent president, sure to lose.

Peter looked into the hotel dining room, half hoping to find Ernest

Cuneo. But that depository of secrets was elsewhere, spinning webs. Eight years earlier, thanks to war and Willkie, Philadelphia had staged one of the great political dramas, involving all the star players as well as the secret dramatist, President Roosevelt himself. Now there were nothing but secondary politicians and party leaders in town for a wake. The age of President Dewey had seized the nation by its throat.

Virtuously, Peter determined to skip lunch. Then he telephoned Aeneas in Washington. What was the latest news?

"You're on the spot." Aeneas sounded querulous. "You tell me."

"At the moment, I've seen nothing but unhappy faces . . ."

"Well, Dwight Macdonald still hasn't sent us his piece on the Kinsey Report."

That was too bad, thought Peter. The tall giggling Macdonald had made a great impression on him when they met in New York, particularly with his offhand dismissal of *The American Idea*. "Just a lot more court history. Oh, I've read your paper. Bits and pieces, anyway. Washington insider stuff. If you don't watch out you'll grow up to be Walter Lippmann—always wrong. Truman's a subject, I'll admit that. Those loyalty oaths. Sickening. All this trumped-up fear of communism. Why? I was taken in for two minutes. Then saw it was the wrong religion at the wrong time in the wrong place. Sex is the latest politics. The row over the Kinsey Report is true radicalism in action. Facts versus superstitions. Now we're getting to the real roots of real politics. Why is poor Lionel Trilling trying to be so middle-class respectable up at Columbia? What's he scared of? That men are promiscuous? Does he really believe in God? If he does, why not say so? Kinsey's the only politics today. The revolutionary."

"Write it for us!"

"What do you pay?"

The price was met but the piece had yet to be delivered.

Aeneas said that if the platform were too strong on what was known, euphemistically, as civil rights, Alabama and Mississippi would walk out of the convention and, presumably, the Democratic Party. "So with Henry Wallace organizing the liberal Democrats and the South threatening to set up a new party to restore slavery, Truman's left holding an empty bag!"

Inside the hall, the television lights were blinding. Sam Rayburn presided over the convention, snarl more than usually fixed on his face. The party's platform, just arrived from the Hotel Bellevue-Stratford, was now being read to the delegates, who seemed exhausted even though the evening was just begun and there remained hours of speeches up ahead, followed by the voting, followed by a speech from Truman himself, who was said to have just arrived from Washington and was now waiting backstage.

Peter entered the section reserved for the press, to a man furiously as one in their denunciation of the television networks who were blocking their view of the rostrum while, simultaneously, blinding them and—was it possible?—replacing them as the national "medium" of choice. But at least some of the giants of what were known in the latest jargon as the "print media" had deigned to attend this funereal occasion.

Arthur Krock, chief of the New York *Times* Washington bureau, greeted Peter and offered him a seat at the *Times* table. Peter had always liked the somewhat pompous but always affable Krock, who was, on any subject, the absolute font of received opinion. "Well, nothing like this has ever happened before, has it?" Peter tacked on the question, to show deference to the vast if somewhat shallow knowledge of so comfortingly predictable an oracle.

"No." Krock indicated for Peter to sit beside him. They now had a clear view of Rayburn fidgeting at the podium; ready to maintain order. "At least not in my time. Harry's done something no one thought possible. He's broken up FDR's all-powerful coalition of big-city machines, Southern courthouses, and labor unions. Everything's up for grabs now."

"The wonder is it held together so long." A young aide handed Krock a slip of paper, who read to Peter: " 'The Southern delegates are going to vote for Senator Richard Russell, as a protest.' "

"But Truman will win?"

"He'll win tonight. He'll lose in November."

Krock was then handed a copy of the platform, which was still being read aloud. He nodded with the satisfaction of a wise man proven right yet again. "They are keeping Truman's civil rights plank, designed to keep the Southerners happy."

"Slavery is restored?" Peter could not resist.

"Well, let's say the total reconstruction of Southern institutions has been delayed."

But the surprises began almost immediately. There was a sudden roar of disapproval from the delegates.

"Floor fight." Krock went into a huddle with his colleagues while Peter moved on to the *Tribune*'s table, presided over by Harold Griffiths, former film critic, former war correspondent, and now political analyst for the *Tribune*, with a syndicated column. Peter and Harold had ceased to be friends when Harold had become totally attached to the ever-rising fortunes of Clay Overbury while Peter had taken his sister Enid's side. Since no one knew whether or not Peter would one day take over the *Tribune*, Harold always treated him with a certain not entirely mock deference, while Peter never let on that he knew anything at all about the plans his father and Harold had for Clay.

"At last some drama." Harold was puffier than he'd been prewar; and the malicious twinkle in his eye was somewhat glazed-over from drink. "By the way, it's Senator Barkley for vice president. Justice Douglas turned the job down. Said, 'I don't want to be the number two man to a second-rate man.'"

"There go all the lights at the Supreme Court."

"I don't suppose you've seen Clay?" Harold was always tentative when he mentioned Clay to his brother-in-law.

"No."

"He's a delegate. But Burden isn't. Funny, since he's running again in two years. I suppose he's getting old."

"Not fast enough for . . ." Peter cut his sentence short.

"For what?"

Peter changed the subject. "What's the title of that film they're doing about Clay?"

"The last I heard it's still 'Fire over Luzon,' with Audie Murphy."

"The real hero."

"*Another* real hero." Harold was sharp.

"Of course. Why didn't Tim direct?"

"Studio didn't want him . . ."

There was a sudden eruption of applause pounded into irritable silence by Rayburn's gavel striking the speaker's stand. A stout rosy-faced young man had just arrived at the podium.

"His Honor the Mayor of Milwaukee." Harold was now making notes. "Hubert Humphrey. He's all set to drive the South out of the party."

"Maybe a good thing."

"Maybe not. The Negro vote isn't worth a dozen states."

The hall became very still as Humphrey spoke. Party politics in America was now entering a new phase. Humphrey wanted the so-called moderate plank on civil rights replaced by the one that his committee had just written, following closely, he maintained piously, the Truman Administration's original guidelines.

Harold chuckled. "I'll bet old Harry's got murder on his mind. This is the silver bullet that's going to kill him off."

Peter tended to agree. The young mayor was declaring war on states' rights, the engine whereby the Negro population was so efficiently excluded from power in the South. Although Truman had followed Roosevelt's moderately inclusive policy toward the Negro, he himself was every bit as racist as the white Missouri constituency that he had represented in the Senate. He was also as politically expedient as the next politician, and no matter what his personal views he would go where the votes were. Apparently the time had come, if Humphrey was right, to loosen the Confederate grip on the party. Would Truman be sufficiently adroit to weather so vast a sea change? Peter recalled something that Hopkins had told his aunt: "To govern the United States, you must move to the right. To win an election, you must move to the left." This cynical wisdom was now about to be tested.

A majority of the delegates, to Peter's surprise, were now moving to the left. Humphrey's plank was accepted by a thunderous voice vote. There was pandemonium in the hall. The Alabama and Mississippi delegations served notice that they would leave the convention after the vote for president. Presumably, for another party as yet unborn.

During the speeches seconding the nomination of Truman, Peter had only one wish: to get out of the heat of the hall into what some-one had said was a cooling light rain. Better wet than dead of heat.

Peter left the stage for the shadowy space that led to some sort of backstage where Senator McGrath, the national chairman of the Democratic Party, was supposed to have an air-conditioned office.

Beside the door to a corridor that led to the outside, Peter found the Senator, whom he knew through Burden Day. McGrath was mopping his face with a hand towel. He shook Peter's hand with the towel. "I think I'm having a stroke," he said.

"I was told you had an air-conditioned office . . ."

"I've been given a special hot box. I can't stay in it. Nobody can. But I don't want to go up onstage yet."

Peter looked longingly at the relatively cool outside where a streetlamp illuminated a section of railroad track. "Why not go outside? It's stopped raining."

"Can't. He's there. Don't tell."

"Who?"

"The President. My room's too hot and too small to hold him. So he's enjoying the view of the railroad, with Senator Barkley. I must say he's a good sport. They just got in from Washington and now he's going to have to sit there for the next three hours."

Peter, more than anything, wanted to see the world's most powerful man abandoned beside a railroad track. "You don't suppose . . . ?"

McGrath shook his head. "Nobody's going near him."

"Three hours is a long time to be with just Alben Barkley."

McGrath laughed. "If you can keep on like that, maybe . . ." He went outside. Spoke to a seated figure; then he waved to Peter, who stepped, as if in a dream, into history.

The President was seated in what looked to be an uncomfortable kitchen chair while Alben Barkley occupied a sort of red leather throne. To either side of them, almost out of view in the dim light, stood two policemen, like sentries.

Truman was immaculate in a white suit. Barkley rumpled in statesman brown. "Mr. Sanford." Truman had risen; shook Peter's hand, as did Barkley. "Come visit with us for a moment." Truman looked about him. "Pull up that crate over there. And let's enjoy the night air."

Peter placed the crate opposite the President and sat down.

"How's the temperature inside?" Truman looked uncannily cool in his unwrinkled white suit.

"They say it's about a hundred degrees on the rostrum. The television lights are blinding."

Truman sighed. "They said we had to have the television. Whole country watching, they told us. But, of course, everybody sensible is going to be sound asleep by the time the voting's started. Alben, you ever think we'd live to see the day when people at home—if they aren't sound asleep—could watch a convention going on?"

"No, Mr. President. But then I'm still not used to radio. When I started out we didn't even have proper amplifiers. Luckily, I had a voice like a bull in rut. I was built for political picnics in the blue grass."

"You're older than I am." Truman was droll. "I keep forgetting."

"Mr. President, you keep right on forgetting."

"Oh, I approve. It might make me a bit uneasy having a young go-getter for vice president."

"Do you think that's how you seemed to President Roosevelt?"

Truman laughed. "I was his vice president for five months and I don't think he ever figured out who I was. Every time we talked it was always like we were just introduced. Of course, he was dying the whole time. You could tell that. By the eyes. You'd be talking to him and suddenly they'd just switch off. Like a lightbulb."

"Lucky the people never knew."

"Maybe *un*lucky. You know, we should get some legislation on that. A presidential illness or disability act. Of course, if I have a stroke, old as you are, you'll have to take over."

"How? Remember Wilson? We had over a year of a president who couldn't function while his wife ran the country. The Constitution doesn't really take into account what we have to do with a president who's conscious enough *not* to want to be replaced but can't do the job."

In the dim light, Truman smiled. The teeth brighter than the magnified eyes that, due to a trick of lighting, were now inscrutably dark. "I can tell that you've been giving a whole lot of thought to this problem ever since I told you you were my choice tonight."

Barkley chuckled. "What did they say of old Adlai Stevenson? There goes the Vice President with nothing on his mind but the President's health."

Truman turned to Peter. "Tell your father I appreciated his support during all that Eisenhower nonsense."

"I will, sir. He takes the view that military men are not suited to politics."

"Well, I'm not so sure Ike isn't one of the best politicians around. After all, at his level of the military it's nothing but politics. And then, four years of dealing with Churchill and de Gaulle and Stalin is certainly a crash course in foreign affairs. I certainly wish I'd had his experience before I got put in the hot seat."

"The Senate," said Barkley, "isn't exactly outer Mongolia."

"I'm not so sure. I suspect you and I learned more about what made people tick when we were still county judges. Now that's real life. That's real work. Those are real people. You need to be smart to be a judge, while any fool can get to the Senate."

"And stay forever." The two men laughed—at the same inside joke? As always, Peter was charmed at how candid a professional politician could appear to be and yet never give the game away.

"I remember when I first came to the Senate in nineteen and thirty-four. You'd already been there—six? No, eight years. Anyway, I was feeling pretty lost and so I wandered into the cloakroom, where the few senators that were in there, Republicans, of course, just ignored me. So I sat down and looked at a newspaper and wondered just how this adventure was going to turn out. Then old Ham Lewis came over to me. From Illinois. Wore a red wig. Shook my hand. 'Welcome to our clubhouse.' Oh, he was a courtly man. Anyway, we chatted about this and that. Then he must have suspected that I was feeling a bit forlorn because he leaned over like he was going to tell me some great secret and whispered in my ear, 'I spent my whole first year here wondering how on earth I had managed to get to the United States Senate. Then I spent the next thirty years wondering how on earth the others made it here.'" Peter and Barkley laughed. Then Truman gave Peter's shoulder a genial tap. "Nice to meet you, Mr. Sanford. Give your father my regards." The audience was over. As Peter got to the stage door he heard Truman say, in a matter-of-fact voice, "I know you don't believe it, Alben, but I'm going to win this election." Peter could hear no more.

McGrath—was he one of the fool senators?—met him backstage.

"How was he?"

"Cool and candid."

"Did he say anything about Mayor Humphrey?"

"Not a word."

"He used the word 'crackpot' to me."

At the *Tribune* table, haggard in the heat, Harold Griffiths had unbuttoned his shirt. The roll call of the states was almost over. Peter could not resist saying, "I just had a chat with the President."

"Did he confess to being an admirer of your paper?" Harold's nerves, never entirely steady, were fraying in the damp heat.

"I don't think he's ever heard of it. I was simply son of Blaise."

"Well, that's currency of the realm."

It was after midnight when Truman was nominated for president with 948 votes to Senator Russell's 263. Rayburn attacked the lectern with his gavel; then he shouted that there had been a motion to nominate, by acclamation, Alben W. Barkley for vice president. The thunder of "ayes" made the air vibrate. Then a band, led by James Petrillo, head of the Musicians' Union, played "Happy Days Are Here Again," FDR's theme song, while someone released a flock of white pigeons, signifying peace, into the tropical air. For an instant, each bird seemed intent upon attacking Sam Rayburn. Furiously, he fought them off.

As the pigeons, now blinded by television lights, ricocheted around the hall, Barkley gave a short acceptance speech that was no match for his Bryanesque oration of the day before. Then he introduced the President.

Truman emerged from the darkness at the back of the stage, a dapper small figure whose white suit shone in the television lights as if it were illuminated. He was politely, dutifully, perhaps sadly, cheered at what everyone knew would be the end of his career. Truman put his black notebook on the lectern; opened it.

To Peter's surprise, Truman spoke not from a text but from notes that appeared to be scribbled in his own hand. Peter had a good view of his back as he pulled himself up very straight and took charge of the delegates, of the Democratic Party back of them and of the American majority back of them in the country.

"Senator Barkley and I will win this election and make those Republicans like it—don't you forget that." The unfamiliar word "win" took a moment to sink in. Then there was a roar from the delegates. Were they beholding a miracle? Was Lazarus rising before their eyes? Could they really win?

Gone was the statesman's drone that Truman affected when he thought an occasion required presidential dignity. This was a tough Missouri machine politician rallying his troops in order to rout the enemy and seize the crown.

Hands chopped at the air as he listed what his Administration had done for the people. What the Republicans had *not* done or stopped him from doing. He blamed the Eightieth Congress for obstruction. The people had won a great war and enjoyed great prosperity during sixteen years of Democratic rule while the Republican Party had done its best to halt any measure that might serve the people at large. The language was crisp, folksy; the accent that of the hillbilly populist majority of a still rural nation.

It became clear to Peter that the campaign would not be so much against the vapid Dewey but against the Republican Party in the Congress, who said they wanted civil rights but then had done nothing when he called upon them to act.

Truman was now working the audience and himself into a frenzy, at whose peak he dropped his bombshell, near atomic in its effect. "I am, therefore, calling this Congress back into session July twenty-sixth On the twenty-sixth of July, which out in Missouri we call Turnip Day, I am going to call Congress back and ask them to pass laws to halt rising prices, to meet the housing crisis—which they are saying they are for in their platform." He rose to a rhetorical crescendo as he listed other measures which "they *say* they are for." Each got its cheers from the audience. Then he shouted, "Now, my friends, if there is any reality behind the Republican platform, we ought to get some action from a short session of the Eightieth Congress. They can do this job in fifteen days, if they want to do it. Then they will still have time to go out and run for office."

At the end, Truman waved to the cheering audience; then turned away from the lights. He shook the hand nearest him, which belonged to Sam Rayburn. At that exact moment, a dazed pigeon, mistaking Rayburn's bald head for a solid rock to rest on, settled upon the statesman's head. Grimly, Rayburn brushed the bird off. Truman exited, laughing.

"Turnip Day," said Harold Griffiths, after consultation with another journalist, "is a Missouri jingle; 'On the twenty-sixth of July sow your turnips wet or dry.'"

"He sowed them tonight." Peter was looking forward to a copy of the largely improvised speech.

He was fairly certain that at no significant point had Truman mentioned the name of Roosevelt. He was now himself, unshadowed, alone; of course he must still fight and win his Turnip Wars.

3

The brick house in N Street was like all its neighbors in that corner of recently gentrified Georgetown. In front of the house, a large magnolia grew out of the cobbled sidewalk; at the newly painted dark green front door, a guard kept watch over what little traffic there was coming and going. Since Peter was expected, the guard ushered him into a hallway, where he was greeted by the lady of the house, a harassed young woman whom he recognized from large Washington parties where she formed a part of the permanent chorus to great events.

As befitted a member in good standing of the whispering gallery, she whispered even in her own house. "He's very tired, Mr. Sanford. But he does want to see you. He's in the study." She opened a door and motioned for Peter to enter a dark book-lined room, as gloomy as the dark autumn day itself.

At a desk, in front of a window looking onto a garden gone to seed, Henry Wallace, haggard and unshaven, necktie askew, was busy typing on a portable machine. He still had his dedicated admirers who would, in a few days, vote for him as president, the Progressive Party candidate for the sole legitimate heir to Franklin Roosevelt's New Deal.

"Mr. Sanford." Wallace shook Peter's hand. He was taller than Peter had expected; solidly built, with shaggy hair somewhat grayer than it looked in photographs. "Sit down." Peter sat on a horsehair sofa, Wallace opposite him. "I've got too much to say, as you must have noticed."

"I know. I'm grateful," Peter added to his own surprise. He seldom betrayed any partisanship when it came to interviewing, or merely inspecting, national leaders.

"Are you?" Wallace's smile was weak. "Well, it's about over." He looked at his watch. "I have thirty minutes."

"I'll just listen, if you don't mind. This is for after the election, anyway. A sort of final impression. You look, if I may say so, mortally tired."

"I am. The South was quite an experience for me. I'm pretty well used to controversy. But not so used to having eggs lobbed in my direction. Harry Truman's smear brigade has been working overtime." He reached over to the desk; picked up a sheet of paper. "Latest Gallup poll says that fifty-one percent of the American people think the Progressive Party is run by communists."

"It isn't?"

"Have you ever met an American communist who could run a shoe store? Of course, the few communists there are in the country are voting for me because they want peace between us and the Soviet while Truman wants confrontation, or worse. Now I'm not one to psycho-analyze public figures, but a half-blind mother's boy is apt to have all sorts of complexes about trying to act like the way he thinks a tough boy would. When I was in the Cabinet, he always used to brag about how he had really *told* someone off but then you'd ask that someone what happened and you'd find Harry had been his usual affable, quick-to-please-the-customer self."

"But he did write you that tough letter, asking you to resign as secretary of commerce."

Wallace nodded. "That was truly out of character. Unless the rumors are true that he does a lot of letter-writing at night when he's drinking and then, if he remembers the next day, he prowls around the White House looking for stamps; very hard to find stamps there, since the secretaries lock their desks. But if he does find a stamp he'll mail the letter the next morning on his regular walk. I think that may have happened in my case. It was a . . . a low letter."

"Profane?"

"No. More . . . Oh, full of phrases like 'one hundred percent pacifists,' 'parlor pinks,' and 'soprano-voiced men of the Art Club,' whatever that is, whoever they are. It was bar-room drunk's sort of language. Anyway, when I got it, I rang him and I told him pretty firmly that this was not proper presidential behavior and neither of us must ever let the public see his handiwork. That was my mistake, I suppose." Wallace shook his head wearily. "He agreed—he always agrees—and he asked me if I'd return the letter if he sent me a messenger. I said I would and I did. I also gave Harry a three-line note of resignation and that was that. He's been really bad luck for this country."

"More than Roosevelt?"

Wallace looked surprised. "I thought *The American Idea* was pro–New Deal."

"But then came Dr. Win-the-War."

Wallace nodded. "Mrs. Roosevelt and I fell out over that, as you know. While all the donkeys in the press and Congress were braying about the American century, I was talking about the age of the common man. The President—when I say *the* President I only mean Roosevelt—was divided on the subject. But he and I were agreed that there was no difference between us and the Soviets that couldn't be worked out peacefully. Truman's simply not up to the job. He plays to the jingoes. To the haters. To . . ."

Wallace picked another piece of paper off the desk. "J. Edgar Hoover believes that one out of one thousand one hundred and eighty-four Americans is a communist. I wonder who did the counting for him? Anyway, I should doubt one in ten thousand has any idea what communism is. But since Harry has given us all these loyalty oaths and star chamber hearings where due process of law is chucked out the window, Hoover now sees his Federal Bureau of Investigation as another Gestapo with himself as Himmler. Well, I promise you that FDR, for all his faults, would not have got us onto the road to what can only turn out to be a fascist state."

"But he did give us Harry Truman."

"Yes. History will worry about that one, I suppose. The feeling against me was so strong that he . . ." Wallace stared out the window at a brick wall covered in dead ivy. He seemed to have lost his train of thought. "You know," he said at last, "I had a very strange impression when we first really met. In 1932. At Warm Springs. He was looking for a secretary of agriculture and I was looking to be secretary of agriculture like my father before me." He laughed. "I read how mystical, woolly-headed I am. Yet I am the first scientist to be a member of a president's Cabinet. I'm a plant geneticist. I'm responsible for hybrid corn and, if I may boast in the Republican manner, I edited *Wallace's Farmer*. I've met many a payroll and I built from nothing a multimillion-dollar business, while FDR couldn't balance a checkbook. Fortunately, this didn't stop him from being a political genius, unlike me.

"You know, he used to filibuster when he was sizing people up. So when we were down in Georgia, supposed to be discussing agriculture, he started in on this long story of a treasure hunt that he'd had an interest in on some island off Nova Scotia. Well, he went on and on, probably the only subject—buried treasure—of absolutely no interest to me, and I kept wondering, what is this man all about? Was he preparing me with a parable? Perhaps he was, because the first thing he wanted to do was cut my department's budget. I guess that was his buried treasure. He truly wanted a balanced budget. Never got one, of course." Wallace shut his eyes; rocked back and forth slowly.

Then, just as Peter was convinced that he had gone to sleep, he opened his eyes. "At the end, he was not himself anymore. There was something wrong with his circulation. You could tell the way what seemed like parts of his brain would suddenly light up while others would just go dark. The choice of Truman came out of . . . I've talked to doctors, authorities on circulation . . ." Wallace stopped: his own blood not flowing to the Roosevelt area of his brain?

"People thought FDR was arrogant, cold, indifferent to people. I suppose he was all those things up to a point. Certainly he felt that he had to dominate everyone. Felt he had to know more about everything than you did. I always knew, each day, the price of cotton in a dozen markets. But he'd still call me and say, 'I bet you don't know the latest price of cotton on the New York Exchange.' But I always knew. Drove him crazy."

"Why do you think he felt he had to replace you in 1944? With Truman of all people."

Wallace shrugged. "The South mainly. 'Go back to Russia, nigger-lover,' they were yelling at me just yesterday in Virginia. I've never seen human hate in the raw like that. But once you see it, you can under-stand how someone like Hitler can exploit it for his own purposes. Then there was my supposedly mystical bent. The letters that some journalists got copies of to my guru. A joke between me and a theosophist friend. I'm fascinated by theosophy, by Buddhism. Yet I was also probably the only believing Christian in the Administration. But, somehow, there's the idea that if one is curious about such things one must be mentally unstable. When the story first broke, FDR han-dled it very well. 'He's not a mystic,' he said. 'He's a philosopher.' Thank God the press has no idea what a philosopher is, because that could sound pretty bad to a lot of people. Finally, he just let me go and took Harry Truman aboard, figuring that as a four-eyed sissy he would be for peace, not realizing that sissies are driven to appear tough. Harry's got to get us into a war to show how tough he is. Then there was Winston Churchill. . . ."

Wallace shut his eyes; began to rock. "I never hit it off with him. He worshiped that empire of theirs, never suspecting that FDR had every intention of folding it along with the French, the Dutch, the Por-tuguese colonies." Wallace opened his eyes. "You know, Harry's been secretly financing the French in Indochina, one of the first places that

FDR intended to boot them out of. Well, Churchill and I were at a dinner and he proposed that after the war the British and the Americans share a common nationality. I could see how this was a good deal for the residents of those offshore islands but a bad one for us. I was, I hope, polite. I pointed out that this Anglo-Saxondom would be considered elitist by those excluded, not to mention all those Americans who come from different racial stock. 'Of course it's elitist,' he said in that cheery lisp of his, 'because we *are* the superior stock. Always have been.' I said that I disagreed. Later FDR told me that Churchill told him that he needed a new vice president."

"The President was just stringing Churchill along?"

Wallace nodded. "As he did everyone." He smiled. "Last time I really talked to FDR was after the election of 1944, just before he went off to Yalta. We were almost always on pretty good terms. Particularly on one of his good days. Well, this was one. I was waiting for him downstairs in the Map Room. A young naval officer, very nervous, was pushing his wheelchair. I stood up. The President was cheery. We started to talk, then something went wrong with the brakes on the wheelchair. The young man lost control of the chair, which started going faster and faster, with the boy trying desperately to slow it down, to stop it. The President was looking very alarmed at this point. Then the boy aimed the chair—and the President—into an open closet full of filing cases, where the chair came to a full halt. The President's face ended up in a drawer. I rushed over to help. The boy was in a state of shock. Unable to be moved, the President then took charge of the wheels of his chair and slowly backed himself out of the closet. By then he was delighted. "I must say, Henry, I've heard about presidents being got rid of by assassination but this is the first time an attempt has ever been made to simply file a president."

Wallace laughed; as did Peter. The dour mood lifted. Then the door to the study opened, and a radio crew appeared. Peter wished the candidate luck. He was rewarded with an absent smile.

4

The secretary of state–in–waiting, John Foster Dulles, was in mellow mood after dinner at Laurel House. "Essentially we will continue along the same lines that Dean Acheson and I have laid down. After all, our foreign policy has been bipartisan since President Roosevelt died. I must say I have generally worked well with Dean and I'm sure we'll go on working together if the law doesn't take up too much of his time. Poor man. Every time he starts to make a little money, he's called back to the White House."

A dozen guests were seated in the drawing room, listening to President Dewey's secretary of state, a dour, hard-faced Wall Street lawyer. He was, everyone agreed, born to be secretary of state; he was a nephew of Robert Lansing, Wilson's secretary of state, who had himself married Eleanor Foster, daughter of Benjamin Harrison's secretary of state. Foster had been born "in the purple," as Peter wrote when Aeneas, although a lover of exotic words and concepts, had forbade him to call Dulles a porphyrogenite, the word for a Byzantine emperor's son born in a special red marble chamber, signifying his divine right to succeed to the throne. Nevertheless, to annoy Aeneas, Peter had begun work on an ever-lengthening piece entitled "Porphyrogenitism," his word to describe those political dynasties that had decorated or degraded the American republic from the splendid Adams family down to the merry Roosevelts.

Blaise encouraged Dulles to "speak freely," something not in that lawyer's nature. The other guests, among them the British ambassador, were all keen to know what was in store for the world during the next four years. Dewey himself had not bothered to confide in the voters. In three days, on Tuesday, November 2, 1948, the nation would vote but, thus far, the deep-voiced Dewey—"the ideal radio voice" he'd been acclaimed—had no message for the people other than that "unity" would be needed in the days ahead. He did echo the House Un-American Activities Committee by deploring the Administration's "coddling of communists." But to Peter's surprise, Dewey did not endorse Truman's plan to outlaw the Communist Party in the United States. "We'll have no thought police," intoned Dewey.

Meanwhile, Truman had covered some thirty-one thousand miles in his whistle-stop train; he had given over 350 speeches to ever larger crowds who plainly energized him by shouting, "Give 'em hell, Harry!" and he had obliged. Sometimes, overenergized—or was it bourbonized?—he went too far. "A vote for Dewey was a vote for fascism" did not play well. On the other hand, in a nation daily terrorized by press, television, films, communism was the greatest bogey of all, and with broad gleeful strokes he painted Henry Wallace and his Progressive Party bright red. "I do not want and I will not accept the political support of Henry Wallace and his communists. If joining them or permitting them to join me is the price of victory, I recommend defeat." Since Henry Wallace had not proposed an alliance, this seemed excessive, but then it was necessary for Truman to destroy completely the political heir of Roosevelt in order that he alone, a conservative Southerner, could replace the great cosmopolite and all his works in the interest not of a new deal but of a somewhat mysterious "fair deal." Despite Wallace's appeal to liberal Democrats, Truman had managed to hold on to most of Roosevelt's Jewish and Negro support. After the convention, he had integrated the armed services. In May he had recognized Israel, a few minutes after the state was created, in exchange, it was said, for Jewish money to finance his train. It was also said that his secretary of defense, Louis Johnson, had managed to tap the China lobby for whatever other money was needed. Mrs. Roosevelt, who had told Caroline that she could not possibly support such "a weak and vacillating person" whose cronyism reminded her of Harding, finally came around at the last moment in a broadcast: "There has never been a campaign where a man has shown more personal courage and confidence in the people of the United States." Peter had found the last part of the endorsement singularly shrewd. Truman really was one of them in a way that Roosevelt never was nor would have wanted to be.

Harry was *us* the people against *them*. Yet he was going to lose. The final Gallup poll showed Dewey ahead at 49.5 percent to Truman's 44.5.

Dulles held the floor. "I think where we might differ from current policy is in our recognition of the Soviets' master plan to conquer the world. I think Dean has underestimated their tenacity. Whenever we stand up to them, they back down. But that doesn't mean they give up. They simply regroup. As they did in order to seize Czechoslovakia. We should have stopped them."

"How?" Blaise exerted his right as host to address the oracle straight on.

"There were several options that I'm not supposed to discuss." Dulles was very smooth, Peter decided. "But I think there is a general hard-line approach which I find lacking in Dean, good man that he is. Dean is too wary of direct confrontation. I'm not. The Soviet empire in Eastern Europe is essentially fragile. At a signal from us, I don't think it will take much for the Hungarians, the Poles, even the East Germans to simply overthrow primitive Russian masters."

"*You* would signal them?" Blaise was politely inquisitive.

"At the right time, yes. My brother Allen is at the CIA, and according to his information, the Soviet itself is none too stable. Russia was—is—a devoutly Christian nation, and should there be sufficient pressure from outside—yes, from us—even Stalin himself might be overthrown in the name—I'm not ashamed to say it, and I'm not a bishop's son like Dean—of our Lord."

Peter had had enough. He slipped away. In his father's study he put in a call to his sister, Enid. Instead he got Dr. Paulus, the head of the sanitarium. "She's under sedation, Mr. Sanford. We've had a restless day, I fear."

"When can I see her?"

"Sunday, as usual, if you like."

Peter hung up. He had no faith in Dr. Paulus. More to the point, Enid, though admittedly alcoholic, was not in the least insane. She had simply had the bad luck to be inconvenient to those interested in Clay's career. How to set her free?

Peter glanced at the advance copies of magazines and columnists' proofs on Blaise's desk. Henry Luce's *Life* magazine ran an inspiring photograph of Dewey aboard a ferry crossing San Francisco Bay, not unlike George Washington crossing the Delaware. The Luce publica-

tions oscillated between ecstasy and reverence as they hailed the president of earth's most blessed Christian nation engaged in holy war with
the Russian Antichrist. Drew Pearson praised the team of dedicated
apostles that had made Dewey's election possible, their heroic work cut
out for them in the years of strife ahead with relentless communism.
The Alsop brothers were simply impatient. Why wait ten dangerous
weeks for the Dewey installation? Lame-duck Truman, resign! Go
home!

Election Day, Peter and Aeneas stayed in the offices of *The American Idea*. They had now recruited a dozen young people who could
report stories, write and rewrite, sell advertising space, and, otherwise,
do everything that the two editors could do.

Most of them had voted for Wallace. But Peter had had a sudden
change of heart, an illumination just short of a celestial vision in the
Fairfax courthouse. He voted for the Socialist candidate, Norman M.
Thomas. After all, Thomas had originated, in his lonely way, all the
social programs of Roosevelt and Truman. So why not vote for the
true author of change in order to—encourage him? Earlier in the summer, Peter had taken a Manhattan subway at Times Square. Opposite
him, in a linen suit with no tie, was the lean bald sympathetic Thomas.
No one but Peter had recognized the sixty-three-year-old Presbyterian
pastor who had helped found the American Civil Liberties Union; been
associate editor of *The Nation*; Socialist candidate for governor of New
York; and then head of the Socialist Party in 1926 after the death of the
noble Eugene V. Debs, imprisoned by Woodrow Wilson because he
had opposed Wilson's 1917 Espionage Act under which he himself was
promptly tried and sentenced to ten years in prison. While a prisoner,
he got nearly a million votes for president in 1920. Upon election,
good President Harding had freed him. Thomas was now in his fifth
race for president.

Fascinated, Peter watched him rehearse a speech. He made notes;
put them aside; moved his lips silently, shaping the words that he would
presently be speaking to some forlorn New York socialists, mostly ide-
alist Jews and Italians. When Thomas got off at Columbus Circle, Peter

had a presentiment that he would vote for him in November, which he did, hoping that the members of the Ku Klux Klan, lingering on the courthouse steps, would not know the terrible un-American thing that had taken place upon their hallowed lynching ground.

Out of consideration for the youth of his staff, Peter served beer and wine. There was a long night ahead.

The first tally came from a New Hampshire village: Dewey had won it. Aeneas was the first to quote the old joke, "As New Hampshire goes, so goes Vermont."

Peter bet Aeneas that New York State would go for Truman. Aeneas bet five dollars that Dewey would win the state. "The liberals—the Americans for Demonic Action—are so busy smearing Henry Wallace's Progressives as communists that they are going to knock off Truman, too. Guilt by association."

"Ironic" was the best that Peter could do. Dewey was an unacceptable candidate for those who thought that the future role of the United States would now be set for some time to come. Wallace, alone of the candidates, had accused Truman of committing the United States to a never-ending "cold war" against communism, which meant any regime that ignorant Congress and ignorant President could be persuaded to dislike.

In addition to smearing Roosevelt's heir as a communist, Truman had ensured the Negro vote with a vigorous stand on civil rights, while his sponsorship of Israel cut deeply into another of Wallace's natural constituencies. The South's candidate, Governor Strom Thurmond, was simply undercut, as Truman knew he would be, by an ancient Southern voting pattern. Each generation since the Civil War had been "Yellow Dog Democrats," meaning that they would cheerfully vote for a yellow dog if he was on the Democratic ticket. That night Truman's various gambles paid off. Thurmond carried only four states of the old Confederacy. Wallace's liberal enemies split New York's vote, giving the state to Dewey.

At eight in the morning, only Peter and Aeneas were still listening to the radio. The others had gone home. All night, Truman had been at least a million votes ahead in the popular vote, but the wishfully thoughtful commentators and analysts maintained that Dewey would, eventually, win in the number of states carried. At eight-thirty a.m. that dream ended when Ohio voted for Truman. Peter gave Aeneas five dollars. "I lose on New York but I win on the election. I knew Truman would win."

"How?"

"The night he was nominated, I spent a few minutes with him and Barkley, who thought—like everyone else—that they were going to lose. He didn't say so, of course. Politicians don't. But Truman knew what he was thinking and so he said, very casually, 'I know you don't believe it but I'm going to win this election.' I could tell by the way he said it that he meant it. I could also tell that he knew something no one else did."

"What?"

"The people, I suppose. The voters, anyway."

The telephones at *The American Idea* were now beginning to ring. With an American airlift supplying encircled Berlin and loyalty oaths being administered throughout the country in the hopes of trapping spies, Harry Truman would now be presiding, in his own right, over a highly fearful nation that was transforming itself, before Peter's eyes, into something altogether different from what had gone before. Truman, the principal transformer, had dexterously appealed to those who were being reluctantly transformed. Uncanny instinct, thought Peter. Great mischief, too. Yet Peter was certain that Truman had not the slightest idea what he was doing and where the country was going. But then no one, placed in a given period of time, could ever know.

FOURTEEN

I

Peter came to New York and stayed not with Aeneas but at the Gotham in Fifty-fifth Street off Fifth Avenue. Upon arriving, he had lunch with Cornelia Claiborne, as droll as ever. He took her to Robert's across from the hotel. Robert was an elegant Francophone— Swiss? Belgian? He always wore a morning coat and striped trousers and sternly encouraged Peter to practice his French.

Robert announced the arrival of fresh shad roe from the Hudson River and the season's first asparagus. Both were ordered, since Peter's latest vow to diet had been set aside as he entered a restaurant that he had known since childhood.

"Were you taken here for culture?" asked Cornelia; they sat side by side on a banquette, a hedge of yellow roses and feathery green fern separating them from the next booth.

"To Robert's?"

"No. To New York."

"Yes. Mrs. Mason Morton," he said.

"*Miss* Mason Morton." Both laughed. The lady had been a fixture in the Washington of their childhood. Conscientious but "busy" parents would call upon this lean, energetic Baltimore spinster to escort their children to New York City for initiation into high culture, something that Washington so proudly lacked. She would take her charges to museums, to theaters: usually Shakespeare, starring Maurice Evans, whose footlit spittle during long speeches glittered as it fell upon the audience like the girl in the fairy tale who extruded jewels and roses when she spoke, so unlike the wicked girl from whose lips fell only toads and scorpions. Opera was also a favorite of Miss Mason Morton. Peter still recalled the excitement of sitting in a box at the Metropolitan Opera House as it suddenly became still and the lights dimmed and the red plush and gilt all around him darkened and the overture began.

Cornelia's experience had been the same. "Though I seemed to have got more than my share of *The Nutcracker*. What was your first opera?"

"*Madame Butterfly* with Licia Albanese, still going strong."

Each confessed to an early passion for the Hayden Planetarium with its ever-changing starry dome and curious ice-cream-parlor smell.

Cornelia then discussed *The Hudson Review,* which she had helped to found. He had done no more than glance at this elegant academic literary quarterly (*Partisan Review* was his current reading), but Aeneas had found it serious if a bit too strong on what was currently being called the New Criticism, so very like the old except that all historical context—Peter's only interest—was to be sternly stripped away to reveal the text in its shy nakedness, weakly etherized upon a table, prepared for critical autopsy.

"Gore is angry with me because the editors, under the pseudonym 'Shrike,' attacked both him and Capote in the first issue."

"Surely he's used to attacks by now. After all, he and Dr. Kinsey have libeled the great republic as a land of sexual perversity."

"Well, to be exact, he only objected to being linked with Capote."

"He would have preferred Dr. Kinsey, I'm sure."

"Mother thinks Shakespeare is more apt."

As the shad roe arrived, Peter quizzed Cornelia about what seemed to him something of a recent phenomenon. He had noticed that most of the writers for the *Hudson Review* taught at universities while even the politically minded *Partisan Review* was publishing an unusual number of schoolteachers. "We usually steer clear of them," he said. "We prefer freelance writers like Dwight Macdonald or Edmund Wilson or artist-critics like Virgil Thomson."

"Wasn't it always like that? What you call schoolteachers writing about what they teach?"

"I don't remember 'always' very well." Peter put a strip of bacon over his shad roe. "But the English seem to be able to be writers and critics without becoming teachers or at least not admitting it if they are. I suppose the problem with most of our academics is that they don't write very well."

Cornelia frowned. "Possibly because they aren't meant to write but to teach. But then I don't suppose I know anything at all about 'always,' either. I mean I'm not really literary or political or . . . But maybe it's because so many of the young men from the war went to college on the GI Bill of Rights and then decided they wanted to stay on in the colleges."

"Putting down roots in Academe while writing for tenure?" Peter made a note. "But when will they ever get to see the world?"

"They saw the war."

"Most of life is peacetime. Or was until last week."

Peter was already at work on an analysis of the North Atlantic Treaty Organization: a permanent military alliance of West European nations under the control of the United States. This was supposed to be a deterrent to Stalin's known ambition to conquer the earth—so eerily like Hitler's—but actually it was plain to both Peter and Aeneas that NATO was to be nothing more than the outward and visible sign of the military annexation of Western Europe by the United States on the sensible ground that American bases in so many countries would intimidate any Western government from going to the left. NATO's brain was the supersecret Central Intelligence Agency, which had managed, somehow, to take public credit for the defeat of the Communist Party in the Italian elections of April 1948.

A year later, the first secretary of defense, Forrestal, had installed a B-29 base in England in order to protect the British Isles from a surprise nuclear attack: this would have been, Peter had written, a true surprise, since the Soviets still lacked nuclear weapons. Forrestal's airy response to this argument had been that, even so, it was a good idea to get the British used to a permanent American military presence in their vulnerable islands. Forrestal himself was now in a military hospital, suffering from "nervous breakdown": he had been captured running through the streets of Washington shouting, "The Russians are coming!" At least such was the whispering gallery's version of why he was so swiftly removed as chief of the defense of the last free nation on earth. But Peter had then uneasily added: wasn't the United States also as occupied as Great Britain by an ever-increasing military establishment that was costing the earth? Aeneas reminded him of the ancient vaudeville adage "Don't make a joke on a joke." Peter cut the line.

"I'm sorry I couldn't go to the funeral." Cornelia was tentative.

"I hate them, too." Peter had developed several responses to condolences, of which the most effective was changing the subject, but since Cornelia had been a friend of Enid's, he repeated yet again how his sister had fled from Dr. Paulus's institution in the doctor's car (he had left the key in the ignition); just south of Richmond, she had smashed into a farmer's truck containing two cows. "Yes." Peter anticipated Cornelia's question. "She had been drinking. She must have stopped somewhere on the road. She was planning to divorce Clay."

"She was very unlucky." Cornelia ate an asparagus with her fingers.

"Very unlucky. Clay, on the other hand, has more luck than is usual."

"What is usual? Faust?"

"Faust was supernatural. Blaise as tempter-in-chief is more usual. Except I can't see my besotted father as anything so glamorous as Mephistopheles. I'd cast Clay for that."

Cornelia was surprised. "He is so . . . blond. I mean bland." She laughed. "I mean both."

The sommelier poured them the last of the Chassagne-Montrachet. "Blonds can be diabolic, too. Not you, of course."

"I'm borderline blond. Bland, too, I fear."

Peter asked Cornelia to go to the movies with him. "I plan to see at least four today. I seldom get the chance to see even one in Washington. Aeneas usually covers all the arts for us, searching restlessly for an *American Idea.* I'm beginning to think he thinks anything will do. We've given up on the *The.* Tell no one."

Cornelia declined the invitation to go see *The Treasure of the Sierra Madre, Key Largo,* and then, at a small movie house on Broadway, *Fire over Luzon,* starring Audie Murphy "in a real-life story of heroism in war." A larger-than-life-size poster showed Murphy, a handsome youth who had won, in real life, in the real war, the Medal of Honor for killing German soldiers; he was carrying a wounded marine out of a flaming building.

Clay Overbury was identified in the credits as the original hero of this "real-life story," taken from the book by Harold Griffiths, "the GI's Homer." Peter rather doubted if the classical allusion, no doubt Harold's contribution, had done much for the box office. Even so, for early evening, the theater was half full with adolescent males and a few matronly women. Voters.

Apparently Clay—the protagonist—was a youth from the American heartland. He had had his doubts about foreign wars but when the Japs bombed Pearl Harbor he enlisted even though he was supposed to marry a girl who lived, for some unclear reason, far from the heartland in Washington, D.C. Audie Murphy's astonishing feats in the real war made even the most bogus movie scenes of combat come to life. Reel after reel, Clay's luck kept on holding. At the end, grateful neighbors sent the shy Audie with his new wife to Congress to make sure that there would never be another war in the new world that Audie-Clay had so famously risked his life to give birth to. The Harold Griffiths touch was everywhere as the young couple, at the end, loomed like archangels over the dome of the Capitol, a radiant alabaster skull set in lush green. Peter made a note: "Why are greens and yellows so phony in American films?"

Peter took a taxi to the East Side. The sun had just set and the sky was a bright electric April blue.

The offices of Hugh Pendleton, M.D., were on the ground floor of an East Side brownstone. Peter was immediately shown into the doctor's office by an irritable receptionist; it was almost eight-thirty p.m. and long past closing time in the land of healing.

Dr. Pendleton was professionally benign. "I hope you don't mind this ungodly hour but I've had a heavy schedule today. At Memorial." He added the chilling touch.

"Cancer's on the increase?" Peter had a morbid if not quite hypochondriacal fascination with disease. Dr. Pendleton motioned for him to sit in a brown leather chair beneath several museum posters featuring Oriental art. On the wall next to his medical degrees, he had hung a Chinese scroll painting—bird in a willow tree, boldly rendered. "Well, it looks like we're doing more surgeries but I suspect that's only because we're better at early detection." He took off one pair of glasses and put on another. He looked to be Clay's age.

"As you know," said Peter, "I was given your name by my sister's lawyer, Al Hartshorne."

"At Mrs. Overbury's funeral. Yes. Mr. Hartshorne told me that he'd spoken to you. Very sad. Very sad."

"Yes. For some of us at least."

"Yes." Dr. Pendleton's voice was neutral: inquiring for symptoms?

"I've just come from the movies. In the daytime. I'm afraid I feel a bit decadent."

"I seldom go at all. Too tired."

"But you saw what I just saw. *Fire over Luzon.*"

Dr. Pendleton nodded. "I'd been reading about Congressman Overbury these last few years. And I knew there was a book about him, which I didn't read but *Life* or *Look* ran a section from it, about Lingayen Gulf. Naturally, I was interested." Dr. Pendleton was eyeing Peter with some curiosity.

"And, naturally," Peter picked up the conversational slack, "I was interested to hear that Mr. Hartshorne had been in touch with you. He was preparing my sister's divorce case when she died."

"Apparently it was not going to be an amicable divorce."

"No." Peter was not about to give any more details than necessary. "You had told a friend that you were there that day, when—Audie Murphy saved a marine from the burning hangar."

Dr. Pendleton's smile was very small indeed. His eyebrows grew together in a straight line, mark of the devil Peter had been told in youth by certain members of the Laurel House domestic staff, ever on guard against Lucifer and all his works. "No. I wasn't at the airfield that day. I was at a hospital in the jungle, ten miles or so away. Just a Quonset hut, really."

Peter's stomach began to churn from tension. A recent development. Dyspepsia?

"So if you weren't there, how would you know—what happened?"

"I didn't know. But I did know that Clay Overbury wasn't there either. He had cut his foot and the wound was infected—gangrene's always a problem, particularly in the tropics. I was busy trying out penicillin on him. We had just got our first shipment and I'm afraid we were really splurging. Reckless, considering how little we knew about side effects."

"So he could not have been at the airfield when the Japanese bombed that particular hangar."

"No." An odd smile. "But I thought Audie Murphy very convincing. Of course *he* was actually there. I mean on the set, anyway."

"How did Mr. Hartshorne find you?"

"We have a mutual friend. I'm afraid I'd told her how funny I thought the story was. She told Mr. Hartshorne."

Peter was thinking hard. But then so, apparently, was Dr. Pendleton. "I'm quite aware of the political and ethical problems involved," he said. "The political, for Congressman Overbury, is obvious. The ethical, for me, is difficult. We're not supposed to talk about our patients, to put it mildly."

"But you *have* talked, haven't you?" Peter was gentle, almost apologetic. "So the story is not only now known but it would have figured, directly or indirectly, in my sister's divorce suit. There's really nothing to be done about what's said and done. Tell me," having made his gentle threat, Peter moved on, "how did the story get out, to begin with? *Was* there a wounded marine in the hangar? Did someone save him? In the presence of a cameraman?"

"At Lingayen Gulf there were many marines, dead and wounded.

And someone did carry one of them out of a burning hangar." Dr. Pendleton removed a glossy photograph from his drawer. "I must say I was curious as to how the mistake was made. So I got this printed up from the original negative. United Press was very helpful. As you can see, there is no way of telling who the rescuer really is. The light from the fire's back of him. So he's in total silhouette. He wears no insignia. Officers didn't in combat. So it could be Clay. It could be me. It could be—well, certainly it was whoever it was, of course. Only he's never recognized himself, that we know of."

"We? You know a lot about this."

"Al got me curious. But the only person who really knows is the journalist who was there and invented the story. Henry—no." He frowned. "I have a block about his name."

"Harold Griffiths."

"Yes. Personally, I preferred Ernie Pyle."

"Who didn't?" Peter rose to go.

At the door the doctor gave him a prescription form with a name scribbled on it. "This might be useful."

Peter took the slip of paper.

"It's the name of the photographer. He's still alive, UP says. *You must lose weight.*"

The following day, Peter met Billy Thorne at the Brass Rail at Seventh Avenue and Times Square. By the time Billy limped in, Peter had already occupied a booth and ordered a roast beef sandwich on rye, a specialty of what was a feeding ground for carnivores. Through the restaurant's plate-glass window, passersby could see chefs at work, slicing joints of beef, ham, turkey.

Peter knew that if he did not eat the famous Brass Rail cheesecake, he could not gain weight simply from lean beef. He felt virtuous already.

"I've never been here." Billy lurched into the booth. He was unnervingly the same. "I've passed by many times. I always think of cannibalism when I look through that window." He shuddered.

"You are simply a repressed vegetarian."

"I'll have a ham sandwich," Billy told the waiter. Then he pushed his wooden leg away from Peter's leg.

"How do you know when your leg's next to mine?" Peter was genuinely curious.

"I always move it even if it isn't."

Peter noticed, with surprise, as he always had in the past, that one of Billy's eyes was brown and the other blue. Although he preferred looking into the brown one, it was the blue that Billy now aimed at him. "How is Diana?" Peter asked the wrong eye.

Billy shrugged. "I guess you haven't seen her since we agreed that she get the divorce. She may have gone to Reno by now. Doesn't the Senator keep you up to date?"

"We've not seen each other for some time. She's quit the magazine."

"To marry Clay. Poor Diana."

"Why—poor?"

"Poor because, among other things, she has no money and so, now that Enid's dead, Clay is going to drop her and marry a fortune."

Peter did not even try to simulate surprise. "Yes. That's exactly what he would do." He repeated, "Poor Diana."

"So then you'll marry her. Frankly, I can't think why she left you to go back to him. You know, once jilted, twice shy—or some such folk wisdom."

Peter's face was growing hot. "I was not there to be left. Clay was not there to go back to."

"He made her think so. For his own reasons. He had to get elected with the help of her father, and so he charmed her all over again to make sure he had the old crook's help in his last two elections, which, along with your dad's money, will see him into the Senate next year."

Peter choked on his beef. Billy joyously pounded his back, the one thing not to do to someone with food lodged in the windpipe. Luckily, Peter was able to cough the gristle onto his plate. With a napkin, he dried teary eyes.

"What," said the now-contented Billy, "did I just say that *most* upset you?"

"That Clay is running for the Senate next year. How do you know?"

"First, because that's what he would do, because it's his last big chance. *Fire over Luzon* is still hot. People think he's Audie Murphy. But by 1952 he's just another congressman. So—go, go, go, Clay."

Peter put horseradish on his beef and, excitingly, burned his much harassed windpipe. "Does Diana know this?"

"Why else do you think she came to New York to see me?"

"To talk about divorce?"

"A nickel phone call covers that. She wanted to know all about . . ."

"The old crook?" Peter's voice broke on the phrase. Horseradish had really burned his throat.

"My testimony is sealed, for what it's worth. But there's one copy floating around, I'm told. I had a problem, you know, getting a security clearance for government work. New rules. They think communists are everywhere. So I made a deal with the Justice Department. I'd be cleared for certain government work I was doing—am still doing—if I'd report what I knew about Senator Burden Day and the Indian land sale back in 1940. That was the year Burden thought he could be president. So he made a deal with this lobbyist . . ."

"Ed Nillson." Peter was not sure he wanted any details at all, wanting all

"The very same. Ed wanted a parcel of federal land, with Indians on it, and oil under it. Land never to be sold. But Burden's subcommittee said that it could be sold for a few beads. When the subcommittee voted, Burden was in Canada. But the decision to sell out the Indians had been his. Ed then became treasurer of the well-financed James Burden Day for President Committee, which, of course, came to nothing when FDR ran."

Peter stared out the plate-glass window at the people walking by, who stared right back in. It was like an aquarium with fish on both sides of the glass. "Does Diana know all this?"

"She knows now. She also knows that Clay knows."

"So what will happen?"

Billy shrugged. "I'm out of it."

"What are you into?" The subject needed changing.

"I write for the *Wall Street Journal*. Analysis of foreign markets. Europe is my specialty."

"Thanks to the Lincoln Brigade?"

"In spite of the Lincoln Brigade. I also do some work for the Treasury. They tip me off. I tip them off."

"It sounds," Peter was pleased to note, "like the CIA."

"The CIO?" Billy had learned to act during his years of lecturing on how he'd been duped by the communists.

"Central Intelligence Agency. It is a clubhouse for the Daughters of the American Revolution, sponsored, as always, by Eli Yale."

"Oh, that!" Billy sucked at his teeth, an old habit that Peter had managed to forget until now. "Well, I do know that as of this month the ladies are on record, in their sorority house, of course, to the effect that the first move of the Soviet towards eventual world domination—their phrase—will be the annexation of China. The mainland of Asia is the Soviet's primary goal."

"Do they believe this or do they just say it?"

"Don't you believe it?" was Billy's question.

Peter suddenly found himself staring into the "honest" brown eye. "I believe," said Peter, "that if Stalin could push a button and annex China, he'd push it. But Mao is slippery. China is a far greater fact in history than Russia. Mao is more apt to manipulate Stalin."

"Which proves my point. Acheson frets over the economies of Western Europe, over the Italian elections, over the Berlin airlift, while the real action is in Asia, which he ignores. You should write about that."

"You write it. You know more than I."

"In the *Wall Street Journal*?" For an instant Billy's scorn almost blew a perfect cover. He quickly readjusted his mask. "They're very good about Europe. But like Acheson, they only think of Asia when Formosa and Chiang Kai-shek are in danger. I can't get them worked up."

Peter looked at his watch. He was due to meet Latouche in half an hour. "Something urgent," was the message. "Why is your CIA—I mean the DAR—suddenly so upset about Stalin and Mao?"

"If I were with the CIA, I wouldn't tell you, and if I was with the DAR, I wouldn't know. Speaking for our little group at Treasury, I can say that we believe there will be some sort of military action soon. Mao's been asking Moscow for planes that can be used to parachute troops. Parachute where? Formosa. Where else?" Peter decided then that the energetic Billy was also on the payroll of the China lobby, which had, in the last few years, siphoned off more than two billion dollars from the American government in order to buy, with American tax money, the American government itself, starting, if the rumor was true, with Truman's campaign train as well as numerous members of Congress, some more notoriously venal than others.

"Why isn't the Administration keeping the same sharp eye that you are on Asia?"

Billy ordered cheesecake. "Just plain," he told Frank, a square-jawed Scandinavian waiter, usually to be found slicing beef in the plate-glass window.

"And you'll have your usual," said Frank to Peter. "The cherry cheese."

Peter's mouth slowly opened to say no; then it shut; Frank was gone and with him the rigorous Spartan regime Peter had intended to inaugurate that very day. Later, he would have to swim twenty laps in the pool at the New York Athletic Club, to which he would jog a few blocks to the north. Yet it was Frank, not he, who had made the fatal decision.

Billy spoke. "Eurocentric."

"Our government?"

"Europe's the whole world for Acheson, as it was for Roosevelt. But it was Japan who attacked us. These people learn nothing. By the way, there's some new material on Pearl Harbor. I gave it to Diana. As a divorce settlement."

The cheesecake arrived. "Stalin's not going to make a move against us in Europe before 1954, if ever."

"Why then?"

"Because by then he'll have atomic parity. He's already got a sort of atomic bomb. Acheson's bracing for that. Sometime this fall it will be tried out and the Alsops' famous balance of power—Truman calls them the Sop Sisters, by the way—will start teetering. Then we rearm, totally."

"We've been doing that since Potsdam."

"You read too much of yourself." Billy was mocking.

Peter's stomach began to rumble. "First," he said, "came the draft. In peacetime. Then the rearmament of Germany . . . ?"

"A few policemen. . . . Anyway the draft, so far, isn't producing much. We've got maybe a hundred thousand more men, all in need of serious training. Four years ago we had twelve million seasoned troops. Now we've got less than two, all because the mothers of America got to their congressmen, who made Truman send them home."

Peter belched, softly. "If he hadn't they would have mutinied. The war was won. They knew our republic was never intended to be permanently militarized."

"Old intentions must yield to new realities, as crafty old Lenin used to say. George Washington thought the Atlantic and Pacific were impregnable defenses. Anyway, all that's going to change this year because it's a matter of survival for us. Already, Stalin and Mao control more of the world than we do."

"A couple of billion impoverished peasants between them? No. The power's with us. And . . ." Peter saw the familiar expression of the dedicated hawk staring at him over the cheesecake. But Peter did not provide sufficient pause to allow for the usual citation of statistics: hawk and dove were nowadays engaged in such stylized debate that each could make his case—or that of the other—without a moment's thought. "The figures that the Daughters of the American Revolution so much enjoy quoting, how the Soviets are spending over thirteen percent of their gross national product on war and the United States only seven percent, make no sense at all considering the wealth of the American economy and the poverty of the Soviet economy, at its best famously inefficient and ineffective." Peter filibustered Billy into silence; then he addressed his colorful cherry cheesecake.

Billy was mild. "I think you're wrong. Luckily for the Administration, McCarthy's Red Scare has given the National Security Council all the excuse it needs to do what it's wanted to do all along, which is the largest, most expensive military buildup in history, whose crown jewel will be the several-billion-dollar hydrogen bomb."

"Who pays for all this?"

"The people. Who else? Thanks to the atomic bomb, they've never been more prosperous. So now we shake them down to pay for a hydrogen bomb and even greater prosperity, which will make them feel wonderfully secure as they pay the highest taxes in our history."

"Not even the Russians-are-coming crowd will buy that."

"We're not selling. Fact, we're not giving them any choice. Why should we? After all, we're redesigning the country to save *their* lives. Defense. Security. Freedom. Democracy. These are the four horsemen of absolute peace . . ."

"Achieved, presumably, by war."

Billy ignored this. "Of course, it will cost us a lot, but it will bankrupt the Russians. So maybe the average American couple may be reduced to only one and a half Chryslers per year, but that's only for a decade or two. A mere generation at the outside. Meanwhile, our defense industries will grow richer and richer as they pay more and more people more and more money to build weapons of every sort while, thanks to the withholding tax, Roosevelt's one stroke of genius when it came to financing all-out war for all-out peace, the newly rich working class will gratefully finance through their humble little taxes the federal machine that hires them to build these weapons that we need to defend freedom and democracy, forever. What Truman's people learned from Roosevelt's act of necessity in wartime is how to use, in peacetime, the same methods to finance an ever-expanding federal apparatus to save us from a savage adversary, longing to destroy us. Oh, they have the nation by the balls, which is why they are grateful for Senator Joe McCarthy's demented ravings." Out of breath, Billy lit a cigar.

"I had not believed," said Peter, gulping the last bit of cheesecake, "that you were so sincere an employee of the *Wall Street Journal*. You have actually come full circle from communism to capitalism."

"The scales have fallen from your eyes at last." Billy blew smoke across the table. "Taken to their logical conclusion, the two are nearly identical. Where the ideal communist's socialist state would use th(

national wealth for the good of the citizens, strictly regulated, of course, by a centralized money power, we are now, in the interest of defending ourselves against an enemy both Satanic and godless—very important point, 'godless,' in selling high taxes to simple Americans of deep religious faith—we are creating a totally militarized socialist state by ignoring such frills as the welfare of the people themselves. After all, the *true* American likes to stand on his own two ruggedly independent feet, which our nuclear state will encourage him to do. He is also free to go to the church of his choice, unlike the communist Russian slaves. I must say the accidental brilliance of our leadership still astonishes me. Haberdasher Truman and Lawyer Acheson and Soldier Marshall are creating a militarized economy and state that leaves those two bumblers Stalin and Mao far behind in the dust, staring skyward at our B-29s, soon to start darkening their red skies. Peter, you have made me poetic."

"Save it for the *Journal.*"

"They would never use a word of it. We're not supposed to give the game away, ever. But, to be fair to my editors, they believe what they write even though it's always wrong, as the masters of our new nation intend it should be."

"Militarized Keynesianism," Peter said, as the change for five dollars was brought him.

"Not a bad phrase." Billy was in a good mood.

"So you don't think that in this new world order there is room for World War Three?"

"Who knows? We do keep pushing the Russians. And it's possible that one day they'll really push back. But I doubt it. They had their chance over Berlin only to discover that our airlift worked. Next month they'll accept our terms. No more airlift and we win again, for now. Then Congress will start implementing National Security Council order number twenty-something-or-other and you'll see every last Republican—penny-pinchers to a man—voting in the name of national defense for the biggest amount of government spending the world has ever seen. We are now inventing *mega*-socialism in order to protect the free world."

"It sounds more like reinventing fascism."

"Mussolini wasn't from Missouri." Billy put out his cigar. "Not only is industry going to be supported by the federal government but the universities, too."

"How?"

"Huge federal grants to higher learning to find new scientific ways of defending freedom. Also, new ways to silence the so-called humanities. We're even planning to set up independent journals and newspapers all around the world to counteract reactionary, un-American papers like yours. Our periodicals will be known as 'liberal,' of course, in the Americans for Demonic Action sense. At last true *benign* socialism."

"What was wrong with socialism before?"

"It was Russian and they were far too poor and dim-witted to do anything with so noble a concept. They also wanted to look after the education and so on of their people. That's not for us. Ever. What's good for General Motors . . ."

"Is good for General Electric. Yes. I understand you, Billy." And Peter thought that now, finally, he did.

At the door to the Brass Rail, they parted. Billy's last words were, "I'm fairly sure Clay's going to run against my ex-father-in-law next year. I hope Diana doesn't take it too hard. Ruthlessness is part of Clay's charm. He's going to be president, you know. If not by 1960, '64. . . . Read his book."

"I have. *Fire over Luzon* . . ."

"No. No. That's Harold Griffiths' great gushing tribute. Read Clay's *Vision for America.*"

"I haven't seen it."

"That's because I haven't finished writing it."

Billy stumped down Seventh Avenue towards Times Square. Peter went back into the Brass Rail and rang Latouche and canceled their meeting. Apparently, the movie star John Garfield was being fired from a film because he had known communists in his youth. Peter said that he would do what he could, which was very little. As he hung up he wondered if the bill for a militarized state, based on keeping the citizens in a constant state of panic, might prove, in the end, more devastating than World War Three, which so many, so excitedly, predicted was at hand.

Although the New York *Post* was the oldest and most liberal of New York's newspapers, its plant looked rather the worse for wear—from time or liberalism? Peter wondered if it could survive the new printless world that he saw up ahead. Certainly, it would be a pity not to have the *Post's* hectoring voice, day after day, warning of crime in high places, celebrating virtue in low.

The publisher's office was small and strewn with proofs. Dictionaries and a copy of *Who's Who* crowded a small table. The publisher, Dolly Schiff, greeted him at the office door. She was a slender handsome woman in early middle age with a square jaw, a thin mouth, and more or less blond hair. "I'm so glad you could come by."

She pushed proof sheets off a sofa and indicated for Peter to sit beside her. "Wechsler tells me you'll say no but I'm always for trying. We need a young writer. We particularly need someone in Washington who knows Washington. Murray Kempton's marvelous on the subject but he's got all of New York to worry about, too."

Peter listened attentively. He'd already decided to turn down her offer to be a columnist on a regular basis. He had too much work as it was. But, at a certain level, the idea appealed to him. There was something satisfyingly immediate about appearing in print along with the news instead of waiting a month or more to be heard from on a subject of ever-lessening urgency.

Peter wondered if the rumors were true that she wanted to sell the paper. Dolly had inherited a fortune and so could keep the *Post* going no matter how hard the times were for other newspapers. But she was said to be flighty or, as Aeneas put it, "First, she'll want you to be managing editor. If you fail at that, she'll want you to marry her. If you fail at that, she'll give you a column."

Peter declined an invitation to dinner. "I must get back to Washington." He reached in his pocket for his train ticket, found the stub of a movie ticket instead. *Fire over Luzon.* Would he dare? He should. For

Enid's sake. But not yet. He declined Mrs. Schiff's offer. She walked him to the door.

"Remember me to your father. And to your Aunt Caroline. She was the first woman in this business. I really admire her."

2

Caroline had always liked Blaise's Italianate palazzo on Massachusetts Avenue. Since it was next door to the elegant ivory-colored Embassy of Japan, the Japanese had tried to buy it from him just before the war, as an embassy for their newly acquired "nation" of Manchuria. Righteously, the Roosevelt administration refused to recognize so recent an acquisition. Blaise had then rented out the house and moved, permanently, he had thought, to the Potomac Palisades. Now he was back and Laurel House was the property of Mrs. Samuel I. Bloch.

The drawing room was splendid as summer light played off a series of millefleurs tapestries from Saint-Cloud-le-Duc, a present from half sister to half brother. With an effort that had given her a terrible headache, Caroline managed not to limp. Doctors had spoken of recent surgical miracles where an artificial hip could easily replace the faulty original. Caroline had declined the generous offer. A wheelchair would do her very well at Saint-Cloud-le-Duc. After all, Franklin had governed the world from a wheelchair and she saw no reason why she could not run the chateau just as well, if not as easily, as Franklin had done. Of course, he had had rather more help than she, not to mention an easier opponent in Stalin, who was mildness itself compared to the truly villainous communist mayor of her village. Now she had come to say goodbye to Washington, to the United States, to that exciting if somewhat rustic world in which she had for so long played a part, sometimes as a principal but more often, lately, as privileged spectator.

"Time for me to go home," she said to Blaise, who stood beneath two of the four Poussins that she had sold to buy and re-create the *Tribune* during the days when her then enemy, Blaise, had successfully kept her inheritance from her. Once she had made a success of the paper (with some help from Hearst), she had made her victory complete by taking in Blaise as her co-publisher; then she had bought back the four paintings, given Blaise two, and kept the better pair for herself. Now, a half century later, her American adventure was done.

Blaise embraced her warmly. In the background, Frederika was doing the honors as hostess. All Washington—*le gratin* as Irene would say in her powerful French—was gathering to say farewell to one of their own who, without having lost an election, had mysteriously chosen to move far, far away from the only world that mattered to its residents, particularly now that their rustic town had become the world's capital.

"I am eccentric," said Caroline to Blaise, who looked somewhat blurred. She needed new glasses.

"Well, if Washington's our natural center, then you are moving to the outer edge—to France, and that's literally eccentric."

The room was filling up with familiar faces from her past as well as those made familiar thanks to *Time* and *Newsweek* magazine cover stories that brought what seemed, for the one so noticed, true fame when, actually, it was only a week's notoriety in a given year that contained, dishearteningly for the thoughtful, fifty-one other weeks and faces.

"I've had an offer for the *Tribune*," said Blaise. "What do you think?"

"How much?"

"That's still being discussed. I'm getting old and you're going away and Peter . . ." He frowned.

"He's peculiar. Yes. I know." She wondered if she had an aspirin in her handbag. "He wants to be a voice. A power. But says no to a newspaper. Does that little magazine of his break even?"

"A bit better. Anyway, he's come into another small trust fund. From Frederika's aunt. The one in Watertown, Connecticut. They made brass buttons in the Civil War. He can now lose bits of money forever."

Caroline was tempted to ask why Blaise hadn't considered leaving his shares to Clay, but she was not certain that this was the sort of thing that could be safely asked even by a departing half sister. "Do what you

think is best," she said. "There is a time for everything, including letting go."

"What news of Tim?"

"Let go!" Caroline laughed; and lightly rubbed the back of her
neck. "He's making a film in Hollywood. Something that hardly anyone does anymore. Everything's on location these days. Or made for
television. The old studios are all letting go, too."

"I saw Emma out at Chevy Chase last week."

"Did you speak?"

"She spoke for two. As always. She's working for Joe McCarthy. It
seems that Alger Hiss was only the tip of a very large iceberg. She has
proof that Dean Acheson is the brains of the communist conspiracy in
the United States."

"Surely," said Dean Acheson, who had heard this last, "the real
brains are those of President Truman. I only carry out orders. A loyal
foot soldier." The elegant Secretary of State bowed to brother and sister. "I never see you," he said to Caroline, "and now you're going
away."

"I can go, contentedly, knowing that a loyal foot soldier is in charge
of the State Department."

"Foot-in-mouth soldier, I think one of your columnists called me."
Acheson's smile was like that of a cat not yet determined whether or
not to yawn, the cat's signal that all is well, or to hiss and claw.

"Well, Dean, you know the press." Blaise was offhand.

Caroline was direct. "You deserve every sort of medal for your
duels with McCarthy."

"*That* is what I most like to hear."

Caroline seated herself on a sofa while Blaise led Acheson off to
greet some Senate admirers. As always, she was struck by how busy
everyone had become in what had been for so long a sleepy town with
an African climate now banished—indoors at least—by air-conditioning. The government seemed never to stop humming away, so unlike
the long quiet afternoons when Secretary of State John Hay and Henry
Adams and she would sit in old Henry's splendid study and discuss
Racine, with Caroline providing the right, she hoped, Comédie
Française readings. There had been limitless time at the start of the cen-

tury. Now, at the middle, the days were too short even to do what needed doing while the calendars seemed to contain not only fewer but ever shorter months. But then in the half century since she had first come upon the Washington scene, this leisurely world, hardly much different from that of John Quincy Adams, had been jolted by the First World War and the attendant corruption that war always brought; then jolted yet again by a second world war that had made the entire world, like it or not, an American responsibility.

Who could keep track of Acheson's activities? He had just taken three pieces of western Germany, stitched them together, and made a new republic. Next he had put in order the disorderly French house. He had even helped finance their attempts to regain control of France's Southeast Asian empire of Indochina, now at risk to the rising tide of communism. He was also supporting the British. This busy-ness was exciting if one were young and a part of it. But she was neither. She missed the old Washington, "the city of conversation" as Henry James had noted, not entirely in ironic mode. Unfortunately, she had no one left to talk to. For her, the gallery was now still. The headache in the back of her head was definitely unimproved by the icy air-conditioning that Blaise had installed in the drawing room. Then her nephew sat beside her and *he* talked to her.

Peter was surprisingly interesting, she had discovered in the last years of what she had come to think of as a long Bernhardt-like farewell tour. "Are you really going?"

"Certainly. At least in the actuarial sense." She saw a familiar figure in the middle distance, a short thick man with lion's head and mane. "Isn't that Senator Borah?"

Peter smiled. "He's been dead ten years."

Caroline's face felt cold: as if a blast of winter air had singled her out on this bright June day. "Now you know why I am leaving. I can no longer tell who's dead and who's not."

"It's a problem for the whole town. After all, to be out of office is to be out of life."

"Out of town first was always the best policy. But it's nice seeing ghosts. I saw Harry Hopkins in Fifth Avenue the other day. He looked better than he had in years. I'm sure he recognized me. They must give them some time off—you know, for bad behavior."

"Or maybe we're just allowed to think we see them."

Again the blast of cold air against her cheek. "Now *that* is macabre." Caroline abandoned the ghost world. "I hear that you refuse to take over the paper that I invented, with so much effort."

"It would do no good. You see . . ." He paused, as if uncertain what next to say. He began again. "The problem is there aren't going to be newspapers in the next ten, twenty years, not like before, not even like now."

"Television?"

"That's where what news there is will come from. By the time you get to the front page of the *Tribune*, you've already been told as much as you want to know about Mao's meeting with Stalin."

Caroline's "No!" was emphatic. "Television's nothing but surface. It also involves looking straight into a lightbulb, which is bad for the eyes, not to mention concentration. Who remembers what he's seen five minutes after? They are doing tests now. On how TV shuts off the mind. Damages memory. I don't think Mr. Sarnoff is encouraged."

"But his audience increases. Ours decreases."

"We can still analyze the news."

"Does anyone really care what Harold Griffiths thinks about General Eisenhower's plans to be president? Or what the Sop Sisters, the Alsops, that is, think about the Yellow Peril?"

"Lippmann's worth reading." Caroline wondered why she was so uncharacteristically weak on her own subject.

"If he really is, he'll end up on television. No, I see the city with one morning paper, the *Post*. One evening paper, the *Star*, full of predictable opinions and wrong guesses. Then the evening paper will give way to television news and the morning paper will be a sort of court circular."

"*You* will go to television?" Caroline felt as if she were in an H. G. Wells science fiction story or, better yet, one of E. Nesbit's glittering trips to the future or past. Hard to tell the two apart now that the room was filling up with dead faces while long-silenced voices were murmuring insistently from who knew what limbo, carried upon the persistent cold wind of Blaise's terrible air-conditioning.

"No. I'll write history." Peter was now looking at her curiously. She wondered if her mouth was on straight. She shivered in the wind.

"Father doesn't understand what I do," Peter continued. "Doesn't care. He does care about news, no matter how old. I don't. I only care about history . . ." Peter's voice was now drowned by a roar of icy air that announced the arrival of Henry Adams.

"Dear Henry." Caroline rose unsteadily to greet him but he had not seen her; he passed her by. She hobbled after him until, halfway across the room, the floor seemed suddenly the most desirable of resting places; and so she rested there: headache quite gone at last.

3

Blaise accompanied the body back to France. Emma had wanted to come, too, but Blaise forbade her with the relevant news that since she was not in her mother's will, she need go to no trouble. Peter and Frederika saw Blaise and the oblong box off at the airport. On orders from the secretary of the Air Force, a military transport plane had been assigned to fly them to Paris.

Blaise waved to wife and son at the top of the steps. Then he entered the plane. Frederika wept with no sound. Peter was still stunned. He had never seen anyone dead, much less anyone die in mid-conversation. Apparently, she had suffered a massive cerebral hemorrhage, much like the one that had carried off her friend Franklin Roosevelt.

"Well, it was quick," he said, inadequately, as they got into the car.

Frederika stopped weeping; told the driver to take them straight home. "Quick or slow is all the same when you go. There's hardly anyone left now. But then if she had gone back to live in France, we probably would never have seen her again anyway. So it's probably all the same to us."

"She thought she saw Senator Borah just before . . ."

"How awful for her," said Frederika, suddenly recovered. "We must remember that along with all the people we cared about who are dead there are millions and millions of crashing bores and, between us, Caroline and I must have met them all. I don't think," she said with a secret, knowing look, "that death is going to be all that relaxing for any of us."

Frederika got out of the car at Massachusetts Avenue; and Peter went on to Rock Creek Park.

Everything was in flower at Senator Day's house. Kitty was at the edge of the woods, feeding two squirrels a biscuit. She gestured to Peter: make no noise. He slipped into the house. Diana was in the living room.

They embraced like the lifelong married couple that they had so abruptly become on her return from Reno. It was only during their time apart that Peter had become convinced that they were intended to be a permanent couple, to which Diana had agreed. Thus far, neither had mentioned Clay, and Peter hoped the subject might be permanently postponed.

"Father's in the loggia. Waiting for you."

Peter was surprised. "Isn't the Senate in session?"

"He wants to know about your aunt. He's . . . very edgy these days. I don't think he's ever quite recovered from that fainting spell he had."

Diana led Peter into the loggia, where new green grapes were growing in tight hard jadelike clusters. Beyond the loggia Peter could see banks of deep purple irises in full lemon-scented bloom.

"Forgive me for not getting up. I'm still a bit lame." James Burden Day held a cane in his left hand while with the right he shook Peter's hand. The grip was strong; and the old man seemed vigorous enough.

"I gather you've just been seeing Caroline off to Europe." He could not have been more matter-of-fact.

Diana left them. "I must go back to the office," she said.

Peter sat in a wicker chair; a bright gold ray of sun fell diagonally across his chest like the chain of some celestial order.

"Yes. Mother and I saw them off from Andrews Field. The Military Air Transport Service found room for them. Father's . . . struck dumb. That doesn't mean he's stopped talking. Far from it. But dumb in the sense he doesn't know what to do and say about what's happened. There had been, after all, as Aunt Caroline would say, no rehearsal. I was the last to talk to her. She was fine. Except she kept seeing people who had not been invited to her farewell party. Literally, as it turned out, farewell."

"What sort of people?" Burden was unnaturally controlled, even casual.

"The dead."

"Oh!" He frowned. "Anyone I know?"

"Senator Borah crossed the room, or so she thought."

"Let's hope Alice Longworth saw him too. Who else?"

"She got up from the sofa to follow Henry Adams across the room. But she never caught up with him. Instead, she just sank to the floor. And never spoke again."

"Not bad." Burden seemed to be scoring Caroline's singular method of departure against those of others that he had known about. "I wish I'd been there. . . . But I had a session of the Finance Committee."

"Would you have persuaded her not to go?"

"Hard to say. When it's time . . . Funny, I once saw my own father a few years ago. His ghost, that is. Or, more likely, my hallucination. It was near the river at Fort Marcey. You know, up above the Potomac. Just north of Laurel House." He shut his eyes. Shuddered. Then he looked at Peter. "I'll be campaigning soon. That time of year. Back to the state to see if anyone remembers me."

"You're sure to win the primary."

"Only fools are ever sure in this business."

"Your speech at the State Historical Society got you five points higher in the polls."

Burden smiled. "Didn't use a single note, either. Didn't have to. I just remembered what it was like when we were putting together a brand-new state so that we could join it to the Union that most of our fathers had tried to get out of. Did Emma go home with Caroline?"

It took Peter an instant to remember who Emma was. Then he

recalled the strong hand relentlessly scraping mayonnaise off a lobster at the Blue Angel. "She wanted to but Blaise said no."

Burden shook his head. "Pity they never got on. I should've done more." This was the closest that he had ever come to admitting his paternity; then he changed the still, for him, dangerous subject. "Well, Peter, the big military buildup is underway. Except we haven't given the President the money. And we can't while McCarthy's out of control. It would be nice," said Burden, thoughtfully, "if someone shot him."

"Why doesn't the Senate expel him?"

"Too terrified. The whole lot of them. The whole lot of *us*. Come November he's threatening to defeat Tydings and Lucas, and this one and that one. He may even pull it off. I've seen some very disturbing polls. Half the country think that communists have already taken over our government."

"I know. In fact, I wrote a piece saying how if the communists are already in charge of the White House and Congress, not to mention Harvard and Yale, they've already won on points, so why not just go along with them?"

"Irony is un-American. But then everything is un-American now. I thought we'd lived through the worst of it back in 1917 when sauerkraut became 'liberty cabbage' and no orchestra could play Beethoven or any other German music, but this is far worse, more insidious, more . . ."

"Calculated?"

"Calculated. Yes. But by whom? *Cui bono?* Harry Truman wanted to scare the American people so he could start his buildup, but he certainly has nothing to do with that drunken buffoon going on about how Harry and Acheson lost China, never ours to have much less lose. No, there's always been a streak of madness in our folks. And there have always been demagogues who know just how to press all the right buttons to scare them out of what wits they have and turn them against their own government. . . ."

Peter knew the litany; he, too, recited it, in different voices, in different places. "What you just said, Senator, is what we all say, but listening to you now, I started to hear something else. McCarthy's babbling about communists in the State Department or the Army or wherever is nonsense, of course, and we know it because we know how Washington works, but what *I'm* now hearing is something else, something really serious. The people's fear of the government because they are starting to believe it's no longer by them or for them."

"Well, that's been the Republicans' line since '35. You know, when we first presented social security to Congress, they said it was just plain communism and they warned the people that if our bill passed everyone's name would be replaced by a government-assigned number." Burden chuckled. "That's your classic plutocratic smear. Big business never wants to pay any tax of any kind or be regulated for any reason or allow a penny of their profits to go to anyone at all, even if they're starving. That's an ancient battle with pretty clear rules for both sides. But now McCarthy's gone and broken every rule and Harry Truman's too weak to know how to put things back on track."

But Peter was sensing something entirely new in this familiar equation. "The fact is that, starting with Acheson's briefing, which, thank God, sir, you so usefully recorded . . ."

"Usefully and secretly." Burden was still uneasy about his memo.

"*Top* secretly. Something strange was set in motion. Part of the famous scaring hell out of the people has been our own government's prompt interference in everyone's life. Loyalty oaths. A peacetime military draft. Deciding who can or can't go abroad. A nonconvertible dollar. Increased income taxes. Then, in the interest of Americanism, all sorts of independent publications like *Counterattack* and now *Red Channels* are deciding who can work in film, television, theater."

"Well, those vigilante efforts are hardly government-sponsored."

"They couldn't exist if they weren't government-inspired and -sanctioned. I mean, how could they be allowed to deny others free speech, assembly, right to work, due process?" Latouche had been sending Peter a good deal of information about a professional blacklist which was getting ever longer and ever blacker. "Several pages," he had written, no doubt with a winsome smile, "are devoted to my own treasonous activities."

Burden had pulled himself up straight in his chair; the cane was now placed across his knees, like a weapon. "Do *you* really believe that our government has become our enemy?"

Peter evaded a direct answer. "I believe that it has come to enjoy so much . . . un-American." Peter smiled: at last a correct use for the word, "power over us that it will never ever let go."

"Never? No. Nothing lasts forever."

"We certainly don't. But, for now, *American Idea* is on the Attorney General's list of—what was their latest category?—'subversive' periodicals."

Diana entered the loggia.

Condolences duly expressed, Peter said goodbye to the Senator, who remained seated. But, Peter was happy to note, his cheeks were now a healthy pink and his eyes bright.

"You missed it," said Aeneas, switching off the television set as Peter entered the office.

"Missed what?" Peter sat on his side of the partners' desk. Diana had her own office on the floor above where she dealt with their youthful staff.

"Representative Clay Overbury has just made an announcement from the Caucus Room at the Old House Office Building. All the press was there."

What Peter had feared would happen had finally happened. "He's declared for the Senate."

Aeneas twirled his wedding ring round and round. "Were you really so certain that he'd do this?"

"Yes." Peter was thinking hard. "Did anyone question him about his promise never to run against his mentor—I believe that's the word he likes to use—Burden Day?"

"Harold Griffiths did."

"A setup. Go on."

"Harold asked the question and Clay was all boyish charm—he's even starting to look like Audie Murphy. He did say one thing interesting. He would never be declaring had it not been clear to him that

Senator Day's health problems would make it impossible for the founder of their state to make the sort of powerful race that people expected of so great a statesman, and so forth and so on."

Peter frowned. "There's a missing piece here. Either Clay knows something about old Burden's health that no one else knows or he's . . ."

Peter rang Diana in her office. Told her the news. "Go home. Tell your father. Find out why Clay's so sure Burden isn't running when, just now, he was all set to stump the state . . ."

Aeneas interrupted. "Clay did say that if the Senator was really willing to risk his health in what was bound to be a long hard election, he—Clay—would stand aside, of course."

"Of course." Peter repeated the message to Diana. Then he put down the receiver. "Well," he said to Aeneas and to himself, "we are at the brink, as Harold Griffiths would write."

"Who falls in?"

"*I* won't," said Peter, awash in uncharacteristic anger.

Clay's office was a reasonably modest shrine to its hero occupant. Only one *Fire over Luzon* poster was visible in a corner. Next to it there were several decorations under glass. Peter noticed that the Silver Star for heroism was not one of them, despite Harold Griffths claim; but a Bronze Star for marginally less heroism was on display.

The usual politician's photographs. One with President Truman, one with General MacArthur . . . plainly a statesman–hero president was impatiently serving time in this rather dingy office. Peter could see why members of the House of Representatives were so eager to move up to the Senate with its spacious offices, wide corridors, marble fire-places, and, as someone had once noted, comforting air of serene mega-lomania.

Clay came out from behind his desk and shook Peter's reluctant hand. The blue eyes glittered in the light of what was, so far, a perfect spring day. "Well, this is an honor." Clay's charm could never seem forced because it was never not on display.

They sat in black leather armchairs, a table between them on

which was a photograph of Elizabeth Watress. Next to it was a photograph of Clay holding up his daughter, whose eyes, eerily like Enid's,
made contact with Peter's.

"Yes," said Clay, as always getting the unstated point. "She's very
like her mother. She's still with Blaise and Frederika. But Elizabeth and
I hope to have our own house by this winter. She'll have a proper home
at last."

"You're marrying Elizabeth?"

"That's the plan. After the election, of course."

"That was the exact same plan with Diana." Peter could not resist.
"Wasn't it?"

"Yes, it was." Clay's smile was intimate, even boyish. "But then I
figured out it was really you she was interested in."

Peter was struck by the boldness, not to mention aptness, of the lie.
How could he now, once again with Diana, acknowledge that she had
always preferred Clay to him and that only after Clay had dropped her
did she return to him? Meanwhile Clay had moved on to the heiress
that everyone knew he would need to finance his rise once he was rid
at last of Blaise, the surrogate father and paymaster and, if Enid was to
be believed, lover. This last, if true, must have been a distasteful business to Clay, but business was business.

Clay picked up a folder. "Your old friend Billy Thorne's a wonderful writer. He's been . . ."

"Writing a book for you."

"Well, that's one way of looking at it, though we're supposed to tell
everyone how I slaved over the text, plumbing the depths of our political system. Unfortunately, he couldn't finish my testament."

"Why not?"

"He's been giving secret testimony to the House Un-American
Activities Committee. He's naming names. Thousands of names. He's
now home—free. But I can't have an ex-communist, no matter how
patriotic, writing . . . I mean doing research for me. Can I?"

"Why not?" Peter shrugged. "It's very much the thing nowadays.
Look at Whittaker Chambers."

"I've got someone else. But Billy was certainly bright. I don't think
Diana ever appreciated him."

"Well, he's found a home at the CIA."

Clay affected puzzlement. "He's at the Treasury, isn't he? When he's not writing for the *Wall Street Journal.*"

"That's the cover story."

Clay smiled: the old charm had been polished to high gloss. "Better cool it, Peter. That's becoming too much your style. Conspiracies everywhere. You're getting like poor old Joe McCarthy."

This was Peter's lead. "But there *are* conspiracies. Thousands of them. Everywhere. Particularly in Washington. Look at you. Conspiring to be a senator. Then president. You never stop . . . whispering to this one and that one."

"I'm not so partial," said Clay easily, "to that word 'whispering.' I tend to speak out. The way I did in the Old House Caucus Room the other day. Everything's in the open." The blue eyes turned unblinkingly on Peter, who turned away. Clay was uncommonly hard but then so was he himself, at least when engaged in such work as this.

"But you lied to the press, once again, when you said that you were in the race because Burden wasn't going to run, due to . . . what was it? Ill health?"

Clay's smile was close to a baring of teeth. "That's the truth. I also said if he wanted to run again I'd pull out, of course."

"But has *he* pulled out?"

Clay looked at his watch. "He'll have a statement by five o'clock. In time for tomorrow morning's papers. I guess we got our wires crossed the other day. I must have misunderstood him. Anyway, we had a nice meeting, yesterday. After all, I do owe him everything, practically."

"You owe him at least whatever it is that you don't owe my father."

Clay laughed. "Don't tell me you're jealous."

Peter's face was hot. Mustn't get angry. Easy does it. "No. You've certainly given Father a great deal of pleasure. You and . . . your career. I've given him none and nothing for nothing is the law of relationships while something for something is the absolute law."

Clay chose to bypass this potentially dangerous line of argument. "What did you mean when you said I'd lied to the press 'once again'?"

"There it is, your truly great lie." Peter pointed to the silhouetted man carrying a marine from a fiery inferno.

Clay laughed. "Well, to start with, that's not me, that's Audie Murphy!"

Peter opened his briefcase and removed the photograph that he'd got from United Press. "Here's a new print from the original negative. I got it from the photographer who was there—when you were not there."

Clay took the photograph; he was still smiling. "The problem is," he finally said, "you can't really tell who it is."

"Luckily for you."

"What are you up to?" The smile was gone. He dropped the photo to the floor, to show he was done with it. But Peter retrieved the print and put it back in his briefcase.

"I want you to ring Burden and tell him he won't have to make any statement, that you've changed your mind about running."

"No. I'm going for it. So . . ." A long pause. Then, Clay picked up *Fire over Luzon* by the GI's Homer. He opened to several pages of glossy stills from the Lingayen Gulf airfield. "How do you explain these? Pictures of me at the airfield. Me with the wounded. Me with a Jap bomb going off. All taken that same day."

"Taken the *next* day. Someone has even airbrushed out your bandaged foot." Peter shut the book. "I've found your doctor. I've found the photographer. I've unmasked *your* conspiracy." Peter smiled at his own neatness. "Why don't you just wait another two years as originally planned? I'm sure Blaise isn't in all that much of a rush. He's certainly enjoying things the way they are, now that Enid's dead."

Clay sat back in his chair, legs stretched out. He yawned. Then he said, "You know about Ed Nillson?"

"Yes. I also know he's not eager to be mixed up in this."

"He has no choice if Burden runs. I won't give him any choice. I won't give either of them any choice." Clay stared at the photograph of himself and Truman. "Why now and not in two years? Because after Truman we're going to have at least eight years of a Republican president. Probably Eisenhower or MacArthur. Then a Democrat. Someone new. Born in this century, not one of these old folks, these holdovers from the coach-and-buggy era. It's all going to change. Well, for me to be ready in 1960, I'll need at least eight years of national exposure in the Senate. So that's what I mean to have."

"Why?"

"Why what?"

"Why is all this necessary? Why must *you* be president?"

"Some people are meant to be. Some are not. Obviously you're not."

"Obviously. It's the last thing I'd ever want. My sort of work is more apt to be useful."

"Like Dr. Schweitzer in the African jungle?" Clay was on his feet. He stretched. For an instant, Peter thought that Clay had actually arched his back. "Everything's now in order for me to start the long march. There's also no one else, which is a help."

"Hubert Humphrey?"

"Too far to the left. The South won't take him."

"Lyndon Johnson?"

"Texas? A bribe-taker? Never."

"Your fellow congressman Jack Kennedy? His father can outspend my father any day."

"He'll be dead by 1960. He's got no adrenal function. 'Yellow Jack,' they call him. Just look at him. He's a skeleton. No, the field is clear for me."

"Ten years is a long time to keep any field clear."

"I know. That's why I've got a lot to do. That's why I suggest you . . . lay off."

Peter rose. "Perhaps you'll rethink your position once I write about what really happened at the Lingayen Gulf airfield."

"Why bother? Burden's taking himself out of the race."

"But if he doesn't?"

"Ed Nillson will suddenly be a very famous man and Burden may go to jail."

"So what about you? The phony hero. The invention of Harold Griffiths."

"And of your father. It takes at least two to give birth to a national hero." Clay was unexpectedly droll. "I am one and there's nothing you can do to change that."

"Let's see what I can do."

"Do you really want to never see your father again?"

Peter laughed. "What a weird thing to say! I hardly see him now. Anyway, he's yours. A present from me to you. A funeral present, you might say. From Enid's funeral. After all, it took the two of you to give birth to that."

Peter left Clay standing in the middle of his office, still smiling.

Billy Thorne was seated at the partners' desk.

"Aeneas had to go up to the Hill, so I said I'd wait for you here."

"Reading our next issue."

"Well, trying to."

Peter sat opposite Billy, who did not move. "Actually, I came to see Diana but apparently she's in Rock Creek Park, commiserating with her father. So I certainly don't want to go there. But I have some business with her. Marital nonsense . . ."

"She's commiserating?"

"Yes. He's pulled out of the race. An hour ago. It'll be on the news."

Peter rang the Burden Day house. A weary Diana answered, "Yes," she said. "It's all over. The statement's gone to the press."

"But I told him he wouldn't have to. That . . ." Peter looked straight across the desk into the ill-matching eyes of Billy Thorne. "That it wouldn't be necessary. That Clay was bound to change his mind."

"Mr. Nillson came by after lunch. He said the only way to keep things quiet was to . . ."

Then Peter interrupted her. "Billy Thorne's in the office."

"How lucky for you," she said.

Billy handed Peter an envelope. "Tell her I'm giving her this joint insurance policy we had. There were two of them. I'm keeping one. I'm giving her the other."

Peter said, "I'll tell her." Then into the receiver he said, "I'll be working late." He hung up; turned to Billy. "Is there anything else I can do for you?"

"No." Billy pulled himself to his feet. "I assume you won't be blackmailing Clay now."

A spasm of anger caused Peter to shudder. "Surely that's more Clay's line of work. And yours."

"Not according to Clay. We were going to touch on it in his book, in a general sort of way. But then I had to quit, as you know. We had no choice after my testimony to the House committee." Billy paused at the door. "Do you still have that coat of mine?"

Peter indicated a closet. Billy retrieved his coat as well as a Borsalino hat. "Don't forget to give that insurance policy to Diana."

"I won't. Goodbye."

"By the way, Clay's got a new writer, a really good one, I think."

Peter prayed Billy would go, quickly. "Only the best for Clay."

"I guess you don't know yet who it is." Billy was most pleased with himself. "It's Aeneas Duncan." Then Billy was gone. Peter continued to stare, as if in total concentration, at a copy of the Mundt-Nixon bill, calling for the sequestration of all American communists in concentration camps as yet unbuilt.

Finally, Peter switched on his intercom. The secretary answered. "Yes, Mr. Sanford?"

"Please get me Mrs. Schiff. At the New York *Post*. I gave you her number the other day." He switched off the intercom, and began to make notes on a yellow pad of legal paper, becoming more and more relaxed. There was something very satisfying—even ennobling—about writing the political obituary of Clay Overbury.

4

Aeneas was not in the least defensive. "I want to go to work in the engine room for a while. When Clay's elected to the Senate, he'll be the leading politician of his generation, which means . . ." Aeneas blew a perfect smoke ring. "It's your fault, really. Always quoting Henry Adams and his friends until I started to find attractive what they found irresistible. Creating a president by educating a politician."

"Hardly possible in the case of a 'villain.'"

"Don't exaggerate. By an accident of time and place, Clay is simply force concentrated and personified."

"Henry Adams would have demanded more."

"Would he? I thought that the one lesson you wise men of the republic had learned was how nothing matters in the end except force and energy."

"You astonish me," was the best that Peter could do. Aeneas was seated in his old place at the partners' desk. He had come back to finish out the month of June; then he would return to New York for good, with a job in publishing. Peter already missed him. But Clay—the wrecker, as Peter now thought of him—had done his work yet again.

"What will you write that anyone will believe?" Peter's story was due to appear in the New York *Post* on Monday the 26th of June. It was now Sunday and Peter and Aeneas were putting together the next issue.

"Well, this is a vision for America, not the story of what a politician must say and do to get elected." Aeneas twirled his wedding band. "There won't be much of anything personal as I see the book."

"Just a program?"

"Or another way of looking at things. Pretty much what we've been trying to do here."

"Clay can't have another way of looking at things that's at all different from what the Gallup Poll says is how the American people look at things as of that morning."

"We'll see. Billy actually did a great deal of good work. I'm keeping a lot of it. We publish in October. When do you?" Aeneas stared at him through cigarette smoke.

"Monday. After that, I don't see how . . ."

But Monday brought its own surprise. On Sunday, the army of communist North Korea invaded South Korea, whose army promptly fled and whose capital, Seoul, was soon in enemy hands, causing its American-sponsored dictator, Syngman Rhee, to withdraw to the relative safety of Taegu.

Peter found it unnerving to have Aeneas sitting opposite him just as his own story about Clay was breaking. Diana had stayed the weekend at Rock Creek Park with her father while Aeneas was living at the Negro boardinghouse down the street, the only place, he maintained, where one could get a decent meal in Washington.

Peter was brought the New York *Post*. "Here it is!" The young man beamed at both of them, unaware that Aeneas was now in the enemy camp if not yet a spy in theirs.

Aeneas affected to be busy with a manuscript from a young historian in Madison, Wisconsin, while Peter absorbed the shock that his story was not on the front page, crowded out by dark war headlines. Ninety thousand North Korean troops had crossed the thirty-eighth parallel, the dividing line between the Red dictatorship to the north and the free world of the south, under the benign protection of General MacArthur at Tokyo.

Peter swiftly read what little Korean news there was. The President had returned from Independence, Missouri, and was now at Blair House (the White House was undergoing repairs). The National Security Council was meeting. The United Nations had been advised. It was expected that the President would go before Congress and ask for a declaration of war. Meanwhile . . .

Meanwhile, at the center of the tabloid *Post*, there were two full pages of Peter's story, as well as pictures of Clay, Audie Murphy, the airbrushed foot. Even downplayed, the story did its work. After a quick professional look, Peter shoved the newspaper across the desk. The equally professional Aeneas read the text slowly. "Is all this true?" he finally said.

"No. I made it all up. Exactly the way the GI's Homer does."

"I think you're wrong."

"About what happened or didn't happen?" Peter felt a great relief now that the story was finally told. The score was even at last. "Don't worry. I'm right. Now it's up to the voters. That's if Clay should stay in the race."

"He'll stay all right."

"And lose?"

"Maybe. Maybe not."

Suddenly, Peter was exasperated. "What on earth are you doing with this monster? Why are you helping him?"

"In a monstrous time we need our own monsters, don't we?"

"That's honest but no answer. Why Clay?"

"There's been no one else since Henry Wallace sank out of sight . . ."

"Clay? A New Dealer?"

Aeneas shrugged. "Labels don't really matter. He'll be what the times require, and what they most require is someone with a sense of his own destiny, someone who will shift this way and that until the time is right to move."

Peter laughed. "Well, that could be Roosevelt or that could be Hitler. . . . No. I don't think a run-of-the-mill opportunist in politics is much of a novelty out there in those amber fields of grain."

"But a superb opportunist, like Roosevelt, is just what we need. Clay's the closest we've got."

Peter was astonished by Aeneas's apparent seriousness. "Where, and at what point, on that long ride to Damascus did you behold this vision?"

Aeneas's smile was visible despite the cigarette between his lips. "When I realized that Harold Griffiths' hero was a fraud."

Peter could not believe what he was hearing. "I thought you were the moralist and I was the relativist."

"Whatever. But I'm the one who has been studying the arts. Remember? The golden age that I said—you said—we are due for. The civilization that we've never achieved before but now . . ." Aeneas stopped; stubbed out his cigarette; shoved the *Post* back across the table. "Clay is the highest sort of artist: the self-inventor. That's better than being an assembly-line product put out by a political party or class."

"My father doesn't count?"

"Your father definitely doesn't count. It is a part of Clay's art to use him just as he is using you."

"Me!" Peter hit the *Post*'s picture of Clay with his fist; the partners' desk gave a satisfying creak. "How?"

"This is all going to serve him in the end. Wait and see. For now, it's something of a setback, but like Roosevelt . . ."

"You're not going to compare this to Roosevelt's polio?"

"I hadn't thought of that. But why not? Anyway, this story isn't over with yet."

"Aeneas, you have, after all the time we've known each other, managed to amaze me."

Burden Day led Peter into the Senate dining room, blue with cigar smoke. There was a strong smell of charred beef and vinegar. Senators sat at tables with one another or with constituents. A Negro waiter led them to Burden's usual table. Various senators greeted him as he passed. He was well liked at the heart of the small club that unofficially controlled the Senate. Due to seniority, he dominated the Finance Committee, chaired Agriculture. Peter was very much aware that, for the first time in this august dining room, with its nineteenth-century white tessellated floor, he had been recognized by almost everyone in the dining room. He was no longer Blaise's son; no longer *American Idea*, still unread by the conscript fathers; no longer unofficially affianced to Burden's daughter. Rather, he was the dragon-slayer. He had, in a thousand newspapers by now, exposed as a fraud a great hero of the Second World War, not to mention current congressman as well as senator and king-to-be. After the first shock of the North Korean attack, which had overshadowed his revelations, the press had begun to pick up the Overbury story. Harold Griffiths had denounced Peter in the *Tribune*, presumably with Blaise's blessing. Father and son had broken off all relations. Finally, Frederika had rung to say that Emma was trying to break Caroline's will. "Too typical," she sighed over the telephone. "Your father's so annoyed with her."

"Along with me?"

"Why with you?"

"The Clay story."

"Oh, that. I cut it out of the Washington *Post*. And I'll read it as soon as I can. I've hired Dorothy Draper to fix up the house here and she doesn't give me a moment's peace. Everything for her is *stripes*. Green and white stripes. I hate stripes."

That was probably the real world's point of view. What was important in the Senate dining room hardly mattered to a lady with an expensive decorator hard at work across town.

Peter ordered the Senate specialty, bean soup—with chopped raw onion for those who liked that sort of thing: both Burden and he did.

Burden seemed neither pleased nor displeased by Peter's handiwork. "No matter what, this is going to be a close election, and if Clay loses, the Democrats could lose their Senate majority."

"Will the sky fall in?"

"No. Have you heard from Clay?"

Peter shook his head. "I don't think I shall."

"He's been in the state. Issuing denials. Well, I'm out of it."

"I wish you were back in it."

Burden put oyster crackers in his soup, proving he was, at heart, a Southerner still. "No, thank you," he said.

They were joined by Tom Connally, an implausibly broad caricature of a Texas senator, with wavy white hair that curled over his collar like a nineteenth-century statesman's while a pair of huge pink ears seemed capable of flight at any moment. "Brother Day." He shook Burden's hand; gave Peter a blank stare that turned, swiftly, to recognition. "Oh. You're the *young* Mr. Sanford. I begin to tremble in your presence, sir. Will all my malfeasances be exposed by you to the public gaze?"

Peter assured the Senator that no one as virtuous as he could ever be so libeled. "Real shame," Connally turned to Burden, "that the boy didn't break his story *before* you pulled out of the race."

"I was still checking it out." Peter saved Burden the embarrassment of answering.

Connally got down to business. "We've got us a constitutional problem here. This Korean thing happened when we weren't in session, which always suits the White House just fine. So while we're off preparing our Fourth of July speeches back home, old Harry has pushed us into a brand-new war." Connally pulled a Government

Printing Office document from the pocket of a brown linen suit that floated about him like a circus tent. "Have you seen this yet?"

"No." Burden took the pamphlet.

"Obviously, Harry was supposed to come over here today and ask us for a declaration of war . . ."

"I thought last week that he said he was just going to go over to the United Nations and collect an international sanction for war." Burden stirred his soup. Peter wondered if he could ask for another bowl.

"That was last Tuesday. Then last Thursday he orders up two of our divisions and sends them off to Korea. So where the hell are *we* in all this? Congress does the war-declaring, not the President."

"He's not addressing us today?"

"Not today. And not tomorrow." Connally indicated the pamphlet beside Burden's plate. "Brother Acheson, our international lawyer, has sent us this special brief for our instruction and edification. Apparently, on eighty-five occasions in the past, presidents have got us into wars without a declaration from us, as required by the Constitution. Seems we shot up pirates in Florida. Overthrew undesirable governments that might, one day, be a menace to Standard Oil in Mexico, Central America, the Caribbean. Now, in the same frisky mood, our thirty-third president is planning to go to war on the mainland of Asia, *without* our sanction. Because," Connally put on a pair of wire-framed spectacles and read, " 'North Korea's a threat to international peace and security; a threat to the peace and security of the United States and to the security of United States forces in the Pacific.' "

He took off his glasses, and looked not at Burden but at Peter, who boldly asked, "How?" without ever himself having been elected to the Senate. "How a threat?"

Burden sighed. "Some things, like the Trinity, are too sacred and mysterious for the mere human to comprehend."

Connally accepted Peter's self-election to the greatest debating society on earth; and responded in the name of Texas. "The answer to your 'how' is that Acheson has convinced himself and Harry that Stalin's given orders to every communist everywhere on earth to keep whittling away at us until we cave in. I heard it all with my own two ears at Blair House last week when those two were busy working the congressional leadership over. They're sure as can be Stalin's behind North Korea's attack. They're also afraid Stalin's gonna order Mao to come to the aid of North Korea. Even so, they have gone and turned down Chiang Kai-shek's kindly offer of troops. Apparently, a big war with China isn't in the cards—*their* cards—just yet."

"You know, Tom, for the first time I'm actually glad I'm getting out of here. We aren't even junior partners anymore. We're just the chorus. A Greek chorus, at that."

"Well, if there's gonna be a Greek kind of tragedy it will be because we're letting the United Nations shove us into their wars . . ."

"No. Harry's shoving *them,* not the other way round. He's making the case that the entire globe is ours to do whatever we want with. Now he's asking all our dependent states at the UN to follow him into Korea." Burden indicated the memorandum. "Is this going to be read to us today?"

Connally nodded. "It's supposed to take the place of an actual visit from the President to ask for a declaration of war."

"Which he could have got so easily." Burden shook his head. "Even Taft is willing to go to war . . ."

A bright blue light from the doorway illuminated the dining room. Television light. Reflexively, senators checked their wigs; pushed at their hair; adjusted smiles. In his shadowy corner, Joe McCarthy seemed to expand like some huge bullfrog in the glow of the source of his power, television. Peter also noticed that his head was trembling. Delirium tremens, it was said. Two young men at his table sat up very straight.

But the lights were not for him, nor, indeed, could the cameras have been allowed into the dining room. Only certain Capitol corridors and the rotunda, with permission, were available.

All eyes in the dining room were now on the door. As Clay Overbury entered, there was a general intake of breath, then, once everyone was aware that he wore the uniform of a colonel in the American army, with two rows of ribbons over his heart, Joe McCarthy began the applause.

"Well. I'll be damned," said Tom Connally, giving a perfunctory clap. "I'll be damned."

"I *am* damned," Peter muttered while Burden crumbled a cracker and looked at his plate.

Clay came straight to their table; pulled back a chair. "May I?" he said to Burden, who nodded.

"Senator Connally." Clay was polite. "Peter."

Connally's smile was wide, gracious, old-school. "You have, my boy, flocked, as it were, to the colors, to defend the free world for yet a second time."

"I had no choice, really. You see, yesterday, Sunday, I was with Frank Pace, the secretary of the army." He glanced at Peter, as if he expected him to be taking notes for an interview. "At my request he had my orders ready. More important, he told me that a huge army of North Koreans has now crossed the thirty-eighth parallel and that President Truman has ordered General MacArthur to come to the aid of the South Korean government. That's all going to be in the President's message today."

"So you will be going to Korea?" Burden's tone was matter-of-fact.

"I'm flying out tonight. To Tokyo. Then—who knows?" He looked at Peter, all patriotic innocence.

Peter indicated the television crew in the hallway. "What are they doing here?"

"Frank Pace is using me as a sort of recruitment ad. The Army's got all three networks to cover my going off to war. A second time. I'll be a field officer, like before. But this time, I'm a colonel."

"You're out of the Senate race?"

"Oh, no!" Clay's smile glittered as he turned toward the lights in the hall. "I've just announced that I'm still a candidate but that the only campaigning I plan to do will be in Korea, fighting communists. Gentlemen."

Clay rose and shook hands all around the table. The entire Senate dining room was focused on him.

"Good luck," said Burden.

As Clay strode to the door, Tom Connally gave a loud whistle. "Jesus H. Christ," he said. Then, with wonder, "I have met the perfect bastard at last." He turned to Peter. "Your story's forgotten already."

"Yes," said Peter. "I know."

F I F T E E N

I

At exactly nine in the evening of a sharply cold November day, Peter and Diana, each carrying a small suitcase, were met at the main entrance to the Union Station by four Secret Service men, who greeted them politely, took their suitcases, and led them into the station, nearly empty at this hour. Capital of the world or not, Washington was hardly a hub of commerce or, indeed, of anything except politics. As a native, Peter could never understand why, in good weather, so many people were eager to come as tourists to the city. Certainly, springtime beside the Potomac was agreeably tropical and the Japanese cherry blossoms, at such risk during the furies of war, still bloomed, but he wondered what the city actually yielded to the average citizen. The Lincoln Memorial was splendid, and even accurate in scale, but Jefferson's memorial was curiously out of kilter, the statue too large and clumsy for its Palladian lean-to. The obelisk to General Washington looked as if it would be more comfortable beside the Nile than the icy Potomac, while the mile or two of pseudo-Roman colonnades created an inhuman monotony of effect as they rose from what had once been a swamp to the Capitol, high on its irregular hill, all brown mud and leafless trees.

A uniformed man from the Pennsylvania Railroad opened an iron-grill gate to the shed where all tracks began and ended. The Secret Service men led them to Track 15, which the police had blocked off. Back of them, Secret Service men guarded the cars of the now legendary campaign train whose name, *Ferdinand Magellan*, was printed in gold on Pullman dark green.

The police let them through. Peter was surprised at the number of people who were also making the journey west aboard the *Magellan*.

One of the Secret Service men observed, "This time we've got a whole car for the Signal Corps. We're tapped in to everywhere on earth." The man's breath hung in the cold air like smoke.

"Is there much press?" asked Peter.

"Just the wire services, sir. And some television."

Then Peter and Diana were handed over to a Pullman car porter, who put their suitcases into the first car beside the gate; then he helped them aboard. Although Peter had never seen a private car as elaborate as the *Magellan*, the familiar Pullman car smell was as comforting as always: a combination of the toy Lionel trains of his boyhood, an acrid battery smell, combined with whatever the porters used to clean carpets and the dark green curtains that at night were drawn to cover upper and lower berths. But there were no berths in this car, only staterooms, like a ship; and an oak-paneled dining room with half a dozen chairs around a mahogany table. Through a swinging door, they could see the galley, where two chefs in white were setting up. Diana indicated the dining-room chairs, covered in green and gold damask stripes. "Dorothy Draper has been here. What would your mother say?"

A butler offered them something to drink. Peter asked for bourbon.

After the dining room, there were four staterooms, A, B, C, and D. Apparently, B was "hers," C was "his." D was theirs. D proved to be a comfortable bedroom with a double bed and a telephone "which only works when we're in a station," said the porter, stowing their baggage on racks. He pointed to the rear of the train, just past their stateroom. "That's the observation lounge. You can sit there if you like."

Once they were alone, Diana promptly went to the bathroom while Peter partially unpacked. They would be getting off at American City the next morning; then the train would go on to California. "I suppose," said Diana, coming out of the bathroom, "that this is what marriage is all about."

"One stateroom instead of two?"

"One *Ferdinand Magellan* instead of none." Then they went into the observation lounge, where the chairs and sofa were done in blues and browns and a smiling butler served Peter his drink.

"Can I take this *before* he comes aboard?" Peter was worried about protocol.

The butler smiled. "He'll probably be joining you. The Missus isn't coming so things are pretty relaxed."

Through the window of the car, Peter could see more and more people, many in military uniform, hurrying to get aboard the various cars up ahead. It was like the war, come back.

"What must *his* mood be like?" Diana's mood was quite apparent to Peter. She was pale; eyes dark-circled.

"I shouldn't think too happy," she said. "China's in the war, and there are so many more of them than us."

" 'A mere peasant's army,' as Harold Griffiths says. Easily defeated by our superior forces led by Colonel Overbury. I wonder who he'll rescue this time."

"General MacArthur. From a flaming pagoda." Diana looked about the observation car. "I can't say I like the combination of blue and brown."

"That's because it reminds you of your ex-husband's treacherous gaze."

Diana laughed for the first time since Burden's death. "You do know how to cheer me up."

"This *is* our honeymoon."

"A very peculiar one. Because . . ." A commotion on the siding below distracted her. A long black limousine, surrounded by motor-cycle police, had stopped beside their car. Police opened the back door and then led the occupants, quite invisible behind a row of massive policemen, to the front of the car, where flashbulbs went off. The engineer of the train gave a warning hoot: all aboard.

A tall, heavy-fleshed man in an overcoat came into the observation car. He was chewing on an unlit cigar. "I'm Harry Vaughan from Battery D. The Chief's on his way. Make yourselves comfortable. Sorry, Mrs. Sanford, about the news." Then he went down the narrow corridor to the stateroom next to the President's.

Not quite knowing what to do, Peter and Diana remained standing, as several Secret Service men did a perfunctory search of the car. Then the President, wearing an overcoat and, respectfully, holding his hat, entered. "Mr. and Mrs. Sanford. I'd hoped to see you under less sad circumstances." A valet relieved him of coat and hat and vanished into Cabin C.

Harry Truman gravely shook their hands. The President paid especial attention to Diana. "Your father was always very kind to me when I was new to the Senate. You don't forget that."

"He admired you very much, sir."

"Oh, we had our differences. But that's politics." A secretary stood in the doorway. Truman said, "Tell the Korea group I'll meet them in the dining room after we start." The secretary vanished. "No rest for the weary," said Truman, making himself a drink from the sideboard. "Sit down. Sit down, please."

The President placed himself in the middle of the blue sofa while Peter and Diana sat opposite him in brown chairs. With a lamp beside him, Peter could see how pale and drawn Truman's face was, so unlike the recent newspaper photographs of a smiling jaunty president on top of the world. "I must say I'm never so happy as when I'm on this train *leaving* Washington. Roosevelt loved it, too, only he had the engineer just creep along, afraid for his balance, I suppose, while I have him tearing along full speed ahead. Someone said I covered thirty-two thousand miles in this train, during the campaign." He smiled at the memory of his triumph of only two years before. Since then the Korean War had begun while, two weeks earlier, on November 1, a group of Puerto Rican nationalists had tried to kill the President at Blair House.

A series of blasts from the engineer; with a jolt, the train began to

move. Truman drank; then gave a contented sigh. "I feel like Jean Val-
jean must've felt like when he got out of that dungeon." The President's
reading was known to be wide; its depth was a matter of conjecture.
Peter knew that Truman liked giving lectures on American history
which, according to the journalist Richard Rovere, who would later
check them out, were almost always a bit off.

Once the train was smoothly free of the station, a steward drew
down the window shades. Truman sighed. "That's the sight I most like,
speeding across the country at night. Through all the little electric-light
towns, seeing how large the whole thing is. But . . ."

"The Secret Service?" Peter could see that since the assassination
attempt, security was intense.

Truman nodded. "Pair of precious damn fools, those Puerto
Ricans."

"Because, sir, we've always been willing to turn over Puerto Rico
to the Puerto Ricans?"

"No. Because if they'd only waited twenty minutes more, they
could've got me coming out of the door of Blair House. It was in the
papers, for heaven's sake, that I was going to be speaking at Arlington
that afternoon. If they'd had any sense, they could have sent me there
in a box." He shook his head at Puerto Rican incompetence. Then the
secretary placed a pile of papers on the coffee table in front of him.
Truman picked up a fountain pen. "Hope you'll forgive me but I've got
seven thousand letters to sign. From well-wishers. You know? After the
shooting. I said I'd sign each letter personally."

This was exactly what he was doing, expertly and quickly, dropping each signed sheet onto the sofa to dry.

"Roosevelt always called this doing the laundry. Poor man. For a
long time he had to sign every officer's commission and then all the
promotions, but when we got up to thirteen million in the military,
they let him use a stamp or something."

There were a thousand questions Peter wanted to ask but did not
know how. What was protocol? They were the President's guests. As
soon as the story had broken in the press that Senator James Burden
Day had been found dead in the shallows of the Potomac River, Truman himself had called Kitty and invited her and the family to return

to American City, aboard his private train. Kitty, all serene dignity, had declined for herself and accepted for Diana and Peter. She would fly to American City.

It was generally assumed that the story of Burden's driver was accurate: the Senator had taken a walk beside the river, where he'd fainted and fallen in. Although there was no suggestion in the press of suicide or foul play, the whispering gallery had read Harold Griffiths' recent eulogy of Senator-elect Clay Overbury, "the fighting Solon," now a colonel in Korea with no immediate plan to leave the war for the marble halls of Congress. According to Harold, Clay had been obliged to run in place of Senator Day, who was under investigation for his part in the "giveaway" of oil-rich Indian land. Prompt denials of any such investigation from both Justice and Interior Departments, not to mention from the Senate itself, did not undo Harold's original charge. Peter was quite sure that Burden had killed himself. Diana disagreed: she believed her father had had one of his fainting spells at river's edge and drowned. But, bitterly, she acknowledged Harold's contribution. Peter wondered how much of this the President had worked out. True, he was due to address the military on the West Coast and American City was on his way, but he had no obligation to show presidential favor to anyone accused of corruption. On the other hand, when his onetime sponsor Boss Prendergast of Kansas City died after a time in prison, the new vice president had gone, defiantly, to his funeral.

"Also," Truman's thoughts were plainly running parallel to theirs, "Burden was the last founder of one of the forty-eight states." Impatiently, he waved a letter back and forth to force the ink to dry more quickly. "As you know, I'm not one to complain about the press." Peter dared not look at Diana. Truman's hatred of the press was often pungently expressed; although he was kindness itself to the regular journalists assigned to him, the columnists, from Drew Pearson to the Sop Sisters to Harold Griffiths, were a subject of constant savage diatribe. "I was disturbed to read that swipe at Burden in your father's paper. I can't say I take it seriously, any more than I do what's-his-name who wrote it, but since he's syndicated that does make it serious, to the public." Truman put away his pen and drank bourbon. The ever-watchful butler, hidden nearby, came to fill his glass. But Truman waved him away.

"Work to do tonight." He took off his thick glasses and the eyes, unmagnified, were the dreamy blue of acute myopia, the whole impression quite at odds with his—affected?—usual sharp staccato performance. "What happened?"

Peter told the President as much as he thought safe; once or twice he turned to Diana, but she was silent. Truman listened, eyes half shut. Then: "Well, that's pretty much the way I put it together. I figured that Indian land sale business was a lot of hooey. Too much out of character for the Burden I knew." In the chair next to Peter, Diana gave a small strangled gasp which the President seemed not to hear. He turned to Peter, "I still can't see how your father could let what's-his-name publish what he did in his paper. But then that's his business, not mine." There was silence as Truman neatly stacked the signed letters on top of the unsigned ones. "Mr. Clay Overbury," he said finally, thoughtfully. "He's in too big a hurry, I'd say. He's got the bug." Truman looked at Diana, who smiled wanly.

"Well, we have a majority of two in the Senate and Mr. Overbury's half of our plurality." Truman was all business. "So he's important to us, particularly since, thanks to MacArthur, we nearly lost both houses of Congress."

"You mean McCarthy, sir."

Truman put on his glasses. "Did I say MacArthur? Well, I do have him on my mind tonight. And, of course, MacArthur did harm us in the election with all his letters to those Republican leaders, saying how he should be allowed to cross the Yalu River and invade Manchuria and China when he isn't even able to stop the Chinese already in Korea. Now they're biding their time. Waiting for some kind of settlement, I'd say. But we're not going to settle. If we did, that would be Munich all over again. Stalin's just the same as Hitler. He's using one of his satellite states to test us. Actually, two satellite states, now that China's come in." Truman finished his bourbon, face slightly flushed. "History taught us all quite a lesson back in the thirties. You can't deal with totalitarian countries because they only believe in force. Ends justify the means. That's their religion. Well, we're responding with more force than they ever dreamed of. Last thing I ever wanted to do was set off those atom bombs on Japan. But if I hadn't we would have had to invade Japan—

a minimum of a million men—on both sides—would've died. Now we got us a different problem. We have to show force right now, show we've got the will to win, which is why Joe McCarthy's basically a traitor to his country, because he's made a lot of our people doubt the loyalty of their own government at a time when we could lose all Asia to Stalin, maybe the whole world, too."

Peter found it hard to discern any logic to the curious template that the President seemed to be carrying around in his head. Munich. Make no deal with Hitler because he will break it as he is a dictator who wants to conquer the world. Stalin is just like Hitler: so make no deal with him either because . . . Yet Peter saw no compelling analogy between the two. It was Truman, euphoric with his new atomic weapons, who had decided at Potsdam that the United States need never live up to the terms of the Yalta agreement or, indeed, any other agreements, since it was now, Peter knew, American policy to conduct no meetings, ever, with the Russians on the ground that, like Nazis, the Soviets would cheat. This was fair enough propaganda at election time, to keep the people frightened so that they would keep on paying for the ever-expanding military buildup. But Peter was alarmed at the apparent rigidity of Truman's mind unless—a vain hope?—Truman was acting a part. Nevertheless, even if he was, there had been quiet exultation at the State and Defense Departments when the North Koreans had invaded the South: now Congress would be obliged to appropriate the many billions of dollars needed to build hydrogen bombs as well as planes and ships and military bases all around the world so that "trouble spots" could be quickly tended to. Had Henry Wallace been right? Was the nation now embarked on an endless war?

"This is all off the record," said the President, "though none of it's hardly secret. Anyway, history teaches us that things go in cycles. Look at Mesopotamia."

Since neither Peter nor Diana had a Mesopotamia at hand to contemplate, Truman helpfully explained. "If you don't resist with force the Egyptians, let's say, they are going to conquer you and take you into slavery, real quick. Well, now we've got the United Nations, something new, just begging us to come to their aid. To stop Stalin. At least in Korea. But thanks to McCarthy and some other traitors, no other word, we couldn't ask Congress to declare war. So we're doing this at the request of the whole free world. That's our job, like it or not. To keep the peace everywhere, even if we have to fight to do it. Vandenberg just wrote me about this so-called Russian peace feeler we got. I wrote him back—he's pretty sick, sad to say—that this whole thing is just an exact imitation of Japan when it was in Manchuria and Hitler was in the Rhineland and Mussolini was in Ethiopia. All totalitarian societies are alike and once they start getting together, get ready for war."

The secretary was in the doorway. "Mr. President, the group is ready if you are, sir."

Truman handed the stack of letters to the secretary and rose; Peter and Diana did the same.

"I'm glad we had this little chat and I'm sorry your honeymoon had to be like this. I'm afraid history has a tendency to tie us in knots when we least expect it. You know, if I hadn't got into politics after the war, I'd have wanted to be a history teacher."

"Surely, sir," said Peter, "it's more fun making history than teaching it."

Truman smiled. "Well, from what I've seen of history-making up close, an awful lot of it is really history-*teaching*, if you try to do it right. We seem to have—the human race has—a kind of built-in amnesia. So we go through the same trials and tribulations over and over again. Good night." Truman vanished into the corridor.

Peter poured himself some more bourbon.

Diana made herself a drink. "I am no longer temperance," she said.

"Does he believe what he's saying?" Peter was uncertain.

"I'm afraid," said Diana, "he does believe every word and he has no doubts, of any kind."

2

The ceremony at the state capitol was solemn but brief, since the President was due to leave before noon. Peter and Diana were led through the surprisingly large crowd by the Governor, along with a number of other officials, many of them surviving witnesses to the birth of their lively state. A north wind blew steadily across American City, so called because the Indian tribes had finally objected to the promiscuous use by white usurpers of their languages as well as land, nations, oil. So the blank adjective "American" had been proposed by Burden. "It has an Italianate ring to it," he used to say, to the puzzlement of the descendants of the original Scots-Irish settlers of the nation.

Inside the capitol rotunda it was still cold but they were, blessedly, out of the monotonous continental north wind. At the center, directly beneath the gray fluted dome, the closed coffin was set on a catafalque. Kitty stood beside it. She wore full mourning, complete with black veil.

Diana gave her a quick professional look. "She's had her hair done," she said to Peter, with relief. Next to Kitty was the Governor's wife; at the opposite end of the catafalque was a small platform covered with red-white-and-blue bunting.

The inevitable television lights were also in place. Peter noted that in addition to local television both NBC and CBS were on hand. Since the assassination attempt, security was intense, and state troopers guarded the entrance to the rotunda. Mourners were obliged to present tickets.

"I flew," said Kitty "I've always hated that train ride from Washington. Now I won't ever have to make it again." Diana embraced her mother as did Peter, whose eyes were inexplicably full of tears while Kitty, inexplicably, was cheerful. "We have a lovely lot," she said, "at the cemetery. Quite near my father's. We've also got a monument that Burden commissioned years ago. He was always prepared. Except for that bastard Clay." The ladies nearby stirred, not quite sure just what the word was that Kitty had used. Kitty continued, "We've also got plenty of room for both of you but you'd better let them know now. It seems everyone's dying at once these days, so reserve your space."

Diana changed the subject. "How are the gray squirrels?"

"Mange!" Kitty's voice echoed in the rotunda, which was now almost full. "Of all things! The doctor insisted on giving them penicillin, of all things. They do look so forlorn with their moth-eaten fur."

The Governor had climbed onto the platform. State troopers stood at attention behind him. Beside the platform stood the Episcopal bishop of American City, ready to perform those sacred rites that spring the locks to paradise.

"Ladies and gentlemen." The Governor's voice was a mellow baritone. "Pray welcome with me the President of the United States of America, the Honorable Harry S Truman." A sudden burst of television light at the entrance to the rotunda illuminated the President. Truman wore a dark blue suit and a solemn expression. Back of him was General Vaughan and a quartet of Secret Service men, eyes anxiously looking this way and that for enraged Puerto Ricans; but there appeared to be none that day in American City. The crowd in the rotunda started to applaud the President until it was recalled that this was, after all, a funeral and a shushing sound stilled the applause. Truman smiled briefly in acknowledgment. A red carpet had been laid from entrance to platform, and he walked down its center, precise as always, even a bit mechanical, as if he were still the Army captain of Battery D in France.

At the platform, he stopped. The Governor said a few words of introduction. During breakfast on the train, Harry Vaughan had told Peter how these things could become a nightmare if you let the locals talk first: "Every candidate for sheriff is going to talk for hours, knowing the President is sitting there and no one's gonna leave till he gets up. So we said we wanted only a few words from their *Republican* governor. Then *we* say a few words and we go."

During the Governor's remarks, the TV camera panned about the coffin, stopping, finally, at Kitty, flanked by Peter and Diana. At this most solemn moment, from behind her black veil, Kitty said, in a normal voice that sounded like the voice of doom in the echoing rotunda, "In my day mange was cured with a dose of sulfur and maybe lye. The vets nowadays are simply killers!" Even Diana was shaking, trying not to laugh, as Peter realized that the television audience would think that Burden had died at the hands of a rogue veterinarian.

Now Harry Truman was on the platform. He had a written text in front of him. He had a tremor of the hands—nerves? hereditary pre-

disposition? or, as the talkative General Vaughan had confided at breakfast, "The Chief starts the day with a swig of bourbon. Gives him
energy. Then he walks a mile and goes to work." To Peter's surprise,
Harry Vaughan, the crony of cronies in the White House, was a non-
drinker. "That's how I'm able to look after the Chief."

The Chief was a bit rapid in his delivery. But he drew a convincing picture of the opening up of the West. The settlers coming into
what had once been Indian land that had now, somewhat mysteriously,
become federal property due to a series of broken treaties, acts of Congress, and the interventions of suspect courts. Needless to say, Truman
did not dwell upon the dispossession of the previous inhabitants; rather,
he spoke warmly of the courage and energy of those who had slept outside on the ground of cities which were then no more than lines drawn
in the dust until the morning when they could start to build their
houses on lots created by government surveyors.

"James Burden Day was there. In the Senate, he was always there
for your new state. Now he is still here, for you. Home for good."

Kitty sighed. Diana wept. Peter cleared his throat, recalling that
Burden had had a job of some kind at the Treasury in Washington
when the state was invented, largely by Kitty's father. But Burden had
been, for so many decades, the most visible living founder that few
recalled who had actually done what.

The Governor then led the President to the entrance, where they
shook hands. As the President marched from the capitol, the crowd
cheered him while national television abandoned them to follow him
back to the *Ferdinand Magellan*.

Kitty, Diana, and Peter were driven in the Governor's car to the
cemetery. En route, on Day Avenue, they passed the Sunflower Hotel,
a twelve-story mustard-colored brick building which, at election time,
had always become the Burden Day "home" so that he could vote for
himself. Clay also claimed the Sunflower for his official residence. The
folks didn't much mind that their representatives lived not among them
but a thousand miles away at the capital. Kitty, however, had caused a
bit of a scandal when, at a ladies' tea during Burden's last campaign, she
was asked how long they expected to be in town this time and she had

airily replied, from who knew what eccentric recess of her brain, "Oh, we just drove over from New York for the day." Even Kitty had astonished herself. "Since I don't suppose I've been three times to that city."

Even in November, the cemetery was more green than dun-colored. Burden's white marble monument dominated a small hill. The grave was open; coffin beside it; flowers banked everywhere. Several hundred people, more curious than mournful, stood about the tomb. Now the bishop took charge. Peter was somewhat surprised that Burden was not a Baptist or Methodist. He always sounded as if he were an evangelical Protestant on the rare occasions that he could be got to perjure himself and publicly abjure his lifelong atheism, thus endangering his mortal self.

A large blond woman moved in beside Diana. "I'm Emma," she said. "Your half sister." Fortunately, Kitty was singing along with whatever hymn the bishop had called forth and did not hear this exchange. Diana stepped away from her mother, drawing Emma with her.

"This is very . . . filial," said Peter.

"I know." Emma was benign, as always, in her self-righteousness. "I thought I owed it to my mother."

"Caroline?" Peter was surprised. "I hadn't suspected that there was debt of any kind on either side."

"Oh yes. The gift of life is the gift of God." Emma crossed herself dramatically, causing several nearby Baptists to turn their backs upon a representative of the scarlet strumpet of Rome.

"You did that very well," said Diana. "You must have been practicing."

"I've been a Catholic for years. Even before I married Tim." Another hymn had begun.

"Is Tim here?" Peter had seen neither of them since the night at the Blue Angel.

"Oh, no. He's in New York. Directing plays for television. I'm in Washington with Fortress America. We've been working closely with Senator McCarthy, much good that it can do now. I'm afraid our homegrown communists have really done us in this time."

Happily the hymn was louder than Emma's voice.

"Done who in?" Peter kept his voice low, hoping to encourage her to do the same.

"The Chinese have crossed the Yalu River. Hundreds of thousands of them. Our army's retreating. Korea's lost. It's a total defeat for us. Our first ever. Truman and Acheson sold us out to Stalin. It was all I could do not to boo that dreadful little man in the capitol."

"Why," whispered Diana, "must you keep talking? After all, it is your father's funeral and respect must be shown him, even by you."

The bishop's voice vibrated in the air as the remains of James Burden Day were lowered into the grave. "For I am the way and the light. He that believeth in me . . ." Where, wondered Peter, in a kind of panic, was God or anyone in the great nothing of eternity?

S I X T E E N

It was John Latouche who reconciled Aeneas and Peter. Although Aeneas's book, signed with Clay Overbury's name, had helped elect the betrayer of Diana's father, Aeneas was still a valuable contributor to *American Idea*. All was never forgiven between Aeneas and Diana, but two years after the rise of Senator Overbury, Aeneas met Peter and Diana in the lobby of the Phoenix Theatre, recently renovated as an alternative to Broadway not only in its geography, far below Forty-second Street, but in the sort of works that it wanted to mount. After three or four years of relentless auditioning for money, John Latouche and the composer Jerome Moross had finally managed to assemble a production of their musical comedy, *The Golden Apple*.

Over the years, Peter had heard Latouche, at home and at parties, play and sing various songs and numbers always identified as being from the difficult second of two acts. Latouche's clear somewhat toneless voice could handle the wit of his own lyrics though not the emotion of the ballads of his composer, Jerry Moross, who always listened with a sad smile to what his collaborator was doing to his music. Now, after much struggle, and many false starts, the opening night had come and all of New York that mattered, to the theater world at least, was on hand.

Peter and Diana were dazzled by the colorful figures in the brightly lit lobby. Somehow, these impersonators or inventors of fictional characters seemed more real and positively essential than the actual, and equally theatrical, rulers at Washington.

"Touche made me stay away from rehearsals." Aeneas was as excited as if this had been his own opening night. But then Aeneas had already delivered up his hostage to critical fortune when he had written, in 1950, that the musical comedy would prove to be the American century's greatest achievement. As intended, he had opened up a controversy that still smoldered not only in *American Idea* but, from time to time, in most serious American journals. Although hardly anyone championed the postwar novelists, poetry still had many fierce supporters, though poetry readers seemed to have died out as opposed to the audience for poets who gave readings, preferably while drunk. This recent development was largely due to the performances of the Welsh poet Dylan Thomas, dead the previous year in New York, of drink and overexposure.

The graphic arts still had their hard-eyed money lobby in Fifty-seventh Street as well as their own highly rigged stock exchange, dominated, suitably, by a Rockefeller who had invented something called the Museum of Modern Art or, as Wallace Stevens liked to intone in his most poetic voice, "a mus-ee-um of *mod*-ern . . . ? art . . . ?" —the words "modern" and "art" each ending with a bewildered sigh. But the museum, like most Rockefeller institutions, had a vital financial function: to publicize and endorse those artists that its patron collected and so drive up their prices. It was all, Peter had once written, like the Defense Department's symbiotic support of the numerous weapons industries that supported, in turn, the Pentagon and their cheery go-between, the Congress.

As they took their seats, Peter asked Aeneas the usual Broadway question. "So what do you hear?"

"Everyone connected with the show's ecstatic, of course."

"Of course."

Peter must have sounded mocking, because Aeneas's response was sharp. "Everyone's working for a hundred dollars a week or less."

"Well, it is a . . ." Peter could not find the word.

"Showcase," supplied Diana, cheeks pink from excitement. "What's it about?"

"The Trojan War," both Peter and Aeneas answered her. Peter laughed. "Aeneas has heard Touche play most of the numbers. So have I. Once, with a bailiff at the door, come to collect the furniture. I think Touche talked him into investing."

Aeneas was scribbling in his notebook. "It's about the Trojan War and the Judgment of Paris. Set in the town of Mount Olympus, Washington State. Time of the Spanish-American War. Ulysses is a local boy who goes off to fight. The story starts when he comes home to his wife, Penelope . . ."

"No *Odyssey*?" Diana sat between them.

"That's *after* the war. When Paris . . ." Aeneas was now studying his playbill. There was loud chatter in the aisles as the people who wanted to be seen took their time getting seated. In the pit, the orchestra was warming up.

Aeneas continued. "Paris is a traveling salesman who arrives by balloon. He awards the golden apple to a local Venus married to a military man, of course, and so Paris upsets the local Juno and Minerva. Then Paris flies off with the prettiest girl in town, Helen. So Ulysses and a half-dozen ex-soldiers go after Paris, to bring Helen home."

"Isn't all this a bit pretentious?" Peter wanted Touche to have a success, but to use a classical story, like the *Odyssey*, seemed like asking for it from an American audience proudly cut free from the classics.

"It's basic mythical stuff. So why not? Cole Porter did pretty well by Shakespeare. *Kiss Me, Kate*'s going to be around forever."

"Forever," said Peter, "is a long time. In ten years it'll be forgotten."

"*Madame Butterfly*'s still around."

"But that's Puccini . . ."

"Oh, do shut up, Peter." Diana was brisk. "Don't be such a snob." Then house lights dimmed; overture began. Moross's music tended towards the melodic ballad, alternating with turn-of-the-century blues, ragtime, waltzes. Peter was charmed despite his vow to himself not to be overwhelmed by Aeneas's enthusiasm for what, Peter was certain, had to be the most intrinsically banal of collaborative efforts, the musical comedy, which, at its best, was neither music nor much in the way of comedy.

The curtain rose. Loud applause for the set. Since the audience was mostly made up of theater people, they cheered their own. But even Peter was struck by the brightness of the stage and the sense that it really was 1900 and that a new century was beginning. Wars are all ended. Boys are all coming home. Girls are all waiting. Mother Hare, a local witch, is distressed that no one is dead.

Then, suddenly, up flared Touche's wit, which had got him entirely banned from working in films or television; fortunately, the national censors had no power as yet over Broadway.

Ulysses and his fellow "Boys in Blue" reminisce about the late war with Spain. Ulysses began:

"It was a glad adventure
The Philippine scenes were so sweet
Them wee Igoroots
In their birthday suits
Made life just a Sunday school treat.

"Wherever we went they loved us
So dazzled were they with our charms
The folks in them lands
Ate right out of our hands
But why did they chew off the arms?"

THE BOYS IN BLUE *(chorus)*
"Oh, why did they chew off the arms?"

ULYSSES
"The same held true in Cuba
Where gaily we bombshelled a port
Though harsh blows were dealt

By Ted Roo—se—velt
They knew it was only in sport.

"Wherever we went they loved us
They tucked us in rose-petal beds
They welcomed our troops
With their dances and whoops
But why did they shrink our heads?"

THE BOYS IN BLUE *(chorus)*
"But why did they shrink our heads?"

ULYSSES
"Wherever we went they loved us
They cheered when they saw us arrive
They loved us so much
Their affection was such
We're lucky to get home alive!"

THE BOYS IN BLUE *(chorus)*
"Oh, we're lucky to get home alive!"

A great wave of applause swept from the back of the theater across the orchestra pit and onto the stage, where the hitherto edgy actors began, suddenly, easily, even joyously, to play. That's why, thought Peter, astonished by his own revelation, they call it play—a Play. He turned to pass this wisdom on to Aeneas, who was too busy writing, small flashlight illuminating small notebook.

Peter wondered how different this New York audience of known theatricals would be from the rest of the country. Certainly different from the audience at Washington's National Theatre, where the lyrics for Ulysses and the Boys in Blue would be considered treasonable by the Red-bashers who were now in full command of Congress and press. The defeat of the United States in Korea had given ammunition to those who saw Stalin's hand everywhere. McCarthy was still formidable, his enemies mostly chastened; then after the election of 1952, Truman had gone home to Independence, his place taken by the famously bad-tempered General Eisenhower, who had concluded, as euphemistically as he could, a surrender to the North Koreans, back of whom were China's Red demons backed, in turn, by the Satanic puppet-master in the Kremlin.

Thirty thousand ill-trained American troops had died. Meanwhile, the American Communist Party leaders had all been locked up even though their party was a legal one. But then most laws of the land had been set aside during this terrible emergency in which the United States, with no military nor economic rival in the world, was, somehow, in terrible danger from an atomic Pearl Harbor for which schoolchildren were being prepared by government-sponsored drills so that when the mushroom clouds sprouted across the land they would know enough to duck under their desks and so survive to fight the Asiatic hordes with rulers, chalk erasers, baseball bats.

Onstage a slender middle-aged man was doing a soft-shoe number. Simultaneously, he was singing, in the character of Hector, the defeated Trojan hero. The actor had much the same charm and style as Fred Astaire and came, no doubt, from the same school of vaudeville. He was in pensive mood as he contemplated the perils that Ulysses and the Boys would face on their way home.

HECTOR
"Some can be bought for money
And some there are that glory can buy
Some yield their purity
In search of security
And some drown their dreams in a bottle of rye.

"Some go for empty knowledge
And some think sex will set their body free
The man of the hour
Will settle for power
Yes, every soul alive has his fee.

"Except for noble people
Lovely people

Wonderful people
Marvelous people
Exceptional people
Like you
And like
Me."

There was applause as Hector strutted offstage.

"Jack Whiting," said Aeneas. "He's . . ." But Peter could hear nothing more through the applause.

A thin bubbly lady scientist was relentlessly cheery as she predicted last earthly things to a triumphant chorus of

"Oh, we're doomed
Doomed, doomed
Oh, we're doomed
Doomed, doomed
Oh, we're doomed to disappear without a trace!"

Later, Mother Hare sang the devil's song, with feeling.

"Good is a word that fools believe
And evil's a word that the wise achieve
Fools who are good fools try to deny
That evil exists—they pass it by.

"But life without evil is empty and strange
Without evil how can the good ever change?
Without change how can any man ever grow?
Ask Ulysses. He's clever. He'll tell you it's so."

Peter rather wished that Touche had had the nerve to show just how well evil could flourish in America's atomic world, but then if he had been so bold, he would not even have got to the stage of the Phoenix Theatre.

At the final curtain, the vaguely familiar tune from the first act was reprised, and Peter realized that Touche had played it for him when they first met, years earlier, in the Chelsea Hotel. It was a love-is-all-that-we-have duet between Ulysses and Penelope, united at last.

"It's the coming home together
When your work is through . . ."

Now the entire cast was onstage as Penelope and Ulysses sang.

"It's to love the you that's me
And the me that's you."

The stage was bathed in a shimmering gold light in honor of that golden apple, so idly given to love, as all the players sang:

"It's the going home together
All life through!"

When the music stopped, the audience was still hoping for more. But the curtain fell. Cheering. Stamping. Whistling. Actors took their curtain calls. Aeneas hurried up the empty aisle; only the daily news-paper reviewers had left. By the time Aeneas got them to the lobby, Diana had blown her nose loudly and Peter had dried his eyes with the back of his hand.

"What is it that works?" Peter asked Aeneas in the brightness of the lobby; behind them the audience, still at their seats, continued to applaud.

"The war is over," said Aeneas. "That's what works." He put away flashlight and notebook; dried his glasses.

"Only it's not. The Russians are still coming. We all know that."

"The war," Aeneas growled, "is over on the stage of the Phoenix Theatre as of March eleventh, 1954. That's why everyone's cheering in there. That's what everyone wants. That's what we thought we had when World War Two ended. We were all ready to start up our lives again. Then, we got Korea and . . ."

"But," said Diana to Peter, "it's really over now. And we can," she reprised the song, "*go home at last.*"

"I wouldn't count on it." But Peter could tell that there were all sorts of conflicting emotional crosscurrents at work in the American psyche, and Latouche had certainly tapped into one. Then a smiling man in tuxedo—a producer?—told them, "There's a small party downstairs. By the johns."

The small party was gradually joined by much of the cast and Latouche's numerous friends. Waiters, out-of-work actors, served champagne. The room filled up, everyone talking at once.

Tim Farrell was standing with Gore Vidal at the foot of the stairs. Gore, Peter noticed, with some pain, was still lean while he himself had never been heavier or hungrier. He had already finished off a paper cup of peanuts from the bar despite a warning sound from the watchful Diana beside him. Diet tomorrow.

Peter greeted Tim and Gore. Greetings on such an occasion involved numerous "wonderfuls" on all sides as Latouche's triumph was duly celebrated, not to mention that of the composer, Jerry Moross, who was also standing at the foot of the stairs, with his wife, Hazel, waiting for Touche. Sooner or later everyone was obliged to wait for Touche, who led a dozen simultaneous lives, making the weather for others.

"Where is Emma?" Peter asked.

"In Washington. Doing her bit for McCarthy."

"If I knew Tim better," said Gore, "I'd suggest he divorce her."

Tim laughed, somewhat weakly. "Well, that's a bit drastic. Anyway, we're Catholic."

Peter wanted to know what had brought novelist and film director together. *"Studio One,"* said Gore. "I'm writing plays for TV. To survive. Tim's one of the regular directors."

Tim turned to Peter. "Have you ever seen a play on television?"

Peter admitted that he had not. "We have what President Truman calls a 'television machine' in the office. To watch McCarthy's Senate investigation of our Army. Infiltrated, it would seem, with communists."

Tim looked somewhat glum—loyalty to Emma?

"Actually," Gore was helpful, "only the Dental Corps appears to be riddled with communists. There's something about dentistry that makes faith of any kind plausible."

Tim frowned. "It's nothing to joke about. Also, remarks like that get heard upstairs."

"Where's upstairs?" Peter was intrigued.

"The upstairs of the Columbia Broadcasting System." Gore seemed more amused than alarmed. "Somewhere, upstairs in the CBS building here in town, they have full-time censors, checking everyone's loyalty. This means that when somebody's wanted for a show, his name is submitted upstairs, where they decide if he is or was or might be a communist."

"Actually, this is all hearsay . . ." Tim looked very uncomfortable.

Gore shook his head. "Naturally they deny that they vet anyone when, of course, they vet everyone. But what's truly demented is how someone who's unacceptable in February is suddenly acceptable in March. The dramatic change often means that he's gone to Syracuse to see the Butcher."

"The Butcher?" Peter wished he had taken notes; or was Gore sending him up?

"The Butcher owns a chain of grocery stores and he hates communists, which means that anyone named in *Red Channels* or even by Walter Winchell or Lee Mortimer in the Hearst papers *cannot* be hired for television, because if he is, the Butcher will refuse to sell the products of the network's advertisers. My solution, for what it's worth," Gore was plainly having a better time with the inquisition than Timothy X. Farrell, "is to work only for *Philco-Goodyear Playhouse* on NBC. Their sponsors are Pontiac cars and Goodyear tires, neither on sale in Syracuse grocery stores."

At that moment, John Latouche descended the stairs. He had been drinking; he had also been weeping. He was surrounded by his usual outriders—friends, admirers, total strangers, all swept into his private force field. He embraced Tim. "Now we can make the film at last!"

Touche embraced Gore. "The Lope de Vega of television! Every time I switch on, there is another play of yours. De Vega wrote five hundred plays. Or do I mean Calderón?" Latouche settled himself on the bottom stair. Someone brought him a large snifter of brandy: mottled hands shook as he held it to his lips and drank deeply. What would have knocked out Peter or any person of normal constitution refreshed Touche. Although the blue eyes were bloodshot and drying tears glistened on pale round cheeks, he suddenly beamed. "A glass of milk now, as a chaser, and I would be a walking Brandy Alexander."

Behind him on the staircase, Dawn Powell leaned forward and put her arms about his neck in what he pretended was a stranglehold; his head lolled hideously to one side.

"Dear Touche," she crooned; and pushed his head to a vertical position. "It's your own tiny Dawn."

"They ruined the second act." He began to sob. Since this was not play-acting, Peter and Diana moved on.

Diana asked Peter if Gore was going to write regularly about the theater for *American Idea*. He had done one piece already on how, no matter what the situation, the contemporary dramatist's only solution was love, preferably between man and woman within suburban marriage. "Take my hand, Doris," he had concluded. "I'm here, Bruce."

"He says he will if he has the time." Peter frowned. "Imagine Tim Farrell, the great innovative film director, ends up directing TV plays."

Peter and Diana joined Tim on a bench, midway between the gentlemen's and the ladies' rooms. Tim answered for himself. "There's no work in Hollywood these days. At least not for old directors. They also think I just do war documentaries. Of course, I'd love to work with Touche, but he's blacklisted. No Hollywood studio will touch anything he's connected with."

Peter refrained from denouncing his cousin, yet again, to her husband. Besides, it was tactless—even brutal—of him to criticize Emma, whose mother had left her entire estate, including Saint-Cloud-le-Duc, to Peter, as tribute to his good sense in a nation notorious in recent years for confusion at every level. Caroline had made only one condition in her will: "Peter Sanford must keep on publishing *The American Idea* now that he has the money to keep it going until, at least, the end of the century, during which time he will have been a voice arguing for reason in a society that is now susceptible to every sort of manipulation. He once said to me that he hoped to live long enough to see a civilization strike root in our somewhat arid land. I said that I'd hoped to see the same, though I can't say I ever totally shared his admirable optimism. Now, I will never know what comes next, but Peter Sanford may live to see and—enjoy?—what I would not in the least mind coming back for a brief visit to witness, preferably on some All Saints' Eve guided tour. But I suspect that the rules of another place require one's constant presence at the heart of Henry Adams' beloved Dynamo, where one is simply swirling atomic dust, fueling energy and creating power in order to achieve metamorphosis from what was human to . . ."

The last will and testament of Caroline Sanford Sanford had ended with an ellipsis. Like life? Open-ended.

In the center of the room, Latouche was embracing the lantern-jawed song and dance man who had played Hector.

"Baby. You were . . . you were . . ." At a loss for compliments, Latouche turned to Peter and Diana. "This is Jack Whiting. Mr. and Mrs. Sanford, who are *American Idea.*"

"Glad there is one," said Whiting amiably.

"How's that crazy son of yours doing?" Touche was now in devilish mode.

"The *boy?* Oh, not too bad. Having a last glorious fling, I suspect. He's a good lad, all in all."

Latouche and Whiting were then surrounded by well-wishers. "Imagine," Aeneas was laughing. "He calls *him* the boy!"

"Well," said Peter, "if it's his son, it's a boy to him."

"It's his stepson. I told you in the theater who it was."

"Didn't hear you."

"Winston Churchill. Jack Whiting married Churchill's mother, Jenny Jerome. Churchill's old enough to be Whiting's father, grandfather. Once, after the war started, Whiting was in a cab when the Prime Minister was on the radio. He asked the driver to pull over to the side of the road. 'I want to hear my son, if you don't mind!' He was nearly taken off to Scotland Yard as a security risk."

At the bottom of the staircase, Peter waited while Diana said good night to Latouche, who was now holding court in the half-open doorway to the ladies' room: those ladies who were in distress were obliged to use the gentlemen's room.

"I must get home," Aeneas said. "Shouldn't have stayed out so late."

Peter was still enjoying the spectacle before him. Sono Osato, the star of *On the Town*, was dancing with an actor whose face Peter had always known but whose name he had never learned. "How is Clay?" Peter had had enough to drink to mention the unmentionable.

Aeneas shrugged. "I thought he might be here tonight. But Elizabeth's spirited him off to Long Island."

"He's Oyster Bay gentry now."

"No," said Aeneas, suddenly precise, "*she* is. He goes along for the ride."

"There's money there, too." Peter could not resist. "A brass ring at the end of that ride."

"Mostly Republican."

Peter gave a mock sigh. "I'd hoped he would find another sponsor. Take the heat off poor Blaise."

"Don't worry. Clay's all set for 1960. Support keeps building. Your *Fire over Luzon*'s gone out."

"No smoke? No sentimental embers?"

"I'm sure they'll be fanned again. But he's long past that now. After all, he's twice a hero now. You really did him a great service. Forcing him off to war again. That was the real making of President Overbury."

Peter winced, as Aeneas intended he should. "He's not got it yet."

"There's continued to be, as I keep reminding you, no one else."

"Do the two of you still think Jack Kennedy will be dead by 1960?"

Aeneas shrugged. "At the moment he's back in the hospital. Spinal surgery this time. He may not come out. But if he does, will the people vote for someone whose health is so dicey?"

Peter had been impressed by how thorough Clay's long-range campaign had been. As a superpatriot, he was listened to on the Military

Affairs Committee, where he could be counted on to champion every Pentagon procurement request; unfortunately, Kennedy was no different from Clay on the few occasions that he had been well enough to make an appearance in the Senate. In fact, he seemed every bit as reactionary, politically, as Clay; no doubt due to the influence of his bootlegger father. Although there was not much to choose between them politically, Peter found Kennedy marginally more interesting.

"Two American Ideas," proclaimed Dawn Powell. "You can't hide from me, try as you might in the pages of that very small magazine."

She turned to Peter. "You must be Mr. Duncan."

"Peter Sanford . . ."

"Oh." She beamed. "The rich one. I like to encourage the rich. It is the true charity of the poor. We give them something to live for *and* lots to pay for." She turned on Aeneas. "Mr. Duncan. Without sounding like the kindly old Mother Hare, based upon Touche's deep reading of my character over the years, how could you have written such fraudulent nonsense about my old buddy and drinking partner Ernest Hemingway? Yes, I know that like the rest of us you thought he was dead in Africa, where he somehow truly belongs, in deepest jungle, in a crashed plane with Mary the boy-wife in sections beside him as saber-toothed clichés poke about in Mr. Duncan's girlish prose, but even *de mortuis*, truth must at some point make its shy appearance. Yes, into the most trivial book-chattering the odd truth or, as Bill Faulkner prefers, *verity* must fall. I knew even as we were drinking memorial martinis to our dead friend, a self-confessed giant that once walked the earth, our very own earth, too, except when he was at the Ritz Bar or browsing in Torcello's gardens, a contessa knotted loosely about his bull-like neck, and so, unlike us mere pen-persons . . . Where was I? My train of thought . . . Oh! That weekend when we thought he was dead, we wept and drank to his lifelong self-reported courage. We drank to those terrible crack-ups from which he always managed to walk away to write the tale while someone else got hurt. And so it came to pass that, by Monday, silly old history had repeated itself. As we nursed our hangovers, Ernest and boy-wife Mary swam out of the jungle in a sea of newspaper ink, all of it favorable, too. Oh! It broke my heart to realize that he was alive, because if ever he muffed anything it was not having left the stage in the heart—the horror—the heart—the horror of deepest Africa! Mistuh Ernest he dead. Only he's not. He's alive. And doomed. And you, Peter Duncan . . ."

"Aeneas," said Aeneas, like Peter overwhelmed by the verbal cascade at the bottom of the staircase.

"We left Aeneas behind us when the curtain fell tonight. No. Ernest muffed his death. He got all the great to-do and raving praises *before* the actual fact. Now he will have to face the shrinkage of everything. The result of a lifetime of back-stabbing everyone who had ever done him a good turn. At least he was pure in that. But you, Duncan . . . Oh, Duncan is in his grave; after life's fitful fever he sleeps well; treason has done his worst, nothing can touch him further . . ." Dawn stopped; finished off what was in her glass. "Duncan, you deserve to die. You praised *A Farewell to Arms*. And so I read it again, tears streaming down my cheeks as I thought of Ernest impaled on a mango tree like a canapé on a toothpick. Even so, through my tears, I realized the book was just as awful as ever. More wooden than Walter Scott. More clumsily written than any other writer we know of in English. In *English!* What am I saying? Ernest writes pidgin English, the way he thinks real men talk and write, consummate sissy that he is. Oh, how I loved him! Love him still. He loves me, too. Daughter, he squealed in that high cojones-less voice of his, if ever woman could be great writer, you are she or did he say you are her? No matter. Where was I?"

"Write for us!" was Peter's impassioned cry.

"What about, dear?" Dawn's voice was suddenly nasal flat like that of a contented housewife in a television commercial. "Land's sake, child, between the laundry in my brand-new Bendix with just a dash of Rinso White detergent, my morning is so full but afternoons are never too fraught thanks to labor-saving devices from General Electric that leave plenty of time to read to the children *and* heat up the doggy-pack blue bowl special for my husband, home from a hard day at the office, malingering."

Gore Vidal joined them. "Gore, you can't imagine what Mr. Duncan has said to me about poor Ernest Hemingway, and to think,"

Dawn's smile shone at Aeneas as she slowly mounted, with deliberate steps, the stairs to the lobby, "I've always defended you. Now—betrayal. But I don't hate you. I just pity you."

As Gore moved in beside Dawn, Peter said, "Keep in touch."

"You can't really mean that," said Dawn.

"I will," said Gore; and did over the years.

From the top of the stairs, Peter could hear Dawn's voice. "I can't understand why your generation has it in for poor old Hem."

"Could it be that he's boring? Or is it that we don't drink enough to enjoy him?"

"*Touché,*" she said. "Oh, God! I forgot to say good night to Touche."

As they disappeared into the lobby, Peter turned to Aeneas. "I must say I didn't care for your Hemingway threnody either."

"It must be annoying," said Aeneas thoughtfully, "to know how much better you are than someone like Hemingway but, because you're a woman, you're not even in the running."

"We'll see," said Peter, the spirit of old Mother Hare entering his soul, "who runs farthest in the end."

"Speaking of running," he turned to Aeneas, "will Clay offer himself to the nation in '56?"

"Too soon, we think. Besides, Adlai Stevenson's going to run again."

"He says not." Peter had been charmed by the civilized Stevenson, who had lost so eloquently to General Eisenhower.

"He says ten conflicting things a day. But we know he'll run again and we know he'll lose and that suits *our* plan perfectly for 1960."

"*Your* plan?" Peter was amazed to find the once unworldly Aeneas so entirely at home on the political heights.

"Yes, *our* plan. Clay sees a lot of the Governor. He advises him."

Peter's inner alarm sounded. Was Adlai Stevenson to be yet another victim of the sweet cheat? "To what end?"

Aeneas smiled at Diana, who was approaching them; then, before she could join them, he said, "Clay will be Adlai's running mate. So you know to what end that must be."

Diana said, "Time to go. How is Rosalind?"

Aeneas was amiable. "Busy preparing a brief on mental health—for Clay."

"He has the whole family," said Diana, taking Peter's arm as she hummed, *"It's the coming home together when the day is through . . ."* They went home.

S E V E N T E E N

I

Iris Delacroix carefully steered Peter into the study. Assured by specialists that there was nothing actually wrong with his legs, he took comfort in the fact that the arthritic pains in his ankles and feet were, if nothing else, reassuringly constant, exposing him to no serious trauma other than an ongoing uneasy relationship with the idea of gravity. Ever since he had watched his Aunt Caroline sink into eternity, he had taken against floors. Head down, he eyed suspiciously the carpet beneath him. Persian. A Kirman—he recalled the name and that meant whiskey as reward in the nonstop memory sweepstakes; even so, he knew that this apparently harmless blue and sand-yellow rug was capable of ambushing him from its neat place on the floor of his O Street house, bought, both rug and house, at the suggestion of Joe Alsop, who had also liked to exchange Peter's guests with his own N Street pilgrims. Edgy friends for half a century, they had proved to be agreeable neighbors. But Joe was dead now. Or was that his brother, Stewart? "Iris," he asked slyly, "*when* did Joe Alsop die?"

The six-foot-tall blond Iris said, "Five, six years ago. Ten? I forget. Time's such a blur nowadays." Iris's smile was radiant. An impoverished cousin, she had proved to be, if not perfect secretary, ideal companion and support, literally, in his long war of attrition with gravity.

"It isn't really forgetting." Peter picked up the thread of his own last thought but one. "Nor is it due to any loss of the proverbial marbles. No. It's more like a sudden readjustment—a shifting of the marbles— of people and places no longer where you expect them to be in their glass case. Like those prehistoric insects preserved in memory's amber. I must use that."

"Actually, you have. A number of times. In fact, Barbara quietly removed one from your last *New York Review of Books* piece. We didn't tell you."

Peter sighed. "How kind everyone is." An orange-and-blue fire blazed in the Adam fireplace that Joe had so openly despised because it was a copy. "*And* a poor one!" he would thunder. Above the failed mantelpiece hung the portrait of Aaron Burr that had played such a significant role in the life of their family. The hole from Enid's bullet had been so expertly repaired that only a slightly mischievous gleam in one of Burr's eyes suggested that he no longer looked as he had when, gravely, he sat to Vanderlyn for his portrait two centuries earlier.

Peter eased himself into a chair beside the fire. Iris poured him whiskey. A small television set on a console flashed mute image after mute image. The millennium was now circling the globe from east to west. Peter had already published his farewell to the twentieth century in *American Idea*. The fact that he himself had now lived through three-fourths of that unlovable century seemed hardly real to him. So many fading, flashing images and making as little sense as the television set. He toasted Iris. Sipped whiskey. Shut his eyes and found himself in Philadelphia. The fire's heat became summer's heat. Summer 1940. He was in the convention hall with Joe Alsop, dapper and superior. They were discussing history while actually swimming—well, treading water—in its stream. Dreamers aware they were dreaming. Theme: better to make history or write it? For the first time in sixty years of remembering this occasion, Peter noticed that Joe was wearing a white straw hat . . . a boater? A floater? What did they call them? Every man in those long-lost summers wore a white straw hat. Then, after the war, there were no more straw hats. All gone, along with the smell of pre-war Washington streets—of asphalt baking in hot sun. He turned to speak to Joe, who was sitting in the chair to his right. But Iris had taken his place.

"Why am I thinking about Joe Alsop tonight?"

"Because you know how furious he'd be at having missed the changing of the centuries."

Peter nodded. Tonight he was definitely one up on Joe. But then Joe had been much older than he and so was doomed from birth to remain forever fixed in the 1900s. Peter was solicitous of Iris. "You're sure you don't want to go to the Mall and watch the Clintons watch the cameras?"

"We can watch them here at home. Anyway, your descendants will be coming in with the new year. We've got supper for them."

Peter still found it hard to believe that not only did he have four grown grandchildren but their mother seemed much older to him than ever did her Aunt Caroline, for whom he'd named her. Iris switched on the sound to the television. Excited voices. Fireworks on the screen. An American network was tracking the dawn all around the globe.

"There will be a river of fire," reported Iris, "in London."

"That was Hitler's Wagnerian dream. Airpower," Peter heard himself repeat something that he had been told many years before, "can never win a war."

Iris pressed the mute button. "You said that on television. On your program. Remember? When NATO was bombing Kosovo."

"Of course I remember." Once a month Peter would talk for an hour on television with a lively young journalist who was eager to recreate the solemn stately dialogues that Walter Lippmann and Eric Sevareid conducted before he was born. The learned Lippmann, now forgotten, had been as commanding a presence on television as he had been in journalism. He knew many things that the audience did not know, and in those simple times there was no objection to knowledge, no insistence on the part of television programmers that an "in-depth" interview could never last longer than seven minutes while shallow was now measured in seconds. Each weighty question, even to Peter on his own program, was invariably prefaced by the stern if smiling command "Now, briefly." This was in stark contrast to the academic historians with their equally stern "Now, lengthily." Such a one was Dr. Robert L. B. Sturtevant, a middle-aged history professor from a New England college. Tall, with a great deal of ash-gray hair, he had been commissioned by a university to write the life of Peter Sanford. "A witness to our times," he had declared upon his first meeting with the bemused Peter, who had immediately started to wonder just what it was that he was thought to have witnessed as opposed to what he had simply observed as time kept moving, ever faster, past him. It seemed like only months had passed since the hapless Clintons had arrived in the whispering gallery; now two terms were almost over and, journalistic scandals to one side, nothing of any consequence had happened in *their* eight years as opposed to the eight years in which they had lived, like everyone else, as swift new means of communication were daily invented and then concentrated in fewer and fewer hands. The politics of the sort that had dominated Washington from the beginning had ceased to matter. Internet, like heaven, was indifferent to who was, or wanted to be, king of the castle.

Now Dr. Sturtevant—Peter wondered why anyone not practicing medicine would use such a title—was on hand to observe the historical Peter Sanford at a significant moment in world history. "The end of *your* century," he said, pointed tongue licking, lizardlike, thin lips. In the one year that Peter had been submitting himself to Dr. Sturtevant's questions, he had found him agreeable if uninteresting. Although a trained scholarly researcher, Dr. Sturtevant did not appear to be much interested in getting to know anything that he did not already know. Very much a court historian, he did not question the prevailing myths about the nation-state in general and the United States in particular. Yet he had been drawn to Peter Sanford, an unglamorous subject whose worldview was hardly congenial to the one that prevailed in the land of tenure, foundation grants, and, sometimes, showy government service. But then Dr. Sturtevant had been a student of Aeneas Duncan. Since the Kennedy Administration had replaced, as it were, the Overbury Administration-that-never-was, Aeneas had attached himself to the youthful melodramatists. Although Aeneas's literary services were not needed, the Kennedys had set him up in the State Department as a mandarin in residence. Then, after the President's assassination, he had resigned to become a distinguished professor of, presumably, distinction, on a range of subjects in which occasional degrees were given: hence, Sturtevant's doctoral dissertation on "The Overbury Challenge to New Deal Orthodoxy" had been the making of Dr. Sturtevant.

"I've never been in this room at night." Fortunately, Sturtevant's voice, even at its most incessant, was a pleasant one and Peter sometimes napped when drawn out at nonbriefly length. Now Sturtevant toured the room; he paused before the life-size portrait of James Burden Day, looking ruggedly handsome. "I hadn't realized what a good painting this was."

"It needs artificial light," said Peter. "Like most good portraits. In print as well as on canvas."

Sturtevant's hand went to his jacket pocket. Peter barely heard the click as a small recorder was switched on. He wondered if he would ever have the energy to read the eventual transcripts, as agreed. Even the thought was wearying. "My wife thought her father's life had been ruined by Roosevelt. Every time Senator Day was ready to fulfill his destiny and run for president, FDR was there ahead of him. The bitterest time was 1940, of course. By '44, Senator Day was too old."

"And so was President Roosevelt." Dr. Sturtevant moved on to a portrait of Diana.

"That," said Peter, "was painted the year my wife died. She was only sixty. She looks much younger, doesn't she? She never dyed her hair."

"I can see the resemblance to your daughter."

"You can? I can't. Caroline is like me, poor child." Happily, neither father nor daughter was stout this season.

Sturtevant rejoined Peter beside the fire; miniature recording machine in hand, containing a Silicon Valley chip that could store a hundred—or was it a thousand?—hours of talk.

"I must go fuss with the buffet." Iris's tolerance for the raw stuff of biography was slight.

"Do you find it odd, being here, tonight?" Sturtevant's manner, at times, was that of kindly adult with slow child. He was certainly a born speller-out of the obvious.

"Odd to be at home? On New Year's Eve? Or odd to be still alive at the age of . . . How old am I?"

"Seventy-seven and two months. I forget how many days. No, I meant still at the center of your world but with so many of its characters gone."

"You would be amazed . . ." Peter began; then paused. How much should be—or could he—amaze the good simple Sturtevant? He selected a midrange rather run-of-the-mill arrangement of mild surprises. ". . . how little the old miss anyone. We have long since learned to take it for granted that the crew's bound to skip ship and that's just what they do and, by and large, one no longer cares. Out of sight, and so on. Certainly I miss Diana. To talk to. Without her, I simply talk to myself, which is probably all that the happily married ever do." Peter thought of old Kitty. "Diana's mother talked to birds and small animals. She also said aloud what she was thinking. Senator Day would be terrified when the fit was upon her and she was in chatty mood."

Sturtevant removed a notebook from his pocket. "When I was writing my book on Clay Overbury, I discovered that the reason Senator Day did not run for reelection in 1952 was the fact that he had taken a bribe from some oilman and . . ."

"All that," said Peter firmly, "is suitable for a life of my father-in-law or of Clay. *Not* of me. Clay was, as I have perhaps suggested to you, a very gifted man with a superb instinct for blackmail—whitemail, too, if I may invent a new crime of sorts. The ability to whitemail an emotional older man like my father into falling in love with him so that he would help him rise. I suspect all major politicians have this gift. Certainly FDR was a master of his own kind of whitemail and practiced it on the likes of Harry Hopkins. But he never—as far as I know, of course—operated at Clay's visceral level." Peter had not intended to say any of this but, once it was said, he felt as if a burden, small but real, had been lifted.

"I know that you never liked Overbury because of your sister, Enid . . ."

". . . When it comes to politics, I'm not that personal." Peter wondered if what he said was true. "Anyway, once Enid was dead and Diana and I were married, Clay was out of our lives—and very much into that of the public. Do you see his widow?"

Sturtevant shook his head. "No. I never really knew her. She moved to Cuernavaca after the . . ." He stopped, "I see Clay's daughter Alice sometimes. Aeneas liked her."

"So do I. My favorite niece." Peter poured himself more whiskey. On television the Eiffel Tower was cascading fireworks. Peter looked at his watch. "Six hours to go before we, too, are catapulted into the future. How far away all this seemed when I was a boy. Once, in school, when we were about nine or ten, the class passed a resolution that in the year 2000 we would all meet again. We solemnly signed a document. Washington children learn about treaties and protocols with their mother's milk. Now I can't for the life of me recall anyone who was in that class."

"Do you have a copy of the protocol?" Sturtevant was suddenly all business.

Peter laughed. "I don't save everything. I also sometimes wonder if I remember anything at all. Or am I just remembering the last time I remembered an event, which was itself just recalling it from the previous time I thought of it, and so on back to the long-lost original happening."

"A palimpsest, as your old friend Gore Vidal describes the way memory works."

"He's been on *C-Span* all week. They keep repeating one of his . . . what does he call them? State of the union speeches."

Sturtevant nodded. "I watched it, Christmas Eve. Do you ever see him now?"

"No. He comes to Washington once a year. To speak to the National Press Club, and he only does this because television covers it, which makes up for the fact that no one at the National Press Club has ever reported a word of what he says to them, which is peculiar, since he does draw a crowd." Peter suddenly recalled having recently met a television executive who was eager for Peter and Gore to appear together—on a program—two old Washingtonians, in conversation.

Sturtevant aimed the recorder at Peter. "You're still a member of the Press Club?"

"I think I can never not be. After all, when my father died, I was the publisher—the reluctant publisher—of the Washington *Tribune*."

"The paper that could not be saved?"

"Not by me. Blaise was . . ." What word would best describe his father in those last years? "Mad" suggested King Lear. "Deranged" was not the same. ". . . *emotional* in his last phase. When *Time* magazine offered to buy the *Tribune* in '78, he was in what I called his militant leftist phase . . ."

"Which started with Clay Overbury?"

"Clay was never a leftist. He was a . . . well, a Clayist. No. My father was simply emotional in those years. He turned against the war in Vietnam. Which was odd, because that was the sort of show of power he usually liked. He had a terminal row with Dean Acheson—the hawk of hawks. In those years Washington dinner parties were battlefields. One night Joe Alsop, in a rage, right here, in the dining room, shouted at me, 'Out of my house!' I was never to return. As tactfully as I could, I reminded him that since we were in my house, *he* would have to go."

"Did he?"

Peter chuckled at the memory. "Not before he'd finished a half bottle of brandy. Anyway, Father had his row with Henry Luce and so *Time* magazine bought the *Evening Star* instead of the *Tribune*. But it would have made no difference. In four years, Luce lost eighty-five million on the *Star* and shut it down, by which time Father was dead and the Washington *Post* had the town to itself."

"But you had *American Idea*."

"Which still flourishes, if that's the verb for what it is we do. You know, it was Aunt Caroline who created the *Tribune*. Then, just like Hearst, she found movies more interesting and left publishing to Father. She was like no one else."

Sturtevant agreed. "It's curious how little sense of history Washington—of all places—has. Even people who should know better think Kay Graham, at the *Post*, was the first woman publisher, but long before her there was Cissy Patterson and before her Caroline Sanford."

Peter nodded, recalling a conversation with Mrs. Graham. She, too, was surprised at the shortness of Washington's memory. Then, unexpectedly, she gave the crown not to Cissy or to Caroline or to herself but to Cissy's relative Alicia Patterson, who had successfully founded a *new* newspaper on Long Island. "She started with nothing!" To which Peter, for the sake of accuracy, added, "Except a fortune."

Peter's own fortune came not from his father, who had left everything to the Overburys, but from Caroline, who had made it possible for Peter to finance not only *American Idea* but almost anything else that engaged his sympathy; she had also saddled him with, after Versailles, the greatest white mammoth in all France, Saint-Cloud-le-Duc. The will stipulated that he was not allowed to sell it or give it away. He was bound to it not only by his gratitude to Caroline but by deeply caring lawyers, schooled in all the arts of entailment. Fortunately, a grandchild now preferred a French life to an American one and so Caroline's great-niece had taken her aunt's place, for which the will had thoughtfully allowed. On Peter's rare visits to Europe, he knew that he had the wing of a museum to himself where he could read and write far less comfortably than at home in Georgetown. But, then, with each passing year, he did less and less of either. For one thing, he knew fewer and fewer people as opposed to those unknown to him who put themselves in his way with projects and schemes all based on hopes which he was too often obliged to confess he could not share, unlike his fears, which he could but did not share since they were so often remote from others'.

The new people took for granted a world that had grown ever tighter and more controlled, not to mention crowded. Currently, he was reading about the ancient Mayan cities, whose temples, altars, pyramids were once thought to be ceremonial centers set apart for the religious life of a sparse population scattered about in leafy jungle lean-tos. But, lately, generations of received opinion had been overthrown by new evidence. Apparently, the surviving monuments had been central to huge cities where millions of people were jammed into vertical compounds, victims of a Malthusian nightmare of overpopulation in a land of limited resources. Since dogs and deer provided too little protein, human flesh was crucial to their survival and never-ending war became a dietetic necessity. Finally, too many died off, leaving the too-few to lead brutish lives in ruins that still reverberated with old stories of what the world had been like at the start of *their* civilization's millennium, to be neatly completed on the eve of December 31, 1999, according to a made-up Christian calendar not applicable to most of mankind, much less present-day Mayans no longer able to interpret those intricate ancestral calendars that had once rung time's changes for a slow-mutating race nourished, at the end, by its own warm blood.

"Now, Mr. Sanford, I've never brought up the subject before . . ." Nervously, Sturtevant stirred champagne with his forefinger.

Peter knew what the subject was. "Yes, Dr. Sturtevant?" There was, he hoped, a bit of the judgment of God in his voice.

"And, of course, there have been so many theories over the years . . ."

"About what?" Let him dangle.

"About the plane that crashed in late October of 1958."

"November first," Peter murmured but Sturtevant did not hear him. Clay had been running for what looked to be an easy reelection to the Senate to be followed by preparations for the presidential race two years later. But one bright morning, as a chartered campaign plane came in for a landing at American City airport, an engine caught fire. The plane crashed into a motel just short of the runway. Clay and a dozen members of his staff were killed on what proved to be, for once entirely by chance, prime-time television. He who had lived his life in bold exciting images had ended his in spectacular flames, not unlike those on Luzon from which he had pretended to emerge a hero in order that he might, in triumph, walk up and down the earth until, in real flames, he crashed and departed.

"Of course, the plane was entirely destroyed. But there was sufficient . . . uh, forensic evidence that one of the engines had been tampered with. Who do you think . . . ?"

Forty-two years had passed since the so-called accident at American City. Suddenly, Peter was more intent upon time's brutal passage than on the old murder, if such it was, of Clay Overbury. But Peter was willing to indulge Sturtevant, up to a point. "First, who benefits? Naturally the Kennedys would be our first suspects. Particularly now we know their record in the political assassination line. In 1958, Clay looked unbeatable for 1960. It is quite possible that Bobby might have engaged someone to remove Clay from the vale of tears as he would, later on, with the dedicated help of our many secret services, do the same or try to do the same to Castro and Lumumba and the Diems and other demons. But I seriously doubt that at this point in their adventures they would have dared do anything so excitingly creative."

Sturtevant was doing his best to disguise his shock. "It's also perfectly unthinkable, isn't it? I mean, after all, they were serious political figures . . ."

"Surely, Dr. Sturtevant, there is nothing," said Peter, enjoying himself too much, "more serious than political murder?"

"Yes. In Chile. But one doesn't associate our people with that sort of thing."

Peter affected surprise. "Surely political murder is the only thing one ever associates with the Kennedys. Poor bastards," he added more for himself than for the record. "Jack and Bobby were both murdered along with Martin Luther King, and no matter what suspicions many of us have had we will never know for sure who was behind any of the three killings, which may be just as well."

"We can rule out the Kennedys . . ."

"Rule out no one." Peter felt suddenly cheery. "It is New Year's Eve . . ."

"Who else would, as you put it—*cui bono?* Benefit?"

Peter decided to go all the way if only to test Sturtevant's nerves and intelligence. "Who else was on the flight with Clay?"

"Just aides. People working on the campaign. And . . ." He frowned.

"Yes," said Peter. "Go on."

"Well, it was tragic, certainly. Aeneas's wife Rosamund . . ."

"*Rosalind.* Yes, she was aboard. She traveled everywhere that season with Clay. They had been lovers for several years."

Sturtevant spilled his glass on the hearth rug. Tried to mop it up with a handkerchief. "Don't bother," said Peter. "That rug's day is done."

"I thought Overbury was very promiscuous—like they claim Jack Kennedy was."

"The promiscuous have love affairs, too. She was no beauty but she was very intelligent. She was also a child psychologist, much the best kind for a man who lusts for the presidency . . ."

"Did Aeneas know?"

"I'd rather hoped you'd be able to tell me something *I* didn't know. Yes, he knew, and, unlike the Kennedy cuckolds, he was not proud of the horns Clay had set upon his brow. Aeneas had, as they say, motive, but I shouldn't think he had the resources—or the skills—to eliminate both wife and lover. So that leaves only one suspect." Peter rose. "I'm going to take a nap before the celebration. Then, tomorrow, if you like, you can join me at our New Year's Day party. Come to the offices at noon." Peter started slowly toward the door.

Sturtevant hurried after him. "That leaves only who, Mr. Sanford?"

"Who?" Peter gave him a calculated blank stare. "Oh, the most intriguing suspect. That leaves only me. That we know of, anyway. Clay was responsible for Enid's death. Could I let him be president?"

"You're joking?"

"Of course I am," said Peter. "I'll see you later. When that crystal ball drops into Times Square or wherever it's supposed to, and we undergo metamorphosis, to hear the journalists run on about this night."

At noon, January 1, 2000, Peter made his by now traditional New Year's appearance at the offices of *American Idea* on Capitol Hill in what had once been a prosperous middle-class black enclave but now resembled some bombed-out European city in the throes of a corrupt restoration. At least, the offices had survived the civil war of the 1960s when the heart of the "capital of the free world," as the presidents liked to call the peculiar white official city set in the middle of a black one, had been well and truly broken. Currently, there was an irritable truce between the races as those blacks who had not yet moved to the suburbs viewed with benign neglect the overwhelming presence of their white masters, well defended by a black police force rooted in a black national army.

As Peter was driven past the Supreme Court, he wondered, for the thousandth time, who benefited by an American race war. What joy was derived by the combatants on either side? In half a century, *American Idea* had published hundreds of symposia on the subject not to mention learned as well as defiantly unlearned essays on the subject. Lately, academic zealots were once again peddling the crude racist line that the Dark Other was, somehow or other, genetically inferior to its pale cousinage and no matter how much money it was given or even earned for singing and dancing prettily, its children's academic scores would always be lower than those of whites, while overconcerned zealots, eager not to be thought racists, pretended to abase themselves before the hordes of clever Asians who were currently getting the highest marks of all in the sciences.

Peter's idling mood was suddenly concentrated by the sight of old Vernon; he was seated on his usual brick stoop; and he waved at Peter, who waved back. Vernon was at least a hundred years old and had claimed to have been born a slave until Peter persuaded him that the dates didn't work out. "Well, I reckon I was the next best thing," he had said, "you could find in Fairfax County."

For a good portion of the century, Peter had watched Vernon push his cart around the neighborhood, sharpening knives and scissors on a round sandstone wheel. He also soldered broken metal over a blue flame. Upon appearing in a street, he would announce his presence with a high-pitched cry followed by a song whose words were meaningless but whose overall meaning was clear to the homeowners who hurried to him with all sorts of wounded metal objects to be made whole. But now, time-crippled, he could only watch the street where once he had reigned.

"Happy New Year!" Vernon shouted; and Peter shouted back.

Two connected brick buildings housed *American Idea*, while in their joint backyard a modern wing had been built to give shelter to several small publishing houses, each capable of creating more disturbance than its modest size might suggest.

The driver helped Peter out of the car. Today's arthritic pains were as exquisitely varied as the next day's weather promised to be. If nothing else, arthritis ensured that he would always be given dramatic notice of any meaningful rise or fall of the barometer. Numerous medical specialists, to a man and one woman, assured him that as he aged everything would get worse. What to do? The obvious thing was not to overdo aging; a process that was, in any case, predicated upon an abrupt stop of its own feckless choosing. Meanwhile, at home and at his office, he had wheelchairs reserved for rainy days.

Education. SAT: that was the acronym for the tests that were now given every schoolchild in the country. To measure intelligence. To determine further "education," if any. Peter was still looking to publish the ultimate analysis of a test that he was convinced had been devised by the mediocre to advance the mediocre through a common educational system designed to maintain in passive ignorance the general subpopulation for which there was nothing much of interest to do and nothing at all of interest to think about once they had learned what little they were expected to know to get through dull repetitive days; to *float* through like . . . From childhood, he recalled one of the aquarium tanks in the basement of the Commerce Building. Large flat brown fish floating in cloudy water. Electric eels slumbering on pebbles. He used to wait hours for them to light up but they never did. Fish in tanks. Mayans crowded together . . .

"Who was *Time* magazine's man of the year for 1999? Or was it the century?" he asked the new editor, Doris Oenslager, a onetime history professor at the same university in Oregon where her mentor, and Peter's late unique contributor, the historian William Appleman Williams, had taught. The current fashion to hire women for all highly visible jobs had been a lucky one for Peter. He was more at ease with them than he had ever been with Billy Thorne or Aeneas Duncan. The fact that President Clinton had made so many terrible rainbow-hued melting-pot appointments did not undermine the principle, at century's end, not so much of "equality," an impossible notion at best, but of interchangeability, modern society's one valuable discovery. It was not that a member of a minority could now be proudly hailed as every bit as good as a member of the old white male ruling class; rather, one could say proudly, that the current woman secretary of state had achieved gender parity by proving to be every bit as bad as her male predecessors. Once the idea of excellence had been abandoned and competence was judged by SAT scores or IQ tests, the mediocre could then move freely from foreign affairs to hospital administration to brain surgery . . . perhaps not brain surgery just yet. But most of the showy occupations were as easily filled with interchangeable citizens as the less showy jobs had always been, while the huddled masses . . . How did the Mayans maintain order in their crowded tenements?

Apparently, *Time's* man of the year had "invented" the retailing of consumer goods on the Internet, selling things from farthest space over telephone lines and off satellites. Well, that must be changing the way people lived; certainly, the way they bought and sold things. From out of a mostly lost past he heard the voice of Herbert Hoover at Laurel House on a summer's day, prescribing an antidote to depression as well as to civil and world wars. "What America most needs now is a great poem," he had said. Peter had been too astonished to ask, A poem like what? *The Man with the Hoe*, of an earlier America? *The Waste Land* of the time before theirs? No. Not Eliot. Frost? Folksy, yes, but perhaps too dark for a would-be age of gold. He must ask Jimmy Merrill, the best of the midcentury poets. Then he recalled that after communing for years with the dead, in verse, by Ouija board, Jimmy was dead, too.

"Doris, we need a great poem. And we need it now."

Doris was making tea in her office. In the conference room next door, editors and contributors were gathered for eggnog made from an eighteenth-century recipe, inherited from Frederika.

"So hard to come by," said Doris vaguely. "Assuming one knows what is great when one sees it. I'll ask Helen Vendler. She's bound to know if someone has written one, or could write one."

"On commission?" Peter sat at the partners' desk that had been in the editors' office since the beginning. "But then I suppose Pindar also worked on commission."

"He just did athletes, didn't he?" Doris poured them tea; laughter from the conference room. "Winners of the Olympic Games. That sort of thing."

Grimly, Peter pressed the various go-buttons of a mind that had once, so swiftly, summoned words onto . . . There was a slight hitch as the weary custodian within sought the latest word as it rattled about, probably unfiled. *Kaleidoscope?* Word-pictures as projected on the . . .

what? Inner—*screen?* No. *Computer* screen. Bull's-eye: A late arrival in his consciousness, unlike Pindar, who was an old secure memory. No problem there. He recalled a discussion with . . . The custodian was put to work. On the screen loomed a round bald freckled man. In bathing suit. Body covered with apish orange hairs. Maurice Bowra. Classics don. Translated Pindar. Sardinian beach. Wind. Cloud of flies. Bowra's beautiful unstoppable voice. Great gossip. Great Britain. Greats . . .

The custodian is now showing off. Produces ravishing if pointless picture of an all-black sea with whitecaps, wind- rather than tide-driven. Picnic lunch at a trestle table on a beach. The young Peter and Diana and a half-dozen others. Umbrellas. Slyly, the custodian zooms in on bottles of black peasant wine—black due to memory's eccentric lighting. Sudden glimpse of the melancholy pug-dog face of Cyril Connolly . . . once edited a "little" magazine. Which? *New Writing?* *Hudson Review?* No. *Hudson* was Cornelia Claiborne's. She was long since lost to a marriage that had taken her life, in another country. Now Pindar is on the soundtrack. The custodian is showing off.

"Who, in his tenderest years, / Finds some new lovely thing, / His hope is high, and he flies on the wings of his manhood: / Better than riches are his thoughts.—/ But man's pleasure is a short time growing / And it falls to the ground / As quickly when an unlucky twist of thought / Loosens its roots . . ."

Peter spoke aloud the next line even before the custodian could get to it: *"Man's life is a day. What is he? / What is he not? A shadow in a dream / Is man*—is man . . ." The malicious custodian switched off the audio. "I can't recall another line." Peter sighed.

"That was better than I could do." Doris was impressed, as Peter had intended her to be. "Was that Bowra's translation?"

"I think so. It's flat enough. He had no ear. But I like 'an unlucky twist of thought.' Diana and I saw a good deal of him one summer back in . . . when Sardinia first opened up. He was a friend of friends. Grand friends. Those old English dons seldom missed a trick. I never learned Greek." Peter did not listen to Doris's response.

Sturtevant's ash-blond hair was windblown into a small haystack set atop a round, Mayan skull which meant Mongolian or, Peter rather hoped, possible Egyptian ancestry. "Are you going to join the party?" He was holding a silver cup of eggnog.

"*I* am," said Doris, rising.

"I'll be in presently. Sit down." On the wall opposite Sturtevant was the framed cover of the Potsdam issue that had been the making of *American Idea*. Billy Thorne. Wooden leg. Ill-matched eyes. Unasked, the custodian perfunctorily flashed odd bits of information onto the screen. Peter asked the biographer if he had, as yet, netted this peculiar fish.

"No." Sturtevant switched on the recorder. "I suspect Mr. Thorne's dead. I was told that there's an ex-wife who might know. So I tracked her down to a nursing home. She has Alzheimer's. There's no record of him after 1980."

"We should try—*you* should try the Freedom of Information Act. I'm sure he has an imposing dossier. I'd be curious to know if he was actually CIA, or just a fellow . . ." The word fell off the screen. The custodian, taking a well-earned nap, hurriedly punched out "voyager," which Peter irritably rejected, along with a dozen other wrong words. By the time "traveler" appeared, the need for any word was gone. Aunt Caroline had said that Eleanor Roosevelt had taken concentrated garlic pills every day of her life for memory. Should he?

"I've got a friend from Langley looking into it. Thorne also stayed close to Clay Overbury even though he and Aeneas never got on. Had Overbury become president instead of Kennedy, Thorne would have been a key player. He was known to be a great cross-puncher . . ."

At the thought of life in the real world, Sturtevant tended, like so many sheltered academics, to indulge in Darwinian metaphors and jock-style language. Peter suspected that "cross-puncher" was probably the wrong phrase but he was not about to ask his exhausted custodian to check it out. But "check it out" gave him unexpected pleasure. Obviously, he himself was still with it, *with it*. So much so that he did not hear Sturtevant's question. All that he caught was the end: ". . . hope to solve the mystery?"

Peter stalled. "Mystery?" What was? Clay's death? Yes.

"Aeneas knew more than he ever let on. But I could never get anything out of him. I know that Aeneas had fallen out with Clay the year before Clay's death."

The year before what? Peter's normally slow pulse was beating faster. "Did Aeneas ever tell you why, exactly, he broke with Clay?"

"I came into his life long after. But you knew him then, knew him all along. From what you said last night, I assume it was over Rosamund. I mean Rosalind."

Peter guiltily drank heavy cream and egg with cinnamon from the silver cup. "We saw very little of each other those last days. Obviously, I wasn't enthusiastic about the Clay for President movement. I preferred Adlai Stevenson. Yes, he couldn't make up his mind, but at least he had one to make up or not. I think Aeneas came to see me, to ask us to support Kennedy."

In the chair beneath the Potsdam cover, a gray Aeneas materialized. He was nervous. He chewed on the stem of a pipe. No more cigarettes. Emphysema. "I suppose you'll say, I told you so . . ."

Peter had been quietly smug. "I'm never so obvious. Anyway, you lasted longer with Clay than I thought you would. Jack Kennedy is much more your style."

"I think he's what we need now." Aeneas twirled his wedding ring only, Peter had noticed with some surprise, he was wearing no ring at all: this was now an automatic gesture, like a tic.

"And what do we need now?"

"Energy. A new generation . . ."

"Yes. Yes. Everyone's agreed. So we have a choice between two young men with rich fathers. Only Clay's rich father is actually my rich father. On loan, you might say. Anyway, you've gone over to Kennedy . . ."

"I hope I can persuade you to do the same."

"Don't even try. I'm forever Stevenson's man because he turned down both Clay *and* Jack to run with last time."

"For Estes Kefauver!" Aeneas's coughing fit filled, first, Peter's memory and then merged into the noise of the party next door. Iris had opened the door.

"Time to shine," she said. "Everyone's waiting."

With Sturtevant not quite clinging to him, Peter made his way into the party, where he was given, for no apparent reason other than longevity, a small but apparently sincere ovation.

Then Peter held court with the contributors that he knew. Thanks to the intensity of Aeneas's early efforts, they still had the best arts section of any review, liberal or otherwise. "I think," said Peter, quizzed on the subject by the stylized skeptic from the Washington *Post*, "that this is partly due to the fact that we keep politics, when not relevant, out of our reviews. We also keep on and on with those good critics who want to keep on and on with us."

"That means," said the man from the *Post*, "you must pay them better than the other magazines." Peter chuckled; changed the subject. He was, of course, in Aunt Caroline's debt for the salaries he could pay that others could not. But no one need know.

Over the fireplace someone had placed a banner with *2000 A.D.* emblazoned in gold on red. Someone else had, predictably, tacked *C.E.* under the *A.D.* Much energy was spent conforming to ever-shifting fads in a language that each year lost more and more words, particularly useful irreplaceable ones.

Peter sat in a throne in front of the window that looked out on the backyard, now front yard to the modern annex, their miniature "publishers row." Doris brought him people to talk to. He did not, he decided, regret in any way his life. Except for Diana, he missed none of those who had defected to death. Old people sobbing in graveyards struck him as either the height of hypocrisy or else of solipsism, since they were mourning nothing more than their own approaching change of estate.

Suddenly, a small dark-haired young man appeared. Peter had not seen him earlier, or ever before. "Mr. Sanford." As they shook hands, Peter stared into a sharp intelligent face. Dark hazel eyes glittered beneath dark hair combed straight back from a brow which, due to youthful baldness, was higher than nature had intended. A white smile was framed by full lips. "A. B. Decker." He identified himself. Peter recognized the name; found the face mysteriously familiar. "I am your something-or-other cousin, sir."

"Emma's son. Aunt Caroline's grandson . . ."

"Great-grandson."

The generations were sweeping over him like the great wave at Rehoboth Beach, Delaware, that had nearly drowned him when he was six years old, a powerful memory that stimulated the custodian, unbidden, to roll some stock footage of a huge wave, as seen by a child, a great green collapsing white-laced wall that fell with a heavy crash upon him: flung him hard against the coarse sand of the beach. "You are the very image of . . ."

"Aaron Burr. I know. So people tell me, the few who know who he is." The young man sat in the chair next to Peter.

"The last time I saw your grandmother Emma . . ."

"Was at the funeral of her real father. Senator Day."

"You know everything?" Peter was mildly irritated not to be able to break so much sensational news to this supremely self-assured young man.

"A. B. Decker," Peter repeated the name. "Aaron Burr Decker?"

"Yes. I was even assigned the name. I can't think what nature is up to."

"Or what your grandmother Emma was up to. Well, Burr started our nineteenth century off with a bang. He elected Jefferson president and himself vice president, and heir. How do you plan to start up our twenty-first century?"

A.B. laughed. "Nothing so historic. So fundamental. ABC TV has a new series—*dialogues*. With the old and the wise. I've got the green light for you and your old friend Gore Vidal to chat together."

"Which one is old? Which one is wise?"

"You both are both. Two survivors of the now forever vanished twentieth century. 'The American century.' Can you tell from the way I just said that that I was putting quotes around it?"

"Now you mention it, yes. But at least you didn't make quotation marks with your fingers on either side of your newly ironic face as the young like to do. I must say, I wish Henry Luce had been more tongue-in-cheek when he minted that bit of fool's gold. Has Gore agreed?"

"If we come to Italy. Next month. Yes."

Several lively journalists from the Internet from—what was it called? Saloon? Salon?—had arrived. He would have to play host. "Well, Italy was—is—part of our global empire. At least we won't end up posing against the Jefferson Memorial."

"Or standing in Arlington Cemetery." This was sharp. Definitely a Burr.

"We are ancestral voices, prophesying . . ." Peter began.

"War?"

"No. That game could be over. For us, if not others." For the entire twentieth century, from the sinking of the *Maine* to Serbia's intolerable defiance, whenever American leaders could think of nothing else to do, war was the diversion of choice. But ever since conscription had been abandoned, few Americans now voluntarily chose to take up arms for their nation; they were also laying down ever sterner rules in order to ensure not only their physical safety but comfort as well. Under none of the traditional circumstances (particularly, war far from home in places hitherto unknown) were their lives to be put at risk either by an overwrought enemy with no sense of irony or by maladministered vaccinations. During the last of the century's Balkan adventure, American bombers had flown so high above their targets that they had missed nearly everything of military consequence while doing considerable damage to random civilians in the way below.

"Since we have too much fire and nuclear power, I suspect we'll leave the actual fighting to our third-world clients. Let them provide the evening news with rich luminous reds."

A.B. grinned. "Let TV be our Colosseum and the third-worlders our gladiators? Say that to camera."

"You say it." The television reporters were starting to converge on Peter. He braced himself.

"Will you do the program?" A.B. asked. "Last week in February?"

A nameless yet familiar television face was now eye to eye with Peter; others joined them. Questions and Answers. Q and A. Most urgent of all the questions was whether or not the President's wife would be elected to the Senate. Yes? No? Maybe? The journalists fired more names at him. He felt as if he were the wall against which various worthies were to be executed by a "World News from Washington" firing squad. Briefly, very briefly, the great subjects were addressed. The price of a campaign for president. The price of a *winning* campaign for president while, just under the surface of such dull trivia as foreign affairs and the public welfare, lurked those issues that would determine the leadership of nation and globe, drugs and adultery.

It was A.B. who changed the subject to something even more

interesting to the questioners than the approaching presidential election. Television. Its role. Its power. To a man, the journalists praised the anchorperson who had, the day before, stayed on air to follow the sun for twenty-four—or was it forty-eight?—hours. Endurance was admired. The sameness of everything around the world was also duly noted, to Peter's surprise. Were they really so observant? Somewhat timidly, he remarked upon last night's apparent absence anywhere on earth of that mournful Scottish air "Auld Lang Syne."

"Perhaps," said A.B., "our century was one old acquaintance that no one wants to bring to mind, ever again."

"But now that we've got to the morning after, will anyone from our time be remembered?" Since Peter could see that the most familiar of the television faces had a list of sure-to-be-immortal names to submit, he headed him off with, "Our President is said to be worrying about his place in history. It's as if he had a reservation which might not be honored if the hotel changes management. But shouldn't he really be wondering if the United States is going to be remembered? You know, for old time's sake? Or for any other sake that comes to mind."

Since none of the journalists had ever before encountered such a nonsensical question, Peter's animating thought did not register. They instead continued to fire names at Peter-the-wall.

A.B. to the rescue. "What politician today, not just here but anywhere, is going to be remembered? It's the global economy, stupid, as the President might be tempted to say now that we've got to the year 2000 in one piece and with the Dow Jones over ten thousand."

Peter made his move. "Certainly, those of you who make the news—or those who hire you to create it—are literally history-makers, as William Randolph Hearst was the first to discover."

"But who," asked the best-known face, "would remember Hearst today if it weren't for Orson Welles?"

"Arson who?" asked a puzzled latecomer to the old century.

Peter avoided the endless trap of who was who. And promptly crashed into a new one. "You are Shelley's dream come true . . ." Shelley! Talk fast. Get swiftly free of that elephant pit. "You—the media—

are what he wanted poets to be, the unacknowledged legislators of the world."

This, happily, went unrecognized and unacknowledged; and emptied their corner of the room just as Peter's smile gave out. He turned to A.B. "Yes. I'll go to Italy . . . to . . . Rapallo?"

"Ravello." The black eyes glittered like polished onyx. "That will be the true confrontation."

"Do you think so?" Peter had his doubts.

"Yes. Time to come full circle." A.B. led Peter to the street, where Dr. Sturtevant helped him into the car.

Old Vernon's stoop was empty. So were the streets around the Capitol: a strangely empty New Year's Day. An omen?

Dr. Sturtevant had had a great deal to think about since the previous evening. "Concerning Clay Overbury's . . . uh, death . . ."

Peter now regretted his late-night appearance of candor. "What," he shifted the subject, "was Aeneas's theory?"

"If he had one, he never told me." They passed the Commerce Building, whose basement contained the aquarium where Billy Thorne's wartime coven of agents met in secret conclave. Then, slowly, the car's driver took the long way around the cordoned-off White House area. Thanks to something called terrorism, officials lived under siege. Early in the present regime, the First Lady of the Land had complained to him that presidents were now prisoners of the Secret Service. "We'd be a lot happier, he told me, if the President lived in a bunker and only rode in a tank when he goes out. He wasn't joking either." Peter thought of President Roosevelt in his open car, being driven around the city with no guards to speak of, a lady beside him and a battered felt hat in hand to wave cheerily for his subjects. At this recollection, the inner custodian outdid himself. Unbidden, he superimposed upon FDR in his car another image: a golden godlike man wearing an elaborate crown.

"Pacal!" Peter exclaimed with delight. "That's his name."

"Whose name?"

"A Mayan emperor. They found his tomb at Palenque. In Central America. He lived almost a thousand years ago. Now that we can read what the Mayans wrote, we can bring him back to life for us. For those who are interested, of course."

"You are—of course." Sturtevant was staring at him intently. "Do you feel that history repeats itself?"

Peter was annoyed by the verb. Intellectuals were not meant to feel. They were meant to think. To imagine. To deduce. "I *feel* nothing except interest in the fact that there have been other empires before us in this part of the world and that Pacal's people, in time, became too many and when they did, they devoured each other."

"You feel . . . I mean you *think* that cannibalism will be our fate?"

Peter laughed. "There are many more ways of devouring one another than culinary and I'm quite sure that we'll try them all out. Anyway, nothing ever really repeats itself except . . ." An acidic fireball in his stomach burst. ". . . my sainted mother's eggnog."

Dr. Sturtevant withdrew a bound manuscript from his briefcase. "I found this waiting for me at the Cosmos Club. Aeneas's daughter was going through his papers and . . ."

Peter opened to the title page. *The Golden Age*. Subtitle, *1945–1950*. He was aware that Sturtevant was watching him intently.

"Did you know about this?"

Peter nodded. "Aeneas was always threatening to write something along this line."

"Was it really so short a time?"

"Well, he thought it was, obviously. I'm more interested to know if there ever was such a thing." Peter suddenly thought of something. Randall Jarrell had written in that long-ago time: how, in the most glorious of golden ages, there would always be someone complaining about how yellow everything looked. He chuckled at the thought, which his biographer was plainly eager for him to share, but Peter was not about to break his rule, which was never, ever, demoralize with a joke the literal, the dogged Robert L. B. Sturtevant, Ph.D.

O N   A I R

After an aggressively dismal winter, one now wakes to what at first looks to be spring but then, by misty noon, the cold sun goes, and the false spring with it. From my study window, the Gulf of Salerno is a battleship gray that exactly matches the sky except where the bright morning sun has burned an imprecise round hole in high clouds. The far shore of the gulf is enveloped in a gray mist that obscures the temples of Paestum rising from their field of artichokes. In Italo Calvino's last book he describes refracted sun rays on the sea as "a sword of light" that seems to remain pointed toward the watching eye from every angle. This morning, the sword is more a highway of glittering spangles, connecting the seashore some four hundred meters beneath my window to the broad deep gulf that ends in a wall of gray nothingness. Silver sequins glittering against gray-black. Where have I seen this effect before?

Childhood memory. I am in "a wood near Athens." It is Midsummer Night's Eve. Sun is setting. Mortals are lost in woods where magical creatures now awaken; among them, Puck—boy actor Mickey Rooney, role model to my tenth year. At full moonrise, two towering figures on horseback ride through black woods toward each other, long trains billowing and sparkling against every shade of gray, against absolute black for foil. The sword of light, as I look southward to the Tyrrhenian Sea, is now producing the same effect that Max Reinhardt created on film in 1935.

"Ill met by moonlight, proud Titania." At the window, I repeat to myself Oberon's cold greeting as he meets his estranged wife, Titania. Oberon is the somber hawk-faced lord of the night; Titania his queen. I was never to forget them. Forty-one years later, I flew from Rome to Atlanta, Georgia, to meet the touring company of a play of mine in revival. The Oberon of 1935 had metamorphosed into a former president, invented by me. But then transformation is the name of the acting game; of life, too, if one stares long enough, as I did this morning, at the sword of light, realizing that Shakespeare's Oberon and my President Hockstader were the same actor, Victor Jory, at different times. As luck would have it, the midsummer night forest king has been preserved on film while my president has long since gone to dust along with his protean impersonator.

At supper, the star of the national production of *The Best Man*, E. G. Marshall, told me that "Victor found true love last night. In a singles bar." I smile, with some wonder. Victor was the same age in 1976 that I am in the year 2000; that is, ancient, with dyed black hair. But the image I shall always retain of him is one of shimmering light emergent from grays and black, aquiline face most regal as he summons Puck to fetch him an herb called "love-in-idleness." Puck takes to the air with a shout, "I'll put a girdle round about the earth in forty minutes . . ." And does.

It has taken the television pickup crew from Rome more than forty minutes to set up in the salone where, over the years, I have done so many programs.

A.B. is admirably professional. He has already learned enough Italian to be able to tell the crew what he wants. Today, he is producer-director; questioner.

While A.B. and the crew move furniture about and arrange their lights, I set out for the piazza, which can only be reached by foot; this detail astonishes American visitors not used to walking. But Ravello is a mountain village and we walk almost everywhere, usually up and down steep gray steps.

The long cypress alley from villa to gate glows in the morning sun, dark greens and pallid golds, just as it did that other February morning when I first walked its length and decided that, somehow or other, I would acquire the villa as yet unseen—at its end. A cypress alley and a view: demure title for an Edwardian novel by one of the young English writers who spent time in Ravello at the start of the century. E. M. Forster wrote "The Story of a Panic" about our woods.

After many attempts at beautification in the last few years, the piazza now has a brand-new pale stone paving whose dark lines suggest a painting by the early Chirico while the ruthlessly restored cathedral looks somewhat astonished, like a recently raped nun. Our retired priest, Don Peppino, strolls on the high porch above the piazza; at least eighty, he looks half his age. When he came to bless the villa one winter, room by room as is the local custom, he was received by an American girl who was house-sitting for us. When he came to her room, she remembered too late that she had left her vibrator on a table. With a straight face, Don Peppino carefully blessed Satan's instrument, then, as he was leaving the house, he gave her a cheery smile and said, in English, "Be a good girl now."

At the Bar San Domingo, I order coffee. I am often astonished by the neatness of coincidence in my life. When I look unsuccessfully for one thing, I usually turn up another that is much more useful. Graham Greene used to say that if he couldn't unravel, at his desk, a tangle in a narrative, the solution would arrive the next morning, after a good night's sleep. He was, of course, what movie scriptwriters call an "early settler": one who tends to settle for whatever he thinks of first.

A friend has sent me the playbill of the York Theatre Company's *Taking a Chance on Love*. There is a photograph on the cover of John Latouche: he's seated in a bathtub whose wooden legs appear to be his legs coming through the bottom of the bath. He clutches a Chianti bottle in his left hand; he scowls at us while smoke from a cigarette in his right hand circles his head, upon which, in the original photo, a

Santa Claus hat was set, now airbrushed out. Finally, after the next best thing to a revival of *The Golden Apple*, there is now a revue entitled *The Lyrics and Life of John Latouche.*

Peter and Iris joined me at a table in the bar. "They make pastry every morning," I said, playing to Peter's regnant vice, gluttony.

"I'll have one," he said. "And a cappuccino. Where's A.B.?"

"At the house. Setting up lights. Look." I pushed the playbill at him. "Just arrived. Right on cue."

"I did hear something about this." Peter stared at Touche's picture. "Weren't you at the opening of *The Golden Apple*?" Peter is as vague about time as I but then how could he—we—not be?

"Yes. We were both there. Now, after forty years or so, Touche is being rediscovered . . ."

But Peter had put the playbill to one side in order to describe, as visitors tend to do, the horrors of air travel in our long-awaited twenty-first-century future. Suddenly, we all—the quick if not the dead—awakened in the year 2000 where everything was supposed to work fabulously well. Instead, we find that we are trapped in a technological Calcutta. Crowded air terminals whose vast, confusing distances must be negotiated on foot by the anxious traveler who moves from delay to cancellation to, at the bitter end, lost baggage after a harrowing flight in a narrow ill-maintained metal cylinder, breathing virus-laden recycled air, all the while wondering anxiously if he has boarded one of the now too frequent carriers doomed to be hurled from sky to earth as over-worked pilot loses his bearings, or a structural fault, known but unat-tended to, causes a fiery wire in the fuselage to make exciting contact with fuel supply. Commercial aviation (my father's invention as much as it could be said to be anyone's) is now the one thing that binds together huddled masses and huddled—what? asses?—in a unanimous spirit of perfect hatred for the disintegrating process. Worse, there is no alternative means of travel. Railroads were deliberately allowed to become extinct along with travel by ship while even the humble ple-beian Greyhound bus has been encouraged to wither away. The crowded skies over our Calcutta-world are like some demented pinball machine where the marbles are shot into ever-wilder trajectories until one hits another and the search begins for tape recordings of the pilot's last musings, often to be found full fathom five in deepest ocean.

But Peter had a new horror story. "Each time I fly, there is, of course, the problem of fighting terrorism. To do so, you must have complete identification, including a photograph."

"I can't think why he fumes so." Too young to recall what it was like to live in a free country, Iris is quite accustomed to being stopped and asked why she wants to fly, say, from Newark to Philadelphia, admittedly a high-security route irresistible to bomb-carrying Arabs bent on destroying all that is good on earth for the sheer joy of serving Allah.

Peter gave me a meaningful look. "Iris doesn't believe me when I say how different things used to be. Remember what it was like when after the ship's party, you could take a nap and wake up at sea, without a ticket or a passport, and then be issued both, paid for with a check."

"No," I said. "I don't remember those days and neither do you. You're talking about the twenties. Our parents—if they had the money—enjoyed that kind of liberty. We had Hitler and Mussolini to contend with."

August 1939: With a number of boys from a Washington school, I crossed from Italy into France on the last train before the border was shut. Fascist police examined our maroon-colored American passports with apparently the same intensity that an employee of Continental Airlines had recently studied Peter's passport and baggage at the gate to the admittedly top-secret shuttle from Washington to New York, known to the FBI as the terrorist-targeted "Mata Hari run."

"I'm afraid," said Peter, "I was short-tempered. I asked this person when he thought that these travel restrictions might be lifted. I got a long speech to the effect that terrorists were everywhere, all set to blow American carriers out of the sky it if weren't for tight security like this. I pointed out, sweetly, let me say . . ."

"You may say," said Iris. "But we reserve the right to wonder."

"Sweetly," he repeated, both amused and annoyed at the memory. "I said that since it was notoriously easy to get a forged driver's license or passport, all this nonsense was simply the state's deliberate harassment of its citizens. The man then howled. Yes, howled. Didn't I know the threat to the United States from *them?* Who, I asked, were *they?*"

"You are an idiot, Peter." Iris looked mildly alarmed at so much banked fury.

I intervened, to ward off stroke. "I must say, the Washington–New York shuttle must have been having an uncommonly quiet day for the two of you to have held a seminar."

Finally, on the torn-up private road to our gate, Peter calmed down. "The worst thing about an encounter like that, with this airline idiot, is that there's no way to conclude it."

"What do you mean? Here you are. Concluded."

"No, it's not over. The man still doesn't realize that everything he thinks is true is untrue."

"How do you know what he really thinks?"

Peter stumbled over a hoe that some less than dedicated farmer had left in the rutted roadway. Iris steadied him. "The worst thing is," he said, turning to me, "I keep right on talking to this fool in my head. I go on and on trying to get in a last word but he's always ready with some stupid line that he's learned like a parrot."

"Feel compassion," I said. "As if you were a Republican candidate for president this year."

The villa is built on a stone shelf, its back attached to the mountain. To the left, a terrace of olive trees and a drop to the sea; to the right, a porous cliff covered with ivy, home to violent bees that produce no honey. Rose bushes are sprouting shiny new red leaves. The first daffodils are coming up. Two camellia trees, for some secret eco-reason of their own, have shifted their flowering from late March to mid-February. Between them grows a datura tree, somewhat the worse for wear. When we first came, it put forth powerfully scented white blossoms, like elongated bells. Then the soft pithy branches dried up and broke off and the velvety skin-smooth leaves developed holes.

"Every morning, when I pass the datura, I think of Paul Bowles."

"Bowles?" Peter stopped his inner quarrel with airline security. "Why Bowles?"

"Because Paul's wife, Jane, fell in love with a terrible woman in

Tangier called Cherifa. Jane was besotted with her. Jane even used to take her place, selling barley or whatever it was in the marketplace while Cherifa would go off for mint tea, leaving the Jewish princess from New York to sell grain to the veiled ladies of Islam. Auden always maintained that only lesbians were capable of grand passion. 'Look at Tristan and Isolde,' he would say. 'Whole thing actually takes place in a girls' school. Tristan is the head girl, good at games, and Isolde is the passionate clinging beauty, fearful of the king—the headmistress. Naturally, the lovers are immolated by their passion.' Unfortunately, this particular romantic agony of the soul came to a crescendo when Jane told Cherifa that she was in her will. Cherifa promptly turned murderess. Very Bowlesian this. Both Jane and Paul liked to set themselves up so that others could victimize them. At first, the sly Cherifa resorted to magic pills and potions. Only when they failed did she turn to that most effective killer: a tisane made with leaves of the datura tree. Cherifa offered Jane her poison-leaf tea, which Jane, love-glow in her eyes, drank. And drank."

"So what happened?" Iris was fascinated and even Peter seemed to have put Continental Airlines on hold.

"Jane didn't die right away. But she lost part of her vision. Then she had the first of a series of strokes that eventually landed her in a Spanish Catholic nursing home, where she died. Paul liked telling the story of Cherifa and Jane. With no moral, of course."

I plucked a leaf from the datura; there were lacelike holes in the leaf's deep green. I gave it to Peter, who put it in his pocket. "What happened to Cherifa?" he asked.

"I don't recall."

Just before last Christmas, I was in Seattle to give a speech. For old time's sake I went into what had been the Snake Pit Bar of the Olympic Hotel. The lowlife bar of the war years is now an elegant oyster bar where I ordered Dungeness crab and looked about the room in search of myself, a nineteen-year-old first mate of an Army ship en route to the Aleutian Islands. My last night ashore, I had discovered the brightly lit bar, packed with soldiers, sailors, marines. Strong smell of beer, sweat, wet wool, vomit, cigarette smoke. Contemplating so many ghosts, I opened my newspaper and read that Paul Bowles was dead; promptly, his unlikely dapper ghost made an appearance at a bar that was definitely not his style even though a handsome military youth called Harry Dunham had been Paul's one great attachment— Latouche's as well. Harry had been married to an agreeable plainly pretty or prettily plain young woman, Maggie, who died not too many years after her husband's death in New Guinea. Harry was killed by the Japanese at Port Moresby. In Paul's first novel, *The Sheltering Sky*, he calls his protagonist Port Moresby. Good name.

A.B. led Peter and me into the salone while Iris settled by the fire in the study. From past adventures, the three-man crew was very much at home with our numerous flawed electrical outlets, which they had once so excitingly burnt out.

"We'll do this in sections, if you don't mind." A.B. and the sound-man wired Peter, who stood staring straight ahead, frowning, talking to himself. I caught a sentence: "If you spent as much money on the prevention of accidents as you do on the retrieval of wreckage . . ." This was promising. He might yet win what could be a world-class *mano a mano* exchange.

A.B. looked at the portable monitor: then, "I'm going to be a voice off-camera. So look at each other when you talk, or wherever seems natural."

Since neither Peter nor I liked to know in advance what we were going to be asked, A.B. started us off cold. "Let's get Pearl Harbor out of the way. Mr. Sanford, *American Idea* has endorsed, I suppose that is the word, a recent book by Robert B. Stinnett, *Day of Deceit*, in which, after years of research, he has come to the conclusion that although the Roosevelt Administration knew that an attack was coming, they did not warn . . ."

With practiced ease, Peter made his case or, rather, his defense of the admiral who had written an indictment of Roosevelt in the pages of the usually pro–New Deal *American Idea*.

At burdensome length, Peter and I put the case for Roosevelt's amoral mastery of world politics and his ability to get what he wanted. I admired him quite as much as I deplored him.

A.B. was cheerful. "We have plenty of time to edit. I've got a great editor. He'll get rid of most of this."

"Why cut?" Peter rubbed his eyes.

"Pearl *Harbor?*" A.B. made a comic face. "Pearl *Bailey* is better known."

"Was," I said, "until she died." The past for Americans is a separate universe with its own quaint laws and irrelevant perceptions.

Our cook served lunch to us in the dining room, where we sat on metal chairs that I had found in a Rome antique shop. "They were made for the Maharajah of Jaipur," said the shop owner, smoothly. "Around 1857, I should say."

"No." I was delighted to see the chairs in life rather than on-screen. "They were made around 1957. At Cinecittà. Here in Rome." Once the owner was satisfied that I had served time, for art's sake, as MGM's contract writer on *Ben-Hur* in Rome, he graciously increased his price. In those profligate days, if one wanted metal chairs, for a film, one got them. Now, of course, the green wood beneath what looks to be hammered silver is warping and strange bubbles are distorting the elegant ram's-headed backs to the chairs. Peter and Iris and A.B. dutifully appreciated those outward and visible signs of the glory that was Cinecittà where, at the same time *Ben-Hur* was being made, a plump young man with large dark eyes was preparing *La Dolce Vita* and visiting, secretly, with my connivance, our top-secret imperial sets, which later turned up in a number of other Roman films though in none, alas, by Fellini.

"I suppose I've come in late," said A.B., "but why are you two so much concerned with what Roosevelt did or did not do at Pearl Harbor?"

"You've come in far too late." Peter was gruff. "He did what no president has ever done. Set us up. To be attacked."

"But didn't it all end well? We won the war. We got the world. We saved as many of Hitler's victims as we could. So some old ships got sunk."

The cook's show dish is baked eggplant, layered with slices of hard-boiled eggs and black olives. Peter had a second helping. "Some three thousand men got sunk, too," he said. "And died."

"Drop in a bottomless bucket." A.B. was blithe.

Even I winced at that. "The fact that you take all this so casually is the principal fallout." I became sententious: something that can happen when one means exactly what one says with no iron door left ajar to escape through, like quotation marks.

After lunch, A.B. and I went out on the balcony that overlooks the sea.

He shuddered with cold; the sun was about to slip behind the high cliff to our west. Inside the salone, the TV crew had set up a new lighting arrangement. A.B. looked at me curiously. "You are in your parallel universe. What does ours seem like to you?"

"What does mine seem like to you?" It is not often a character frees himself from the text. "After all, you are in my narrative."

"And I *think* you are in mine. I suppose that's how every being— invented or not—perceives the world."

But I hardly know what I actually think as my inventions now circle me. Inside the salone, Peter was again being wired for sound. On the far wall the black-and-white mosaic hippocampus—part horse, part fish—seemed to be swimming past us, back to its primal origin in the mid-earth sea. Mediterranean.

I opened the balcony door. Let A.B. go through first. As he did, I said, "You're Aaron Burr, aren't you?"

A.B. grinned. "If you say so."

We stood facing each other in the open doorway between the evening chill and the warmth from the house—limbo? "You started our nineteenth century off with a bang. You were the vice president who made Jefferson president. So how do you plan to start our new century?"

"Like this. With a television interview. You and Peter Sanford . . ."

I laughed. "Aaron Burr as Larry King? No!"

But A.B. was serene. "Remember how I . . . that is to say, Burr . . . took on every sort of case as a lawyer before I made my deal with the devil, Thomas Jefferson."

"You really are back, aren't you, Colonel?"

"If you think so, yes. I'm nothing more than energy to be put to use because, as Jeremy Bentham liked to say, without such energy there is nothing. Anyway, this time around I shall ignore parish-pump politics. That's for puppets. Power to make the sort of world I dreamed of is elsewhere."

"Where?"

A.B. gave a sweeping gesture that included the invisible temples at Paestum and the last of the sword of light and the entire dark Gulf of Salerno. "Nation-states are finished. The answer is now the round earth itself with all those billions waiting to be connected by . . ." He stopped.

"By you?"

"By energy."

"On the Internet?"

"Oh, it will go far beyond that. But wherever it is, I already am."

"Leading it?"

"Who knows? This time."

After the taping, the TV crew went back to Rome. A.B. and Iris walked into the village, where Peter and I would join them once we'd recovered from our complementary rather than competitive monologues to camera. The cats, one tortoiseshell and the other white, slept on the suede sofa, their claws extending and contracting in their sleep.

Over Peter's shoulder, Harry Truman and I are grinning at each other in a photograph. Truman came to Dutchess County in the late autumn of 1960 to speak for the Democratic ticket. I introduced him to the cheering faithful. He told the audience how he had recently gone to see my play, *The Best Man*, the story of two candidates for president at a convention where a former president is king-maker.

"Funniest thing," said Truman. "There we were, Mrs. Truman and I, walking up the aisle, and everyone's staring at me in the most peculiar way. Can't figure out why."

This got a laugh. It was generally believed that I had based the old president on Truman even though Eleanor Roosevelt had said, "He seems much more like Mr. Garner to me."

But that night in Fishkill, I was thought to be introducing one of my characters to the Democrats of Dutchess County. Truman played along with the joke. Then, when it came time to endorse me for Congress, he forgot my name and said, "Now you all gotta vote for this young man here for Congress because he's . . . Uh, he's got the words." I thought that a fair description.

Peter was amused. "Personally, I always liked Truman. You know, he once gave Diana and me a ride in his train . . ."

"I know," I said.

Peter nodded. "Of course you do. You made him up. Then you made me up, too. How does it feel to play god?"

"Unreal," I said. "Do I wake or sleep?" I picked up Aeneas's book. "Hard to recall now just how serious we were when we thought we could turn all those V-E and V-J Days into something new under the sun." I looked at the title page: *The Golden Age* by Aeneas Duncan. "Well, we did have five years of peace. That's quite a lot, really. From the Japanese surrender to the Korean . . . what?"

"Defeat." Peter shook his head. "After that, we went to war full-time. We had to save everyone from communism. Then communism went away, so now we have to save them from drugs. From terrorism. We are all under constant surveillance. Do you know that at every airport . . ."

"I know, Peter." I headed him off before he yet again confronted the security guard from Continental Airlines.

"Well," he gave me a hard look, "you should have constructed a better universe for us."

"One works with what one has and knows, as you know as well as I, in *your* universe."

"Do I really have one?" Peter sighed. "I suspect that I only have a few random memories. If they are memories. For me, the golden age came and went one spring day in 1948, when I had lunch at Robert's in Fifty-fifth Street."

"With Cornelia Claiborne?" I thought of yellow roses. "You live in the past; don't you?"

"The only place," said Peter, "where you can get a decent meal. Shad roe from the Hudson." He smiled at the memory.

I looked at the playbill of Touche's revue. "You know, I thought I caught a glimpse of what we might have become that night at the Phoenix Theatre, with you and Diana and Aeneas . . ."

"And Latouche, weeping about his second act. Oh, that night was unforgettable. But the golden age, if there had ever been one, was already shut down by then—1954, wasn't it?"

"Yes. Which means that what we thought was a bright beginning was actually a last flare in the night."

"Well, it hasn't been all that dark since." Peter was judicious. "Do you understand the Internet?"

"No." I was firm. "And neither do you."

Peter rose and stretched. "We must consult A.B. He's the future, not us. Our revels now are ended. Why do you keep letting Shakespeare leak in upon us?"

"Why not? He gives names to things, real and unreal. He understands how the actors—the Roosevelts and the Trumans—are simply spirits and once their scenes are acted out, they melt into air, into thin air, as we shall presently do, still hankering after what was not meant to be, ever, other than a lunch at Robert's for you and then, for both of us, two hours in a far-below-Broadway theater called the Phoenix—at least the name indicates hope, doesn't it? A cleansing fire followed by a dazzling rebirth: also the logo of a thousand dishonest insurance companies. The phoenix could well be the sign in which A.B. conquers where Aaron Burr failed. Burr wanted to be a mere emperor of Mexico. A.B. wants the great globe itself—all cloud-capped towers, gorgeous palaces, solemn temples, the whole lot bound together by waves of energy of which we are insubstantial, interchangeable parts. Now—should I let you go?"

Peter was silhouetted against the fire. "Go where?"

"Does it matter?"

" 'What Is the Matter with Matter?' was the title of a piece I published, by a physicist, right after Hiroshima."

"What *was* the matter?"

"Nothing," said Peter. As his host—and creator—I let him have the last word, which is something.

As for the human case, the generations of men come and go and are in eternity no more than bacteria upon a luminous slide, and the fall of a republic or the rise of an empire—so significant to those involved—is not detectable upon the slide even were there an interested eye to behold that steadily proliferating species which would either end in time or, with luck, become something else, since change is the nature of life, and its hope.

A F T E R W O R D

For those who mistakenly regard history as a true record and the novel as invention (sometimes it can be precisely the other way round), the "historical" novel does seem to be a contradiction on the order of Thomas Jefferson's famous "true facts." Yet I think it is fair to ask of a given writer, "What did you make up and what did you take from the agreed-upon historical record?" In *The Golden Age* I found myself unusually situated. I had lived through the period. I had been at the convention that nominated Willkie. I knew a number of the historical figures that I describe. Also, as one who had grown up in political Washington, D.C., I was an attentive listener to the many voices which sound and resound in that whispering gallery. Later, as an adult, I listened to some of the principals in other settings. Eleanor Roosevelt's aria on jealousy is not word for word what she said to me in the early 1960s at Hyde Park, but I suspect that my memory of what she said is a lot closer to her actual words than, say, a reconstruction of a Periclean speech by even so great if interested a writer as Thucydides. The lives of such invented characters as Caroline and Blaise and Peter Sanford intersect with those of "real" people like Roosevelt and Hopkins. What the real people say and do is essentially what they have been recorded as saying and doing, while the invented characters are then able to speculate upon motivation, dangerous territory for the historian.

I realize that in these American history narratives, over the years, I have broken a number of taboos. For instance, in *Lincoln* (1984) Abraham Lincoln tells his law partner, William Herndon, where and with whom he had once contracted syphilis. Since I use the language that Herndon himself used, I thought that all this was very much to the point, since mercury was the "cure" for syphilis in those days, and Lincoln's later melancholy and odd health could well have come from mercury poisoning. Unfortunately, the Lincoln brigade in academe was outraged by my reference to this "maggoty story." Apparently, no great American could ever have caught a venereal disease or been untrue to his wife, and so on. It was then that I discovered how many bold fictioneers reside in Clio's grove.

It was well known within the whispering gallery of the day that FDR had provoked the Japanese into attacking us. In fact, our preeminent historian, Charles A. Beard, was on the case as early as 1941 with *President Roosevelt and the Coming of War*. Needless to say, apologists for empire have been trying for fifty years to erase him. But he is indelible. Finally, did Roosevelt know that the inevitable first strike would come at Pearl Harbor rather than at, say, Manila? I leave this moot.

Over the years, I have been publicly advised by no less a personage than Dumas Malone that as no gentleman in the antebellum South would ever go to bed with a slave and as Thomas Jefferson was a very great gentleman indeed, he could not have had children by his slave Sally Hemings. Thus a national tall tale is firmly based on a false syllogism. What I wrote of the Jefferson-Hemings affair (*Burr*, 1973) has now been proved true through DNA testing. Burr's latest academic biographer believes that my intuition as to what Hamilton had said about Aaron Burr that led to the fatal duel appears to be true. But enough of I-told-you-so boasting. The real problem here is why so many American historians become so frantically unhistorical when a national icon is placed in too severe a light.

President Eisenhower may have solved this mystery when he warned us against the military-industrial complex. Eisenhower acknowledged the costliness of modern weapons; then he alluded, unexpectedly, to the complex's influence on the universities, once "the fountainhead of free ideas and scientific discovery." This has changed, he noted. "Because of the huge costs involved, a government contract becomes virtually a substitute for intellectual curiosity. . . . The prospect of domination of the nation's scholars by federal employment, project allocations, and the power of money is ever present, and is gravely to be regarded." There it is or, until recently, was.

The vast amounts that government spends on research and development in the science departments cannot help but affect the fragile humanities. Hence, the ongoing revisions of our history and the inevitable fury that truth-telling often evokes. I don't believe that the good Professor Dumas Malone actually wore a cloak and carried a dagger for his country when writing his life of Jefferson, but I do know that the "intellectual" operatives in the CIA of his day liked to refer to their busy establishment at Langley, Virginia, as "the ministry of culture," from which they founded literary magazines like *Encounter* in Europe, funded culture at home, and even made Hollywood films like Orwell's *Animal Farm* in order to demonize our enemy, who, rather meanly, folded in 1990, leaving our propagandists at such a loose end that there are now furtive signs of a revival among younger academics of the realist historians—anti-ideologues like Richard Hofstadter and William Appleman Williams. With luck, a golden age of historians may now be at hand, freeing novelists to return to the truly great themes— how a sensitive, innately good person was wrongly accused of political incorrectness and so failed to get tenure at Ann Arbor, while his wife left him for another. . . . Shakespeare country up ahead!